I0562817

On Deadly Ground

by

Susan Vaughan

*Devlin Security Force, Protecting
Priceless Treasures, Vol 1*

This is a work of fiction. Names, characters, places, and incidents are either the product of the author's imagination or are used fictitiously, and any resemblance to actual persons living or dead, business establishments, events, or locales, is entirely coincidental.

On Deadly Ground

COPYRIGHT © 2023 by Susan Vaughan
1/19/2015; ©TX008856142 Susan Hofstetter Vaughan

All rights reserved. No part of this book may be used or reproduced in any manner whatsoever without written permission of the author or The Wild Rose Press, Inc. except in the case of brief quotations embodied in critical articles or reviews.
Contact Information: info@thewildrosepress.com

Cover Art by *Kim Mendoza*

The Wild Rose Press, Inc.
PO Box 708
Adams Basin, NY 14410-0708
Visit us at www.thewildrosepress.com

Publishing History, First Edition, 2023
Trade Paperback ISBN 978-1-5092-5006-6
Digital ISBN 978-1-5092-5007-3

Devlin Security Force, Protecting Priceless Treasures, Vol 1
Previously Published: 2015 by Gullwood Press
Published in the United States of America

Dedication

This book is dedicated to my friend and the best editor in the world, author Linda Style, without whom this book would still be a hot mess. Thank you, Linda, for more than you know.

Chapter One

Dulles International Airport, Washington, D.C.

THE GIG WAS right up his alley. Recover an artifact with a curse—Kizin, the Maya god of earthquakes, no less. Deliver it in tandem with the rescue of a kidnap victim somewhere in the Costa Verde jungle. And outflank that damn smuggling ring. Only hitch was the time frame—beat an earthquake.

And, oh, yeah. The client. Make that two hitches. *Talk to the boss on that one.*

Max Rivera adjusted his back pack and grabbed his duffel bag from the carousel. Slinging the strap onto one shoulder, he headed toward the coffee kiosk by the car rental desks. The new client must be damned important to Devlin Security Force if Devlin himself took the time to make the introduction. Max searched the crowd as he wove past people gabbing in a dozen languages.

He paid for the coffee, downed a big gulp, and burned the crap out of his mouth. He needed a jolt but not blisters.

"Need waking up?" Thomas Devlin's deep voice turned him around.

Brown eyes crinkled with amusement, probably at Max's beach-bum look. A definite contrast to the other man's dark suit and open shirt collar. Devlin might dress civilian, but his bearing was all military.

Max threw back his shoulders and gripped his

former captain's hand. "No shit. But right now I need caffeine." He barely stopped himself from adding *sir*. "I just dragged my butt off a sixteen-hour flight. Surrounded by a family that never stopped talking."

"You can sleep on the flight to London." Devlin pounded him on the back and nudged him through the building toward the escalators.

"You know me, Thomas. I'm up for anything. I know Costa Verde. England, not so much. But a chance to jam up Centaur and return a bit of history to its rightful place, I'm in." Especially Maya history. If his old mentor was looking down, he'd approve. "Hazardous situation, potentially explosive, even better."

"So you say, but I hear doubt in your voice." Devlin stuffed a boarding pass in Max's shirt pocket.

"No problem with the mission." Choosing his words, Max drank more coffee. "Not for me, I mean. But damned dangerous for a museum executive type. I'd rather handle the job solo."

He knew his own capabilities. Other people let you down, left you high and dry. You didn't know who to trust, who not to trust.

"No can do. Here's the part of your job I didn't tell you because I needed to check with Interpol. You're to find out what you can on our kidnap victim's black-market dealing—subtly."

Max pressed his lips together. He shot a glance toward the high ceiling before nodding. "And for that, I need Doug Fontaine's sister Kate. The client. Get her to spill on her brother while I protect her in London and Costa Verde. Roger."

He scraped knuckles across his jaw. A run-in with Fontaine two years ago in Istanbul had left behind a bad taste. If traveling with the sister meant a way to nail the guy, he'd suck it up.

"One more thing," Devlin said as they left the escalator. "Don't mention the other players to Kate Fontaine until you know more."

"Or until sharing that becomes necessary." More danger to the client might put her on the sidelines. Something to keep in mind.

The wait in line at the ticket counter was short, one couple ahead arguing in French. Max checked the duffel, glad to have the weight off his shoulder.

"Twenty-one days before that earthquake's supposed to hit? But come on, Thomas, an earthquake curse?"

"Right. There are tremors. The client will explain further." Devlin led the way toward a central hallway and the escalators to the security checkpoint. "The quake's the biggest danger... but not the only one. People will kill to possess the artifact. DSF has no contact in Costa Verde to verify, and I can't send in a team. This op has to be low key. Kate says certain parties there want the statue for the powers they believe it possesses."

"I'm not surprised." For many, ancient Maya beliefs mingled with others.

They wove past other travelers to the checkpoint, and Devlin tipped his head toward a pillar. "There's our client."

Max's gaze followed his boss's as he tossed down the last of the coffee. He stopped mid-swallow. Shit. Not the hot blonde. "Her?"

"Katherine Fontaine, Assistant Director, one of three at the National Cultural Museum. Your traveling companion. Your principal."

Cell phone to one ear, she stood tapping her foot. Mile-long legs encased in slim black pants. Fitted jacket. Designer and pricey. An attitude that shouted hands-off. A body that equaled distraction. Distraction meant trouble.

Elegant. Educated. Probably pampered. Trouble in capital letters? Yeah. Big time.

I'm awake now.

Clunky shoes—practical. Okay. Maybe the woman had some sense after all.

"London, yeah, but can you see that female in the interior jungles of Costa Verde? Nope, *de ningún modo*, no way."

Devlin's mouth quirked up. "DSF does a lot of work for her museum. She's a valuable client. And Kate Fontaine is tougher than she looks."

Max gritted his teeth. Tossed his cup in a nearby recycling bin.

She'd better be tough. His job was protection, not babysitting.

****

"You have no idea how much this is upsetting me, Katherine."

Kate did, but it was too late to change anything she'd done or failed to do. She switched the cell phone to her right ear.

"I thought you hired someone to rescue poor Dougie."

"I did, Mom, but to accompany me to England and Costa Verde, not to deliver the statue. I'll be okay. Try not to worry. Devlin Security Force is a reputable firm. They specialize in protecting and retrieving art and artifacts. The museum has hired DSF many times to protect exhibits en route. I have every confidence in their man to protect and guide me." Every. Confidence.

"But why do *you* have to go?" Without stopping for an answer, her mom continued her complaint.

Kate stepped closer to the pillar and away from passengers filing into the security line. She shifted the shoulder strap of the carryon and readjusted the phone. No sign yet of Thomas Devlin and his agent, and her mom could talk longer than the life of the battery charge.

If only she'd taken the time to attend the London auction instead of sending Doug, everything would've been fine. He wouldn't be suffering from a broken leg and a head injury, and his life wouldn't be in jeopardy. That Doug didn't blame her for the injuries and neither did Mom made no difference. Her fault. All of it. Tears burned her eyes and she willed them away.

Ten days ago, because Doug hadn't returned her call, she'd driven to his condo. No Doug. No wheelchair. No meds. Only a printed note that read, *"We have Fontaine. If you want to see him alive, no police. Call."* Then a phone number. A disposable phone, the police detective said, untraceable. No witnesses, no clues, no leads. The damn scum thought of everything. The FBI could offer nothing better. Time was short so she had little choice. DSF was excellent at protecting artifacts, but…

A man in a black leather jacket approached on her left. Kate edged aside but relaxed when he discarded a sandwich wrapper in the trash. *Calm down.* Except… oh, wait, didn't she have every right to be jumpy and suspicious? She huffed and turned her back.

"Mom, Scotland Yard will tell me nothing. I need to find out the names of possible suspects some other way."

And the British collector who sold the statue to Doug knew the business, knew other collectors. Even some who might do whatever necessary to obtain a rare artifact. She pressed her free hand to her roiling stomach. She wouldn't think about what could happen to Doug.

"All well and good," her mom continued. "England is civilization. But the jungle?"

No kidding. Scorpions in the tent, snakes, and— Minor hazards of nature compared to an earthquake. True, all true. Enough to terrify her, but not enough to stop her. She'd do whatever it took to save Doug's life. She fisted her free hand so tightly her nails bit into her palms.

"I have to follow the kidnapper's instructions." It was more complicated than that, but no point in elaborating. "I have to do this myself, Mom."

"But earthquake country? Didn't you say the tremors were increasing?" her mother whined. "You're not equipped, Katherine."

Kate tuned out the same old song. But Mom was right. She wasn't tough or brave or experienced like Doug and her dad. Going through the jungle was beyond risky. God, she'd give anything to be at her desk where her only concern was placating a temperamental curator.

Her mother sniffled. "How can you go off and leave me all alone? *Anything* could happen to you. I need you."

Anything could happen, yes, but she couldn't— wouldn't—let herself dwell on worst-case scenarios. And Devlin's operative would guide her. He'd protect her. And Kizin, once she recovered it. She couldn't afford second thoughts, not with barely three weeks before the deadline. At the inadvertent word choice, a shiver went through her.

"You'll be okay," she said gently. "If I had a choice, I'd stay here."

More sniffs and the brush of tissues. "You're going on a wild trek just like… like…"

Like my father. Like my brother. She studied a crack in the tile floor. "It's not the same as one of Dad's expeditions, Mom. I *have* to go." The loudspeaker blared. "They're calling my flight. Try not to worry. I'll bring Doug back. I promise. Love you. Bye."

She dropped the phone in her bag. The announcement was about a truck blocking the fire lane, but she couldn't bear listening to more pleas. And about her dad… Her throat closed.

The leather-jacketed man returned. He stood by the pillar, looking her way. Swarthy complexion, stocky. Maybe Hispanic. When she caught his eye, he turned away abruptly.

Her pulse kicked up and a band tightened around her chest.

His gaze scoured the crowd. Like her, waiting for someone? Or—

Had he been watching her? Could he be with the kidnappers? Her heart pounded double time. Edging away, she searched the baggage-laden crowd again for Thomas.

A group of women in brightly colored saris walked toward her. Behind them… At last, Thomas Devlin. She sighed and relaxed the tension in her shoulders. She'd recognize that military stride and piercing stare anywhere. The commanding confidence that drew every eye.

But no more than the man with him. Her protector? About her age, early thirties. Close to six feet like

Devlin. Macho and muscular. Good.

In contrast with Devlin's GQ looks, he wore scuffed Western boots, cargo shorts, and a shirt as rumpled as his jet-black hair. He was shaggy, slovenly, and unshaven. And very hung over, judging by his pained expression. Not good.

Please, not him. An inarticulate grumble escaped her throat. She searched for some other likely candidate, another eagle-fierce male nearby. No one. Only a Greek or Italian family, all shorter than her five eight.

Clutching her bag against her side, she hurried toward the two men. "Thomas, there's a man." She flapped a hand toward the pillar. "He was watching me. Maybe for the kidnappers?"

Devlin took her arm and pulled her aside. "Where?"

"There, by the pillar. I—" She searched the area. "He's gone."

"What's he look like?" Devlin's agent dumped his backpack onto the tile floor. A scowl storm-darkened his blunt-featured face.

The man looked more frightening than the watcher, yet a frisson of awareness rippled through her. "Small, dark, maybe Hispanic. Black leather jacket."

People streamed behind them on the concourse and ahead to security. Kate caught sight of a short man in a leather jacket hurrying away through the crowd.

"There!" She pointed. "By the Iberia ad. That's him."

"Worth a shot." The agent took off at a trot, past the sari-clad women, who fluttered aside like flower petals. Kate heard his "Sorry," as he ran on, weaving around the travelers in his path.

"Kate," Devlin said, pulling her attention from the

now disappearing agent and the swarthy man. "Why do you think that man was watching you?"

She drew a deep breath, then described the man's behavior. Her pulse settled to normal, but suddenly her tablet and overnight necessities weighed more than the *Queen Mary II.* She slid the bag to the floor. "He looked my way more than once, but maybe I'm overreacting."

The grim look tightening his straight, dark brows softened. "In your situation, probably not. Our bad guy could very well be keeping tabs on you to make sure you're following instructions." He placed a hand on her shoulder. "Don't worry. Max will protect you."

As if conjured by the mention of his name, the agent rejoined them, barely breathing hard. Disreputable, but rugged and fast on his feet. Okay. She could live with that.

"Guy's gone," he said. "Too much of a head start. I checked the nearest men's room. Nada."

"Too bad," Devlin said. "Almost like that thief in Kabul."

"Yup." The agent stepped closer. The aroma of coffee and the light tang of sweat emanated from him. Framed by thick, sooty lashes, eyes the color of melted chocolate swept her with male interest. "That one didn't get away, ma'am."

His drawl—Texas?—slid into her like red wine. The man radiated sex like heat rays.

"Kate Fontaine," Devlin said, "this is one of my best operatives, Max Rivera."

Max Rivera held out a hand. His expression smoothed to polite blandness. "You okay?"

"I'm fine." She accepted his handshake, registering strength, the rasp of calluses, and a surprisingly gentle warmth. "Thank you for coming to my rescue, Mr. Rivera." *Max Rivera.* The name seemed familiar. Thomas must've mentioned him before.

"No problem. And make it Max, Kate."

They'd be traveling together for days. Formality was out, but she could ignore him as a man, regardless of her initial reaction. She was no lonely female looking for a fling. Especially with an adventurer like the men in her family. A man who'd take over, who'd pat her on the head—figuratively—and tell her she was out of her element. She was, but still.

"If things go according to plan, you shouldn't need rescuing again, you or the statue." Humor glinted in Max's dark eyes.

She managed a smile. "Like you say. As long as nothing goes wrong." Great. What could go wrong? Her stomach churned.

She thanked Devlin and shook his hand. The two men performed some sort of guy handshake, and she and Max joined the security line.

He didn't seem inclined to chat and neither did she. They inched forward through the rope line until finally they reached the checkpoint. She deposited her gear in bins. Behind her, Max untied and kicked off his boots.

What was it about his name that niggled at her? She set her handbag and tablet case on the conveyer. Something about Doug. *Max…. Max Rivera.* Her breath caught. *That's it!*

She spun on him.

"What is it? You see that guy again?" He gripped her arm.

She jerked away. "No, not that. I recognize your name."

His eyebrows shot upward.

"You're the man who cheated my brother."

Chapter Two

SHIT. THE SWEAT trickling down Max's back had nothing to do with the security check. She *knew* about Istanbul? Figured her sleazy brother'd put his own spin on what happened.

Kate glared at him. "Well?"

People behind them were piling up, pushing their bins forward. The elderly woman ahead of Kate eyed them with suspicion over her reading glasses.

Max dumped his boots in a bin and bent close to Kate's ear. "Not here."

Color flared on her high cheekbones. "Yes, here," she said through clenched teeth. "I need an operative I can trust. Apparently that's not you."

Fuck, this was no time for true confessions. Or hasty fabrications. For more than one reason, the mission required her trust. He couldn't blow this. "What happened with Doug was a misunderstanding. Look, the plane boards in thirty minutes. And how long before that earthquake anniversary?"

"Twenty-one days, as you very well know." She shook her head as the short time frame seemed to snap her back to the situation. Tears welled up in her pretty eyes. "But my brother…"

Tears. Aw, dammit. "Kate, you can trust me. We can talk on the plane. Devlin'll verify."

The impatient clamor grew louder. The X-ray

machine was sucking Kate's bags into its maw. The TSA dude ushering people through the imaging machine gave them a hard look.

Her brow furrowed. She was weighing his words, but before she could speak, TSA hurried her forward.

Max blew out a breath. He passed through the checkpoint and collected his belongings. While Kate was occupied with stowing her tablet in her carryon, he texted Thomas Devlin. Now, if she phoned, he'd covered his butt.

When they continued on to the gate, Kate took out her phone. A look over her shoulder at the screen had him sweating again. Devlin's private number. A moment later she huffed in frustration and stowed the device in her bag. The call had gone to voice mail. Either Devlin read Max's message first or he turned off the phone while he was driving. Bullet fucking dodged.

Neither of them spoke until they settled into their seats on the British Airways flight to Heathrow. Because Kate had sprung for business class tickets, Max could stretch out his legs. The cushy seats sure as hell beat the coffin fit on his last flight. *Thank y'all, darlin'.*

When the attendant offered flutes of champagne, he passed. His mouth tasted like Texas road kill, so he went for a cola. Kate ordered mineral water. She wasn't looking at him but the displeasure pursing her full lips made her look even more buttoned-up. When she removed her jacket, he caught a scent both sweet and spicy. The impression of lace peeked through an off-white silk blouse smoothed over breasts as classy as she was.

Whoa, hoss. This was the client, and not one of his good-time, good-bye girls.

Once their drinks had arrived and the attendant left them alone, she turned to him. "You promised to explain." The crisp edge to her soft voice said she'd waited long enough.

He downed a swallow of soda and rubbed his gritty eyes.

Hard to tell what exactly ol' Dougie told her. All Max had was the truth, minus a few details. "Like I said, what happened in Istanbul was a misunderstanding. I met Doug in the Starbucks near the Sultanahmet Hotel. We recognized each other as Americans and started talking. I'd just finished a delivery to the archeological museum so I was free. He hired me as protection on his buying trip to a dangerous part of the city."

"And you accepted employment from a stranger, just like that?"

"If you're thinking I set him up, no way. I knew the name as a guy who traded in antiquities. The son of the famous archeologist."

She gawped. The attendants launched into their pre-flight explanations, and she leaned closer, giving Max another whiff of her scent. "You've heard of my father?"

"While Douglas Fontaine was alive, nearly every *American Journal of Archeology* issue had an article about one of his finds." He poured more cola into his glass.

"Esoteric reading." Her tone and hiked-up eyebrow said she was impressed.

"Guatemalan guy I worked with when I was in school got me interested." He'd followed up on the ancient lore Nestor shared. "Took a few courses in archeology and ancient history. Fascinating stuff. Comes in handy in my work." Like helping him spot pilfered shit.

"Of course." She sipped her mineral water. "Doug bought three items that trip, I think."

"A wrought-gold bottle, a copper vase, and a bronze snake head," he said. "The guy selling them didn't mention the snake head came from the excavations for the new railway tunnel under the Bosporus. When I recognized the piece, I insisted on handing it over to the authorities. Doug was out the snake head and the money. But it was the seller who cheated him."

"Not you." She studied him, seeming to look for dissembling.

He held her gaze. Shit. She still didn't trust him. And probably wouldn't. "Not me. A misunderstanding, like I said."

On a muffled roar, the jet took off into the skies over D.C. Both of them leaned back until the G-force evened out.

Kate gave a little sigh of resignation. "We'll see how it goes in England. I still plan to phone Thomas Devlin."

"No problem." Change the subject before she quizzed him further about Doug's aborted deal. He liked her voice, smooth as cream when she wasn't on the attack. "An awful lot of people are hot for Kizin. Theft, I get, but attempted murder and kidnapping? Damned extreme."

After a sip of mineral water, she slid a photo from the tablet case at her feet and handed the eight-by-ten glossy to him. "This is the photo from the auction catalog. Carved figures like these aren't idols."

"They were created as offerings to the gods and later smashed to bits. An intact one is fu— *very* rare."

"Unique, in fact."

He heard the smile in her voice but continued looking at the picture.

Kizin, Maya underworld god of earthquakes. Devlin's report hadn't contained a picture, only a brief description. Other versions Max had seen were stone. He couldn't take his eyes off this image. Carved of polished jade, it gleamed. Offset lighting flashed on gold inlay in the shape of a skeleton. The rough-cut emerald eyes, disproportionately large, seemed to stare with malevolence. And he couldn't stop staring back. No fucking wonder thieves went for this guy.

"Emerald eyes. How valuable are ones that size anyway?"

"The best emeralds are worth more than the best diamonds. That large a stone, cut and polished, could bring more than a hundred thousand. Maybe twice that amount."

"Whoa, that much. Unusual and valuable." He tore his gaze from the picture and handed it back. "But there must be more to the story." He knew some of it, but he liked hearing her explain in that sexy voice.

Her index finger traced the moisture on her glass. "Yes, the legends surrounding the artifact and its history make the statue the most storied prize for Meso-American collectors. Sixty years ago, when archeologists were beginning to restore the ancient Maya city of K'eq Xlapak, a thief stole Kizin from the temple pyramid." She leaned closer as she warmed to her story. Was her skin as soft as it looked?

"Before the international agreements about not removing antiquities from their countries of origin," he said.

She tilted her head. "Yes, exactly right. One of the

16

guards at the site stole the statue and other artifacts. One day later an earthquake partially destroyed the temple and leveled the nearby native village. The chief archeologist was killed by a falling palm tree. Professor Gregory Douglas Fontaine, my great-grandfather."

Hoo boy. "So that's why you and your brother wanted it."

"Definitely. Completing that restoration would've capped Gregory's career. They'd barely begun when he was killed. Dead, he couldn't recover the statue. The local people said he died because Kizin cursed him and caused the earthquake." Her voice was liquid with emotion.

"Coincidence." Max set aside his empty glass. "But enough to start the quake curse legend."

"Twenty years after the theft, a fault rupture caused a massive quake across Costa Verde and Guatemala. Seven point nine on the Richter scale. More than twenty-two thousand deaths and a million people homeless."

"Always a threat along fault lines. Significant because?"

"The date of the quake was the anniversary of Kizin's theft. Curse Day, they call it. *El Día Mal....* something."

"*El Día Maldito.*" He searched her gaze. "I reckon that wasn't the last earthquake."

"Another less devastating quake hit the region twenty years later." She wrapped her hands around her glass. Her knuckles gleamed white. "And twenty-one days from now is the next twenty-year anniversary. Seismologists detect increasing pressure along the fault lines, and the tremors are growing in strength."

"Scientists can't accurately predict quakes, but the

data are damned scary. No wonder the locals believe in a curse. And Kizin?"

"A series of collectors owned it, even a museum or two. The statue disappeared about twenty years ago. Dad set aside his book royalties, hoping to purchase it." Her breath hitched and she looked down at the photo in her lap. "Then I took over."

Max gave a low whistle. "And last month the statue showed up at that Paris auction."

"I couldn't get away and the auction house didn't take internet or phone bids. Doug went instead, but arrived late. Alistair Sedgwick had already bought it."

Judging from her tight expression, it wasn't the first time her brother'd been late. "And then Doug paid big bucks to buy the statue from Sedgwick."

"Yes. Doug had just purchased it the day before it was stolen."

And then somebody wanted the artifact as ransom. Too many players. "My notes don't say much about your call to the kidnappers. Could y'all spell that out for me, darlin'?"

Her eyes flashed electric blue. "I'm not your *darlin'*."

"A harmless Texas expression." Slip of the tongue, but riling her had its rewards. Her flare of temper was a hell of a turn-on. "What about the voice?"

"Male, I think, but muffled somehow."

"Electronically altered?"

"I don't think so, just indistinct. He said to go ahead with the trek through the jungle to K'eq Xlapak. He recited a new number to call when I have a satellite phone number. Then he'll call me after I arrive in Costa Verde. I don't think he knows the statue was stolen or about my trip to London to search for it. He seemed to assume Doug had left it with me for safekeeping."

Yeah, that had been in Devlin's report. But what did it mean if the kidnapper was really unaware of the statue's theft? "He speak with a drawl like yours truly or a foreign accent, anything distinctive?"

She looked down, frowned at her glass. "A Spanish accent, maybe. His English seemed limited. He made his demand like he'd rehearsed it or he was reading the words. I did tell Thomas all this."

"Sure 'nuff. He put people on it. They'll locate your brother." Tracking Kizin, buying it from Sedgwick, losing it again—all that so she could return it to its temple after her brother's rescue. "Tell me you don't believe returning a jade statue can stop an earthquake."

"What I believe doesn't matter" She shook her head as if shaking off the curse. "The Maya believe. Returning Kizin is my responsibility as a Fontaine. The Maya value faithfulness, honesty, integrity."

He couldn't argue with that. The same Maya ideals old Nestor impressed on him. Since then, he'd known allegiance like that only with his Special Forces team and DSF. But here he was deceiving her. No choice.

Her voice and gaze held loyalty and desperation. And fear. Oh yeah, she believed.

A hell of a lot in this mess didn't add up. And not just thieves and kidnappers. Returning Kizin to its temple ran a close second to saving her brother's life. Why? For Max, family ties had only unraveled, leaving him shredded. But for Kate, maybe not. Or else something more drove her.

"I'm sorry about your brother." He gave her hand a pat. Skin as soft as he'd imagined. Softer. *Shit.* "I'll do everything I can to get the statue back. And I'd like to see that jungle temple myself."

She smiled as if she believed him. "Thank you."

He yawned. "Now I need some shuteye. My boss met me at baggage claim just before this flight. I haven't slept or showered in forty-eight hours. Hell, maybe longer."

She looked him up and down, apparently only now making sense of his attire. "You just returned from a trip."

"Egypt. Had to retrieve tomb artifacts hijacked as they were being returned to the government."

Avid interest shone in her eyes. She ate up this ancient shit like he did. "I hope you were successful."

"Always." He reclined his seat and closed his eyes. If he didn't cut this off, she'd make him relive breathing all that sand. And he'd be sucked in by eyes the color of Texas bluebonnets.

****

Shafeton Manor, Hampshire, England

Art and artefacts filled the walls and tables everywhere Kate looked. The cavernous room, which a century ago might have been a banquet hall, smelled of the must and dust of ages past. Locked, security-wired display cases of pottery, carvings, and jewelry alternated with tapestries along the carved-panel walls. Larger pieces topped pedestals—masks, urns, a feathered headdress from indigenous cultures in the Americas.

She and Max had arrived at Sedgwick's estate half an hour ago. His sprawling conglomeration of stone and mortar was more castle than house. A servant had opened the massive door and led them down a wide marble corridor, up a set of stairs and down another long corridor to the owner's private museum.

"Sedgwick actually lives here?" Max ended his circuit of the exhibits on the museum's other side. "This entire pile of stones is a damn museum."

"Impressive, isn't it?" Kate said, amused his reaction was the same as hers. "I think he has a flat in London and divides his time."

She halted her tour before the brick fireplace and held her hands toward the flames. This whole situation had a chilling effect. She had to persuade Sedgwick to share ideas on who might've attacked Doug and stolen the Kizin statue.

She sucked in a breath against the tightness in her chest. Goosebumps rose on her flesh. She rubbed her arms.

"Cold, Kate?"

Definitely. The fireplace sent more heat up the chimney than into the room. A better source of heat prowled the other side of the room. "I'm fine."

Mostly Max's default expression was stony detachment. At the moment, one side of his mouth twitched. Flirting? Ill at ease in Sedgwick's opulent mansion? Maybe, but doubtful.

His hard-case demeanor struck her as a deliberate barrier, a ploy to keep people at a distance. If the scowl didn't work, his blunt features would. She'd done a double take at breakfast, then tried not to check out how broad his shoulders looked in the tobacco-colored suede jacket. Or how his jeans hugged his taut butt. Or how the cleft in his smooth-shaven chin seemed to lure her touch.

No touching. Distance worked for her too. Max was a security expert and an investigator, a professional, and she had to rely on him. Thomas Devlin had vouched for his version of what happened in Istanbul. When this was over, she'd ask Doug about that misadventure. Yes, this *would* end with Doug's rescue, dammit.

Max peered through the glass doors of an oak display case that rose at least eight feet from the polished oak floor.

"Something special?" She stayed put, preferring to warm herself by the fire.

"Dozens of clay, stone, and jade figures. The pantheon of Maya gods." He snapped a photo with his cell phone. "With one notable gap."

She frowned. "And yet he sold it to Doug."

Max murmured something she couldn't catch. He was opening drawers in the lower half of the case. He aimed his phone at something in a drawer. What on earth was he doing?

"Max." She started toward him. "You shouldn't be—"

He shut the drawer and put a finger to his lips. Shaking his head, he crossed to her.

She heard the scrape of shoe leather in the corridor two seconds before the museum door opened. Alistair Sedgwick strode into the room. The energy and sharpness in his gaze made him look like a man who'd drive a hard bargain. With Doug, he'd demanded—and got—twice what he paid for Kizin.

Sedgwick introduced himself. "My apologies for the delay. I thought you might enjoy my collections while you waited."

Kate shook his extended hand and introduced Max. "Thank you for seeing me."

"I'm delighted you came, Ms. Fontaine." A thin smile split his long face. His eyes gleamed from beneath amber eyebrows that matched his thick hair. Pink cheeks completed his very English good looks. "I had the honor of meeting your distinguished father a number of years ago when he lectured at the British Museum. He was responsible for great contributions to the field of archeology. You must miss him terribly."

Her breath hitched. Miss him? Only every day for the last three years. Even now whenever someone offered condolences, her chest felt constricted, as if a great boulder got in the way of her lungs. "Yes, I do. Thank you."

"And I was so sorry to learn of your brother's tragic accident. I hope he's recovering."

"Exactly why I came to see you, Mr. Sedgwick. I'll try not to take too much of your time."

Sedgwick ushered them to leather armchairs and a cocktail table on an Aubusson carpet before the hearth. Kate took a chair facing the fire, and their host sat beside her. Max seated himself off to one side, a strategic place to observe. She wouldn't need his protection here, but having his support comforted her for a reason she didn't care to examine. His thumbs flew over his phone. Texting? An unreadable look on his face, he gave the barest shake of his head before stowing the phone.

A uniformed maid whisked in with a tray of tea and the little cookies Brits called biscuits. She set the tray on the cocktail table.

After Sedgwick served the tea, he said in upper-class fruity tones, "I can't imagine what our business might be. Perhaps you've recovered the Kizin statue and wish to sell it back to me?"

Kate sipped her tea, stronger than she liked. She set the cup and saucer on the table. "Hardly. Neither Doug nor I would sell Kizin. The statue is to be returned to Costa Verde. Doug made that clear."

He lounged in his club chair. "A shame that now neither of us possesses Kizin."

She glanced at Max. He selected a biscuit and dipped his head as if to urge her onward. Her stomach clenched. "Exactly. And I need to recover it as soon as possible. The police will share no information with me. I'm here because I need your help."

"I fail to see how I can be of assistance." Sedgwick crossed his ankles. Beneath an arched brow, his eyes gleamed with shrewdness. "I was dining in the West End when your brother was attacked. I knew nothing of it until a Scotland Yard detective questioned me."

"Yes, of course. But I can't wait for the police to solve the crime." If they ever would. She licked her lips. "Perhaps you can think of someone you told about the sale to Doug."

"I wish I could offer you hope, Ms. Fontaine, but I told no one. Given my extensive collection of artifacts, I'm extremely careful about security. Perhaps your brother divulged our deal." He cast a glance at Max as if urging his agreement.

Max studied the tea in his cup.

Doug had claimed he told only her, but his injury muddied his memory. "When you and Doug concluded the sale of Kizin, did you see someone hanging around outside the British Antiquities Society? Maybe someone followed you?"

"The club was quiet that morning. I saw no one outside."

"But—"

"See here, I'm sorry about your brother's injury and

the loss of the statue, but I have no idea who could be behind the crime. There are other statues of Kizin you can purchase, but of course none with, shall we say, the cachet of that particular one with its little curse."

She clasped her hands in her lap and sought calm. "Let me explain my real reason for needing this statue of Kizin and no other. You must know its history."

"Taken from a temple in the Costa Verde jungle sixty years ago. The ensuing earthquake started the curse legend. Wasn't your grandfather the archeologist?"

"My great-grandfather. My father spent years trying to find Kizin so he could return it to K'eq Xlapak. And now someone has kidnapped my brother and demands Kizin as the ransom. If I don't hand it over, they'll kill Doug." She swallowed against the hot, hard lump in her throat.

Sedgwick set his cup and saucer on the tray and splayed his hands, palms up. His long face was sorrowful. "Ms. Fontaine, I do wish I could help you. You have my sympathies."

"Everyone in the antiquities world knows about the auction sale. And of your success in purchasing Kizin."

He sat up straighter, his puffed-out chest endangering his vest buttons. "Indeed."

"Not you, of course, but some collectors will stop at nothing to obtain a piece they want. Can you think of any of your British Antiquities Society colleagues who could be involved?"

His smile flattened. "Certainly not. All of our members are honest collectors."

Kate's temples throbbed. She bit her lower lip. "I'm afraid professional criminals are behind the theft—black-market smugglers. Given your connections among collectors, you could inquire. Others might've heard rumors or have suspicions. Please, Mr. Sedgwick, I need your help."

His gaze skittered away. Then he stared at the carpet before again meeting her eyes. "Black-market smugglers? In that case, I advise you to leave everything to Scotland Yard."

He pushed to his feet. "I cannot help you. It's much too dangerous. For anyone."

Chapter Three

Dorchester Hotel, London
"ALL THAT THINKIN', I expect to see smoke rising from your head." Max snagged an apple from the fruit basket the hotel provided and crunched into it.

He slid off his backpack, then eased onto an armchair, a sorry excuse for furniture but not as prissy as the settee beside it. Stretching out, he admired Kate's hips as she paced from window to window in the suite's parlor and closed the drapes.

"Sedgwick's out, but I do have that appointment at the U.S. Embassy. I'm hoping that in person I can get the FBI agent to leverage pressure on Scotland Yard." Her red-gold mane rippled across her shoulders as she shook her head. She crossed to the matchstick-legged settee. "And there's another collector I can contact, a friend of my father's. Like Sedgwick, he belongs to the British Antiquities Society. Maybe he heard rumors or will have some ideas."

He dragged his gaze from her sleek legs before his blood steamed hotter than a Houston July. Finished with the apple, he tugged his tablet from his pack and fired it up.

So far Kate had been too occupied to mention his snooping in Sedgwick's little museum. He'd texted and sent his photos to the DSF research department. Mara Marton had replied she'd have something fast, the kind of research she really got into. He pictured the intensity on her exotic face as she hit the keyboard. A sexy *chica*, but hitting on a colleague could stab a guy with more thorns than a patch of prickly pears. Too bad.

Yo, here was her report and the Interpol background info. He read the bullet points. It was all there, except for putting a few things together. He set the tablet aside and went to the mini-bar.

He'd devoured his pub lunch of fish and chips in Hampshire, but Kate had only picked at her beef pie. She spent most of the drive with her hands knitted in her lap and her mouth tight. Downed aspirin and spoke only to comment on the GPS lady's directions. Clearly brooding over Sedgwick's refusal to help. Back at it now, massaging her temples and staring at nothing.

He rummaged in the mini-fridge. Came up with one of the bottles he'd purchased at the pub. "A local brew. Hope it's a good beer."

Kate looked up, the skin between her brows pleated, as if his voice yanked her from the thoughts. "I recognize the red-and-white label. One of the better local brews."

"Want one? Or there's a complimentary bottle of wine."

"The local, please."

He opened another and took it to her. "Wait, you probably want a glass."

"If you don't mind." She kicked off her heels and tucked her feet beneath her.

He delivered her bottle and glass and sank onto his chair. Savored the first taste from his bottle. Decent, full flavor.

Kate looked much too inviting curled up on the seat, drinking beer, even if she wasn't cowboying it like him.

Hair loose, although she wasn't. Uptight and high maintenance. Had to remember that.

"You don't need to contact your father's friend," he said.

"What? Why not?"

"I know where the Kizin statue is. Sedgwick has it."

Her eyes rounded and she gaped at him like he'd grown two extra heads before realization flickered in her gaze. "I meant to ask about all that at Sedgwick's. You saw something in that display case. Then you texted. Tell me."

She caught on quick. He took another pull on his beer and set down the bottle. "Sedgwick's maid slacked off on the cleaning. The middle shelf of the case not only had a gap, but also a smudge in the dust where a statue had been. Seemed about the right size for Kizin."

"Then you opened drawers." She raised an eyebrow. "And?"

"Answer this first. When Doug took possession of Kizin, how'd he carry it? Was it in a case or something?"

"No case. It came wrapped in a large jeweler's cloth, apparently what the previous owner had used to protect it in storage."

"One of those anti-tarnish things?"

Her brow furrowed. She huffed and reached in her bag on the other end of the settee. "I have a photo. Doug took it with his phone and sent it to me from the hotel the night he— That night." She swept a finger across the screen a few times, then handed him the phone.

Max peered at the screen. "Too small to see what I need. You mind if I send this to my tablet?"

"Be my guest. But—" At his upheld hand, she shrugged and sipped her beer.

After sending the photo, he returned her phone and retrieved his tablet. In a moment, the photo appeared. Its emerald eyes glittering, Kizin stood on the brown jeweler's cloth.

Hoo-yah. Game on, Alistair.

Just how far would Kate go to get Kizin back? Did she have the guts?

"Here's the photo enlarged." As he handed her the tablet, he could smell her sweet-and-spicy scent. He leaned forward to get a better whiff and his blood supply took a detour south. He sat back, gripped his bottle. "What's that design on the corner of the cloth?"

She glanced at the image. "*J. L.* The initials of the previous owner."

"An elaborate script," he said. "Distinctive, maybe?"

"Yes, very. Custom made. What are you getting at, Max?"

He selected another image. "This is the picture I took inside the display case drawer."

Her mouth didn't drop open but only because she clapped a hand over it. "Oh, my God! It's the same cloth."

Max held his breath and watched as the full impact sank in.

Tears gathered but didn't fall. She finished her beer. Chin up, she set down the glass. "Sedgwick must've sent some… some thug to attack my brother and steal Kizin."

"Yup, hired help. The fu— Sedgwick wouldn't get his hands dirty. Even set himself up an alibi."

She pounded a throw pillow. "Thief. Prick. *Bastard*!"

Damn, so Ms. Uptight Museum Director had some

fire in her belly after all. Righteous anger, a good thing. Max swiped a hand over his almost grin. He worked his mouth, stared at the wall. Her last words to Sedgwick echoed in his head. "You pull those black-market smugglers out of your hat to shock the Brit or do you know something?" Like Devlin's "other players."

She huffed. "Only a suspicion, and yes, I wanted to shock him. In recent years, various professional journal articles in the museum and collecting arena have warned of an international black-market syndicate called Centaur."

That set him back on his heels. But on second thought, word must've circulated in her world about them. "DSF's been running up against Centaur. Interpol suspects them in hundreds of art and antiquities thefts and sales. A shadowy group though. Seems Sedgwick wants his cake—Kizin—and the money too. Chances are Centaur has a finger in that cake."

"You think Sedgwick is involved with them?"

"Centaur finds items for less than scrupulous dealers and collectors. For a finder's fee. Interpol's been looking for certain pieces. I spotted two of them in the museum— an Inuit mask and the totem beside it. Maybe Sedgwick obtained Kizin for Centaur, but Doug made him a better offer. Maybe he changed his mind. Or Centaur changed it for him."

She frowned. "Or Centaur has Kizin. How will I get it then?"

"Nu-uh, Sedgwick's got it. Couldn't stop himself from glancing toward his hidden safe."

Her gaze angled upward and she squinted as if picturing the scene. "He kept looking at something next to the hearth. There?"

He didn't think she'd noticed. "Not your ordinary wall safe but a hidden room like a damn bank vault fitted into the wall."

A knowing gleam lit her eyes. "That's enough for me. Now Scotland Yard will have to listen to me." She hustled with her phone into her bedroom.

Max went to the bar for another Fuller's. He saw only one solution and the cops weren't it. He sucked on his beer and texted Devlin to send the kit for Plan B.

****

Kate made her way through a series of automatic relays and intermediaries. She paced the length of the bedroom. Her stride grew stiff and her shoulders tight. Finally she reached a detective and asked to speak to Sergeant Witherspoon.

He had her spell her name for him and explain what the case entailed, then said, "My apologies, madam. Witherspoon's away until next week."

"Yes, but this is urgent." She launched into what they'd found at Sedgwick's mansion. "The photographs are proof."

"Possibly, but it's not my case. You'll 'ave to wait to talk to Witherspoon."

Closing her eyes briefly, she lifted the hair off her neck. "Detective, you don't understand. A man's life is at stake. My brother—"

"Wish I could 'elp you, ma'am. My case load's all I can 'andle. I'll pass on your message to the sergeant. Or you could make an appointment for next week to show 'im your *evidence*."

She could practically hear the man yawning with boredom. Or worse, he thought she was a crackpot calling with a bogus tip. Dammit, she needed action not delays. She took a deep breath and released it slowly. "I'd like to speak to your supervisor."

Two more conversations later, she disconnected. Shoulders slumped, she stared at the screen. Now what? A couple of ideas occurred to her but nothing seemed viable. She tossed the phone on the bed and returned to the sitting room.

Max stood behind the bar, a beer in hand. From the look on his face, he guessed she'd had no luck. "Looks like you struck out. Want another Fuller's?"

Shaking her head, she sat on one of the two bar stools. Slammed both fists on the wood. "Scotland Yard put me off. The detective on the case is away and the one I spoke to didn't grasp the urgency. I could hear *so-called evidence* in his tone." She relayed the other conversations. The supervisor said what they'd found wasn't enough to authorize a search, but he'd consult with the FBI. Next she phoned the embassy. The special agent said basically the same thing. Not enough for a search. "He did offer to press Scotland Yard to put a man on Sedgwick, in case he made a suspicious move." She huffed. "Like driving around with Kizin on his dashboard?"

"Doesn't leave many options." He propped his elbows on the bar and regarded her with a steady gaze.

His nearness brought her the scents of soap and something woodsy. She straightened before the smell of his skin distracted her. "You knew about Sedgwick's vault."

"Guilty. DSF obtained the house plans. Don't ask how." He swallowed some beer. "We knew of Interpol's suspicions about Sedgwick and Centaur. Nothing concrete. Devlin likes his people to be prepared."

"And are you still prepared to help me recover Kizin?"

"That's my job. The cops won't move. What do you have in mind?" His expression unreadable, he picked at the beer label with his thumb.

She bit her lower lip. "Confront Sedgwick with what I know. Show him the pictures, tell him I'll take my proof to Scotland Yard."

"You think he'll open his vault just like that?" He snapped his fingers. "He's too cool a customer. Too slick. He'll deny everything."

"But the jeweler's cloth with the initials."

"Scotland Yard and the FBI nailed it. Not enough evidence for anybody but us. By the time you got the cops to act, he'd destroy the cloth or say there were two and he gave Doug only the one or we faked the photos. Any delay and he'll stash the statue somewhere else. Or pass it to Centaur. Tackling that passel of cutthroats would be even riskier."

She narrowed her eyes. "I assume you have an idea what to do."

"Only one way left. Plan B." He slid the bottle aside and leaned closer as if to gauge her reaction. "We have to steal Kizin."

Kate's pulse pounded in her ears. She jumped to her feet.

Steal it? She couldn't. They couldn't. Had she made a terrible mistake in trusting Max? In hiring Devlin Security? Thomas had the mansion plans. He'd suspected there'd be no recourse except to do what Max suggested. He knew her desperation to rescue her brother. There must be some other way.

All that came to mind was the image of her brother

in his wheelchair. Where was he? Were the kidnappers feeding him, giving him his medications? Were they hurting him? She pressed a hand to her throat. Now this. Oh, God.

She clutched the edge of the bar. "Max, have you done this sort of thing before?"

He shrugged. "Something like it. Always legit. DSF has an arrangement with some governments and Interpol for off-the-books covert jobs."

"So you could carry out this, um, caper." She swallowed past the hard knot in her throat.

"Not me, Kate. *We*."

"W-w-we? I've never… I mean…. n-no. No." Damn, she sounded like a dying outboard.

He shook his head. "Reckon expecting you to do second-story work's asking too much. Maybe DSF has an agent available. Somebody who can hang tough." His eyes as dark and hard as obsidian, he folded his arms.

"Not equipped…. not capable." Her mother's words floated through her mind and she drew a deep breath. "I run and work out in a gym. I used to do gymnastics."

"Not the same thing. For this I need somebody I can depend on, somebody who won't freeze or wimp out on me. In this op *and* in the Costa Verde jungle."

Her stomach tightened as if she'd swallowed a rock, and she hugged herself. Max was challenging her to prove she could handle the challenges, the dangers, especially the jungle. He didn't think— Hell, why should she care what he thought? He was her employee, not the judge of her skills. Or her courage.

She could stay here at the Dorchester while he broke into the safe.

But should she?

Could she trust him? He'd clearly not told her the whole story about Istanbul. If he'd commit this crime, what else might he do? Would he return with Kizin?

"But, Max, *stealing*?"

Something shifted in his eyes as if his doubt that she'd go for the *op* had morphed to certainty. He picked up his beer. "Stealth, yes. Breaking and entering, yes. Safecracking, yes. But stealing? The statue belongs to you. I like to think of it as recovering stolen property."

On a sigh, she sank onto the stool. "I'll have that beer now."

Chapter Four

Shafeton Manor

KATE CROUCHED AMONG the shrubbery at the edge of the manicured parkland surrounding the mansion's walled garden. Gritting her teeth against the wild fluttering in her stomach, she focused the night-vision binoculars and peered through the midnight veil of fog and drizzle.

"He left yet?" Max said from behind her.

An owl hooted as it took off from a dead tree, a misshapen skeleton in the drifting mist. The BMW still idled at the gatehouse. "Not yet."

"Keep checking." He stretched out with their equipment pack as his pillow.

Camouflage paint darkened his face and his black commando jumpsuit outlined every sinewy muscle. Awareness shivered through her. Not eye-candy? He was, but she'd stop at looking. She'd trust him to guide and protect her—and Kizin—but that was her limit. Even if he were attracted to her—which he obviously wasn't—he was her bodyguard. Not for her, any man who pursued danger like an Olympic medal.

Devlin Security had overnighted a high-tech burglary kit to the hotel, including black jumpsuits and black knit caps. And a Taser. If Max had to put Sedgwick or one of his minions out of action, he said it'd be without bloodshed. Thank God. *Bloodshed?* Just thinking of the possibility roiled her stomach more. She'd have demanded a Plan C. But dammit, as much as she hated the break-in, Max was right. If they waited and tried to devise something else, she could lose Kizin.... and Doug.

For two days they'd plotted their foray into Sedgwick's museum vault and studied the house diagrams. Neither the exterior nor the museum had video cameras probably because of so many black-market pieces.

He drilled her step-by-step on his plan. "Same goes in the military. Be ready for the unexpected."

They'd chosen this evening because Sedgwick would be in London giving a banquet speech to a gathering of antiquities aficionados.

She hadn't counted on this trip to England entailing physical risk, but here she was with Max and his backpack of burglar tools... and with her heart trying to pound its way out of her chest. Should she go through with this? Could she? Or should she wait here while Max did the B&E? No, she *had* to go in. She'd come this far. This wasn't about her.

Shaking off her doubts, she raised the binoculars. The BMW sedan rolled down the graveled driveway toward the motorway. "There he goes."

Max didn't budge. "Give the servants time to settle in their quarters. Wake me in a few."

She changed position, sat on her heels, drummed fingers on the binoculars. Adrenaline pumped through her like an open fire hydrant. Jerk. How could he relax, let alone nap?

Shifting to her knees, she strained her eyes for any movement in the sprawling mansion.

The great pile of stone—complete with battlemented towers, chimney stacks, and mullioned windows—heaved above the sea of fog like an ocean liner. The south side, spider-webbed with scaffolding up to the roof, was their target. Sedgwick had told them as they left the other day, he was having the stonework re-mortared. Spotlights illuminated the entrance, but there was no other security lighting.

"Disconnected for the construction," Max had suggested. "Or the son of a bitch is overconfident."

On the east side, a massive gatehouse formed the main entrance with twin round towers on the northeast and southeast corners, remnants of the original fifteenth-century building. The plans indicated the present-day residence dated from the eighteenth century, including two more gray stone towers on the west corners. Maybe added in a bout of nostalgia or an attempt at architectural balance.

The west wing housed the museum. Once inside, they had to make their way undetected from the south side.

One by one, lights winked out in the residence wing. This was it. She worked up enough saliva for speech. "Only low-wattage lights in the corridors. I can't see the servants' wing."

He jackknifed up, alert as if he'd never closed an eye. "Kate, last chance. Y'all in?"

Her heart throbbed in her throat and her nerves were jumping. But she was ready. Not trusting her voice, she nodded and donned her night-vision goggles. The world brightened in shades of green and silver.

Below the goggles propped on his head, the scowl didn't waver. She'd watched earlier as he'd checked his pistol, but his demeanor now—hard features, competence and battle-ready control in the set of his jaw—drove home the knowledge he was a warrior who'd protect her.

"A final warning," he said. "We've planned, but there's always the unexpected. Be ready."

She cleared her throat. "So you've said over and over and over. I'm in."

He slid down his goggles and shrugged on the pack. "Then let's rock and roll." He headed through the bushes.

She jogged beside him. She didn't have his expertise but she was in shape. Everything had to come off like one of her themed nights at the museum. Better. Perfect. Because if she froze, as Max feared, she could ruin everything. They could lose their chance at Kizin. They could be arrested. Even though Max had discounted that possibility, she couldn't.

Or they could die.

Sedgwick had to be behind the attack on Doug. Finding Kizin would be proof enough. Gooseflesh pricked her arms beneath the black microfiber, but she kept her legs pumping to stay in tandem with Max's longer stride.

Keeping low across the wide parkland, they scuttled from tree to tree. Their rubber soles swished across the wet grass.

He'd asserted that they ought to be damn near invisible in their commando gear but it was good he seemed to be taking no chances. An overhanging tree served as cover as he scaled the garden wall.

He turned and held out a black-gloved hand. "Alley oop. This ought to be as easy as that climbing wall you said you have at your gym."

She ignored his offer of a hand up. "Easier." Lower by far. She dug her fingers and toes into the cracks. A soft thud came as he dropped to the other side. She heaved herself onto the top and over, and he lifted her down.

He released her as soon as her feet hit the grass, but she still felt the strength of his hands on her waist and the heat of his muscled body against her. He'd hauled her down with ease, and she was no feather.

They zigzagged through the garden paths until they stood beneath the construction scaffolding below the rows of windows. The mist carried the scents of roses and the muddy dankness of a nearby marsh—and her nervous perspiration. She watched Max listening for movement. Only the whish of wings and the squeak of a hunting bat came to her ears.

The windows were tall, four-over-four Tudor panes. The top ones arched and the lower sections opened outward casement style. From this angle, the inside was dark as a cave.

"We're going up the inside of the scaffolding," he whispered, "close to the building where we're less likely to be spotted. Don't touch these two lower stories of windows. They're wired. Third story's clear."

She knew. They'd gone over and over the plan. She didn't need him to keep asking and reminding but she said nothing. She hated the whole venture but would do her part, dammit, despite the gathering collection of rocks in her stomach.

"The scaffolding looks solid," she said. The base had settled into the ground, and the framework appeared level. A workers' platform lay on the ground, to be hauled up by pulley for the next day's labors.

"Yup, lookin' solid." He gestured upward at the metal spider web. "The sections on this scaffolding are too far apart to climb like a ladder. We'll have to shimmy up the poles and across the diagonal supports to each higher bar. Can you manage?"

"It's like uneven parallel bars. No problem." She rolled her shoulders.

When she reached for the first bar, he covered her gloved hand with his. "The bars are wet from the fog. If you get in trouble, I'm here. Take your time. We have hours."

In the shadows of the manor, he appeared as merely a denser outline, but she could see his eyes crinkled with concern. His worry for her warmed something inside her. Damn, more likely he was worried for the mission, worried she'd wimp out. Warmth faded.

She inhaled deeply and flexed her fingers. "I'm good."

He jumped for the first bar. His grip set, he hoisted himself up and waited. Reverberation from his weight shivered the structure, but didn't rattle the metal. Bless quality construction.

He extended an arm to her. Too risky not to accept his help. She clasped his hand and climbed. She followed him, scooting over a diagonal span and up the second vertical.

Like a monkey up a coconut tree, she shimmied up another vertical and reached for the next bar.

Her hand slipped on the wet metal.

Her left leg banged into a crosspiece and the framework trembled.

Her heart thudded loud enough to wake every

servant in the mansion. She wrapped her right arm around the upright, grabbed the bar, and held on. *Dammit!* Where was rosin when she needed it?

Before she could get her bearings, Max was beside her. He hooked an arm around her waist in support. "Hang quiet and listen."

No voices broke through the fog. No doors banged.

She breathed deeply and concentrated. His body heat permeated her thin jumpsuit, and she felt his heart beating in tandem with hers. She couldn't see his face but pictured the scowl contorting it. Somehow that was comforting. *I can do this.*

"Okay. Only one story to go."

Careful to grip each bar and strut tightly, she continued upward. With Max beside her, she made it the rest of the way up to the third-story windows.

Using a circular cutter, he sliced a hole in one pane large enough for his arm. He reached through to the latch. Seconds later, they were in and Max closed the window behind them. Their headlamps showed an elaborate, carved-wood chimney piece that filled an entire wall of the cavernous room.

"Empty," he said. "How could anybody have enough furniture to fill a place this size anyway?"

They stayed low as they moved away from the windows and toward the far wall, where carved-wood panels surrounded a door. Kate opened Max's pack and exchanged both sets of goggles for head-mounted lamps and flashlights. She pulled out her phone and scrolled through the plans for the layout of this floor.

Sure enough, the carved door led into a hallway. Someone's stern ancestors glowered from the walls as they padded toward the tower. Sedgwick's family might have photo albums, but not gilt framed oils. Maybe they came with the mansion.

That way, she motioned.

Past the landing, stairs led down a floor. A right turn took them into the west wing. Creeping past more elaborate doors, they reached the double doors of the museum.

Max shrugged off his pack and went to work.

She didn't understand the technology, but watched, fascinated, as he applied a digital lock pick. The device was a small remote control with a wire to attach to the lock. In only moments, it opened the doors and another gizmo disarmed the security system.

They were in! The door closed behind them with a soft click.

His beam outlined the Inuit mask in otherworldly light. Other objects on pedestals stood sentinel in the dark museum.

Intrigued, she reached out a hand to the glowing mask.

Max's hand closed over hers. "Don't touch. The pedestals have weight sensors. I noticed the wires the other day."

"That's not in the plans," she snapped. "And you didn't mention it."

"Reckon not, darlin'."

Be ready for the unexpected. More challenge to her alertness and nerve.

Before she realized he'd left her side, he'd ghosted across the room to the wall where the safe was hidden. He tapped and fingered the panel edges.

She joined him as the wall panel slid to the left, revealing a solid-looking metal door with an electronic keypad in the middle. He applied the digital pick.

When the device appeared to give him trouble, she held her breath. She flexed her fingers. *Please, please!*

A moment later, a code slid into place on the lock pick's readout. A series of clicks came from the metal door. Max pulled down on the handle and the door opened. Fresher air than the museum's musty smell blew out on the hum of a fan.

"Magic!" Kate whispered.

"Nu-uh, electronics. But it's damned slick," he drawled. "Now it's your show. Where would Sedgwick stow the statue?"

Their beams played over the vault interior as they entered. Drawers lined the left and rear walls like safe-deposit boxes. The right wall held shelves on which stood various small pieces—boxes with jeweled inlay, carvings, clocks.

No Kizin.

A metal table took up the center space. Max mentally pumped a fist, recognizing the sculpture on the table, a foot-high bronze horse. "Interpol will want to see this one." He snapped a picture, then watched Kate take stock.

"If I were a Maya artifact with emerald eyes, where would I hide?" She made a sweeping gesture at the drawers. "You start in the back and I'll start on the left."

He listened for approaching footsteps but heard nothing unusual. The wind whined in the windows of the ancient manor. A brass carriage clock on the shelf ticked away the minutes.

They opened drawers and examined their contents. Some drawers held cash in several foreign currencies. Some had jewelry and loose stones protected with velvet bags and padding. He snapped more pictures as he poked in box after box.

Surprised the hell out of him Kate went through with this. As stiff as a cottonwood but serious enough about setting her brother free that she didn't let fear stop her. This time.

What if Kizin wasn't here? What if he was wrong? To tell the truth, he wanted to see the damn little god. And get out before they got caught.

If they made it out of here okay, it wouldn't be due to his expertise. Kate had thrown off his usual concentration and made him wish he wore cargo pants instead of the form-fitting microfiber jumpsuit. Hers molded to her long, lean curves like shrink wrap. The camo smear couldn't hide the pallor on her cheeks. Her translucent skin showed her every emotion. Including fear. The woman was petrified but damned if she'd let him know it.

She hadn't needed help down from the garden wall but it gave him an excuse to hold her and inhale her fragrance. Hell, she wasn't his type. She was the kind of female men of good family took home for dinner with mama, not the no-strings kind that guys with no family and no history took home for a few hours.

He opened another drawer. Hot damn, there on a velvet pillow was the gold snake arm band on Interpol's list, a black-market piece from Syria they suspected Doug Fontaine sold. Not the time to share with Kate. He took a quick snapshot, then stowed his phone.

Ay, she was so earnest and scared for her brother, had no idea he was bent. She'd find out soon enough. Not Max's problem. His duty was to Devlin, not any sympathy for her. Or thoughts of getting her naked. *¡Qué* *lástima!* What a shame.

He finished rifling through a drawer of small gold coins and was about to close it when he heard her gasp.

Chapter Five

MAX SPUN TOWARD Kate.

No Sedgwick, no harm, no foul. He slid his hand from the Taser and grinned at the sight of her running her fingers over the jade statue like it was a lover. He should be so lucky.

"This is it, Max. Isn't it beautiful?" She touched one of the emerald eyes. "Emeralds are a type of beryl. Traces of chromium form the different shades of green. These stones' deep green says they probably came from Colombia."

The emeralds were as large as robins' eggs, irregular ovals and polished, but with only a few facets. He frowned. "Not what I pictured. They look like jade but clear."

"These are rough-cut stones." She raised the statue so her headlamp beam caught the minute inclusions in the center. Then she bent to their pack on the floor and zipped Kizin securely inside a padded pouch. "You think the ancient Maya had gem-cutting tools?"

"Good point. Now let's get the hell out of here."

Before they could move, lights blinded them. All the illumination in the museum room flashed on at once. Overhead fluorescents in the safe glared in their eyes.

Son of a bitch! Max felt for the Taser at the small of his back.

Kate raised a hand against the light and edged closer

to him, placed a hand on his arm. "Max?"

The man stepping into the vault's opening blocked the harshest light. He held a semiautomatic.

"Ms. Fontaine? Indeed it is. I should've known you'd not give up so easily," Alistair Sedgwick said with plummy-toned disdain. His sharp features and blond mane came into focus as Max's eyes adjusted to the glare. "So you guessed my little secret."

"Your *dirty* secret." Kate said.

The collector inclined his head in a slight bow. "As you wish. A fire at the hotel canceled my meeting tonight. Bloody lucky for me, as it turns out. And bloody lucky I decided to take my brandy up here."

Max smoothed his features. Play for time and look for an opening. Or this could go from bad to fugly real fast. "And you just happened to bring your pistol."

Sedgwick smiled, a spread of lips without humor or good will. "Yes, the gun. I keep it handy just inside in the museum door. One never knows."

"Do you plan to use it? Messy in the safe."

"I could shoot you both with impunity. The constables would find two dead burglars."

Kate's hand trembled on Max's arm. Hell, he'd pushed her to show she had what it took and neglected the first rule of security—*protect the principal*. His gut twisted.

He tugged her behind him, blocking her body with his. Sedgwick's gun hand wavered. He was sweating. An amateur. Even more fucking dangerous, but he'd neglected to demand they show their hands. Max kept his right on the Taser. "You won't shoot us. There's too much you wouldn't want the cops to see."

Sedgwick's grating cackle echoed in the vault. "The

local constabulary wouldn't recognize the *Mona Lisa*, but I suppose you know all about it."

"Some. And so does Interpol." The collector had been a busy boy buying stolen shit from all over the world. Max had photographed five more from the list. He tipped his head toward the bronze horse. "The second-century Han Period horse stolen last year from the Tate. I can point out others."

Sedgwick's pink face blanched to a sickly gray. The gun barrel angled down as he seemed to consider his dilemma. "Perhaps we can reach an accord after all. Leave the Kizin statue on that table and go."

Behind him, Max heard the faint clinking of metal. The drawer of coins? What was Kate doing?

He grasped her arm with his left hand, ready to tug her out of the way and use the Taser.

"Be ready," Kate whispered to Max. Before he could stop her, she shook off his grip and stepped toward the collector, her right hand closed at her side.

Be ready? Max's pulse cranked to fifth gear. Was she trying to get them both killed?

Forcing himself to breathe evenly, he rotated his shoulders. Other than the rush of adrenaline in his system, he heard only the normal creaking of the ancient house and the chiming of the hour—ten. Nothing else. Sedgwick hadn't raised an alarm. Yet. Max kept his stance loose and watched the collector.

"The statue doesn't belong to you," Kate said to Sedgwick. "I will *not* let you keep it. You're a thief and you tried to have my brother killed." Her voice trembled, yet rang with determination.

"He gave me no choice. He wouldn't sell it back to me. I need that statue."

The intensity in the other man's eyes said Max had guessed right. Centaur wanted the statue and Sedgwick had screwed up by selling it. If Max and Kate could get out of here with Kizin, the Brit'd be in deep shit.

Kate's chin shot up. "Need is a relative term. The statue will save my brother's life. I intend to leave with it."

"My dear Ms. Fontaine, you forget who has the gun."

"I told Scotland Yard we found the jeweler's cloth here in your display case. Kizin was wrapped in it when you sold it to Doug. If anything happens to us, the detectives will arrest you for your crimes." She took another step forward, blocking Max's chance at a clear shot.

He swallowed a groan, gripped his weapon. *Dios mío*, what the hell game was she playing? Sweat trickled down his spine.

Sedgwick might shoot them anyway. He'd clicked off the automatic's safety. Getting rid of the bodies would be no trouble for this rich dickwad and a couple of cooperative servants. In a hundred years or so, archeologists might find their bones in the marsh.

"Put down your gun." She raised her closed hand waist high. "We're leaving now. Aren't we, Max?"

"No! What are you doing?" Scowling, Sedgwick took a step closer. He and Kate stood a mere three feet apart.

Max eased closer behind her, ready for whatever the fuck she planned.

She tipped back her head, aimed her headlamp's beam at Sedgwick's eyes.

When he blinked in the glare, she raised her arm and

heaved a fastball of gold. The spray of tiny coins flew at Sedgwick's head.

Coins hit his face, his shoulders, his arms. Coins pinged on the floor. He threw up his hands, blocking the attack.

Max lunged. He snatched away the semi-auto and passed it to Kate.

Sedgwick reeled. He turned in a fighting stance.

Max fired the Taser. Wires shot out, darting the probes through the other man's expensive cotton shirt and into his chest.

Sedgwick screamed, went as rigid as the bronze horse, then dropped like the fucking bag of shit he was.

Another five-second ride put him to sleep.

Kate stared from the pistol in her hands to Sedgwick and back.

Max scratched his head. Damn, the woman had come through when he thought she'd pull an armadillo and curl up into a ball. Surprising. Hot. And fucking terrifying. No way would he let her hang onto that pistol. "I'll take that off your hands, darlin'."

He could hang onto the semi-auto, toss it in the woods, but he didn't need the extra weight in the pack. He dropped the clip in his pocket and the semi-auto in a drawer.

"But, Max, is he—"

Grabbing his pack and her hand, he dragged her with him. "He'll live. Let's beat feet."

****

They retraced their steps to the scaffolding in what seemed to Kate like seconds. Max swung down ahead of her and she followed. She jumped the last span into his waiting arms. Still shaking, she held onto him as his arms tightened around her and held her fast. His dark eyes were radiant, intense, but with emotion she couldn't discern. She felt every pounding beat of his heart and every ridge of his muscle as he slid her downward until she stood, still shaking, wanting to sink against his solid strength, safe and warm.

"Keep low," he said, his voice rough. "We have to get out of here."

She reeled as he released her, her chest light, one burden lifted.

She would whoop with joy, except they might hear her in the manor, and she needed all her breath to keep putting one foot in front of the other. They ran across the garden and the parkland. In moments they reached the woods beyond the estate and the safety of their rented British SUV.

Max jerked a nod toward Shafeton Manor. "Shit, he's up. That place's lit up like the London Eye. Sedgwick's hunting us."

Kate had no time to catch her breath before they were speeding away on the dirt track toward the highway.

After a few miles down the highway, Max turned onto a smaller country lane. Then he pulled off where a farm road disappeared into the dark, cut the engine, and slammed out of the SUV.

She stepped out and leaned on the fender, dragging in air. She flung her arms wide. "We did it, Max. We did it. I have Kizin. One step closer to rescuing Doug. Thank you for keeping me safe, for everything." She removed the knit cap and shook out her hair.

No hint in his expression he appreciated her thanks. His dark eyes glowered above the dark smears on his cheeks. Anger simmered in his hard stare and tight mouth. He rounded the vehicle and yanked her against him. He was so indelibly male, so macho, so physical, a look from him fluttered her pulse. Then something else burned in his gaze, something molten that stopped her breath. Dangerous.

She stilled in his arms, her breasts against his solar plexus, her thighs against his. His scent—earthy, salty, male—washed over her. She ought to step back, but instead flattened her palms on his chest. She fought the urge to knead the slabs of muscle straining his jumpsuit.

"What the hell were you— Aw, shit." He tangled one hand in her hair and brought his mouth down on hers.

Heat flashed through her, from her lips down to her core. He tasted hot and untamed and she wanted the kiss to go on and on, but, like a lightning strike, it ended after only an instant.

Blood thundered in her head, and her senses struggled for balance as she pushed through the sensual fog. Her fingers still dug into the fabric of his jumpsuit. No, she didn't want this—*him*—and *he* didn't want her. Not really, even if she felt evidence to the contrary against her belly. What *did* he want?

She pushed against his chest to step away but she might as well have been struggling against steel. Her pulse raced and she glared at him. "Let me go. Why did you do that?"

"Heat of the moment." Chest heaving with labored breaths, he held her a beat longer, then backed away in a stiff motion. He folded his arms.

His scowl said he wasn't going to offer a further explanation. Anger? Relief at the escape? Her lips still tingled from his kiss and her pounding heart made her rib cage feel too tight. "See that it doesn't happen again," she said through gritted teeth.

"What the hell were you thinking back there with that damn coin toss? You're lucky he didn't blow a hole through you."

She could scarcely believe what she'd done. An acidic lump lodged in her throat. "He was going to shoot us. I couldn't let him win. My brother... I had to do *something*." She tried to inhale deeply, but her lungs didn't want to cooperate.

His scowl remained adamantine. "I didn't take you for impulsive. A surprise."

A trait hidden from herself, it seemed. But *he* saw that? What else did he see in her? More wild fluttering in her stomach.

Then the reason for his anger hit her. "I wasn't thinking about the Taser. You had it ready, didn't you?"

If not approval, at least understanding softened his eyes before he nodded. "Next time, trust me. Now let's go. This detour back to London will take longer."

Once on the road, he spoke again. "Nice follow through. Where'd you learn to pitch like that?" His tone was level, annoyance apparently dissipated.

She let out a breath. "Long games of catch with Doug and Dad on expeditions."

"The slimy bastard didn't expect you to threaten him, and he sure as hell didn't expect you to hit him with his own coins. Hell, neither did I." He scraped knuckles against his jaw and shook his head. "Element of surprise."

"Be ready for the unexpected." Like his punishing kiss—no, demanding kiss.

"Remember that once we get to Costa Verde. A

Devonshire estate's not the Central American jungle."

No flutters in her midsection, only a sick sensation. Could she handle the dangers, so much unknown? Could she turn Doug's rescue and Kizin's return over to Max and Devlin? An image of her brother tied up, drugged, bloody rose in her mind. No, she couldn't allow anything to stop her from rescuing Doug. She was going, no matter what Max said.

She lifted her chin. "Not the jungle. I know. As you constantly remind me."

****

Two days later

"My employer is distressed you have hidden your latest moves from him," the Frenchman said from his fireside chair. A block of a man whose Algerian ancestry shaded his complexion, Le Noir linked his fingers across the buttoned placket of his double-breasted silk suit coat. He stared at Sedgwick with dead black eyes.

"I hid nothing." Sedgwick's pulse pounded. He had to put off Le Noir and his bloody employer. He took the seat opposite the other man, but the leaping flames didn't dispel his chill.

"You purchased the Kizin statue and then you sold it. At my insistence, you recovered it and now you 'ave lost it once again." Le Noir's lips were pressed as thin as a guillotine blade.

How could the Centaur syndicate know? Did they have spies everywhere? But Sedgwick *would* have it. He shook his head. "Monsieur Le Noir, I—"

"A prize such as that could pay your debt in full. *Enfin*, my employer is most concerned about the debt owed."

"I paid your *employer* almost a million American

dollars." What Fontaine had paid him, less a hundred thousand. Compensation for his trouble. "I have other assets as valuable as Kizin, ones easily liquidated."

Le Noir made a clucking sound. "Monsieur, it seems you do not understand. He will keep your cash as down payment, but it is Kizin you were told to obtain. Kizin is what he will have. He collects certain artifacts *aussi*. Ancient items of... power."

Sedgwick studied him. Le Noir never joked, and he wasn't joking this time. The head man of Centaur believed in ancient legends and curses? Such superstitions made him unpredictable. And more dangerous. He swallowed a laugh. Christ, how could the leader of this cut-throat organization be even *more* dangerous?

Le Noir lifted one shoulder in a purely Gallic gesture and examined a manicured and buffed fingernail. "You will have the statue soon, *n'est-ce pas*?

Deals with Centaur had shackled Sedgwick to a bloody gang of thugs in Italian tailored suits. An impasse he had to overcome. He'd kept Kizin too long, had no luck finding an artisan to craft a duplicate. But if he could recover the statue, he still had a way out.

But first he would produce the real artifact at the November meeting of the British Antiquities Society. His childhood had been spent above a pub, not in the comfort of a manor like the other members. His public-school education hadn't the cachet of Eton. Regardless, he'd made his fortune and a name among the titled elite who collected art and antiquities. Possessing Kizin would cement his status. They would respect him.

Then Centaur could have the damn thing. He would buy another.

Nausea at the other man's heavy cologne sifted inside him. He resisted the urge to swallow the bile creeping up his throat. He reminded himself the Frenchman carried concealed blades sharper than shark teeth.

Sedgwick's shoulders sagged. "Kizin will belong to me in a matter of days."

Le Noir cocked one dark eyebrow.

"I meant to say, belong to your employer. I shall turn it over, of course."

"*D'accord.* We will expect your call within a week." Despite his muscular bulk, or perhaps because of it, Le Noir rose to his feet as lightly as a cat. "Please summon your butler. I am ready to depart."

He wandered around the museum, stopping before an antique Japanese screen depicting peacocks in a garden. Raised a hand toward it.

Fingers on the keypad, Sedgwick opened his mouth. He'd protested already as much as was wise. His stomach rolling, he swallowed his words and pressed the button.

Centaur's man ran fingers over the fragile silk. "My employer grows impatient, Monsieur Sedgwick. Make no mistake. Your debt will be repaid one way or another. Given your background, you may have limited experience with literature. I suggest you peruse *The Merchant of Venice.*"

The threat twisted like a dagger. When the dapper thug had left, Sedgwick stumbled to the drink cart. A shot of brandy calmed his heart rate and his shaking hands.

No missing the slur on his background. Le Noir and his so-called employer knew too much about him. More than he'd been able to learn about Centaur. The crime syndicate with its mysterious leader materialized a few years ago. Small and secretive, they began with art and artifact theft and oozed into the art black market with theft-for-hire contracts and high-interest loans. The way they'd sucked him into their web.

He poured another dram and crossed to the Japanese screen. Priceless, and that slimy wanker had dared touch the silk. He spotted a new mark on the largest peacock. If Le Noir had dirtied it... Holding his breath, Sedgwick touched the spot with his index finger. Not dirt.

The peacock's throat had been slit.

Chapter Six

Cabo Grande, Costa Verde

KATE HITCHED HER carryon and camera bag onto her shoulder and wheeled her suitcase a few feet away from the throng milling around the baggage carousel. Spicy aromas from vending carts and conversations in Spanish and other languages swirled around her.

Was it only two days ago she'd returned to Washington? Barely time to pack and placate her mom. No success there. Only the same protests and worries Mom always trotted out, wailing that Kate wasn't tough enough—the time she came down with malaria, the spider that sent her crying in panic. She breathed deeply against the tightness in her chest.

Mom was wrong. That was a long time ago. Stupid childhood fears wouldn't stop her. The threat of earthquakes wouldn't stop her. If she succumbed to fear, who knew what would happen to Doug.

After leaving her mom's condo, she'd returned to her house in Adams-Morgan to pack. And jumped nearly through the eight-foot ceiling when her cell rang. The kidnapper demanded the number of her satellite phone and the time of her arrival in Costa Verde. How had he known she was ready to leave? Were they following her? Did he know about London?

Before she could ask about Doug, he hung up. She sank onto the bed and lowered her head between her knees before she could breathe again. She spent the rest of the evening packing and watching *Brave* and *Frozen*. Twice each.

Finally tonight she and Max landed in Costa Verde.

She sat on her suitcase and turned on her satellite phone. Nothing but a blank screen. Damn, no connection under the roof. When would the kidnappers call?

In the high-ceilinged tin can of a building, air conditioning did little to mitigate the boiling heat. She used her passport folder to fan her face. Max would find her after he retrieved the rest of their luggage.

Today he looked the badass adventurer in his khaki safari shirt. The shadow of beard jazzed her pulse. At the play of muscle in Max's arms as he loaded bags onto a wheeled cart, her mouth went dry.

Kate touched a finger to her lips. His taste, the imprint of his mouth, did they still linger? Her breathing quickened. Just thinking about being in his arms raised her temperature. But they'd barely spoken since that sizzling embrace. Rather, *he*'d barely spoken, playing the tall, dark, and silent bodyguard type. Probably regretted that kiss. As she ought to. As she did. *Yes, Kate, and tell yourself another.*

She could look but no touching, no kissing. Not with a man she couldn't trust except for protection.

Max turned away from the carousel and began wheeling the cart toward her. He stopped dead in the middle of the aisle.

A small boy, about three years old, stood alone. Travelers streamed around him, paying no attention to the child only as high as knee level. Tears fell from

61

brown eyes wide with panic, dribbled down his chin, and onto his Incredible Hulk T-shirt.

The sight punched her in the stomach. She started to rise, but held back when she saw Max kneel in front of the boy. Travelers' voices, loudspeaker announcements, and landing airplanes prevented her from hearing what Max said.

After a glance around, the child sniffed and replied.

Lost, he'd probably wandered away. Mom must be nearby. Kate scanned the crowd but saw no frantic woman, no one who stood out as panicked.

Max pulled a pack of tissues from his shorts pocket and handed one to the boy, who wiped his eyes but not his nose. Max spoke again, a gentle smile on his face, one that softened his blunt features and softened something inside Kate's chest. He pointed to the uniformed guard at the security desk.

The boy studied the guard for a moment, then nodded.

Max pushed to his feet and wheeled the luggage cart out of the boy's way.

When the toddler reached up, Max opened his hand, a soldier's hand, thick with muscle and calloused. A tiny hand—likely wet with tears and baby snot—closed over two of Max's fingers.

Kate's throat closed, and she had trouble swallowing. She craned her neck to see around the throng dragging bags past the security desk.

No sooner had Max and the lost boy walked up to the desk than a heavy-set woman hustled toward them. She wheeled two suitcases, the smaller one covered in super-hero stickers. Her face was just as frantic and tear soaked as the boy's.

Crying out, the boy flung himself into her arms.

After an interchange between the mother and Max, he headed toward Kate.

At what was probably a sappy smile on her face, he said, "You saw that?"

"Max Rivera to the rescue. Nice work."

Scowling, he scraped fingers through his hair. "People shouldn't have kids if they're not going to keep track of them."

Okay, that comment didn't invite further comment from her. But the vehemence of his statement did invite curiosity. Some history there. But asking was out of the question. Definitely more to this man than brawn.

Stick to professional distance. Better, safer to concentrate on the expedition, on ransoming Doug, on steeling herself for that first quiver of the ground. DSF's researcher had reported more frequent and stronger tremors. Her chest quivered as if a tremor had reached inside, and she pulled her shoulder blades together, straightening. No tears. No panic. No turning back.

****

Max eyed Kate as they made their way out of the terminal. Mouth a tight line, eyes straight ahead, back stiff as a private in basic training. Terrified but determined.

Or angry. About the delay while he helped the little guy find his mom? Nu-uh. More likely she was still ticked off about him kissing her. Damn, she had every right.

That night, she'd seemed to accept his smartass comment and brushed off his reckless lip lock. Neither of them had said a word about it since, not even on the flight here. A hard lesson he'd learned early on, females held onto a mad like a rattler on a rabbit. He was a sorry son of a bitch, and unprofessional, but apologizing more now would be lame. And might rile her worse.

But man, he didn't regret the kiss. She'd tasted sweeter than… hell, he didn't know what, and he'd wanted more. Out of the question. All he could do was what she'd hired DSF for. And the extra little matter Devlin had assigned him.

They joined other luggage-laden groups in the taxi waiting line. Shouldn't take too long. Not a problem, except for the heat, even late at night. He peeled his sweat-damp shirt away from his back.

A couple of bored-looking cops in navy shorts and white shirts stood nearby. Palm trees and bougainvillea lined the far side of the airport entrance beneath a star-lit sky. Vendors hawking tours and souvenirs vied for curb space with limo drivers holding passenger name signs.

Devlin's briefing warned that several factions wanted the valuable artifact Kate carried, but nobody made any threatening moves or looked at them, the only obvious *norteamericanos*. And the only guns in sight hung on the cops' belts. A normal airport scene.

Kate drank from a water bottle. Clutched the camera bag against her side. Maybe her silence just meant she was hot and tired.

She liked to be in control. A little organizing ought to perk her up. "So what's the program, boss?"

Her eyes were blank as if jerked from her thoughts. "Um, tomorrow after we collect our supplies, we'll meet the Maya guides. Then tomorrow night's the gala."

Que desastre. He'd forgotten. Hell, he'd deliberately pushed the gala out of his mind. When *Presidente* Aguilar had learned a director of the National

Cultural Museum would be visiting, he sent Kate an invitation to his wife's birthday celebration.

Their low profile was blown before they even got started. Bad omen.

Just the thought of wearing the straitjacket in his suitcase made him queasy. "About the gala. Not a good idea, an evening in a crowd of people. Didn't you say some of those who want Kizin would attend?"

"Not going would be a slight to President Aguilar and might appear suspicious. I want no one to suspect I've brought Kizin with me."

Ah, the statue. He furrowed his brow and wagged his head. "You can't carry it to the gala and I'd bet my boots you won't leave it behind. Whole thing's too dangerous, Kate."

"I'm sure we'll think of something. The hotel must have a safe." She tilted her head and beamed him a dazzling smile. "Besides, you'll be there as my protector. In your tuxedo."

Before he could come up with more reasons to pass on the damn fancy-dress party, a uniformed soldier approached them and saluted smartly.

"*Buenos noches, señor y señora.*" He continued in Spanish, "Welcome to my beautiful country. General Rodolfo Lopez of the Costa Verde Military Forces has instructed me to offer his car and his hospitality." After indicating a limousine idling beyond the taxi stand, he waited at attention.

Kate clutched Max's forearm. "What does he want? My phrase-book Spanish isn't up to this."

As Max explained, his mind kicked out the name Lopez from the DSF file. "This guy works for General Lopez. Isn't Lopez one of the parties interested in the jade figure?"

She gazed with avid eyes at the long white limousine with its smoky windows and Costa Verde flags. "If he could aid in returning Kizin, it would be a coup for him as a presidential candidate in the coming election. But... a limo, with air conditioning. What harm can it do?"

A lot, if the general was determined to have Kizin. Whether he'd return it to the temple was another question. Even baking in the tropical heat, the limo looked inviting. But risky.

He turned to the chauffeur, who looked disconcerted at the delay. "The Cabo Grande Hotel is on the central plaza of Cabo Blanco. Do you know it?"

The man bobbed his head. "*Sí, sí, señor*. But *el general* offers you his humble home while you are here. He promises that *Señorita* Fontaine will be much more comfortable at his estate than in a hotel."

Max pulled Kate aside. "I don't like this set-up. Lopez wants us to stay at his place. At the very least, you'd be in his debt." If she wouldn't trust him on this, she wouldn't trust him on anything. That could mean trouble down the line. Jaw muscles tight, he crossed mental fingers.

Her gaze held calm decision. "Tell the soldier I appreciate the general's gracious offer, but accepting his hospitality would be a slight to President Aguilar, who is my official host."

Max couldn't help but grin at her diplomatic refusal. No wonder she was high up at her museum.

When he translated her speech to the chauffeur, the man snatched off his cap and started to plead. Polite deference ratcheted up to agitated whine. The general wouldn't be happy with Kate's refusal of his so generous hospitality. Not Max's concern. Kate was his concern.

The cab line moved along and their taxi's doors stood open and waiting. Ignoring the soldier's protests, Max helped their driver load bags into the rusting van.

As they drove away into the capital city, he looked behind them. The soldier waved a fist as he talked on his phone.

****

Kate stared at her home away from home. Eleven o'clock at night and muggy heat wrapped around her. Sweat crawled down her back and seeped through her blouse. She could feel her gelled and smoothed hair springing around her head with gleeful abandon.

If the Cabo Grande Hotel was the finest establishment in Cabo Blanco, she'd hate to see the worst. Stucco painted Caribbean blue, white shutters, wrought-iron balconies, as advertised. Strictly speaking. The brochure failed to mention the peeling paint, shutters with missing slats, and balconies so rusty they couldn't support a newborn baby.

If the outside was this bad, what were the rooms like?

Stay in this crumbling hotel? It couldn't be worse than the trek into the Costa Verde jungle. Something dark and heavy settled inside her chest. She pressed a hand to her sternum.

But no tremors so far. Maybe Kizin had settled down to help her. Wishful thinking. There *would* be tremors. She sucked in a shaky breath of the steamy air. Her brother would be rescued. Then she would return Kizin to K'eq Xlapak. She shifted the camera bag, weighted with the jade statue inside its secret compartment.

"Y'all ready?" Max's deep drawl snapped her from her reverie. He'd paid the taxi driver and lined up their luggage on the pavement. Heat didn't seem to bother the big Texan.

Typical of the tropics, the hotel entrance was open-air, from a covered portico into a tiled lobby—*cracked* tile—where two ceiling fans swiped at the heavy air. A bellman in a sweat-stained uniform shuffled toward them with a rickety luggage cart.

She held up a hand in the universal stop gesture. *"Espere un momento."*

She hiked her purse and camera bag straps higher on her shoulder. "Max, this... establishment isn't what I expected."

"The hotel?"

"My uncle stayed here several years ago. He recommended it, but I realize the brochure was old. I should've guessed when the Cabo Grande had no website. I—we can't stay here."

Max beckoned to the bellman and spoke to him in rapid Spanish.

When the man started loading luggage again, she said, "Wait. What are you doing? We're not staying. I'll find another hotel. A better hotel."

"A better hotel? Only if you want to commute from Guatemala or Mexico, darlin'. The Cabo Grande doesn't look like much, but it's safe, the rooms are private, and the sheets are clean. In any other *posada* you might have to share a room with the owner's livestock. I was here a few years ago for DSF. Trust me."

Having matters snatched from her hands added spikes to the lump in her chest. She'd researched everything but the hotel, trusting her uncle, glad to eliminate one thing from a long list. Dammit, she should've been more thorough. She nodded. "It seems I have no choice unless I want to be indebted to General Lopez. I've reserved a suite for me and a double room for you. I'll check us in." She turned and strode inside.

To her right in the bar, patrons occupied tiny tables. One of them carried a massive pistol in a belt holster. Two beer-drinkers were playing chess and another man stared with rapt fascination into a tall drink with ice.

At least they have ice. She made her way left toward the reception desk.

"Buenas noches," she said to the clerk. When the young woman returned her greeting, she managed enough Spanish to say she had reservations. She presented her confirmation letter but the clerk's rapid-fire speech, which seemed full of regrets, lost her.

The clerk pointed to a computer behind her. The screen was blank. Was everything gone?

"Un momento, por favor." Asking people to wait seemed to be the only Spanish Kate got to practice. Throat tight, she headed back to Max.

He stood beside the luggage cart chatting amiably with the bellman. "Yo, Kate."

Familiarity no longer grated. Not after their B&E and that sizzling kiss. Hard to tell whether his usual stony detachment was for personal reasons or a necessity in security work. But at the moment, an appreciative look heated his dark eyes.

She fanned herself with the confirmation letter. "They have rooms, but there's some problem. The clerk doesn't speak English and I don't know enough Spanish to understand her."

"I'm on it." His mouth curved in a charming grin as

he greeted the young clerk.

Kate tried to follow but after three ping-pong exchanges of Spanish, gave up. The conversation took long enough to cover all the ills of the world. She stood beneath one of the ceiling fans but its movement created no detectable breeze. The heat seemed to be expanding, melting her clothes to her body.

The clerk leafed through a worn black registration book. She fluffed her hair and smiled at Max.

He smiled back and gave her a wink.

Kate pursed her lips. She sighed. The heat and the long flight were testing her patience. When Max turned back to her, she touched his forearm. "What were you saying? What's the problem?"

"No problem. Your address is lost in the dead computer so they couldn't notify you they had no suites. But they have rooms. Second floor." He held up two room keys.

"Thank you." She exhaled and accepted a key.

Tension drained from her spine as they headed for the wide tiled stairs. At least the room issue was settled. Not knowing the language was only part of the problem. Arranging things herself usually meant plans worked out as she expected. In the States, she'd thought she had everything arranged, but here in Cabo Blanco, she was facing Max's *unexpected* at every turn. She clutched her camera bag with its precious cargo. If her brother's life wasn't at stake, she'd be on the next plane back to D.C.

At the landing, she glanced back. The man from the bar, the man with the pistol, stood in the lobby. His little black eyes, hard like snaps, focused on her.

Chapter Seven

K'eq Xlapak
PROFESSOR ESTEBAN MORALES crossed the dusty central plaza to the steep pyramid temple, where his assistant Héctor and three crew members were working.

Only nine in the morning and already the heat beat down, shimmering in the humid air like spirits of the Maya who'd built this ancient city. He pulled his hat lower over his forehead as his satellite phone rang. Ah, exactly the person he'd hoped for.

He stepped into the leafy shade of an acacia tree. "Ah, *Señorita* Fontaine, it is so good to hear from you."

"*Hola*, Professor Morales," came the voice, faint but clear enough. "My guide and I arrived in Cabo Blanco last night. The statue is safe."

"*Gracias a Dios* for that. I trust you had a comfortable flight."

"Yes, yes, thank you." Her words came quick and staccato. She had every right to be anxious. "This morning I'll collect the tents and other equipment I had shipped. We should be ready to leave tomorrow or the next day."

Then a hike of several days. Eleven, even ten days was plenty of time. This morning's tremor was barely a wake-up call. But hope was a fool's messenger. The stresses along the fault lines were not easing. His shoulders drooped. "We will be prepared to welcome you."

"And the Maya guides?"

"Ah, *sí, sí*. Arturo and Constantino are in the city now. I shall send word to them through their employer at the pottery factory."

"They are not professional guides?"

"Few of these Maya speak enough Spanish or English for professional work. These are men designated by the Jaguar priest. They know the jungle well. You will be in good hands."

She was silent for a moment before agreeing, and they arranged a meeting at the hotel.

Morales ended the call and hustled toward the workers, feeling as nervous as Kate Fontaine sounded. How quickly was work progressing? This area must be restored enough for the return of Kizin. What happened with the pending earthquake he couldn't predict, but another outcome was certain. If the priest was displeased, he would shut down the restoration.

A dozen or more hieroglyphic stone pillars called stelae had once stood near the temple's entrance, stone guardians carved with images and symbols and painted bright colors. Erosion and quakes had toppled the individual blocks making up each stela. Héctor and the other workers knelt among the stones labeling and measuring.

Some glyphs could still be read. Some blocks lay in pieces, but others remained square. Enough, he hoped, to reconstruct a few more stelae.

As he approached, Héctor beckoned to him.

"*Profesor* Morales, you must see." He set down the digital camera and indicated the top side of a numbered block. The others, a man and two women, lay down their trowels and measuring tapes and sat back on their haunches.

Morales peered at the image carved into the stone. For a better look, he stuck his glasses on his nose and lowered himself to a crouch. Definitely a feathered headdress. His heart raced. He pushed to his feet, a creaky process after so many years at this work. The years had added gray to his head and arthritis to his knees, but had not diminished his thrill at recovering pieces of his country's history.

He removed his glasses and grinned at the crew ranged around the stones. "The headdress is faint but there. This was a royal personage. Well done, *amigos*."

Héctor returned his grin, obviously pleased at the find. "We have five blocks ready to raise." He gestured toward the temple entrance. "We can put another together if we move some blocks."

Morales mopped his forehead with his bandana. "No, each block, each stela must be measured, labeled, and photographed before any is moved. Hurry but follow procedure." He smiled. "Fabiola will have my head if anything is missed."

Héctor laughed, clearly aware of the project illustrator's temper. "*Sí, Profesor.* We will do our best." His gaze drifted behind his boss. "You have visitors from the village, the priests."

Morales turned and walked toward the two men, stopping in the shade cast by the temple. Birds called and monkeys chattered in the nearby acacias. Behind him the *stela* crew returned to their work, their voices a low murmur.

The priests wore striped sashes as belts on their black trousers and matching bandanas on their heads. Ceremonial dress. An official visit. Morales straightened his shoulders and removed his cap. At least he had good news for them.

"*Malokeen,* Don Luis, Jago." Wishing the men good morning, he inclined his head slightly. Such deference along with the honorific of *don* showed his respect.

The younger man, Jago, nodded and stepped back a pace, deferring to the chief Jaguar Priest.

Don Luis clasped his hands together. In recent weeks, the lines on his countenance seemed to have deepened. He returned the Mayan greeting. "*Profesor,* my friend, have you word from *Señorita* Fontaine?" he continued in Spanish.

"I do indeed," Morales said. "She has arrived in Cabo Blanco."

"And the Kizin statue?"

"She has brought it with her. She and her guide will leave tomorrow or the next day."

"My people are frightened. Two tremors yesterday, another this morning. Kizin is warning us. *El Día Maldito* approaches. Will the *señorita* arrive, will the statue arrive in time?" Don Luis's Adam's apple leaped in his wrinkled throat as he swallowed hard.

"The journey is arduous but not long. She will arrive with time to spare. Do not fear."

Brown eyes intense and wary, the assistant priest stepped forward to stand beside his mentor. When Don Luis nodded, Jago said, "*Her* guide? I thought our men would guide her on the old limestone *sacbé*, as Don Luis directed."

Morales frowned, searching his memories of previous communications. Ah, yes, the theft. "This man is her personal guide and bodyguard. She fears an attempt to steal Kizin. The American will protect her and Kizin, and Arturo and Constantino will lead them here, as agreed. All will be well."

But Don Luis was no longer listening. The two priests looked around, eyes wide, and Jago hustled Don Luis away from the stone walls of the temple.

No animals called. No birds. And then Morales heard the rumble.

Adrenaline flooded his veins, scrambling his pulse. "Héctor, bring the crew! Everyone, get out into the open, away from the buildings, away from the trees."

They knew the drill but he couldn't help warning them anyway. All knew the story of how sixty years ago an uprooted palm had crushed Gregory Fontaine.

He hurried to join the priests in the center of the plaza. The ground shook, and he stumbled to his knees. Arms lifted him and he found himself herded along by Héctor and a graduate student. She made the sign of the cross as they ran.

Dust floated up, trees swayed, and the ground rippled like a shaken blanket. The rumbling crescendoed in a deafening roar as if a monster bore down on K'eq Xlapak. Morales and the others planted their feet and held onto each other. He prayed this was only another tremor and not the major quake he feared, the one that would crumble the ancient ruined city to pebbles and open the earth for Kizin's Underworld to swallow them all.

He'd told Don Luis all would be well. *Ay, Dios mío, if only I believed it myself.*

****

Cabo Blanco

Max paced the flagstones in front of the hotel steps. After arranging a meeting with their Maya guides, he'd suggested to Kate they check out the plaza. A good way for him to scope out the hotel's neighborhood. An early morning shower had brightened the plaza but not his mood.

He kicked the base of the nearest pillar. How long could it take for Kate to fetch her sunglasses from her room?

Damn. That wasn't what steamed him like this climate. The woman operated like an Army CO. Assumed everything was going to skate along because she organized it.

He'd set them up with rooms overlooking the plaza so he could keep an eye on comings and goings, but she nixed the adjoining part. What, she thought he'd sneak in and jump her bones? Not that he'd mind some horizontal tango with her. Shit, he'd never forced a woman and never would. Fucking miracle he managed a calm reply.

Told her the Cabo Grande might be secure from bedbugs, but he couldn't count out bad guys after Kizin. Probably shouldn't have added the rest—that she was paying DSF for him to protect her and Kizin and how could he do that from down the hall... darlin'.

She'd pursed her luscious lips and tapped her foot before yielding, but giving in had obviously chafed like sandpaper on sunburn. Just remembering chafed the hell out of him.

Although the hotel was their best choice, the Cabo Grande had no safe for guests' valuables. Like a jade statue with emerald eyes. Not that she'd let it out of her sight or trust him with the damn thing. She insisted Kizin was secure in the base of the camera bag, and with her.

She wasn't making his job easy, for damn sure. Once in his room, he'd checked on his knife and his 9mm. Made sure the pistol was in working order, loaded it, and set the safety. If he needed more weapons, he'd buy them here.

She'd handled the general's offer without a blink but the hotel-room snafu threw her. Only the first shock, he reckoned. He pictured the fear pinching her face when she saw the gun-toting drinker. She recovered fast enough then. Guts and determination. Or was her stubbornness due to a need for control?

He shouldn't let her tick him off. What could he do? *Nada.* If only she didn't know about Doug and Istanbul, it'd be easier to ask her about her brother's artifact trading without her realizing he was gathering info.

He turned from the plaza to see her crossing the lobby toward him, the camera bag slung over one slim shoulder. Her wide smile when she spotted him made her beautiful face glow and whacked him right in the solar plexus. And lower. *Hell, I get a hard-on when I'm supposed to interrogate her?*

He jammed on his aviators at the same time she slid on her sunglasses.

They strolled across the steaming pavestones. Children called out, hawking chewing gum and hard candy.

Small shops ringed the square—clothing, fruit and vegetables, ice cream, jewelry. Aromas of peppers, onions, and unidentifiable spices floated from a café. Vendors at kiosks and tables, women with shopping bags, a few men in a group smoking near the central fountain. No other *norteamericanos*.

Kate set her sunglasses on top of her red-gold hair, bound in a ponytail, and examined embroidered handkerchiefs in a vendor's stall.

A lanky man with a stringy mustache ambled toward them, and Max turned to observe him. Mustache crossed to the fountain and joined the smokers. But his gaze kept returning to Max and Kate. The man's bearing marked him as former military. Unemployed, if he was hanging around on a weekday morning. Maybe he was just admiring the beautiful woman. Or maybe he'd been paid to watch them.

Max would rather admire Kate's legs, on display in a knee-length khaki skirt, but kept Mustache in his peripheral vision. Somebody, even Sedgwick, could've hired a mug like him, and it'd be nuts to discount Centaur. The black-market ring sent their thugs all over the world. And hired extras in places like Costa Verde.

Mustache left the smokers and entered a bar on the other side of the plaza.

Kate withdrew a small purse from a side pocket of the camera bag. She paid the vendor for five handkerchiefs and slid on her shades. *"Gracias."* To Max, she said, "Something for my mother, even though she deplores my coming here."

"But the family must've gone with the professor on expeditions."

"We did, sometimes." Her shoulders twitched in what might be irritation or defense as they wandered along. Aromas of grilling goat meat wafting from a vendor stall made his mouth water. "Mostly Central and South America, but a few times to South Africa. Mom fretted about the dangers then too."

"Any fieldwork since? With Doug?

"Definitely not with my brother on his treasure hunts. And nothing since I started work at the museum. My last digs were as a summer intern in grad school. Anasazi pueblos in southwest Colorado."

He snorted a laugh. "Summer camp."

Lips pursed, she whipped off her sunglasses. "Yes, I know the jungle's not the same. I *know* I haven't your experience or expertise. I *know* the trek'll be hot and exhausting and dangerous. If *you* don't know by now I won't fold, keep it to yourself. Dammit, Max, I'm paying you to do a job, not question my competence."

He held up his hands. "I give. Just trying to assess what to expect once we hit the bush."

She studied him for a moment, then nodded and replaced the glasses. "Okay, then." She set off toward the blue stucco church.

Max followed, resettling his ball cap on his head. *Competence?* Defensive? Oh yeah, darlin'. More going on with Kate than rescuing baby brother and returning Kizin. The lady had something to prove. Okay with him, as long as the risks didn't mean impulsive moves that'd ratchet up the danger meter, like her coin trick inside Sedgwick's vault.

They meandered past the church and stopped in front of the leather shop. The rich smells of tanned hides invited them inside. Nobody seemed to be paying them undue attention.

Various leather goods hung on racks and covered small tables. Max followed Kate's example and smiled at the proprietor, a small dark woman in the traditional embroidered dress, seated on a folding chair by the doorway.

She returned his greeting but her sharp gaze followed him as he lifted a tooled belt with a silver buckle from a display.

Not his style. Too flashy. He turned to Kate, who appeared focused on wallets. "Rescuing your brother this way is a big challenge. You and Doug must be close."

She slanted him a questioning look. No wonder. His question came out of left field. "Not so much now," she said, "but we were tight growing up. Even though he was a little pain sometimes, he stood up to anyone who hassled his big sister the bookworm." She blushed and lowered her gaze to the leather goods.

"You and your brother partner often for antiquities buys?"

She set down a red fringed wallet and picked up a simple black one. "Once in a while, if he can talk me into a loan." A wistful smile on her lips, she shrugged. "Or if it's a piece that interests me."

"Like what?" He replaced the belt and fingered a leather vest.

Her head tilted as if she searched her memory. "There was a set of three French Victorian jewelry boxes."

Perfect for her. Probably nothing Max needed to take note of. "You bought one?"

"All three. I gave one to my mother." She rifled through a bunch of key cases. "My work for the museum doesn't interest her much, unless there's an opening reception, but she does occasionally appreciate the results of Doug's treasure hunts."

"Like the jewelry box."

She nodded. "I miss haggling with him over his

80

finds. "He's injured, you know. Not just the leg, his head... I—" She fluttered a hand and appeared to sniff back tears.

Dammit, this conversation had taken a left turn. "Hey, he's probably haggling with the kidnappers. Giving them a hard time."

Kate flashed him a wobbly smile. "Sounds like my brother. Thanks."

"DSF will find him, get him out of there." He couldn't tell her not to worry. They both had a hell of a lot to worry about—tremors, animal and human predators for starters.

He left the shade of the shop's awning and checked out the plaza scene again. No sign of Mustache. No point in scaring Kate, so he wouldn't mention the man unless he popped up again. "So Doug twists your arm when he needs help buying some pricey item?"

She murmured assent. Holding up a key case, she signaled to the woman, who hurried over with a waist pouch of cash. A moment later, Kate joined him in the sunshine. "Enough shopping. Small gifts for Mom and a new case for my keys."

One more shot and then he'd back off. For today. "Big-ticket items like artifacts or is Doug into gold coins like Sedgwick had?" he asked as they wandered back toward the hotel.

"No coins." She slipped on her sunglasses. "A while ago he wanted help buying a couple of ancient Greek pieces he found in Alexandria."

His pulse kicked up like a colt let out to pasture. "Like what?"

"A Corinthian bronze helmet and a gorgeous glazed amphora painted with the image of the goddess Nike."

The descriptions sounded familiar. He filed them away to send Mara later. "Cool. I'd like to see those. I bet you went for them for your museum."

She shook her head. "Too expensive and I wasn't certain of the provenance. Doug managed alone." She slid the shades down her nose. "Why are you so interested?"

Tingling spread across the back of his neck. He rubbed his nape and shrugged. "No special reason. Just making conversation."

"Uh huh." She hiked the camera bag higher on her shoulder and walked on.

He let out his breath. Subtle, Devlin had said. Next time he'd have to be more careful.

Chapter Eight

KATE GLANCED AT Max as he drove their rented SUV to the dockside warehouse storing the crate of supplies she'd shipped.

Even driving, he maintained that soldier-like vigilance. And his trademark grim face. Checking the rearview mirror, the side streets, everything, like this morning. As they'd explored the shops, he never stopped surveying the plaza. Protecting her, from what she didn't know, in an open square. And what was his reason for the questions about Doug's artifact trading? Still something to do with Istanbul? She'd pay closer attention if he asked again and press him for a better answer.

"Ah, on our left, there's Our Lady of the Rosary. It's one of the oldest churches in Central America." The ornate colonial Baroque style needed paint but the stonework and statues in several niches were intact.

When Max turned toward her, a bemused expression twitching the corner of his mouth, she shut up, her mouth suddenly dry from chattering like a monkey with what she knew of the country.

It was the third church she'd pointed out. She never babbled. She must be boring him to numbness. Chalk it up to nerves. She unscrewed the top of her blue Nalgene canteen, took a sip, and licked a stray drop from her lower lip.

His scowl deepened. Looking away, he rubbed his nape.

What that was about she hadn't a clue. She shrugged and took another drink.

Once away from the city's central square, the SUV wove through narrow, unpaved streets. Kate shook her head at the tumbledown tin and stucco shacks they were passing. "Costa Verde was once a prosperous country."

Rainwater and—from the rank smell—sewage flowed in a ditch on one side. A skinny dog lapped muddy water from a pothole. Women scrubbed clothes at a communal fountain.

"Earthquake damage and political turmoil have been costly. The old dictator propped himself up, not the country, for too long."

"I think President Aguilar has made reforms, but they have a long way to go."

"You're on the money. The markets in the plaza were selling more goods today than I remember from before," he said, his intent gaze flicking to the rearview and side mirrors, hands flexing on the steering wheel.

"What is it?"

"Don't look, but we have company."

She went still but her mind raced. "Following us?"

"Man in the blue sedan behind us. He was watching us in the plaza earlier. Another man's riding shotgun."

She leaned closer to the door and checked her side mirror, but could see only the vehicle, not the occupants. "Max?"

He squeezed the hand she was white-knuckling on the camera bag. "They seem to be tailing us, not threatening. Locals, maybe hired by the general. I want you to get on the floor. Just a precaution."

Pulse scrambling, she undid the seatbelt and folded her knees so she could scoot down to the floor. She dragged the bag with her and clutched it to her chest. The rough mat smelled of nameless dirt, but she forced deep breaths to dispel the dizziness behind her eyes.

"Hold on. I'm gonna take this next left fast."

Max knew what he was doing. Evasive maneuvers, like she'd seen in a hundred movies. His jaw was set, making him look more hardened than ever. He'd taken out the pistol and placed it on the console tray.

God, please don't let it come to gunfire.

He spun the wheel, rocking the SUV and throwing her off balance against the seat cushion. Her breath blew out in a whoosh but she held onto the camera bag. They were speeding along now, bouncing in ruts and potholes. She kept her gaze on Max, wishing she could emulate his iron control instead of trembling all over.

After two more jouncing turns, they slowed.

"It's okay," Max said, his voice soft. "You can get up now. They're gone."

She levered herself up into the seat and buckled up. "You lost them." If only she didn't sound so breathless. But thank God for his alertness and experience.

He shot her a wry grin. "Not really. They turned off at that last corner. Must've figured I made 'em. Probably weren't supposed to be noticed. Amateurs."

"I'll take it."

"Somebody or more than somebody is too interested in us for safety. We need to speed up this operation as soon as we meet these guides of yours."

"My thoughts exactly." Not that the back country would be any less hazardous, but at least they'd be moving forward. Closer to Doug.

When her pulse returned to something approximating normal, she once again looked around them. More tin shacks lined the dirt road. Returning Kizin would bolster the country's cultural heritage, maybe the tourist trade. Too inadequate, but maybe she could come up with something more. "Where are we?"

"I see cranes and masts ahead. So we're on track for the docks." Max braked for four barefoot children kicking a soccer ball. They scampered aside and waved. "What exactly is in the warehouse?"

"I didn't know what I'd be able to find here, so I purchased all our equipment in the States and shipped the crate. Tents and other camping gear, mosquito netting, lanterns." She held up her list of purchases. "We'll buy food here, of course."

"Of course." They reached the harbor, and Max turned left toward the commercial docks. "Did you consult my boss on this?"

As he steered around three dogs asleep in the rutted street, the SUV's swaying threw her against her seatbelt and closer to him. Sun-heated skin laced with soap. Strong jaw in a hard profile. Sinewy muscles bulging below the short sleeves of his T-shirt. After a beat, she straightened in her seat and returned her gaze to the front. Awareness still filling her senses, she smoothed her hands down her skirt. Now was not the time. Not that there'd ever be a time.

"He suggested I wait," she said. "He said shipping was risky. But I felt waiting was equally risky." She'd preferred to line up everything beforehand. "Why?"

The warehouse lay directly ahead, a rusting metal building with bay doors open wide. A man dozed in the shade, his plastic chair propped against the door frame.

Max switched off the engine and turned to her. "You know Costa Verde is a poor country, but you don't *know* Costa Verde. Be prepared to be disappointed."

The skin on her arms prickled and she nibbled her lip. "What do you mean?"

Without explanation, he shoved open the driver door.

She unhooked her seatbelt and slid out. They circumvented puddles from the night's downpour. In the porous soil, puddles didn't last long so earlier this morning these must've been small lakes.

"Hola," Max greeted the warehouse manager.

The man raised sleep-drooping eyes. The chair legs slammed to the cement floor. He stood, eyeing them with suspicion. *"Hola, señor, señora."*

Max explained what they wanted, and Kate showed her invoice. The man wore a tag that identified him as Manuel. He scratched his shaggy head and said something in Spanish. Max translated that Manuel wasn't sure. Perhaps he remembered such a crate in the back of the warehouse.

Max and Kate tramped behind him through the building past wooden crates and tarp-covered objects piled up at random spots.

The warehouse was an oven. The breeze off the water wafting through the bays at either end kept the temperature just below broiling, wrapping Kate in an invisible heated towel. The air shimmered before her eyes. She dabbed her temples with a tissue. How did Max continue to look so damn cool? If this sauna didn't bother him, what was a Texas summer like?

Finally they reached the building's far end. Beside a pile of unidentifiable metal parts lay a litter of broken wood slats in a puddle. Manuel pointed to the debris and mumbled a few words.

"Manuel says this is your shipment." Max sidled closer to her.

"It *can't* be." She couldn't prevent her voice from rising an octave.

Manuel compared her invoice to the label on one slat, then returned the invoice to her. *"Sí, sí."* This was the right crate. Or what was left of it. His shoulders moved in an elaborate shrug.

The tacit apology seemed at odds with the look on the man's face that said this loss was nothing new. The heat and the theft pressed down on her shoulders. What could've happened? She turned to Max, who was listening to Manuel's rapid Spanish.

"Manuel claims the crate was intact last week. Says you can file a complaint in the manager's office."

"Great. Why not?" An effort probably as worthless as fanning herself with her invoice. She headed back through the warehouse.

They found the manager's office two warehouses along the harbor. Kate completed the paperwork, including a list of the missing contents, and left it with the secretary, who apologized and clucked with concern. Better than nothing.

Afterward, in the rental SUV, she directed the air conditioning onto her face and closed her eyes.

"You okay?" Max handed over her canteen.

She drank deeply. The cool liquid helped almost as much as the concern in his dark eyes. "Sure, just in shock. What could've happened to the supplies? Who stole them? Why?"

"When you don't have much, goods left lying

around are up for grabs. Especially if they belong to rich gringos. Insurance will cover replacements. Chalk it up to experience." He steered around the muddy puddles and away from the harbor area.

"We have less than an hour until our guides arrive." Kate sipped more water. "I hope that works out. You know the saying about bad things in threes."

"In this case, fours. But don't borrow trouble. If they show, they show."

She laughed, surprising herself. "I wish I had your laid-back attitude. I suppose I'm overreacting. It's just that I remember Dad *planning* his expeditions."

His gaze flicked to her before his attention returned to the road. "Not organized like a military campaign?"

If organizing military campaigns meant chaos. Arguments between her dad and mom about whether the kids would go, what to pack, the dangers involved, and a list of other issues. Her dad the general and her mom an officer had done the planning at full volume, leaving Kate and Doug on the outside.

Feeling Max's gaze on her, she straightened. She hadn't meant to reveal her resentment. "I didn't mean that. Only that as a child I wasn't privy to what had been decided until Dad left alone or we flew off together. I felt swept up by a tornado."

"Maybe parents don't keep kids in the loop because they think they're protecting them. Or the parents are too busy. Or tired."

Busy, definitely. Preoccupied with themselves and their plans, probably. And disorganized. In hindsight as an adult, she guessed it was really Dad's assistants who'd carried out the actual organizing. If only her parents had involved her, she'd have felt... what? Reassured? Yes, but what else? She was too hot to examine it now. She shook her head to knock the unsolvable from her brain.

He steered around a wide puddle. "No wonder you like to line things up yourself."

Did she? Was she a control freak? She wagged her shoulders. "I simply prefer organization, planning. Most of the time my work at the Washington Cultural Museum allows that. Managing exhibits and submitting grant applications, yes, predictable and straightforward." She picked at the seal on her canteen.

"And boring? Sorry. I mean, some of it must be grunt work."

She laughed. "To you, all of what my job involves would be boring. Yes, sometimes, like the grant writing. Bringing in traveling exhibits and meeting with the curators to organize them are joys."

"Did you ever want to do fieldwork like your father?"

They were passing a small house painted sky blue, where a gray-haired woman watered flowers in a window box. A simple life with simple choices. And clear paths. "Once, but only briefly. I enjoy the cultural and historical richness of places like this and sharing it through my work. I'll leave it to others to dig up the past."

"I take it your brother didn't catch the archeology bug either," Max said as they pulled into a parking space by the hotel.

"Only the possibility a dig or an exotic location might lead to riches." She sighed. "Doug's kidnapping changed everything. I must be ready—"

"For the unexpected," he finished for her.

"Yes, the unexpected." This journey overflowed

with the unexpected.

****

In the jungle

Doug Fontaine heaved himself up from the wheelchair, braced himself with his good leg, and pivoted to the narrow cot. Lungs pumping like a bellows, he collapsed onto the lumpy mattress and lifted up his cast-bound leg. His T-shirt was soaked. He swiped the worst of the sweat from his forehead and lay back on the pancake-flat pillow.

The guard named Alano—or something that sounded like that—stood over him, hand on the knife at his belt during the process. Apparently satisfied, he yanked Doug's hands in front of him and rebound his wrists with rough cordage.

What the hell? Did the fucker think in Doug's condition he could jump him and escape? The trip across the rough ground to and from the poor excuse for a toilet—a doorless outhouse—had drained what little strength he possessed. He closed his eyes. A tossup which stank worse—the outhouse or this guy's rotten-teeth breath.

But the smell took his mind off the darts shooting through his skull. Neither of his guards paid much attention to his pain. They doled out his meds on their own schedule and not when he needed the pain killers. He was getting better at concealing his agony, reducing its effects, even the accompanying sweats. Forcing himself to breathe deeply and evenly, he pictured the blonde who sunbathed topless at his condo pool.

Soon the vise clamping his skull cranked open and the pain receded. Either he'd fallen asleep or that Zen shit the doctors advised for his brain trauma wasn't crap after all. He'd take it. He was beginning to feel more alert, a hell of a lot sharper than those first days in this thatched-roof hut.

For whatever crap lay ahead, today or the next, a clear head would come in handy.

When he heard noise outside, he turned toward the doorway. No door, only an opening in one wall. At least the one tiny window and the spaces between the skinny, upright logs forming the walls let in breezes—and voices. Must be the changing of the guard.

Al and Franco—his wider replacement—were arguing about something. Could be about Doug, could be anything. He sure as hell didn't speak their language, Mayan, he guessed, mixed with Spanish words.

He had no idea how long they'd held him here. It could be a week, two weeks, longer. Couldn't gauge by beard growth. They shaved him every other day, maybe so the tape would stick to his mouth. So far they hadn't cut him, but who knew about the next time.

Three men had come to his condo. Al and two others. Two had the look of the Maya—broad faces, brown skin, and short stature. The taller Maya introduced himself in halting English as Don Luis, chief Jaguar Priest of K'eq Xlapak.

"The thief took Kizin to my country," Luis informed him gravely. "He will sell to one of the candidates for *presidente*. Must stop. You are rightful owner of Kizin. My people need help from you."

"I'm not in shape to help anybody," Doug protested from his wheelchair. He pointed to the cast on his left leg. "Kinda outta commission."

The priest bowed. "Thief must pay. Come to Costa Verde. I will help you recover Kizin. Then you return

Kizin to K'eq Xlapak. You will stop *El Día Maldito* and save my people."

His solemn sincerity was convincing. Hell, even on mind-dulling painkillers, Doug knew returning Kizin wouldn't stop an imagined curse or a damn earthquake. Recovering the thing would be his chance to recoup his losses. Somehow he'd get away from these super-serious dudes and find a buyer among his many contacts. He'd be flush.

The next day the third man drove Doug and the two Maya to the airport. In Cabo Blanco, Doug was loaded, wheelchair and all, into an old Chevy van. One of the men jabbed him with a needle. He'd blacked out for God knew how long. Until waking up here.

Wherever the hell *here* was.

In the Costa Verde jungle, for damn sure. Bird calls and howler monkey calls blasting through the canopy at all hours.

Operating with his brain only on half speed, he hadn't seen something was off about the damn priest. Off about the whole returning Kizin thing. If that was what these fuckers were up to. He had no real idea what they wanted or what snatching him had to do with Kizin. Nobody spoke to him in any language he could understand. Shit, he had to figure this out.

A low rumble began then cranked up, like a convoy of semis thundering down a rutted road. Pulse revving, he heaved a sigh and wished for the forty-seventh time he wasn't fucking tied up and could hold onto something. Anything.

Here, folks, for your entertainment, the daily shake, rattle, and roll.

The semis roared in and rippled the ground into a

choppy sea of dust.

Pebbles jumped and floated above the dirt floor. As the small table danced, his plastic breakfast bowl tumbled across the room. The cot's metal frame clanked and rocked as if shaken by a giant hand, tossing him side to side.

He stuck out his good leg to brace himself but found no purchase. He bounced half on and half off the cot.

After a light year—or twenty seconds—the tremor stopped. Everything settled.

Franco stumbled inside, squinting through the dust. Apparently satisfied Doug hadn't used the opportunity to escape, the hefty guard left. A creaking noise meant he'd returned to sitting on his wooden chair.

Doug maneuvered to the center of the bed and willed his heartbeat to regulate.

He guessed he wasn't far from the K'eq Xlapak epicenter. And the tremors were increasing. One or two a day, strong enough to knock over the guards' chairs and one of the saplings near the hut.

A big quake was coming, like the one that had killed old Gregory. And nobody knew what had happened to Doug, who had taken him, or where he was. Not the blonde by the pool. Not his mom. Not his sister.

Katie. Dammit, she'd stuck by him every time he screwed up. She stood up for him back when they were kids. And bailed him out of some bigger scrapes later. But hell, not *now*. His sister was the last person who could get him out of this shit storm. His fault he'd lost Kizin and ended up in this prison hut. Maybe— No, he wouldn't think about Katie.

Turning onto his side, he pounded his bound fists on the thin mattress. Fuckin'-A, he had to figure out what the hell was going on and find a way to escape. How, with his leg in a cast? And go where?

He closed his eyes and swallowed against the tightness in his throat. He'd be lucky to survive. Hell, they all would.

Kizin would have his revenge.

Chapter Nine

Cabo Blanco

MAX FOUND THEM a table in the hotel bar where they could wait for the two guides. Something had to smooth out for Kate. *"Dos cervezas, por favor."*

The bartender nodded and reached into the cooler.

First this half-star hotel. Then the supplies. She was holding up better than he'd reckoned after shock number two. He swigged a long drink of his beer. A Mexican brand, Sol. Not bad.

"I wasn't surprised at your military campaign reference," Kate said after a sip of beer. "I gather you and Thomas Devlin were in Afghanistan together."

"And Iraq. Special Forces. He was my commanding officer."

"Delta Force, wasn't it?"

He went still. The Army liked to be low key about SFOD-D. "What makes you think so?"

"The delta on the Devlin Security Force logo." She laughed, that husky laugh that went right to his cock. "I'll let you off the hook and switch subjects. Many security firms employ ex-military. How on earth did Thomas get into the business of protecting art and artifacts?"

He downed a swallow and cleared his throat. "I don't have the whole story. I was still deployed when he opted out of the Army and set up shop in Arlington. But our team went into Iraq a few years after the invasion forces. He was already pissed off about the looting, especially Baghdad's big museum."

"The National Museum's ancient treasures weren't *all* looted. Employees hid most of the priceless ones away once invasion was imminent."

"True, but we didn't know that for a long time. And later looters went after ancient sites and museums all over Iraq. When some of us caught one of our men carting away artifacts at a temple in southern Iraq, Thomas went ballistic. Thief did some time for that. Reckon it psyched Thomas to rectify matters. One of DSF's first gigs was to recover some of the stuff that was actually stolen."

"Impressive." The look in her eyes said the company just went up a notch in her mind. As children's laughter floated in from the plaza, she glanced outside.

He finished his beer and waved to the bartender. To Kate he said, "Want another? Or would you rather have something else?"

"Beer's fine. But one will do. I still have some." She kicked off her sandals and crossed her legs, flashing him an eyeful of tanned and toned thigh. Tendrils of her bright hair curled around her face in corkscrews, soft-looking hair a guy liked to get his hands into. *This* guy.

Max clamped his jaw against a rush of heat. He linked his fingers around his empty *cerveza* until the new one arrived.

She sipped her beer. A gentle smile played on her lips as she watched the shoppers. In the full heat of the day, their numbers had dwindled. Vendors fanned themselves beneath awnings and parasols.

Rather than awkward silence, the interlude felt more like companionable quiet. "Tell me about these men you hired." Another disaster looming? He hoped to hell not. All he knew was they hailed from the village near K'eq Xlapak. Devlin had said Mara rolled her eyes at the impossibility of conducting background checks on Maya villagers.

Her mouth curved in a rueful smile. "I don't blame you for skepticism. I didn't hire them. The project archeologist at K'eq Xlapak arranged it, following the priest's instructions. Arturo and Constantino seemed the logical choice because they're already here in the capital. They came to find work."

Table legs rattled on the tile floor. His full bottle tipped over, sloshing beer onto the cracked tile. The vibration strengthened, shaking the table harder and swinging the overhead fan in an arc. A couple of vacant chairs fell over. Plaster dust rained from the ceiling.

Max gripped the table. *Oh, shit.*

"Max?" Kate's eyes grew big and round as hubcaps. All color fled her face. She clutched the camera bag. Jerked to her feet and booked it out the exit.

Worked for him. He jumped up and followed in the wake of her escape.

Out in the sun, people in the square stood with their feet planted wide for support as the ground spasmed beneath them. Curtains of dust flew upward, whirling like dervishes.

Max caught up to Kate, wrapped an arm about her trembling shoulders. She grasped his arm in a tourniquet grip.

"Just a tremor, darlin', no big deal." *Madre de Dios, tell yourself that, Rivera.*

The shaking subsided slowly, like retreating thunder. A fine layer of soil settled on everything. People around them picked up their dropped shopping bags, crossed themselves, and went about their business. Vendors collected their wares from the ground. The air smelled of heat and dust.

Panting, apparently close to hyperventilating, Kate still held on, her nails digging into his skin.

Max sneezed. "You can let go now. It's over."

"Oh." Color seeped back into her skin in the form of a blush.

They picked their way past a smashed flower pot and returned to the bar.

As the bartender mopped up a broken bottle of tequila, he called out, *"No es un terremoto, solamente un advertencia de Kizin."* He crossed himself.

Kate blew out a breath. "I understood the first part, that it wasn't an earthquake. What was the rest?"

"He said it was only a warning from Kizin."

Her lips curved in a wobbly smile. "Ah, now you see how strong the belief is here."

More than he wanted to, he got it. This expedition had started on shaky ground that was getting more unstable by the minute. What other beliefs did people here have about Kizin's so-called powers and how far would some go to get those powers for themselves?

The bartender delivered new beers, then swept up the broken glass by their table.

Kate downed a healthy swallow of her new Sol. "Sorry I panicked."

"I was damned scared too. But your reaction shot to the top of the fright-o-meter at *Terrified*. It's not *El Día Maldito* yet. What gives?"

"I grew up with stories about the earthquake that killed my great-grandfather. You'd be terrified too."

"And the curse? Are you a believer?"

Those vertical thinkin' lines between her brows, she stared at a condensation circle on the table. "Like I said, I grew up with the stories. More than that, the curse legend has been told and dissected around the Fontaine dinner table since before I was born. It's practically part of my DNA. I consider myself a sensible person, but this…" She looked up and shook her head. "I can't say I believe, but I can't say I don't."

"Too many things in the world can't be explained."

If there was a word for earthquake phobia, he didn't remember ever hearing it. In spite of her fears, Kate came to fault-line central on her risky quests that included some nebulous challenge to herself. A hell of a determined female. "You know the tremors are increasing in strength?"

"And frequency, yes."

Shit, now he was scaring them both. "Change of subject."

"I'll drink to that." She lifted her bottle.

The kidnappers' demands bugged him. Too much made no sense. "Why Maya guides? They could be in danger from the kidnappers. We could use GPS and guide ourselves."

"Don't think I haven't lost sleep over that. When Doug and I originally set up the return of Kizin with the archeologist, the Jaguar Priest had certain requirements. One is that a descendant of the foreigner responsible for losing Kizin must return the figure in person."

He quirked a brow. "Another is Maya guides?"

"Exactly. And walking there on the limestone road built by the ancient Maya. The priest insisted. And now the kidnapper insists I follow the same instructions." She shook her head. "I don't know why, and I don't much care. I want my brother out alive and the Kizin statue back in its temple." Her face crumpled. "Why hasn't the kidnapper called me?"

"Don't head down that bad road. Possible he doesn't know we're here. Or he could be waiting for us to head into the interior."

In that case, it was possible the guides were involved in the kidnapping. Or not, and the whole priest thing was legit. DSF had tracked Fontaine's flight from D.C. but had zip on anybody accompanying him or meeting him. Security cameras in the Cabo Blanco airport were nonexistent. Thomas's supposition was that the kidnappers had hidden their captive somewhere in the jungle. But insist Kate stick to the priest's orders? To draw her into the jungle where she'd be more vulnerable? Or—

Max was getting nowhere. Only guessing. He lifted his beer to his lips. "I've read some on the contemporary Maya. In the remote villages they follow a mix of the old beliefs and Christianity. People have both kinds of priests bless their babies. The priests of the Classic period wielded enormous power that included predicting the future and averting famine, plagues of ants, and earthquakes. A good bet the imminent threat of earthquake increased the Jaguar Priest's role."

"I agree, and many of those remote villages have only the Jaguar Priest. But again you surprise me. Your knowledge about the Maya seems to go beyond antiquities study."

"Not just a pretty face."

She laughed, low music that tightened his body. Again. "I'm beginning to see that. So how do you know to say *Maya* for the people and *Mayan* for their language?"

He studied her expression. Open, curious. No harm in telling her. "When I was a teenager, I worked after school mowing lawns and trimming hedges with a Guatemalan guy. Nestor insisted I had Maya blood and the idea I might got me interested in Maya history and culture." Nestor had done more than that. The old man's encouragement and trust had given him a direction in life.

Grinning, Kate looked him over. "You're no short Maya. One of your parents gave you the height gene. Your dad?"

"Probably. I never knew him." Shouldn't have opened that door but thinking about Nestor had distracted him. He hitched around in his chair. His mom had been short, or did she just seem that way because he'd been tall for his age?

She leaned forward, sympathy shining in her eyes. "Did he die when you were young?"

He stifled a hoot. "I meant I don't know who he was. I don't know if my mom did."

"I shouldn't have assumed. Your mom raised you alone?"

Her question was natural enough. Her blue gaze fixed him with interest, not pity.

He wasn't about to spill about being dumped at age ten or foster homes or any of that. He could barely remember his mother's face or the sound of her voice. The anger had faded, leaving an occasional aching hollow behind his ribs. Like now.

He wagged his head. "We did okay. Happens all the time."

She shifted, crossing her legs.

Better if he focused on the slide of the short skirt on her thighs rather than the implications of his maudlin history.

History? What a laugh. A half-Mexican-half-Anglo kid from the barrio? He'd made it out but had a history shallower than a Houston bayou. A reason to explore ancient history, like Nestor used to tell him.

Her smile was soft. "Well, Max Rivera, kid of a single parent, I'd say you've done damned well for yourself." She placed her hand on his arm.

Tingling, and not from embarrassment, swept up his arm. He covered her hand with his. "Don't worry about the guides, Kate. I'll figure out a way to send them ahead once we make contact with the kidnappers."

Her good humor vanished at the reminder of her brother's plight. She withdrew her hand. "Do you think he's still alive?"

What could he say? "You've followed their directions. When they call, we'll get proof of life and go from there."

"All we can do, I guess." She set away her beer and stared at the tabletop.

A few minutes later two men, ball caps in hand, entered the hotel bar. They wore T-shirts and baggy shorts. Short and stocky, their dark skin and broad features marked them as Maya.

Man, did they ever resemble their fierce-looking ancestors portrayed on countless stone walls of ancient hidden cities. Flatten their foreheads with tight headdresses and dress them in tunics, and they were the same people thousands of years ago who built cities and temples and invented a perpetual calendar. Hell, if

Nestor was right, he shared their ancestry.

"Here they are." Kate stood and beckoned. *"Hola, señores. ¿Cómo está?"* She repeated the greeting in Yucatecan Mayan. *"Bakoosh."*

Max leaned closer. "You speak Mayan?"

"As well as I do Spanish. *Un poco.*" A little.

The two men approached. *"Señorita* Fontaine?" said one. A shy smile gleamed beneath a bushy mustache.

She replied to his question and introduced Max. On a sigh, she said, "You'll have to take over."

"¿Qué onda?" Seeing the men's blank expressions, Max wanted to take back his street greeting. Mexican Spanish differed from other Spanish dialects more than British English did from American. He needed them to relax so he could take their measure. *"Buenos días."*

"Me llamo Arturo Gomez." The one with the mustache introduced himself. Arturo's dark eyes were gentle, like his voice.

The other man was his younger brother Constantino. He'd slicked his hair back with styling gel or thirty-weight. His T-shirt bore Kiss's black-and-white painted faces. He ogled Kate for a second before wilting under Max's death stare. So much for relaxation.

Everybody shook hands, and Kate gestured for the brothers to take seats.

Arturo explained in halting phrases that he and his brother were still learning Spanish. In their village the people spoke only Mayan.

For the next few minutes, Max and Kate questioned them in a jumble of languages. Both men knew their prescribed route and the jungle as well as a couple of villages along the way where they'd be welcome to stay if they didn't want to camp.

Morales, the archeologist, had told them only that two *norteamericanos* needed guides to reach K'eq Xlapak along the old routes. Nada about Kizin. A good sign… if they told the truth.

Arturo struck him as competent and earnest, the younger brother as careless, a little wild. After another round of handshakes, they left.

Max watched them hustle across the plaza. They'd do—under his supervision.

"Finally something has gone right," Kate said afterward as they climbed the stairs to the second floor.

"Once we stock up on equipment and food, we'll be ready. Arturo said they'd meet us here tomorrow morning to show us the best places to buy supplies."

"Perfect." She stopped at her room door. "*Presidente* Aguilar's gala starts at nine thirty tonight. We have plenty of time to rest and have a leisurely dinner."

Max groaned.

"Yes, the gala. I know you'd like to forget it but I need you." She removed her purse from the camera case and dug inside for her key.

"Wait," he said, tugging her aside. "I need to check the rooms first."

He motioned to her to wait while he unlocked his door.

Scratches marred the metal around the keyhole. He wrapped his hand around the pistol in his pocket. "Hold on. Somebody's been here." Could still be here.

Kate gasped. "Inside?"

"Maybe. Stay back." He withdrew the semi-auto and pushed open the door. The mattress lay sideways against the wall. Luggage linings had been slashed. Clothing and toiletries strewed the green tile floor. Heat blasted through his blood. *"¡Cabrones!"* The bastards!

She surged forward into the doorway. "Oh, my God!"

He tucked her behind him and scanned the room. More mess. Stuff scattered over the floor, under the bed. He'd had his tablet with him, so no breach of DSF security. "Somebody searched. A damn thorough job and they didn't care who knew. Nobody here now."

"They must've gone into my room too. My computer!" Another gasp, of indignation.

When she started to rush past him, he stepped in front of her. Blocked her. "No, you don't, darlin', not like in Sedgwick's vault."

Keeping himself between her and the connecting door, he crossed the room. Flung the door wide.

Chapter Ten

BY THE TIME the police finished with the crime scene and interviews, eight o'clock had come and gone. Both their rooms had been trashed and searched, but nothing was missing. Kate couldn't say so to the officer, but the burglar was obviously searching for Kizin.

The police officer dismissed her question about fingerprinting, saying a hotel room either had layers of prints or none because some industrious maid had wiped everything clean. He'd said detectives would investigate thoroughly, but she thought his hasty assurance stemmed from Max's fierce insistence.

Apologizing for his hotel and for every member of his ancestry, the hotel manager moved Max and her to new adjoining rooms on the third floor. He had a complimentary meal delivered to their rooms—fish grilled in banana leaf, a local delicacy. Delicious, but she could choke down only a few bites.

The new room was identical to the last—peeling turquoise paint, chipped tile, bed, bedside table, chair, and a small bureau. Shabby but clean, and the ceiling fan moved the air wafting through the open shutters.

She slipped on her gown for the gala, a metallic gold knit that shed creases—unlike the rest of her clothes, wrinkled as elephants. When she picked up her gold drop earrings, she fought to steady her hands. A shower had removed the sense of violation, but good God, what else could go wrong?

She lifted the small jade carving from the bed, where she'd laid it after checking to reassure herself it hadn't been damaged in their wild ride to the warehouse. The emerald eyes sparkled and the gold inlay gleamed in the lamplight. "Quakes every twenty years a result of rhythms in the faults, or is your curse real? Not answering, huh?"

She sat on the hard mattress and brushed the tablet screen. But she could concentrate on her notes no better than on her dinner. She kept wondering about the next setback, wondering about Doug's condition.

He embraced buying and selling artifacts with same enthusiasm he'd had collecting baseball cards. He'd practically levitated with excitement at the biggest find of his treasure-hunting career. Kate pictured the gleam in his eyes, the same blue as hers. Until she'd played the guilt card about family honor and returning Kizin to K'eq Xlapak instead of selling it. If only she'd gone with him to England.

And why the hell hasn't the kidnapper called? She glared at the satellite phone, willing it to ring.

When she heard two sharp raps, she jumped, pulse racing like a frightened bird's. God, she was an idiot. It was only Max knocking on the connecting door. She sucked in a deep breath and rolled her shoulders. She'd have to hold steadier than this. Who knew what would happen tonight at the palace or in the jungle? "Come in."

He charged in, his broad shoulders filling the doorway. He ran a finger around the inside of his starched collar. "The manager damn well better have the rest of our clothes cleaned and pressed by nine in the morning like he promised. I'm not wearing this monkey suit one nanosecond longer than I have to."

Kate's mouth went dry. Her fingers stilled on the keyboard. She swallowed. Curls of heat wound through her.

Her reaction must have been apparent because he grinned and struck a pose. "Like what you see?"

His Texas drawl melted into her like butter on a hot croissant. The midnight blue silk looked tailored to fit his perfectly sculpted body, and the pleated white shirt complemented his bronze skin. The chin cleft looked oh so touchable. Why did she ever consider his blunt features unhandsome? Testosterone oozed from his pores, making her acutely susceptible to his maleness... Another flutter of awareness flared.

Damn, she shouldn't let herself think this way about him. He was her employee, her protector, and that was all. Even if she couldn't forget that kiss. She needed the same determination against Max's charm as she had against thieves.

His response when she'd confronted him about pressing her on Doug's business dealings had been too quick and too dismissive. He hadn't asked again, but how could she trust him enough, let alone act on her attraction to him?

She cleared her throat. "I'll be the envy of all the women at the president's palace."

"Your servant, ma'am." His languid gaze caressed her body. When he met her eyes, he lowered one eyelid in a slow wink. "As long as I get to escort you in that gold paint masquerading as a dress, wearing this strait jacket is worth it."

"Why, thank you, sir." All she could think of was getting him out of that "strait jacket" and licking every inch of those muscles. She lowered her gaze to the computer screen. "I'm just reviewing my notes on the president and his wife."

He crossed to look over her shoulder at the screen. Scant inches from him, she could feel his body heat and smell his aftershave. Oddly comforting. Her pulse leaped. *Be tough, Katherine.*

He continued around the bed and settled on the straight chair. "Aside from the statue's curse and its history, could somebody be after the emeralds?"

"Possibly, but intact it's worth much more. There is one suspicious character in the hotel. You know, the hard-looking man who hangs around the lobby, the man with the gun on his hip. The police officer just shrugged when I mentioned him."

Max cleared his throat. "The cop didn't care because that man is house security."

Now she felt foolish. Except for her concern about the man's drinking on duty. But she'd leave that particular battle aside. "Anyway, thank God I had Kizin with me." She picked up the statue and extended it toward Max.

He accepted the heavy object, turning it this way and that and examining the fine craftsmanship. "Amazing that somebody created this to sit on an altar for only a short time."

"Even more amazing that this one wasn't smashed and dropped in a *cenote* with the others. They must have been interrupted."

"By an earthquake?" He passed the figure back to her.

"Maybe. Appropriate or ironic, I'm not sure which. We'll never know. He has other names and other guises, the god of death, for one. The earthquake connection seems to come from depictions showing him uprooting trees planted by Chac, the rain god. Other stories, later ones after the Spanish conquest, merge him with the Christian devil."

She wrapped the small statue and re-inserted it into the false base of the camera bag.

Frowning, he shoved to his feet. "This break-in was about Kizin. I hope you see just how dangerous your enterprise is. Things could get a whole lot worse on the trail." When she started to speak, he held up a hand. "Nope, not trying to talk you out of anything."

"Finally, you get it." She held up the camera bag. "I can't take this with me to the gala."

He frowned, looking dubious. "The SUV's glove box locks."

She gripped the bag's strap. "Secure enough?"

"All I can offer short of waking up a banker and renting a safe-deposit box. But I wouldn't trust that much more than the glove box. Plus, tonight's thieves are probably following us." He grinned. "Ready to go dazzle *los selectos*? The elite, that is."

Apparently she had no choice. On a sigh, Kate stood and smoothed her gown. When she touched her hand to his big warm one, she felt a tremor low in her body.

A jungle trek wasn't the only danger she faced.

****

They entered the grand ballroom half an hour later. On the way to the palace, Max had kept an eye on the rearview mirror but spotted no tail. He couldn't assume Mustache and his pal were sloshing it down at a bar, but it was a safe bet they couldn't wangle a way into this gala.

Although more rivals for Kizin had to be prowling around, he'd dug up only two names—President Aguilar and General Lopez. He'd keep a sharp eye for anybody watching Kate too closely. One scum he hoped he didn't have to worry about was Alistair Sedgwick, as long as he was tucked into his fucking mansion an ocean away.

Working for Devlin had taught Max how to conduct himself with kings as well as thieves, a long way from street punk. The gleaming marble floors and gold-flecked walls mocked the poverty and hunger in Costa Verde. Made him long to heave a grenade at the fancy chandeliers. One saving grace. Not spending money on air conditioning. Fans circulated the breeze entering through French doors.

"This place is the freakin' Taj Mahal."

At his side, Kate whispered, "Native stone, polished like marble. Built ten years ago by the dictator. President Aguilar doesn't seem to mind the opulence."

"Hardship duty." He held back a snort.

Men in tuxedos and Costa Verde military uniforms and women in sparkling gowns filled the ballroom and queued for the reception line. The full orchestra played a fast Latin tune for a crowded dance floor.

No surprise other men eyed Kate like jaguars tracking their next meal. Max was checking her out too. Gorgeous anytime, but tonight—hoo, momma, a stunner.

She'd clasped her hair up in back so it tumbled in sexy curls, baring her neck to temptation. He placed a hand on the small of her back. Not only did the gown caress all her curves like a lover's hand, but the back dipped low enough for his fingers to touch bare skin. Skin even softer than her arm.

She flinched at his touch but didn't move away.

His body reacted in a predictable way and he withdrew his hand. Hell, he shouldn't be thinking of her skin. Resisting temptation was tougher than he'd expected.

His life meant daily risks, but the tangible kind, the kind he knew how to handle, not the emotional-attachment kind that could bite you in the ass. Nope, not gonna get that close.

Sharing a small tent would make distance impossible. She'd breached his first line of defense by being nice. He needed to shore it up again. Keep his emotions out of the equation.

"We're next in the reception line," she whispered. "Then you'll go check if *things* are secure?"

"Need to give it a little time. Not be obvious. Try not to worry." He'd have to trust Kizin's hiding place was safe unless a searcher had X-Ray vision.

An official in a tight-collared uniform presented Kate. President Aguilar was thin, about her height, with a slash of a mouth that reminded him of an old-time gunfighter. Not a man to mess with.

As soon as Kate in turn introduced Max, Aguilar presented them to his wife, a tiny woman with loops of black hair piled on top her head, a hairdo that would've done a Houston society babe proud. She accepted Kate's birthday wishes with a sniff.

"Bienvenida a mi bello país, Señorita Fontaine." After welcoming her to his beautiful country, *el presidente* eased into barely accented English. "It is a great honor to host such a distinguished representative of the Washington Cultural Museum. Rumor has it you have brought with you Costa Verde's most famous lost

treasure."

Both Aguilars gave her their full attention, their eyes glittering and narrowed, coyotes freeze-staring a rabbit.

Max edged closer to her side.

"Sadly, you have been misled, Your Excellency." Kate added a slight pout to her regret. "The Kizin statue is undergoing study back in the States. I am here to photograph the jungle trek and the K'eq Xlapak restoration for the museum."

Lying like a pro. When the Aguilars seemed to accept her cover story, Max studied the polished floor to hide his relief. He sent Kate a mental *hoo-yah*.

"You must know the anniversary of the theft is a few days away," *Señora* Aguilar said. "There have been tremors…" Her eyes widened as if she expected a quake in the next moment.

"Yes, I experienced one earlier today." Kate angled her head as if speculating. "Do you believe in the curse?"

The first lady drew up to her full height, barely five feet without the hair monument. "People in my country believe many things about the figure. The chances of my husband in the next election—"

Aguilar's hand clamped down his wife's arm. "My dear, we don't want to bore our visitors with local politics."

"You are right, my husband." *Señora* Aguilar fell silent but her pursed mouth and snapping eyes spoke for her.

The president's gaze softened with apparent concern. "The route to K'eq Xlapak through the jungle is treacherous. No place for a refined young woman. I am happy to offer you the use of my helicopter."

An alternative Kate would probably jump at if the

kidnappers didn't require the Maya way. He pressed his fingers firmly on her spine to send her a silent message of support. If only he could rewind and delete the president's interruption so his wife could finish her sentence. Just how interested in Kizin was the man?

Kate returned Aguilar's smile with a warmer one—probably every bit as real. "You are most gracious, Excellency. I do appreciate the offer but we've made other arrangements."

He bent his head in a small bow. "As you wish, but if you change your mind, my helicopter is yours. Enjoy our small party. I hope you have a pleasant stay in my country."

He dismissed them with a brief nod. *Señora* Aguilar was already greeting the next guests.

"Way to go, Kate," Max whispered in her ear as they moved down the reception line and waited for the next dignitary to greet them.

"Well, of course. A helicopter is out of the question."

Before he could reply, another dignitary turned to greet them. The next few murmured distracted welcomes, and finally they reached the end of the receiving line and were introduced to General Rodolfo Lopez.

A barrel-chested man with a large nose, he beamed Kate a smile that crinkled his deep-set eyes. He enfolded her hand with both of his and bent closer—too fucking close to Max's way of thinking. "I am so pleased you came tonight," he said in heavily accented English. "I fear my earlier invitation was… clumsy."

Kate looked properly contrite. "No indeed, General. I'm the one who must apologize. The flight was long and

I wanted only to go to my hotel." She lowered her voice. "And I feared accepting a rival's invitation might offend my official host."

Her dazzling smile did its job. "I understand, *Señorita* Fontaine. The matter is forgotten. You are here, and I am more than pleased to meet the woman who recovered Kizin."

Kate's shoulders stiffened. "I didn't buy the statue. My brother did."

"But you possess it, do you not?" His gaze flicked up the line toward his election opponent.

"For the time being, but I don't own it. How can one own such a precious artifact?"

His mouth twitched. "Many in Costa Verde would like to own it. I can make it worth your while to place the statue in my hands. For safe keeping, you understand."

Lopez had homed in on the same goal as *el presidente*—possession of Kizin. Prestige, yeah, but more than that. Max sent Lopez his best aw-shucks grin. "Folks here who're interested in the statue of Kizin are thicker 'n fleas on a stray dog. Seems like it's not totally about the earthquake curse."

The amiable smile disappeared from the general's fleshy face. "You are perceptive, *señor*. Costa Verde has more than one legend about the powers of Kizin."

Kate squeezed Max's arm. "Thank you for your offer, General, but I don't have the jade figure with me on this visit to your lovely country."

"Lamentable. Odd that your museum would send such a high-ranking official as photographer."

She winked, one conspirator to another. "The director balked, but I insisted because of my personal interest."

A flicker in his gaze said he considered this a poor excuse. "Also regrettable you had some trouble at your hotel. I hope the rest of your stay is without incident."

"Thank you. We mustn't monopolize any more of your time." Tugging Max along with her, she led the way to the bar.

He blew out a breath. Thank God he'd steered her away from the general's original offer of hospitality. They were served flutes of tepid champagne. After holding his breath while Kate ran the gauntlet, he'd prefer a shot of tequila, maybe two, but in this barrel of snakes, he needed all his wits.

They moved past clutches of chatting people and found space beside a pillar. The music shifted from slow and dreamy to a salsa beat. Kate moved closer, likely for privacy. Regardless, he savored her scent and the feel of her body against his.

"The car? Now, please?" She clutched her champagne tight enough to break the stem.

He winked, shook his arm, and then peered at his shirt cuff. "Damn, I've dropped a cufflink. Maybe it's in the SUV." He mouthed, "Stay here." When she nodded, he handed her his glass and strode away through the dancers.

Shit, protecting Kate ranked higher in his priorities than checking on the statue. But she ought to be okay for a few minutes. Who'd dare try something there, in the middle of all the dignitaries? What would be the point? She couldn't hide a Post-It in that painted-on dress. Besides, security guards—army, from the look of the uniform—encircled the palace.

Outside, he inhaled the cooler air. Cooler was only relative, a couple notches down the Costa Verde thermostat from roasting, and just as humid. Sweat trickled down his spine.

He'd hated turning over the keys to the valet but that was the palace protocol. He nodded to the two guards by the door and waved to the valet, explained his problem. The young man beckoned he should follow and the two of them trotted off toward the parking lot.

Apparently with all the security, they weren't worried about car theft. The SUV keys were still in the ignition. Max made a show of looking on the floor while he scanned the vehicle interior. All intact. The glove box was locked and the key in his pocket, although at the last minute he'd found a better hiding place.

A movement beyond the passenger window caught his eye. A man ducked into the trees and disappeared, but not before Max caught a glimpse of his face in the moonlight. The man who'd followed them before, the man with the mustache. His jaw clenched. Maybe he should buy a bigger pistol.

He'd have no excuse to come out here a second time, but maybe his surprise appearance had scared off Mustache.

He slipped the cufflink from his inside jacket pocket and pretended to scoop it up from the floor. Backing out of the driver side, he held up his prize in triumph. After he tipped the valet, he hurried back to Kate. He'd alert her about Mustache later. No need to frighten her now.

"Thanks for holdin' my glass, darlin'. Found the cufflink first thing." He held up his left wrist and grinned, then swallowed some of the drink. Flat now as well as warm. In a low tone, he added, "Everything's okay."

Her smile was forced but her sigh of relief genuine.

"Could the general be behind our burglary?" she whispered.

"We think alike, darlin'. Could be a slew of crooked in his family tree. What do you think he meant by the powers of Kizin?" He handed their empty glasses to a passing waiter.

That little wrinkle appeared between her brows. Thinking hard again. "As I researched over the years, I ran across several legends about the statue. But not one applies here."

"It's not just the powers of Kizin, but *power* itself, Ms. Fontaine."

At the British accent, Max spun around.

Chapter Eleven

"SEDGEWICK!" KATE'S EYES widened as she too turned.

A thin smile split Alistair Sedgwick's face. The collector wore a tailored tux that had to cost four times as much as Max's. What exactly did he hear? Damned obvious what he was up to. If Max had known he was here, he'd never have left Kate's side. Add the Brit to the collection of snakes determined to possess the statue.

Max missed yanking Kate back before she took a step toward Sedgwick.

Shoulders squared, she glared at the thief. "What are you doing here?"

"President Aguilar invited me, of course," Sedgwick replied. "He and I are old friends."

"You know very well I mean here in Costa Verde."

"When I learned you were on your way, I decided to give you a chance to return what you stole from me."

Kate's hands fisted at her side, but her voice remained calm. "What *I* stole? You are the only one who thinks that's true. You're the thief and a murderer."

He bristled. His tangled eyebrows bunched. "You wound me. No one has died."

"Not for your lack of trying." She shook her head. "Your gall amazes me."

The thin smile turned feral. He lowered his voice to just above a whisper. "You'll not put me off. I shall possess the statue. One way or another."

Max curved an arm around Kate's waist. Sedgwick—and the other interested parties if they were watching—ought to get the picture. "What did you mean about Kizin and power?"

The asshole's laugh dripped scorn. "More superstition. One legend says whoever possesses the statue holds the power of the earthquake and will rule the region."

"Ah," Kate said. "Too bad I didn't bring the statue to Costa Verde."

Sedgwick stared at her as if he could read her secrets. "Somehow, my dear, I don't quite believe you." He turned on his heel and strode away into the throng at the bar.

"Cocky bastard!" Kate hissed.

"Nu-uh. Vein in his neck was jumping like a son of a bitch." A mistake, assuming Sedgwick wouldn't show up to join the others in this barrel. Like a rattlesnake, the fucker had more venom in his fangs.

"Dance with me, Max." Kate's hips swiveled to the band's beat. The gold gown skimming every curve, she sashayed onto the dance floor.

"How can I refuse an invitation like that?" He salsa-stepped right behind her, his gaze riveted on those sweet hips.

He took her hands and turned her, brought her to his side. Grinning, she followed his lead, stepping and swiveling, bumping her hip against his to the music's pulsing beat. Her eyes were bright, her cheeks pink.

Kate grinned. "I shouldn't be surprised a Texan knows the salsa, but a badass Delta Force soldier?"

"Badass, huh?" He grinned. "Darlin', I grew up in

the barrio. Everybody danced. Besides, all kinds of skills come in handy in my work." He tugged her a little closer and turned them in a tight circle, thighs and bellies pressed together.

Around them, couples swayed and laughed as the music rose and fell. Odors of perfume and hot bodies threaded the air. But only Kate filled his senses—the sway of her breasts, her full lips, her unique feminine sweetness.

His blood sizzled and dived south. This might be the only time he'd hold her, so, damn, he had to burn the feel of her into his memory. He turned her into his arms, absorbed the slide of her body against him, the intensity in her eyes. Supporting her with a hand on her back, he dipped her.

She threw back her head, laughing. As he lifted her upright, she twined her leg around his and glided the length of his body. Maybe she was working out her fury at the Brit. Or maybe she felt the same voltage he did between them, the heat that had nothing to do with the sultry night.

The crescendo of horns ending the song penetrated his awareness. Damn. Hard with desire, he couldn't resist full body contact one more time before he spun her out.

****

When they returned to the hotel, the tower clock in the plaza chimed midnight.

At Max's signal, Kate remained quiet while he checked their doors. He'd used a precaution she'd read about only in thriller novels—a single wet hair stuck from the door frames to the doors. The cloak-and-dagger ruse sent a tingle through her.

Someone—maybe the mustached man Max had seen—had rummaged through the camera bag and probably the rest of the SUV, but had taken nothing. Kizin had remained undetected behind an interior door panel. Feeling comforted by the statue's weight back in the bag, she fought the fidgets while Max searched.

"All clear. Come on in."

He'd left his cargo shorts and shirt on the floor. An indent marked the pillow where he'd stretched out earlier. Walking through Max's room to enter hers felt too intimate.

For days she'd told herself she didn't want intimacy, not with this adventurer she didn't completely trust. But she did want. After this evening, she could no longer deny it. Did she have the nerve—if he offered?

She itched to feel his skin. He'd touched her frequently tonight. An arm around her shoulders as demonstration of protection and support. A hand at her waist as they danced. Fingers on her bare back as they walked. Each touch left a burning brand, making her hypersensitive to his nearness and—dear God— culminating in that fiery salsa that lit her up like a torch.

Or was she merely vulnerable? Did guilt for her brother's predicament turn her to the first man who offered strength? At this moment, she didn't care to examine either.

"Laundry's here, earlier than promised." She handed him one of the paper-wrapped packages she'd picked up in the hall.

"The only thing that's gone right today." His tux jacket landed on the bed. He'd yanked off the bow tie and opened his top shirt buttons as soon as they climbed into the SUV.

Kate stopped in the connecting doorway. She'd been skeptical from the start, but Max's intuitive intelligence and resourcefulness were proving invaluable. "Thank you for tonight."

He shrugged, ambling closer. He leaned one arm on the door frame, more than filling the space. But was it his wide shoulders or his commanding presence? "I didn't do much but stand around."

"Your support meant a lot. And dancing with me to keep the wolves at bay until we could leave." She smiled, remembering his expertise and athletic grace. The smooth, oiled power of a panther. Hypnotic. Sensual. Seductive. Heat crawled up her face, and she cleared her throat. "You do a hot salsa. I mean cool."

"Thanks, ma'am. But you were the cool one under fire. If I didn't know better, I'd believe you really didn't bring the statue." His shirt hung open, displaying a sleekly muscled chest swirled with fine black hair.

Max intrigued her. His many layers—his surprising expertise in more than protection, his teasing gallantry, and his pride as a self-made man. She was drawn when she shouldn't be. She wanted him.

If only she could fully trust him. Or was trust overrated? Dammit, she wasn't usually this ambivalent, this… needy. This turned on.

When she met his gaze, he cupped her bare shoulders and pulled her close. "Kate. So cool and yet so hot. You make a man want to know your secrets." His dark eyes and Kahlúa-rich voice beckoned her.

She should stop this, but her pulse throbbed with the heavy beat of desire. She savored the pressure of her breasts against his hard torso. She flattened her palms against his chest, then curved her fingers over the hot bulge of muscle.

In spite of herself, she caressed his skin, threading her fingers in his chest hairs.

Dark awareness flickered in his eyes. The heat and pressure of his arousal against her belly turned her liquid with want. Kisses—or more—didn't have to mean anything. Just a man and a woman. Together for now. His mouth was so close. How could she deny what she wanted?

What they both wanted?

He rocked his mouth over hers, blanking out coherence with a hard kiss that obliterated everything but his taste, his heat. His tongue took possession of her mouth. She quaked. She melted. She was free-falling down an elevator shaft. She should object but she couldn't think why. Then she couldn't think at all, could only hold on and kiss him back.

He released her. His sensuous look morphed into his default blank mask, at the moment, every bit as seductive. "Sorry. But you're too much temptation."

She reeled, breathless and lightheaded. Peeling her hands from his skin, she took one step back. Heat suffused her entire body. "A glib compliment doesn't release you from blame. You're half naked." She stabbed her index finger at his sternum.

"I usually don't do things halfway." He clamped his hand around her finger and held it against his bare chest. "Up to you, Kate."

The hot, wild taste of his mouth lay on her tongue, and frissons of excitement raced from his touch up her arm and down her spine. He radiated heat and sensuality. His obvious desire for her triggered passion too intense to deny, and reckless urges she'd never experienced before, even in her two long-term relationships. Pure chemistry, animal attraction, but impossible to resist.

Dangerous? Maybe.

She ought to retreat to her room and close the door. She ought to do a lot of sensible things, but for the life of her, she couldn't think what they were. Her senses reeled from his heat and touch, and longing quivered deep in her body. She burned.

Sex, not commitment, Katherine. If only for an hour, what harm could come of forgetting in his arms the other dangers?

She flattened her palm on his chest. His skin was as hot as hers. "Your room or mine?"

Max's pulse kicked him like a stun gun. Hot damn, really? She was going for it? For *him*?

Her eyes met his, and his entire blood supply drained south. He hardened with a violent rush that shocked him. He could barely breathe.

"Kate?" How to begin? He was on fire, but he'd have to take his time or his hunger would scare her. "I'm not, I mean—"

Her eyes widened and she pulled back. "Are you trying to tell me you're married or something?"

"Hell no, not even 'or something.' No relationships for me." He watched her eyes to see if she got the full implication of what he said.

Her gaze was steady. She snuggled, the friction of her gown against his skin like flint striking a flame. "Then we're clear. We're just a man and a woman, together. For now."

He held her closer, hyper aware of the lushness of her breasts and the length of their bodies touching— thighs and knees, hips and torsos—as she stood in his arms. He nuzzled her tumble of hair and inhaled her scent.

She felt so perfect that he didn't want to move. Except lust shot through him with a furnace blast. He covered her hand where it lay on his chest and laced his fingers with her small ones. So soft and delicate. Refined. Too refined for the likes of him. But if their differences didn't bother her, why should he even think about it? "Are you sure?"

"I know what I'm doing." Her voice, husky with desire, hardened him to an ache that went beyond desperate.

Her breath hitched, and he tugged her backward with him into his room until he came up against the bureau. "If you change your mind, you can leave."

Her smooth finger trailed across his lips. "I won't. I want you, Max."

"You're the boss." He captured her hand and kissed each finger. Her eyelashes drifted lower as he made his way up her arm. Biting back growls of need, he licked the tender spot inside her elbow. "Tell me what you want."

Her chin lifted, and her lashes. Desire burned with blue fire in the depths of her eyes, as if alight from within, and a mischievous smile tilted her mouth. With one finger, she trailed a sizzling fuse down his chest to his navel. "I want you naked, so I can see if you're this beautiful bronze all over."

"You're killing me." His heart raced, and he clasped her shoulders to stop his hands from shaking. "*Bonita*, I crave you so much I'm on fire." Aflame, yes, hotter than the Costa Verde sun.

She pulled the pins from her hair and let it fall to her

shoulders. With excruciating slowness, she unfastened the black onyx cufflinks and slid the garment from his shoulders and off his arms. She tossed it onto the small pile of clothing on the floor. "This tux looks amazing on you. And off." Her fingers went for his fly, but he brushed them away.

"Later. This will be over way too soon if you keep going. *My* turn." With one index finger, he traced the plump upper curves of her breasts above the gold gown's low neckline. She sucked in a breath when he delved inside to stroke one nipple to pebbled arousal. He moaned when her eyes closed.

He reached behind her and lowered the zipper, and the gown slithered away, leaving her in tiny pink panties. "Beautiful."

"I'll bet you say that to everyone."

"Only women, darlin'."

Her breathy chuckle cranked the heat even higher.

He bent to her left breast, brushing his lips over the puckered nipple, laving and tasting the unique sweetness of her skin, before focusing the same attention on the right. He cupped one hand on the silk at the apex of her thighs and coaxed a sigh from her. Sliding aside the fabric, he pushed one finger into her heat. Ah, perfect. As he brought his mouth back to hers, her little hitch of breath nearly undid him. Her hand reached for him and he batted it away. "Let me pleasure you. We have all night."

A tossup who was more aroused. He growled low in his throat. *Ay*, he might die from the sweet ache. Some guys went right for release, but he loved the slow build nearly as much. With her he needed all the self-control he could muster. It was all he could do not to flip her onto her back and drive into her, hard and fast. He didn't want to rush with Kate. He wanted to imprint on his very cells the sweet-and-spicy scent of her, the catch of her breath, the brush of her skin on his.

He stroked her with one finger then eased in a second. Nudging her legs wider, he circled her center. Her slender hands gripped his biceps and she writhed against him. How could he have ever thought her aloof and cold? Tomorrow she'd wake up and remember who and what he was but tonight passion would obliterate their differences. And he'd dive into her fire.

"Come for me, *bonita*," he rasped out.

He stroked deeper, circled her faster, more firmly, pushed her higher and higher until he felt her climax grip him. He plundered her mouth, stroked her with his tongue, absorbed her sweet cries. She clung to him, arching against his hand and shaking from her climax.

He held her, brushed his lips against her damp temple as she regained her breath and her senses. He'd never forget how beautiful she looked coming apart in his arms. A sleepy bird call floated in on the night breeze. Far away, a deep voice shouted and another answered. The only other sound was the thudding of their hearts.

"Now I want more." Kate's grip on his arms eased and she tugged on his waistband. Heat shimmered between them. She kicked away her panties and stretched out on the sheets, the sight more erotic than any fantasy he could've come up with. "I want to feel the length of you on top of me."

He skinned away the rest of his clothing and extracted a foil packet from his toiletry kit before he joined her. "A different kind of dance, darlin'. Much closer than salsa."

"And hotter." Her small hand gripped him. "Now, Max, *now*."

"*Dios*, you're killing me, woman." Currents of heat swirled in his blood, lapping tension higher and higher. He was close to losing it, too close to exploding. Strange, he never lost control with a woman. Restraint was his rule, but not now, not here, not with Kate.

He donned protection and drove deep into her welcoming body. She gasped as he thrust, and a quiver raced through him. Intense pleasure swamped him, spiking every nerve ending as she wound herself around him like a flaming ribbon. He found her mouth and they thrashed together on the big bed, no stopping, no slowing down, no holding back, only full speed demanding all the other could give. He wanted to give her all possible pleasure but damn, he could hold out only so long.

And then her muscles tightened around him and her nails scored his shoulders and her moan filled his mouth. Finally, oh, finally, he let himself follow her over the edge, going rigid and pouring himself into her.

Chapter Twelve

HER CLOTHING GATHERED in her arms, Kate closed the connecting door behind her and laid her head against the wood. Her lungs pumped like a bellows, and every cell and fiber in her body still throbbed with heat. God, what had she done? Had she lost her mind?

Probably. Possibly. Definitely.

She pulled herself away from the door before temptation could take hold again. Her shoes landed with a clatter on the tile, and she let the gown slither onto the chair.

She hugged herself and took a deep breath. No surprise his scent mingled with her lotion. His hands had been everywhere. *He* had been everywhere. She'd never experienced such total focus as in his every touch, every kiss, every caress. After pleasure beyond any she remembered, she'd surfaced in Max's arms, wanting nothing more but to stay there and explore all those burnished muscles and experience again that heat and liquid fireworks.

But the surprising tenderness in his eyes had jerked her back to reality and a glimmer of sanity. She could list a thousand reasons not to get involved with Max, first and foremost because of what she might face in the jungle, the choices she'd have to make. Her chest tightened, and she knitted her hands together.

But also because they were way too different. The

experience and qualities—suspicious nature, combat skills, rough edges—that made Max ideal on this expedition were the very ones that made him so wrong for her. A man whose middle name was danger? She shook her head.

Once Doug was rescued and Kizin in its temple, she'd return to her museum desk and drinks and dinners with guys in suits at Georgetown restaurants. As she headed to the bathroom, a little voice in her head murmured the word *dull*.

After taking care of necessities, she slipped on her sleep tee and panties. She stared at the cool sheets—the unused sheets—and the empty bed before sitting on the mattress.

Somehow she'd managed to leave his arms. She kissed him and dragged herself out of his bed. Before her escape—she could call it nothing less—what did she say? No idea. A garbled excuse mumbled in the foggy afterglow of amazing sex.

Whatever she said, she glimpsed hurt in those beautiful dark eyes only a millisecond before his default grim mask slammed in place. He must've experienced some deep pain and wanted never to be vulnerable like that again. Was it a terrible loss in combat? Or did his defensive toughness stem from his childhood? No dad, and he'd barely mentioned his mom before shutting off that topic.

Whatever it was, Kate ought to be grateful his barrier was up again. Perhaps the shock of reality had hit Max too, and they would both return to professional distance.

She eyed the door a long moment, then turned off the bedside light.

And yes, his skin *was* bronze all over.

****

In the jungle

Doug's head ached like he'd just taken that half-gainer off the hotel balcony. The morning's ground shudder had been a big one, like Mama Earth was trying to shake off the humans irritating her. His wooden-frame cot had collapsed, so Franco hoisted him into the wheelchair.

The tumble to the boogying ground had whacked Doug's head a good one, but at least he was vertical now. Fuckers still kept his hands tied but didn't uncover his stash. He couldn't move the damn wheelchair with his hands tied, but his headache was receding.

Voices outside cranked his pulse. What now?

Al hustled in with the folding chair and placed it opposite the wheelchair. He backed out of the way as a man entered—the damn Maya priest who'd conned him and kidnapped him. If Luis *was* a priest. But given the bowing and scraping, he must be some high muckety-muck. But no damn way would Doug use the Maya title of respect.

Luis waved a hand, dismissing Al, and lowered himself onto the chair. No cheap suit like when he came to see Doug in the States, just dark pants and a white collared shirt. He sat perfectly straight, his hands on his knees. Unsmiling, he stared as if he could see inside Doug. Fucking eerie.

Doug forced his hands to relax in his lap. Forced his gaze to lock with that of Luis. Forced his breathing to slow. And waited. He'd faced some tough negotiators. It never paid to show your cards or any emotion.

"My men make you comfortable?" the man said in

133

a conversational tone.

Doug held up his bound hands. It was all he could do not to roll his eyes. "Shit, yeah, it's like being the guest of Vlad the Impaler."

A slight frown crimped the other man's forehead, his only reaction. "That is good. You bought the statue of Kizin in England, *sí*?"

Doug nodded.

"From English man named Sedgwick?"

His pulse kicked up again. *Chill, Fontaine.* "Alistair Sedgwick. I told you that in D.C."

"Why he wants Kizin *now*?"

So this *was* about Kizin. Doug couldn't yet see how, but maybe this news gave him some leverage. "Dunno."

"Why he buy Kizin?"

"Sedgwick's a big collector."

Luis cocked his head. "He sold the statue. He wants it again. Why?"

Like Doug could read Sedgwick's mind? He raised his shoulders slowly, lowered them incrementally. "Second thoughts? He here in Costa Verde?"

A blink was all Doug caught, but he figured he'd hit it right. Sedgwick had followed the thief to this backwater. Doug wanted to know the same damn thing this man did. Why was ol' Alistair so hot for Kizin?

"You know this man. Try." He leaned forward, placing his forearms on his knees. The change in posture revealed a huge blade in a belt holster.

Sweat streamed down Doug's spine. Shit, did these Maya still practice blood sacrifice?

He was getting nowhere by stalling. "Probably regretted selling such an important find. Buying it back's no big deal to him. Sedgwick's a rich dude. He could buy

Kizin from the thief for twice as much as I paid him. Who's the thief, anyway?"

The priest heaved a sigh before standing. He turned and strode from the hut.

Crap, Doug had overplayed his hand. Pushed when he should've stayed cool, pulled the dude in, drawn him to ask more questions. Luis saw he had no answers. But he'd be back. Doug would bet his secret stash on it.

He twisted to feel the object in his pants pocket. He smiled.

The tremor had dumped him, yeah, but it also tipped over the table, and his breakfast dishes. He'd cheered inside like he won the Super Bowl when he secreted a dinner fork in his pants pocket. A cheap-o fork but the thing had four sharp tines. The old woman who brought his meals hadn't ratted on him—who knew why—but he'd take what he could get.

Life was good. Hell, at least more tolerable without the lumpy mattress's inhabitants crawling over him. Thank God his brain was healing. He could concentrate longer. Shadows of memory made him think someone had helped him fall. He'd remember sooner or later.

For now he needed free hands and an opportunity to use his weapon.

He stopped there with the impossible wishes. Wouldn't think about escape.

****

Cabo Blanco

Max finished his coffee and snagged a mango from the fruit bowl on their table. A rain shower early that morning didn't cool things off. Instead it stoked up a steam bath. Quiet reigned in the plaza except for pedestrians dodging steaming puddles. Breakfast was in

135

the hotel bar, so he would easily spot their two guides when they arrived.

Kate probably hadn't slept any better than he did after she left his bed. Her eyes and shoulders drooped as she picked at her omelet. Otherwise, she looked good enough to eat in a flowered sundress that hugged her fine breasts and skimmed her knees. Her hair was bound in a ponytail and damp after a shower— No, he wouldn't picture her naked and wet.

A major case of the hots for her had driven out what little was left of his common sense. Hooking up with a client was unprofessional. He'd never done it before. Thomas would have his head. Fine. *He* obviously wasn't using it. *¡Imbécil! ¡Bruto!*

She'd slipped out of his bed saying something about needing to sleep in her own bed. Of course she hadn't stayed the night. Sex was all she wanted. All he wanted.

Except he wanted her again. Wanted the surprising fire in that cool package. He liked her strength. Determination like hers was rare as a flood in the desert. But he'd seen her cool shell crack. A complicated female. Who fit perfectly in his arms, every curve a magnet for his hands. Remembering her sighs as he caressed her hardened his body all over again.

So what if they hooked up for the duration? Why not? As long as it didn't interfere with the job. And as long as he kept it strictly sex. He hadn't gotten in over his head with a woman yet. No reason he'd start now.

What would he say? She sure as hell wasn't talking. Hadn't said more than two words or looked him in the eye. They'd ignited the bed but it was only sex. Only.

So why did he spend the night tying the sheets into knots? Every drunken shout outside had popped his eyes open. After she'd left his bed, he headed for the shower. Cranked it all the way cold. Shit, even a cold shower in this climate was too tepid to cool him off. And sitting beside her was burning him up again.

¡Malditos!

He beckoned to the waiter, who was gabbing with the bartender as he washed glasses. *"Mas café, por favor. Café negro."* No milk for him, even if it was local custom. He needed his caffeine undiluted. Especially this morning.

After both their cups were refilled, he dived in. Needed to get past this thorn bush between them so they could at least be civil. "Kate, about last night, I—"

"Max Rivera, don't you dare apologize." Her fork clattered onto her plate. "I wanted you. You wanted me. We had a fabulous time. And if you're worrying I might sue for sexual harassment, please."

He scratched his chin, fighting a smile and the urge to kiss her. "Whoa, darlin', I never apologize for great sex. It was unprofessional of me and Thomas would have my hide if he knew, but that's as far as my regrets go. What I started to say was I'd understand if you felt last night was a mistake. But if that was our only time together, it'd be a damn shame."

A rosy pink climbed her neck and spread into her hairline. "Unusual as compliments go, but I'll take it. And last night was most definitely not a mistake."

He nodded, conceding he'd have to see where things went.

His phone jangled, and in his haste to set down his cup, he sloshed hot liquid onto his hand. Kate dabbed at his skin with her napkin as he growled a greeting into the phone.

"Easy, big fella." Mara Marton's voice blared in his ear. On some satellite connections, you had to shout. Not this one. Loud and clear. He held the receiver away an inch. "Jungle fever got you already?"

"Sorry." He handed Kate her napkin and mouthed a thank-you. "Late night." He related the events at the gala but didn't go beyond that.

Kate sipped her coffee and was finally eating her eggs. Her gaze flicked to him as he finished his report. She smiled and looked away.

"Sedgwick, Lopez, Aguilar, and some mustachioed local." The DSF researcher clucked her tongue. "And those are the ones we know about. Should I tell Devlin you need backup?"

"I'm good. Better to keep a low profile. What's going on?" He stretched out his legs.

A heavy sigh on the other end. "The tremors, Max, they're getting more frequent, stronger."

"No shit. A couple rocked us here yesterday." Not to mention the quake rocking his bed last night. Damn, now he needed another tepid shower. He grabbed a gulp of coffee.

"Then you know why I'm calling. It's not just the tremors. The stress on the fault lines has increased in magnitude from the date the statue was stolen from the temple to the twentieth anniversary, then to the fortieth, and to now. It's no longer safe, for you or the client." The high pitch of Mara's voice was a measure of her worry.

"Unless Devlin has a man set for an extraction, nothing I can do."

"Lucas Del Rio is poking around there, but no luck so far on locating Doug Fontaine."

"Then we keep to schedule. News on... my other

thing?" Kate didn't seem to be paying attention to his side of the conversation. She was gazing out at the plaza.

"Not yet. I sent descriptions to Interpol. The Corinthian bronze helmet and the Nike amphora. If Fontaine bought those illegally, we'll find out."

At Kate's sharp intake of breath, he groaned. Shit, she'd heard. Maybe not all, but enough. Thanks to Mara's dialed-up volume. "I'll check in later. Gotta go."

"But the tremors—" she said, as he disconnected.

"What the hell was that about the pieces Doug bought?" Kate's blue glare cut into him like a laser, and her mouth was tight. "DSF investigated him? I heard the word *illegally* too."

A wrench was twisting his gut. Hell and high water, no way out of it. He had to level. Shit, he was no good at subtlety anyway. Behind them, the waiter and bartender stopped chatting. Listening? Maybe they understood more English than he thought.

He shot to his feet and jerked a nod toward the archway leading to the plaza. "Not here."

She slung her camera case over a shoulder and stalked outside.

The plaza stretched before them, steam rising from puddles, vendors still setting out their wares, other people striding past the stalls on their way to work. Max urged Kate to the left past a bakery, where aromas of honeyed pastries and tortillas flavored the air.

She stopped in the shade of a bougainvillea the size of a small car and planted her feet among the fallen red blossoms. "Far enough. I need an explanation."

He'd feared from the outset this wouldn't work. *A la madre.* He scrubbed a hand through his hair. "Yes, DSF and Interpol investigated your brother. They suspect he's had dealings with Centaur, and some of his other deals were also illegal."

Her eyes narrowed. "Like the amphora and the helmet."

"Interpol hasn't gotten back to Mara on those." He held out his hands. "Look, I never wanted to mislead you. Devlin ordered me to find out what I could about Doug's business." That wasn't all, but all he ought to say.

She huffed. "Thomas will hear from me about that. And Istanbul? Did you mislead me about what happened there?"

"What I told you was true."

She shook her head. "But you didn't tell me everything, did you?"

"Hell, you might as well have it all. I insisted Doug turn the bronze snake head over to the Istanbul Archeological Museum, and he offered me money." When she shook her head in apparent disbelief, he added, "Yeah, money. He tried to pay me off. When I refused and hauled out my phone, he shoved the piece at me and disappeared into the crowd."

She huffed. "Doug is impulsive and reckless. But he's not a criminal. If he bought a stolen item, he didn't know and panicked when you told him. When we find him, he'll clear all this up. The Centaur part too." She started to walk back to the plaza, then turned. "You *do* still intend to take me to K'eq Xlapak, to rescue my brother?"

Shit, he should've told Mara to tone it down. The truth would've come out sometime, but why'd it have to be now? After last night? Kate's skeptical tone said she was back to square one, not trusting him. For much of anything. He knew about trust, and about betrayal. Nestor had taught him that no matter what others did, a real man kept his promises.

He firmed his jaw. "I made a vow a long time ago to always keep my commitments. I'll keep you safe while we go to the restoration. Count on it. And DSF has sent another agent to find your brother."

"I keep my commitments too. This trip covers two of them." Her chin trembled, then lifted. "This DSF agent, can we contact him, find out what he knows?"

"No can do. Protocol. Safer to keep different missions separate. We go through Mara. When Del Rio gets closer to finding your brother, I'll get the word to be in contact."

"I see." She turned and walked away.

Back to all business. Probably for the best. Then why did he feel like he'd explode if he didn't have her again? He couldn't think of the last time a woman affected him like this. He shook himself back to reality and jogged ahead.

"Kate, wait up. Mara warned me about the seismic data." A few strides and he joined her on the hotel steps. He summarized the increasing danger. "By the calendar we have eleven days, but seismic time may be different. We buy supplies and go."

Her shoulders shifted in a small shudder before she nodded. "No time to waste. Agreed." She pointed to her watch. "Nine-fifteen. Arturo and Constantino should've been here by now. They seemed so eager."

"I know what you're thinking. Another snafu. But time is more fluid in Central America. Give them a few minutes."

Sirens broke the morning's peace as two blue-and-white police cars screamed to a halt across the plaza. A woman rushed out of a store and pointed to the adjacent alley.

"What's going on?" Shading her eyes with one hand, Kate stretched up on tiptoes.

Prickling on the back of his neck warned him to check it out. "Maybe the shop was robbed. Hard to say."

Her forehead crimped. "Constantino and Arturo…"

"Whatever's wrong across the plaza can have nothing to do with them." What about those shouts he heard last night? "If it makes you feel better, I'll check it out. Stay here in case they arrive."

By the time he made his way across the plaza, a crowd had gathered around the cop cars and in front of the shops.

As the sun climbed, so did the heat and humidity. Not like the dry heat of his month in Egypt. Sweat beaded his forehead and stuck his shirt to him like melting wax.

To the crowd in general he asked what happened.

The man beside him shrugged. *"No sé, señor."*

He didn't know. Max rubbed his nape. Damn prickles.

He wove through the crowd until he reached the shop. Everybody was too engrossed in the commotion in the alley to pay him any mind—including the cops. One uniform was interviewing the agitated woman inside her shop. The other three clustered around the trash bins.

Edging around a hanging rack of embroidered dresses placed him close to the alley, where crime scene tape blocked entry. He peered around the corner.

A man sprawled on his side as if sleeping. Even twenty feet away Max knew death when he saw it. Blood spattered the cement around the man's head, his face battered beyond recognition. He wore one sandal and the other lay in a puddle. Max's sense of dread had been right. He pounded a fist into his other palm.

He heard a gasp at his elbow and, "No!"

Kate. She stepped forward, her face white as ashes.

He snapped his hand around her wrist and pulled her against his chest.

"You don't want to see this." No sense reminding her he told her to stay put. He cupped her head and held her.

"But, Max." Her words caught on a sob. "It's Constantino."

"Yeah." He recognized the T-shirt. He shuddered at the image of crimson smears across the four Kiss faces.

Kate trembled against him but held herself stiffly as if resisting his comfort. Couldn't blame her.

Who had killed Constantino? Which of the greedy bastards wanted Kizin enough to beat one of their guides to death?

And where was Arturo?

Chapter Thirteen

KATE DESCENDED THE steps of the *Comisaria de Cabo Blanco*. The police station's cheerful orange stucco walls belied the seedy hostility inside.

A few dusty police cars sat at the curb. A water vendor wheeled his cart down the empty street followed by a couple of skinny cats. Two shorts-clad men seated on the other side of the station steps smoked cigars. One wore an Atlanta Braves cap. Neither man gave her a glance.

She slid on sunglasses against the Costa Verde sun. Doug should be here on such a day. Here to tease her with that glint in his eyes. Here to join her in returning Kizin. She'd give anything to have her baby brother well and safe.

Sitting on the top step, resting the camera bag on her lap, she willed Max to come out of the station.

Max.

A deep ache twisted her mid-section, and she hunched over the bag. Last night had been a mistake. She'd let the mood and the sexual voltage between them evaporate her usual common sense. Why couldn't it have been mediocre sex, forgettable sex, instead of incredible sex?

The wrong time, the wrong man. Dammit, why'd she have to be so attracted to this man she couldn't trust, at least about her brother. He—and Thomas Devlin—

were wrong about Doug.

Nothing she could do for now. She had no choice but to trust DSF's other agent to rescue Doug and trust Max to take her and Kizin safely to K'eq Xlapak. Beyond that, nothing personal, only professional distance.

When she'd questioned whether he'd follow through, he bristled. His tight-jawed assurance that he always kept his commitments triggered old memories. A promise broken, that to this day gave her guilty twinges. Another kept, one that set her course. The third, that led her down this road. The image of her dad in pain never left her. Hands that once were strong and vital had barely been able to hold hers as he demanded her promises.

Her heart pounded an unsteady rhythm, and a shallow throbbing settled deep in her skull. She closed her eyes for a moment, but it didn't help, not in this heat.

She wanted Esteban to know what was happening and started to take out her satellite phone, but it was too soon for Arturo to reach the village, if that's where he went. She fanned herself with one hand and looked back at the orange building.

No Max.

Unease crawled over her skin. Or was that more sweat?

What was taking so long? The police had already taken their statements.

After finding Kate's name and hotel on a piece of paper in Constantino's pocket, the police searched their rooms. She'd held her breath during their cursory check of the camera bag, but no one noticed the secret compartment. Then they were hustled to the *comisaria* for questioning.

First they waited in a drab, hot room with a tiny window and no fan. A room that smelled of rancid peppers and unwashed bodies. She wrinkled her nose, still smelling the rankness. For hours she stewed in her own perspiration. No one told them anything about the murder or Arturo.

Finally the detective took their statements. He accepted Kate's cover story of photographing the restoration as the reason for their presence in Costa Verde and apologized profusely for the delays. At five o'clock the police released them with instructions to notify the police if Arturo contacted them. Max had stopped at the exit, saying he would join her in a minute.

Nerves eating at her empty stomach, Kate looked at her watch. That had been ten minutes ago. Where the hell was he?

As if in response, Max appeared in the doorway and bounded down the steps.

"That took longer than I expected, dar— Kate."

Thank God he was whole. But why the grim face? She wanted to hug him. Rising to her feet, she hugged her bag. "What was that about?"

He guided her leftward along the crumbled sidewalk. "The hotel's only a few blocks this way. Let's walk."

She cut him a sideways glance. He must have something to tell her that he didn't want overheard. "Sure. I need fresh air after that stifling experience."

He halted, giving her the once-over. "They didn't lay a hand on you, did they?"

She couldn't help smiling at his solicitousness. "I'm fine. All the detective laid on me was a glower no fiercer than my mother's."

He gave a sharp nod and hurried her along at a fast clip. After crossing the next street, they passed a small grocery with oranges and mangos piled in outside bins. When they reached a grassy park where mothers wheeled baby carriages and small children kicked balls, he slowed their pace.

He pulled her into the shade of a palm tree. "I have the scoop on what the cops know. They think Constantino was beaten and killed sometime between midnight and two o'clock. The brothers were seen in a cantina near the central plaza talking to two men. The bartender recognized one because of a big scar on his cheek. Said he thought the guy was in the Costa Verde army."

"That points to General Lopez."

"Or *el presidente.*"

Kate shook her head at all the possibilities. "They would tell *me* nothing. How did you find this out?"

He held up a hand and rubbed his fingers and thumb together. "Money talks. Especially American dollars. I'll add it to my bill."

She should've known. "Do you have more to tell me?"

"Not much. The cop said our break-in might be connected or it might not. He wouldn't commit. Constantino and his brother's employer told the cops where they were staying, a thatched hut at the edge of the city. A few pieces of clothing in a rucksack that seemed to belong to Constantino. More rock-band T-shirts. Arturo's pack was gone."

She licked her lips. "If his pack was gone, he might be safe."

"Then we'd better hope he headed home. If he

shows up here, they'll arrest him for his brother's murder."

A hot sunburst kindled in her chest. Not that gentle-eyed Maya, no. "I can't imagine him beating his brother to death. The murder has to be connected to Kizin." The attack on her brother and his kidnapping, and now a death. "Sometimes I wish I'd never heard of Kizin. What now?" She drew in a deep breath, banking her fury.

Max took her arm. "Let's keep moving. We have supplies to buy and we'll need new guides."

She walked faster. "Are you certain we can make it in time?"

A muscle in his jaw twitched. "Not much about this operation is certain."

****

K'eq Xlapak

Esteban Morales sighed as he disconnected the call. Nothing and no one must be allowed to stop this restoration. Forces of nature were one matter, but worse were human greed and cruelty. Poor Constantino. How much of what happened in Cabo Blanco should be shared? His chest ached with the dilemma.

He stood quietly outside the king's palace and let his gaze pan the expanse of the great plaza. His tour of the project's work was his favorite part of the day. Seeing the entire city, not just the plaster floors and ceramics in the palace, reminded him of the grandeur they were restoring.

The city was laid out around the broad limestone square, with the king's palace on one side opposite the temple. *Stelae* the height of the church steeple in Cabo Blanco's central plaza demarcated the other two sides. Beyond them lay the vegetation-buried remains of dwellings and other buildings only beginning to be mapped. To the east, the archeological team's camp. Turning his face upward, he let the history of K'eq Xlapak wash over him with the sun's rays.

Boots scraped across the plaza. He turned to see his wife hurrying toward him.

A smile lit Pilar's fine features. "I have no patients this morning. No stitches needed from chisel cuts and no broken toes from dropped stones. Yet. I thought I'd join you for your morning tour." She handed him a mug of coffee.

He shook off his thoughts. Suddenly he felt very old. Caffeine was the boost he needed. "Thank you, *querida*."

They'd taken only a few steps across the stony ground when Pilar said, "You seem distracted, sad. Was it your phone call?"

Temporizing, he sipped his coffee. *Ay*, so she'd noticed him talking on the phone. And she was too perceptive not to notice his mood. Not because she was the project physician, but because after so many years of marriage, she read him like a *stela*. He needed to decide what to do with what he knew. But if anyone could be trusted, it was his wife.

He halted midway across the plaza. They stood far enough away from the work teams that no one would hear their conversation. He passed a hand over his face. "*Sí*, the phone. I will tell you because you may have advice for me, but you must promise not to share this confidence."

Her dark eyes solemn, she nodded. "What concerns you so?"

"The call was from Kate Fontaine. Constantino was found murdered in an alley this morning. Beaten to

149

death."

Her hand flew to her throat. "*¡Dios mío!* How could this happen? And Arturo?"

"The *señorita* said they do not know. Perhaps he is hiding or perhaps he is coming here."

"What will you do?"

"That is my dilemma. This disaster will delay the return of Kizin."

Pilar flipped her braid off her shoulder. To him she still looked young, but white strands now muted the red of her hair. She stared at the ground, pushing a pebble with the toe of her boot. "And the news might frighten the villagers."

"They are frightened now and every day grow more anxious." As did he. And Pilar, judging from her tight expression. He downed the remainder of his coffee. "The priests will see omens in Constantino's death and alarm the people even more."

"If that is possible." She shook her head. "What about *Señorita* Fontaine? Is she coming?"

"*Sí*, but I do not know much. When I told her there was not enough time to send new Maya guides, she said only they would work out something." A deep breath didn't ease the tightness in his chest. "So should I keep the news a secret—at least until I know more—and say that *Señorita* Fontaine and her guides are on schedule?"

"Perhaps that is wise. But Constantino's family should know of his death. They will want to bring his body home." Her voice was gentle.

"*Sí*, I don't like keeping it from them."

Pilar stared past him. "You must decide fast. Don Luis and his assistant are headed this way."

****

Cabo Blanco

Alistair Sedgewick watched the two sods he'd hired to be sure they left.

Unfortunately he'd been forced to make his arrangements long distance before seeing the pair. They slouched down the hall, their sandals scuffing the tile. They could as easily stab him in the back as rob him. Surprisingly, they'd accomplished what he'd asked, but they'd brought him a new problem.

Fortunately the one called Zaga—appalling name— was just the sort of unscrupulous type he needed. If all went well, he'd have Kizin in two days. Then he could leave this backwater.

He closed and locked the room door. Not that the thin wood could keep out either brigands or noise. He crossed the creaking floor and paced in front of the window with its peeling shutters and view of stray dogs picking through the spilled garbage. Staying at the same hotel with the Fontaine woman and her bodyguard had been out of the question. If this *posada* was the best alternative, a good earthquake might bloody well improve matters. What a pit.

He was no safer here than within reach of Le Noir. But if he didn't return with Kizin, he was a dead man. He shoved that morbid thought away. Now that the men had gone, he prepared to leave for dinner. Not that he could find a decent establishment.

Knuckles drummed on the thin wood. The innkeeper, no doubt coming to apologize for the shoddy accommodations.

When he opened the door, his heart took a flying leap into his throat. He couldn't manage more than a croak. "Le Noir, what are you doing here?"

The burly man's lips curved in a sword-sharp smile. "I protect my employer's interests, *naturellement.*"

Bloody hell! Sedgwick hadn't anticipated this turn of events. He eyed the Frenchman up and down, clad not in one of his silk suits but in a perfectly pressed tropical shirt and white trousers. "You don't expect to go into the jungle with me, I hope."

"If I must, *certainement.*" Le Noir closed the door behind him. "But first, you must inform me what you 'ave planned with the two *chameaux* who just left."

****

West of Cabo Blanco

Max steered over and around potholes. The limestone road arrowed straight through the canopy of trees. What had once been a major Maya thoroughfare was now a country lane that neglect had nearly returned to the jungle. What would've been an easy fifteen-minute drive on any U.S. highway was looking like an hour's drive on this Mayan ruin. Like on Afghanistan's bomb-pocked roads, he could drive no faster than fifteen miles an hour.

But dammit, they'd make it to within hollerin' distance of K'eq Xlapak later today. Kate—and Kizin—would be safe. Barring any more disasters. Still no word from Del Rio about rescuing Fontaine. He worked his tight jaw.

"Jungle looks thick," Kate said. On both sides of the road, trees and vines formed a wall of green. Decaying vegetation and new growth feathered the humid air.

Max's forehead hurt from scowling at the eccentricities of the no-frills pickup as they drove through the heat of the day. Larger than the SUV, it held all their food, camping gear, and other equipment. The hot air blowing in the open windows plastered his neck and nibbled at his eyes.

"Strange," he said. "October usually means the end of the rainy season. I expected thinning foliage and more brown. Kizin must like rain with his tremors." Vines and spider plants draped spiny acacia trees and thin-barked copas. "I'd hate to have to hack my way through those vines with a machete. They cover everything."

"There's a bright spot after all. You won't have to."

The concern in her tone suggested she was thinking of Constantino's death three days before. He wished he had a word of comfort for her but he didn't want to offer false promises. A miracle if Arturo made it to his village.

He slanted her a glance. A white-knuckle grip on her camera bag, frown lines to rival his. She hadn't recovered from the tremor at their lunch stop, a tin-roofed open-air dive beneath a sign reading Gas-Bar-Food. He'd scarfed down his lunch but she'd eaten only half of hers when the shaking knocked their plates to the floor.

To his surprise, she looked natural in hiking clothes. Good to go. Snake-proof boots. Moisture-wicking pants that cupped her sweet tush. Insect-repellant cotton shirt and pocketed vest over a form-fitting camisole. That meant no bra. His blood heated and he shifted in the seat.

"Are you sure we can trust this man?" she said.

She must be balancing on a thread. She was used to controlling events, not having events stampede over her. He passed her a hand-held global-positioning-system device, more complex than the one she probably had in her car. "You know how to handle this?"

"I do." She pushed buttons to bring the screen to life. "I used GPS on my digs out west."

"I've keyed in the coordinates for our destination near K'eq Xlapak. You can see whether we're headed there or Alaska."

Her eyes shone with purpose. "Leave it to me." She yanked back her hair, secured it with an elastic thing, and threaded the gathered hair through the slot in her yellow cap. Finished, she paid him no mind as she became absorbed in the GPS.

During their few days in the humid tropics, Kate's hair had morphed from disciplined and tame to unruly. Sexy and soft and all windblown. Wild. He tightened his fingers on the steering wheel.

Heat—but not from the climate—trickled sweat down his back. His body stiffened. He wanted her. And worse, he wanted to know what made her tick. Dangerous to involve himself for more than sex, but the woman had mysteries. And when he wanted something, he went for it.

Shit, this expedition would be over before he ever saw her naked again or got to know her better. And she'd never speak to him again once she learned the rest about her brother.

"Amazing that most of these ancient *sacbéob* are straight. Some are more than sixty miles long, leading to trade centers or religious sites," she said.

He grabbed his canteen, his old Army one, lightweight like hers but in camo, and sucked down water like a desert rat. Between the muggy heat and the fucking road hazards, the muscles in his neck tightened into steel rods. At the speed they were traveling, a gang of bandits could waylay them on foot. If bandits could find them. Or Sedgwick. Or Lopez. Or Aguilar. Or any other greedy bastards. "You know why they topped the roads with limestone?"

"You have me there."

"Unlike crazy gringos, the Maya knew enough to travel in the cool of the night. The white limestone reflected the moonlight so they could find their way."

Kate curled sideways in her bucket seat and regarded him for a silent moment. "Your ancient history courses?"

He shrugged. "Worked my way through an associate degree before joining the Army. Didn't want to be just a grunt. Figured a degree'd get me in Special Forces."

"That doesn't surprise me, you working the angles, I mean."

That was as much as he'd share. He'd already told her more than he usually divulged. "All Devlin field operatives have background related to art or ancient history. I haven't studied much modern history of this part of the world. I wish I understood more about Costa Verde's politics so I could figure out the who and why of Constantino's death."

She bit her lower lip as if biting back emotion. "Did someone kill him to keep him from guiding us? Or were they trying to beat information out of him?"

"It could be either. Or both. General Lopez is at the top of my list. He wants power. He has men who take orders without question."

"That description fits President Aguilar. And don't forget Sedgwick."

He squeezed her hand in reply and withdrew so he could shift gears. Again. "It sucks, but men like him can always find low-lifes willing to do anything for money."

Then there was the Centaur syndicate. No point in piling onto Kate's load of worry with yet another bad guy. Or team of bad guys. Shit. "Constantino's murderers won't bat an eye at killing us to get Kizin. You sure you won't let me carry the statue?"

"It's my responsibility." She glared at him. "We're still in that much danger?"

"No question. In Cabo Blanco, killing us would've caused an international incident. Out here, no law, no witnesses. If we disappear, we drowned in a *cenote* or a jaguar got us or bandits killed us. The possibilities are endless. And if Kizin happened to show up later at the K'eq Xlapak temple, they'd announce the find as a miracle.

"The pistol you bought yesterday, it's for jaguars?"

"My 9mm's okay as a concealed weapon. But this Glock 17 will take down a jaguar or a javalina." He gripped the holster at his side. "Or a human."

Kate shuddered and lowered her gaze to the GPS device in her lap.

"There's the air field sign." The marker reading *Aeropuerto* was barely discernible in the weeds. He nosed the truck onto the dirt road. A series of bumps forced him to slow the pickup to a crawl. "This is no road. It's a damn goat trail."

Soon the jungle opened into a clearing, weeds covering the stubble and rocky soil of what might've once been a farm field. An ancient Jeep stood beside a tin-roofed hut, over which a windsock sagged.

"Hardly qualifies as an airport." Kate's eyes narrowed when she spotted their transport. "That looks like a military helicopter. An old one."

Smaller four-passenger helicopters looked to Max like beetles with rotors. This craft was a dragonfly on steroids. The helicopter's rotors spun with a low whirr as the engine idled.

The fifty-foot-plus chopper was a thirty-year-old U.S. military surplus UH-1H, better known as the Huey. According to the pilot, the Costa Verde military bought this bird years ago and recently sold it to him. He swore he had to use this remote field because only the government had access to the airport. The junk heap better be as flight-worthy as Julio swore on his mother's grave it was and not *Aerolínea Suicida*.

"Military surplus." He stopped the truck a hundred feet from the chopper. Kept his expression neutral, hoping she wouldn't ask for details.

Chapter Fourteen

DESPITE KATE'S HAT, the full violence of the sun attacked her head like a laser as she descended from the truck. She peered at the helicopter over her shades.

Dented and scratched fuselage, faded camouflage coloring, a swathe of bright blue on the side that contained a crude painting of a hummingbird in flight. Her stomach pitched. "We're going to fly in *that*? That derelict?"

"Perfectly safe. Refurbished and retrofitted. Room for all our gear."

At the strain in his voice, she pivoted to face him. "More of the Texas bull you employed to convince me this was a good idea?"

"No bull, Kate. This is the only private chopper in the whole country." His voice sounded reasonable as he swung on his backpack. "You got an alternative?"

"You know very well I don't."

Flying was their only choice. Dubious and risky to boot. When Max had said maybe his Maya blood would qualify him as a Maya guide, she couldn't work up a smile. A search on his tablet located a cleared field where they could land within ten miles of the restoration. From there, they'd call Morales and arrange for *real* Maya guides for the last leg.

Finally, she'd agreed because they had only eight days before *El Día Maldito*, not enough time to make it on foot.

A slight, shaggy-haired man stepped away from the bird's shadow. He wore shorts, a khaki shirt with epaulets, and the ubiquitous flip-flops. Ambling closer, he waved. *"¡Hola, Señor Max!"*

Max waved. "That's Julio."

"Not Maya." Dust from the whirlwind kicked up by the rotor's wash tickled her nose.

He placed a hand on her shoulder. "It'll be okay. This way we get there on time. Ahead of time."

"Heaven help us."

Heaven wasn't listening, but maybe Hell was because without warning, the ground quaked and shuddered. She stumbled, and Max caught her to his tree-trunk-sturdy body and held on.

His arms held her firmly. "Just another buckin' bronco, darlin'."

Broncos that kicked up their heels with more and more frequency and strength. Heart pounding like the rumbling ground, she gripped his biceps and waited while the surrounding trees swayed. The pilot hooked an elbow around a strut, and the helicopter's rocking lifted him off his feet as if he were a child.

When the rocking and rolling ceased, everyone breathed a deep sigh and brushed off dust.

The pilot released his hold on the metal support and crossed to them.

"Hola, Julio." Max shook the man's proffered hand. *"¿Como está?"*

Kate didn't hear Julio's reply. She was still staring at the helicopter. But she pulled her attention back to the men as Max introduced her in English.

"Mucho gusto, señora," Julio said, shaking her

hand and grinning widely. "Uh, happy to meet you. Thank you for hiring my beautiful *colibrí*, my hummingbird. She flies like the wind."

Kate returned the pleasantries and complimented Julio on his enterprise. "I hope she wasn't damaged in that tremor."

He crossed himself. "No, no *señora*, all is well."

A second man descended from the co-pilot's side. Taller than Julio, the square-shouldered newcomer looked fit in black T-shirt, jeans and new white Nikes. Sunlight gleamed off his opaque black sunglasses and his bald dome, lending it an oily caramel sheen.

Beside Kate, Max stiffened. "Didn't count on an extra passenger, Julio."

The pilot snatched his ball cap from his back pocket and jammed it on his head. "This is my cousin Rufo. He will be my company on the return."

"Hola." Rufo swept off his dark shades. His black eyes didn't change expression when he smiled. "My cousin is superstitious. He does not like to fly the jungle alone." He poked Julio in the arm. "I think he fears the old Maya gods will reach up and get him."

"I hope you do not mind," Julio put in. Sweat budded on his forehead. His shoulders rounded in tacit apology.

"I will help load the gear." Without waiting for agreement, Rufo traipsed around to the truck bed.

She had no choice but to make the best of the situation. She mustered a warm smile. "That's fine, Julio. We can't leave your cousin stranded here for hours. Not a problem. Don't you agree, Max?"

Max clearly did not. He didn't like surprises. Especially the way things had been going. Scowling, he followed Rufo.

After the men loaded most of the gear, Kate ducked beneath the rotor blades and climbed aboard. Clear from the interior this was an old military transport. Bare metal all around, the pilot's and co-pilot's seats forward, a middle section with five passenger seats bolted to the side opposite the sliding door, cargo hold in back. The space smelled of metal, sweat, and someone's lunch of spicy meat. She buckled her camera bag into one of the empty passenger seats. Duct tape covered holes in the upholstery but the frames seemed sturdy enough. She dropped into the adjacent seat.

The cargo hold had straps and netting to prevent gear from sliding around. She had no fear of heights, but a helicopter's tilt-a-whirl maneuvers might be another matter. Willing her racing pulse to calm, she forced herself to relax against the cushioned seat. Everything would be fine. She closed her eyes.

Clicks indicated the rear door was secured. She looked up as Max climbed inside. He had that hard warrior look, insanely masculine, especially with a weapon at his side. Her pulse leaped again. He closed the sliding door, chose the seat on her other side, and buckled up. Despite their differences about Doug, she needed his strong presence, and his familiar sun-warmed scent was comforting.

When Julio and his cousin entered the cockpit, she called, "Julio, do we get helmets and earplugs?"

A hoot of laughter was the only reply.

"Darlin', you're lucky to have a seatbelt in this bird." Max buckled his.

The rotor blades' whirr cranked to a whine as Julio increased the engine speed. He pulled a lever and the helicopter rose, lifting with a deafening *whomp-whomp*. Kate grimaced.

The craft banked and arced out over the jungle, and she drew deep breaths to calm her swooping stomach. As they leveled out and settled into a constant speed, the noise diminished to a bearable level. Breathing more evenly, she lifted the GPS receiver from a camera bag pocket and pushed buttons for the display. On track.

Max tugged on her arm and pointed out the window.

Mesmerized by the view, she forgot her anxiety. The canopy spread five or six hundred feet below, a rolling, verdant blanket dotted with flocks of multihued birds.

For a long time, she simply watched the landscape unfold beneath the copter's landing skids. What appeared to be hills jutted upward here and there. Not hills, but unrestored Mayan buildings, overgrown with roots and trees and as green as their surroundings.

Dragging her gaze away from the panorama, she checked the GPS receiver. She sucked in a sharp breath, then spoke into Max's ear. "We're way off course. Where is Julio going?"

His gaze locked onto the coordinates. Forehead bunched in a storm cloud, he handed back the device and undid his seat belt. He opened his holster and started to take out his pistol. "Just what we need. A freaking scam. Or worse."

When Kate turned toward the forward seats, she gasped and clutched her throat. "Max!"

Rufo leveled a long black pistol at them. "Take the gun out slow."

Her heart slammed against her rib cage.

Max spat curses in Spanish. He held both hands in the air. "You don't want to do this, man. We have nothing valuable. People will be looking for us."

"Perhaps. But I have my instructions." The bald man's black eyes were as opaque as his sunglasses.

"What *are* your instructions?" Max asked in an amiable tone.

"To return with the contents of your baggage." The pistol's barrel remained steady in his hand. "The gun, *señor*. Two fingers."

Apparently seeing no other option, Max lifted out the Glock by the grip.

"Toss it back there, into the cargo hold."

Max hesitated, then complied. The heavy automatic pistol landed with a soft thud. On one of their packs, Kate guessed. Out of reach.

"Now the other." Rufo gestured downward with his gun. His smile chilled her.

Mouth a grim line, Max bent and removed the small 9mm from his ankle holster. He tossed it into the cargo hold, where it too landed soundlessly. He then hooked an arm around her. His support eased the worst of her trembling.

Julio quietly continued piloting the helicopter. No help there. Rufo probably wasn't Julio's cousin any more than she was. What did this man want? The statue? Money? What?

"I have money, Rufo. I can pay you. Put away the gun and let Julio take us to K'eq Xlapak." She barely recognized her thready voice.

Rufo sneered, insulted. "*Chica*, I am an honorable man. I have already accepted money for this job."

She could say nothing in reply to that amazing statement.

"Hang in there." Max squeezed her shoulder. In her

ear, he whispered, "Wait." He slid his arm away, leaving her trembling more than before.

Wait? What did he mean? Did he have a plan? Praying he did, she drew in a deep breath against the clawing in her belly.

The gunman squeezed between the front seats and crossed the cabin. He unlatched the door and shoved it open wide. Air rushed past the open doorway, along with the whomp-whomp of the rotors. His mouth spread in what she supposed was meant to be a smile. "Who will jump first?"

Bile stinging her throat, she shook like a sapling in a quake. "No. You can't do this."

When neither Kate nor Max made a move, Rufo took a step toward them. He sneered and raised the pistol. "I can shoot you first and dump the bodies. It matters not."

Julio erupted in an angry flurry of Spanish. Rufo's staccato reply was a clear refusal. Julio remained silent, piloting the craft. But to where?

Kate leaned closer to Max. "What did he say?"

His smile was grim. "He reminded Rufo of his promise not to fire a gun inside the helicopter."

"But that means—"

"Yes, that Julio gets a cut of Rufo's blood money." He glared at the gunman. "Who wants us dead, *cabrone*? How much did he pay you?"

Rufo shrugged in reply. "You I will shoot. Only one gunshot. My cousin can live with that." He angled his gleaming dome toward the pilot. "Right, cousin?"

When Julio ignored him, Rufo laughed.

Without warning, he flipped open Kate's seat belt. He reached behind her and grabbed her ponytail. Hauled her upward.

Searing pain stung her scalp. She cried out as she stumbled to her feet. Her boots clattered on the strips of metal flooring.

Max started forward. "Kate!" He stopped when her captor jabbed his gun into the tender skin beneath her jawbone. Max sank down, his face a mask of fury, his hands balled into fists.

Rufo released her hair and clamped his hand around her upper arm. His fingers dug painfully into her flesh. He dragged her closer to the open doorway. He kept the pistol aimed at Max, forced to remain seated on the other side of the copter.

From the corner of her eye, far below she saw her leafy grave. The sight blurred. Images of her body impaled on a tree branch or broken on the rocky ground flashed through her mind. Her pulse roared in her ears and she gasped for breath.

Rufo pulled her close. His stale breath nauseated her. He nuzzled her ear. "*Ay, chica*, too bad we have no time. A waste. Close your eyes. It will all be over in a moment."

Insides churning, she jerked away from her captor. "No!"

Rufo reeled her in as if she were a child. He jabbed the pistol hard into her neck. "I have wasted enough time."

She cried out and her heart thumped against her sternum. She would fail in every way. Kizin would be lost. She would die. Max would die. And Doug...

Fighting the sob clogging her throat, she looked to Max for reassurance.

He sat erect, alert and watching, his hands on his

knees. His dark eyes searched for an opening. Knowing she could count on him gave her courage. But what could she do?

Moves she'd practiced in a self-defense class came back to her. She slumped against the gunman. At the same time, she lifted her right foot and stomped hard on his canvas-clad instep.

Rufo howled. The impact of her boot heel threw him off balance. His gun lowered. He released her.

Max dived for the gun.

She fell to the floor. Scrambled into the back corner by the cargo hold. *Oh God, let me reach Max's pistol.* Prayed she could hold it steady enough to fire. Prayed she wouldn't hit Max.

The helicopter tilted and swayed, dipped and wallowed with the shift of weight. An aluminum canteen rattled across the cabin and rolled out the open door, falling to the ground as she could have. She shuddered.

The frame creaked and whined at the strain. Then the angle evened out.

Julio yelled. Kate didn't need to understand his words to grasp his meaning.

Max and Rufo grappled on the cabin floor. Fists landed on flesh and bone with sickening thuds. They grappled for the pistol. Stronger, Max outweighed the other man by at least twenty pounds, but both had skills. And both were fighting for their lives.

Max! Nothing could happen to Max.

Dragging her gaze away, Kate climbed over the net barrier into the hold. Max's big pistol lay atop his pack. She didn't see the other gun. She crawled closer, but another shift in the craft's angle sent her crashing against the fuselage. Pain rocketed through her shoulder, then

166

numbness. For a moment, she couldn't move.

The pistol slid farther aft and landed with a clank.

Far behind the luggage. Out of reach. And still no sign of the smaller pistol.

She rubbed her throbbing shoulder and scooted closer to the cabin. Her gaze locked on the men, she pressed a hand to her mouth. She had to do something more than pray. The helicopter must contain something she could use as a weapon.

Max and Rufo rolled to the lip of the open door.

She scanned the hold. Anything, anything. In this damn bare-bones chopper, nothing. She started pawing through the baggage.

The two traded blows with their free hands and vied for the pistol with the others. Max plowed a fist into the other man's chin. He closed his hand over the pistol, but before Kate could glimpse hope, Rufo snatched the weapon back.

Gunshots rang out. Bullets smacked into the passenger compartment and into the canopy above her. The aircraft dipped and dived. It looped from side to side. Barely able to hang on, she flattened herself behind the tent bag and fought the nausea stinging her throat.

Max! Was Max all right? Did he fall? Did both?

Her heart jammed up into her throat, she crept forward enough to see. The men still fought for possession of the pistol.

More shots slammed into the fuselage.

The combatants rolled halfway out of the plane. Kate could barely breathe as they hung there.

God, she had to find something. There! Sunlight glinted off metal. One of the curved ribs supporting the fuselage had fallen off.

She scrambled over the tent pack and yanked on the rib. The metal creaked but stayed put, trapped beneath the pack. Pain screamed in her shoulder. A twist and a turn and she muscled the tent aside. Metal rib in her hand, she scooted toward the middle section.

Still hanging partway out, Max and Rufo grappled for the gun.

Her pulse pounded. Her stomach roiled. Her hands shook. She gripped the rib with two hands like a softball bat.

As Rufo raised the gun to fire again, she sucked in a breath and surged forward. She swung. The metal strip slammed down on his arm. The chopper tilted, and she crashed backward onto her behind.

His shot went wild. The gun slipped from his hand.

Max delivered a crushing blow to the man's throat. The bald man gagged but reached for the gun, stretching over the edge as the weapon skidded out.

Max hooked his free arm around the strut behind the co-pilot's seat and kicked.

Rufo slid over the edge. His eyes and mouth widened in terror as realization hit him. His arms windmilled.

He disappeared into the void.

Max held onto the strut, chest heaving with effort before he hitched himself back inside.

Kate exhaled and put her head down to dispel the nausea stinging her throat. *Thank God.*

"Something's wrong. Check Julio." Max pulled himself upright and slid the door shut.

Levering to her feet, she mustered the strength to propel herself forward. The helicopter had stabilized but now it dipped and veered to the right. She propped her back against the co-pilot seat and braced her legs.

Julio flicked a switch on the control panel. She had barely been aware of the crackling noise but now that it stopped, she realized he'd shut off the radio.

The left side of the man's khaki shirt was soaked in blood. "I cannot... fly her... my *colibrí*..." His voice was a reedy whisper in her ear. His hands still held the controls but with no strength. Pink bubbles foamed at his mouth.

No, oh no!

"He's been shot. A lung, I think. It looks bad." She grabbed a stained hand towel from behind Julio's seat and held it against his chest. But blood quickly soaked the cotton. She tried to keep her voice even but her vocal cords wouldn't cooperate. "He can't—"

Something black and huge grabbed her throat, her chest, threatening to choke her. Rufo and his gun were gone but they were going to die anyway. The jungle would grow over them as it had covered the ancient Maya ruins.

Chapter Fifteen

MAX GRIPPED KATE'S shoulders. "We still have
a chance."

He wedged past her and took the co-pilot's seat.
Madre de Dios. He hoped to hell the Huey operated like
the newer helo he'd operated incountry. He'd be damned
if he'd let this go south now.

Julio's head lolled as the loss of blood and breath
took its toll. His hands fell to his sides.

The ship tilted. Emerald treetops rushed up to them.

Her boots clattered on the metal as she stumbled.
"You can fly a helicopter?" Her voice was breathy with
fear.

"I can." He injected more confidence in his voice
than he felt in his gut. Hell, he was jacked up on
adrenaline. Focused. He could do this. "Go strap yourself
in."

He felt her pat his shoulder before she made her way
aft.

Grasping the collective control lever, he moved it
forward to increase the power while he moved the cyclic
control stick to climb. He settled his feet on the pedals
and maneuvered the rudder.

The craft bobbled in the sky for a long moment
before the rotors found air again. He stabilized the
position and banked up and away from the lethal canopy.
Nosed the bird forward. *Hoo-yah!*

"Max!" Kate cried as they leveled out. "I can see the western hills in the distance."

They were finally headed the right way. He checked their position on the control panel. "GPS here says we're not too far off course," Max called. "Maybe sixty miles north of the ruin."

"Not much farther away than we'd have been with our original plan. We can get there after all. Today!"

He checked the other gauges on the panel—attitude indicator, altimeter, air speed, RPM. A hard look at the fuel gauge stifled the affirmative reply on his tongue. A cold sweat washed over him. "Shit!"

"Max?"

"Kizin is testing us, darlin'. A bullet must've hit the fuel line. We're losing fuel. I gotta set her down."

"Here? In the trees?" From her squeak, he reckoned she gripped the seat arms with white knuckles.

"A chopper's not like a fixed-wing plane. You don't need a runway, just an open space. Hang tough. We'll make it."

The fuel gauge read a quarter tank and the level was falling faster than Rufo. Max had been in tight spots before but not dangling several hundred feet above the earth. He reduced the collective and eased the cyclic back to slow for a better view of the rough terrain.

No openings, only a solid floor of green. Towering trees and scrubby underbrush interspersed with cactus. Not the most welcoming landing pad. Dripping like a beef at a barbecue, he swiped at his chin and dried his palms on his shorts.

The warning light blinked red on the fuel gauge. The needle ticked closer to *E*. If he landed now, would the trees cushion the fall? Or maybe they'd smash the chopper. And them.

"Up ahead. I see a gap in the trees." Her voice was rough with fear.

"Roger that." Concentrating to maintain the right amount of control, he nosed the bird toward the gap, about a quarter mile ahead at his ten. No matter how small the space, he had to take the chance. "Going for it."

He held the airspeed at sixty knots and the altitude at about a hundred feet as he kept his eyes on the opening.

Slowing as he began the approach, he saw green and more green and some brown. No indication of what lay below. The landing spot was too small, barely big enough for the chopper body. Treetops could puncture the fuselage. The rotors would rake the trees and break off like twigs. The tail section could get hung up and flip them over. God knew what else.

He worked his back teeth apart so he could speak. "This is it, Kate. One hell of a bumpy landing coming up. Pull out a seat cushion. Bend over it to brace yourself. And pray this old crate can take the impact."

"Thank you, Mr. Sunshine. I'm ready."

Her spunk made him smile but the trust in her voice punched him in the gut. Every muscle in his body was bowstring tight. He forced tension from his shoulders and hands so he could control the levers.

He reduced power and brought the nose up to level off. The chopper drifted into position. Easing back on the cyclic, he established a hover. Dangerous. Hovering ate up more fuel than cruising. "Setting 'er down, Kate. Hold on."

Keep the descent slow. Nice and easy.

The tail hit the trees first. Crashing and splintering-wood sounds competed with the motor's whine. Max fought to compensate. Increased the pitch. He would not let Kate die, and he wasn't ready to end it here like fuckin' Rufo.

The rotors sliced off treetops. The blades cracked off with pops as loud as thunderclaps. With no power, the bird dropped the last dozen feet like the proverbial stone. He braced himself.

They slammed into the ground. The impact jarred every bone and tooth in his body. The landing skids snapped like hummingbird bones. Trees splintered and metal crumpled louder than gunshots. The windshield cracked into spider webbing.

With a final heave, the chopper settled at an angle. Fifteen degrees or so. Manageable.

They were on the ground.

He released his grip on the controls and hauled in breath. "You okay? Kate?"

No answer. He felt like a shard of glass was lodged in his throat. Hands shaking, he freed the seat belt and stumbled aft.

She was hunched over the cushion from the seat he'd vacated. Unconscious? Or—?

"Kate."

Twitching in her shoulders started his heart again.

She straightened, her face pale as milk. "Knocked… the breath…"

"You're not hurt?"

She shook her head as she inhaled.

Ay, gracias a Dios. He probably should let her recover at her own speed, but he couldn't help himself. The hell with it. He pulled her to her feet and into his arms. She trembled, the aftermath of an adrenaline spike. He felt her heart racing against his chest. Planting his feet, he held her until both their hearts calmed.

"We did it, darlin'. We're on the ground." He kissed the top of her head.

Looking up, she smiled. "*You* did it, Max. I knew you would."

"No, *we*. You saw we were off course, and we might not be here if you hadn't slugged that bastard when you did. A hell of a swing, darlin'."

Her cheeks pinked and she licked her lips. "Thanks. Playing ball with Dad and my brother finally paid off."

A new threat around every turn, yet not once did she complain. Not once did she back down from her goal. He ached to kiss her luscious lips. Hell, he ached to do more than kiss her. Dammit. "What did you hit him with?"

"Some metal piece from the fuselage. Never thought I'd be glad for the shaky condition of Julio's *colibri*." Worry filled her eyes. "Julio?"

"Gone before we landed. There was nothing we could do."

"I should be sorry, but I can't work up sympathy. He was part of the plot to kill us."

"Yeah. Somebody knew we chartered his plane. Somebody with money paid Rufo well. A toss of the dice who bought him. I shouldn't have let the bastard come along."

"You're not clairvoyant. And he might've pulled the gun on us then if you'd tried to stop him. It would've made no difference." She frowned. "But why fly all this way? Why not just rob us and shoot us at the airfield?"

"I get the feeling we were supposed to disappear. Totally. And we nearly did."

"Should we use the helicopter radio to call for help?"

Max shook his head. "No way, I trust nobody. How would a rescue party get to us? I'll call Mara, fill her in. Then we're back to Plan A."

"Plan A?"

"Trek through the jungle. We have eight days to make sixty, seventy miles. Plenty of time."

Kate grinned, her stiff cheeks indicating her optimism was forced. "As you said before, as long as nothing goes wrong."

****

Kate's shoulders ached where she'd fallen in the cargo hold. She bruised easily and this one would be a doozy, but she had no time for pampering. She collected her camera bag and the GPS as Max shoved at the sliding door.

His praise for her actions echoed in her head. Thank God she'd found a way to help. But he was wrong. He was the one who'd saved their lives. She'd never forget the sight of him, muscles bulging, features taut and dark, as he grappled in the open doorway. After this, she sure as hell could trust him to keep her safe in whatever situation came up. For an instant their eyes caught, and the air between them crackled with heat. Her pulse sped up.

Chalk it up to the danger, she told herself. The attraction between them must remain in the past. She dragged her gaze away.

Max cleared his throat. "Sliding door's jammed. We'll have to exit the co-pilot's side."

As she clambered out behind him, she averted her eyes from the dead man.

Heat and the fecund smells of vegetation immersed her. Humidity pressed down on her and soaked her in sweat. Jungle growth encircled the copter, trailing vines and bright blossoms. Dense foliage blotted out the sky.

"We can't just leave Julio like that," she said, accepting Max's help in pushing through vines and creepers toward the cargo-hold door. All around them, birds squawked and insects droned.

"He would've left our broken bodies for the jungle scavengers to gnaw on."

She shuddered at his matter-of-fact tone, the voice of a warrior who had faced death before. "But Max—"

He raised his hand as if to cup her jaw, but instead stepped back. "We can't bury him. The limestone ground is like cement and we have no shovel. The best we can do is leave him be and close up the helicopter."

Bowing to the inevitable, she nodded.

When he wrenched open the cargo door, his Glock tumbled to the ground.

Their gear stashed so carefully in the hold looked shaken and stirred by a tornado. Kate gasped. "Goody, fifty-two pickup."

Max re-holstered his gun. "Good to know you can see the humor in our situation. Let me do a little recon and then we'll see what we can salvage." He punched numbers on his phone as he headed into the jungle.

She removed her phone from the camera bag and turned it on. Thank God it had sustained no damage. She'd call Esteban later. Surely the kidnapper would call soon. Maybe he'd allow her to speak to Doug. *If they've hurt him...* She curled her fingers into a fist. Damn, as if she could do anything.

After a private break behind an agave plant, she

dragged her pack from the cargo hold and checked inside. Without conversation, jungle sounds seemed louder, encroaching. High in the canopy, a monkey protested their invasion with a staccato, barking call.

Satisfied the contents of the pack were intact, she reached for her tablet. An ominous rattle from inside the case said the electronics hadn't fared well.

Her stomach clenched. She could do this. She was fit enough, prepared enough. A little discomfort wouldn't kill her. Nor would a few bugs. She refused to think about the ground that could convulse beneath her without warning. Or about the men who coveted Kizin. And whoever paid Rufo to kill them. And whoever killed Constantino.

When Max returned, she willed herself to relax. She had to stay strong for the trek. He looked tough and sexy and cool, ready to start a new day, not like he'd just wrestled a killer and landed a helicopter in the jungle. How often did he face this kind of danger? Was this just another day working for Devlin Security?

"Mara's relieved to know we're okay. She notified Thomas when she saw we were off course. Phone GPS signal's still strong." He stowed his phone in its belt holster. "That's the good news. Bad news is one of Centaur's thugs was spotted at Heathrow boarding a plane for Cabo Blanco. Name's Le Noir, a nasty French cuss."

"First Sedgwick and now this Le Noir. Who's next?"

"Wish I knew. Le Noir's probably here to connect with Sedgwick. Mara said Scotland Yard found evidence the Brit owes Centaur big bucks for black-market artifacts. Turning over Kizin may be the payback they demand." He grinned. "Must steam him big-time."

She set down the tablet case and drank from her canteen. "But Max, the GPS? Couldn't the bad guys track us too?"

His dark brows knit as he thought. "A tough call. Requires damned sophisticated technology. Centaur maybe. The identity of their head honcho is a mystery, but the network's extensive, probably computerized big time. Maybe Aguilar or the general. Not likely the kidnapper can, not if he's out here off the grid. He'd need more juice."

The thought any of them would track their position gave her chills, even in this sauna. "Maybe we can disable the GPS?"

"No can do. It's a chip embedded in the circuits, not a separate unit. Removing the battery's the only way. But it's safer all 'round having DSF track us."

She absorbed that as she slathered on an insect-repellant-sunscreen combination. Instead of screaming her head off, she went for confident. "Then we deal."

As soon as she closed up her pack, her satellite phone rang.

Chapter Sixteen

STARTLED BY THE alien noise, a parrot squawked and darted away into the trees. Max dropped his pack and took out his phone. His heart beat with slow, hard thumps, the way it always did at the start of a battle.

Dammit, Kate was making no move to pick up her jangling phone. She stood statue still, eyes wide with shock as she stared like a trapped jackrabbit at the fucking thing.

Unlikely DSF would phone her directly. Before leaving Cabo Blanco, she'd spoken to her mother and Morales. Could be either of them. But Max's gut said this was the kidnapper and the timing was right.

In quick strides, he closed the several feet between them, grabbed up her phone, and pressed it into her hand. "Kate, darlin', you *have* to answer."

The ringing or the vibrations must've reached her because she blinked and shook her head as if to clear the fog. Her hand closed on the phone.

"You okay? Can you talk if it's him?"

"Yes, yes. I'm okay. I can do it."

He nodded encouragement. "If it's the kidnapper, give me a thumbs-up. Keep him talking. You know the drill." He punched numbers on his phone. They'd gone over the strategy for when the fucker called. What to say, every detail. But reality was damned different from planning. Being faced with actually talking to her

179

brother's kidnapper must've grabbed Kate by the throat.

Sinking onto her pack as if her legs couldn't hold her, she drew deep breaths. "It's a blocked number." She rotated the antenna and pushed OK. "H-hello. Who's this?"

Stepping out of the caller's earshot, Max reached Mara just as Kate gave him the *go* signal. Her hand shook but her chin was firm, her gaze steady and locked on his. He smiled back.

"Hey, gorgeous, you finding this signal?" he said to Mara, pitching his voice just above a whisper.

"Hold on, big guy." Clicks and humming came through as Mara worked computer magic.

Shit, yeah, he had to give her time. Too wired to stand by, he crossed to kneel beside Kate so he could hear the kidnapper.

"Yes, of course I have Kizin with me," Kate said into the phone.

"Tell me where you are. We must meet."

The accented voice was muffled. Male or female, hard to be sure. The accent could be Spanish, maybe French. Fucking Le Noir? That made no sense, unless he was calling from Cabo Blanco. But why would Centaur's man want Kate to go to K'eq Xlapak? *Stow that for later.*

At Kate's frown, Max shook his head. Pantomimed stretching a big rubber band.

"Oh, dear, I don't know exactly where I am," she said. "I'm relying on my guides. I could ask them, but you probably want this kept secret."

Gotta love the helpless-female act. Max bit his lip against a grin. If this bastard had seen her whacking Rufo, he'd never buy the performance. Hell of a woman.

"No, no, do not ask," the caller hurried to say.

"We started on the trail a few hours ago." She looked to Max and shrugged as if to say she was winging it. "Maybe if you tell me how far away you are?"

"I will find *you*. Good—"

"No! Don't go." Her chest rose and fell with quick breaths. Her gaze clung to Max's as if the connection could keep her from falling over a precipice. Her hand tightened on the phone. "Please. I've dealt with you in good faith. I've come to Costa Verde with the statue as you instructed. I'm trekking through the jungle. I'm prepared to trade Kizin for my brother. Now you must act in good faith. I need to know Doug is alive and unharmed. Put him on the phone. You have to let me talk to him."

Click. The kidnapper had disconnected.

Kate squeezed her eyes shut. "He's gone. What if my... Doug— Damn them!"

To hell with professional distance. Max pulled her to her feet and wrapped his arms around her. She felt damn good against him, even muttering cuss words into his shirt. He rested his chin on the top of her head. "You did great. Kept him on a long time. He might not be wherever he's holding your brother. Or he didn't expect your demand and had no response. He'll call again. Don't let this throw you."

She raised angry eyes and nodded. Backing away, she flailed her arms as if in frustration.

At Mara's voice calling his name, he lifted his phone. "Anything?"

"Not enough time to get an exact location. I'm monitoring all the satellite phone signals in the general area of the temple. Six phones there—probably the archeological crew—a handful more in nearby villages.

Three phones were active the past several minutes. Now if you'd only ask the guy for his number, this'd be a whole lot easier."

"Damn, I didn't think of that. He'll call again. Thanks, gorgeous."

After disconnecting, he relayed the situation to Kate. "And I won't tell you not to worry, but it's not all bad. This phone call was a step closer to locating the kidnapper. Mara will pinpoint him next time and Del Rio can move in. Your brother will have to face up to what he's done but that makes no difference to the mission. We'll get him out of there. I promise."

He crossed mental fingers.

****

Two hours later, Kate stretched her sore back and mopped sweat from her face. They'd assembled what was left of their gear. The tent and packs with the clothing and food survived intact. Both tablets had been tossed around the hold. As dead as Julio.

They'd left unnecessary items including their formal wear and her cosmetics in the truck. Might as well count those for lost too. She still had Kizin and the essentials.

"You set to head out?" Max had retrieved his smaller pistol and restored it to his ankle holster. He hitched on his pack, looking ready for anything.

And she'd better be ready too. Going for perky, she said, "Got your machete ready, pal?"

"I can do better than that. This gap in the trees is part of a Maya *sacbé*."

"Another limestone trail." Indeed they *were* all over the place. And they all led to K'eq Xlapak. She grinned. "Kizin must be guiding us."

"I'll take whatever help the little guy wants to give,"

he said. "This *sacbé* hasn't been used much so it's narrow and rough but passable."

She pulled her ponytail through the hole in the back of her cap. She stuffed the camera case with its precious cargo inside her backpack and hooked on her canteen. Her boots hadn't left the closet since the last Anasazi dig, but they still fit comfortably. Although her feet felt good, granny knots tied up her stomach and her head and eyes ached.

"Nice boots. Made an effective weapon." Max's features were set in stone beneath his khaki cap, but his voice held a hint of approval. Even affection. "Pack not too heavy?"

"I can manage." Her pack contained only her personal items and some of the food. She couldn't complain about Kizin's heavy weight. Max carried most of their supplies.

"I can tote that camera case for you."

"I won't burden you anymore than I already have." She summoned a confident air. "A few days and we're there. We've almost made it."

What might have been a smile lifted the corners of his mouth and then vanished. "*Almost* doesn't cut it. This from the woman who *almost* did a swan dive from a helicopter. You do know we're not out of the woods yet."

"Max, we're not even *in* the woods yet." The lift of his eyebrows told her he didn't buy her flippancy. Tough. Bravado was all she had. At the sight of their path disappearing into tangled growth, the granny knots tightened. She tried to swallow but cotton wads filled her mouth. The jungle was a green wall but pungent with sun-heated rocks and overripe fruits. Monkeys chattered overhead. Maybe this trek wouldn't be so hard after all.

Tell yourself that, Katherine.

Her heart raced as something else hit her. "We could have two or even all three rivals for possession of Kizin on our trail."

He spat out an expletive in Spanish. "All three? *¡Qué lío!* And Le Noir. A mess if they all show up."

She couldn't tell if he was joking but decided to play along. "Plus bandits. Never mind. I'll protect you."

His dour expression morphed into a wide grin. "We have the advantage."

She felt a real smile curve her lips as she understood. "Unless they can use GPS to track us, they don't know where we are, thanks to our detour."

"Never thought I'd be grateful to our hired killers." He gave her a slow, sexy wink. "Okay, Ms. Explorer, time to hit the trail."

Feeling less like a jungle explorer and more like Dorothy on the road to Oz, Kate marched along the jungle trail behind Max, the rocks crunching beneath her boots.

Jaguars and scorpions and snakes. Oh my.

Max had used the coordinates from the helicopter instrument to pinpoint their location on his map. All they had to do was head southwest to reach K'eq Xlapak.

The trail was level enough, but rough and not straight like most Maya roads. Perhaps to deter the invading Aztecs, this overgrown *sacbé* zigged and zagged like an alpine highway.

She did have Max to lead the way. The only drawback was that his backpack and all its attachments completely hid his fine backside from view. All she could see of him was below his knees. Plus she didn't like being back here by herself. Enough of that. In most places, the trail was wide enough for two. Stretching her legs, she caught up to him.

As they trooped onward, she drew from him the incident in Kabul he and Devlin had mentioned at Dulles. They'd visited an open-air market, where a pickpocket lifted a woman's money. Max tackled the thief and returned the money. No big deal, he insisted. Kate knew better. She related some experiences from her summer digs in Arizona. To her delight, he asked probing questions about the ancient pottery and customs the group uncovered.

He stopped and unhooked his pack. "Let's hydrate."

She slipped off her pack and drank from her canteen. They were drinking a lot. She'd have to conserve.

"You seem to be managing the pace okay," he observed.

"I am, better than Mom predicted. Before I left the States, she reminded me of, um, disasters from years ago on expedition. Said I wasn't cut out for the wilderness. Or adventure. She's right."

"Cut yourself some slack. You've had more adventure than you counted on. Me too." He swigged more water, Adam's apple moving in his strong throat. "No mystery why she's worried. She lost her husband. Her son was injured and kidnapped. She's afraid of losing her daughter."

"And her son." *Doug.* No, she would *not* dwell on Doug's plight.

After another sip she sealed up her canteen. "You're probably right but that's only part of it. Mom hated going on expeditions. The discomforts, the uncertainty, the dangers in remote places. Bugs, snakes, strange food. At home she kept busy with friends, the garden club, university functions."

"She was protecting herself."

She frowned. "I never thought of it that way. Odd she married an archeologist if she didn't understand what that life was like." Her parents had married while still in college, so her mother probably considered her husband's profession glamorous. At first.

He hoisted her pack and motioned for her to turn around. "We'd better keep eating up distance. The map shows a *cenote* coming up in about seven miles. Let's get there before dark."

Cenote, a water-filled sinkhole. They were all over the limestone shelf that made up the Yucatan. "We can clean up and get more water." She had plenty of water-purifying tablets in her pack.

As they continued onward, sultry heat wrapping around them, a memory surfaced. She and Doug had been upstairs, supposedly asleep. She heard loud voices and tiptoed to the top of the stairs. Her mom accused her dad of ruining the children's lives. He retaliated that she was narrow-minded and selfish. The kids' lives would be broadened, enriched, if she'd only understand. Tears streaming down her cheeks at the harsh tones, Kate had crept back to her bed.

She hadn't thought of that episode in years.

None of the chaos or disagreements or lack of explanations bothered her brother. Only her. When she'd told Max about the disorganized planning, he guessed that was the reason she liked to be in control. Maybe. Was that all it was?

A deep baying blasted through the jungle—combination air-raid siren and growl on steroids.

Her pulse jumped. She clutched at Max's

shirtsleeve. "What was that? Hound of the Baskervilles?"

"Howler monkey somewhere way above us." He covered her hand with his. "A male, judging from the basso voice."

To help calm her nerves, she focused on savoring the strength of his hand. Rough and wide, with long, thick fingers. "Howler. I remember. The world's loudest creature on land. They use the calls to keep track of each other. This one's telling the others his location."

He cocked his head, brows raised. "Something you learned on expedition with the professor?"

"Yes, the memory just surfaced. I jumped a mile back then too. Doug laughed at my fright."

"He tease you much?"

"We were about even in the teasing department. I let him get away with that one because the week before at school he stood up for me—his bookworm big sister— against some bigger kids. Doug was a head shorter than them but he backed them down." She smiled at the memory. "But I know not to be frightened if a howler trumpets again."

She had to dig deep for the bravado the howler's call had evaporated. And keep in mind Max's watchword. B*e ready for the unexpected.*

****

They were making good time. Max figured they'd covered almost three miles in the last hour. They'd be okay for the night once they reached the *cenote*.

At the top of a slight rise, he pointed out vultures circling overhead. "The jungle always provides plenty of carrion."

Kate's boots crunched on the limestone as she halted

to have a look. "And those guys do the clean-up."

The songbirds had gone silent. The jungle seemed eerily quiet except for the whish of wings overhead. Max studied the underbrush, saw nothing unusual. He'd stay alert.

Kate mopped her brow with one of the bandannas he'd encouraged her to buy in Cabo Blanco. She was keeping all her fears inside, putting one foot ahead of the other, emotionally as well as literally. Covered in a damp sheen, her face glowed. Clearly fascinated by the vultures, she kept staring upward.

Until she stumbled.

Her backpack threw her sideways. Before he could grab her arm, she grabbed a sapling for support. A strangled shriek tore from her throat.

Then he saw what frightened her.

A jaguar stood in the middle of the trail, a fawn clamped in its jaws. The tiny creature, its newborn spots still visible, jerked and then fell limp. Sunlight gleamed on the jaguar's golden fur dotted with rosette-shaped brown and black spots. A big male, more than two hundred pounds. The black nose twitched as it scented the intruders. Fangs flashed with a curl of blood-stained lip. The tail flicked back and forth. Yellow eyes flickered from Kate to Max and back again.

Cautious. Calculating. Deadly.

Adrenaline surged his heart into a sprint. *Madre de Dios*. He flicked open the strap on his drop holster. Withdrew the Glock and released the safety. He'd hate to kill the big cat. This area was its territory. He steadied his breathing, but before he could sight his target, the tawny-eyed beast vanished into the trees with its prey.

He holstered the pistol. "Reckon he figured keeping

his next meal was better than facing two humans."

She didn't move. Clutched the sapling for dear life, focused on the empty trail where the jaguar had stood.

"You okay?" He stepped to her side, not liking the pallor in her cheeks.

She panted as if she'd run a mile. "So much for being brave." Easing away from her tree support, she nearly fell.

"Darlin', take it easy. He's gone." He grasped her elbows and steadied her. "Breathe."

He unhooked her pack and slid it from her, then shrugged off his. "Hey, jaguars rarely attack humans. Seeing one is a rare thing. The ancient Maya revered the big cat."

She nodded. "I know. There are several jaguar gods. It's just—" She sucked in a breath. "I saw that spotted body. And the poor little fawn…"

"Poisonous spiders and scorpions are a worse threat. Most won't kill you, but you'd be damned sick. Not to mention malaria-carrying mosquitoes."

"What a relief. I'll be sure to tell my mother."

Smiling, he wrapped his arms around her and held her close. His heart slowed to a jog, but hers was thudding. She felt good in his arms. Too good. "Your scream stopped that jaguar in his tracks. That'll teach him to look both ways before crossing."

She let her head rest against his chest. "I'm such an idiot. I'll try not to do that again."

"No big deal. Let's hope that's all you have to panic about." He buried his nose in her hair and breathed in her sweet-spicy scent.

She raised her chin and their eyes met.

Her yellow cap had fallen off in her fright. Sweat

plastered hair to her temples. He pulled curls free and tucked them behind one ear. Of its own volition his finger slid downward and along the plump curve of her lower lip.

Her blue eyes went smoky and her lashes lowered. "Max."

Man, that breathy whisper was a yes. But a kiss wasn't enough. Not by half. He burned to touch her everywhere again, in every intimate way possible. He started to settle his mouth on hers.

A deafening screech jerked him back into reality with a thud. He clawed his way back to alertness.

"Howler." Kate shook her head as if to dispel the mood. The smoke in her bluebonnet eyes cleared and she stepped back.

Cursing silently, he scanned the area but saw only the surrounding trees. A yellow-and-black bird stared at him from a branch. Kate bent and replaced her cap, face pink instead of the earlier pallor.

Beautiful. Sexy. And his desire for her had put her in danger.

"Damn careless and unprofessional of me. Out here, vigilance is key."

"You're right." She blinked and dropped her gaze to her pack. "I forgot, too. My brother's kidnapping, Kizin, the danger all around us—everything. I wanted to forget."

He wanted her still. And she wanted him. Enough that she'd set aside her distrust and his suspicions of her brother. Rotten timing. "We need to get moving."

By the time they slung on their packs, he'd pulled himself together. So, it appeared, had she. Stick-straight back, compressed mouth. They traipsed onward, accompanied by bird chatter and monkey hoots.

Kate's last words replayed in his mind. *"I wanted to forget."*

Forget her troubles? Not a hell of a lot different from what he usually wanted from a woman. He limited himself to casual hook-ups for recreation or escape. Why did it tick him off she was ready to do the same?

Chapter Seventeen

THE SINKING SUN wasn't lowering the jungle's temperature. Or Kate's. Her shirt and camisole clung to her skin like tape. Humidity frizzed her hair into clown curls. Her feet and back hurt, her shoulder ached, and her thighs wobbled. For now, she just wanted to reach that *cenote*, where she could ditch her pack and rest for the night.

She pushed on beside Max, slanting a quick glance his way.

He was fast becoming a dangerous passion, like an intoxicating potion. If she'd resisted sex with him to begin with, maybe she'd have an easier time resisting him now. How could she be with him again, suspecting his attraction to her was only to weasel out information about Doug?

"Your brother will have to face up to what he's done…"

Was Max talking about the amphora and helmet? Or that criminal syndicate, Centaur? Was it possible? Doug was a good guy, but tunnel vision took over when he wanted something. He had such a fixation on ancient treasures and making big deals. If Max—and Devlin— had proof of some sort, shouldn't she ask? But did she really want to know? Her head ached with the dilemma.

As if to remind her why she was here in the damn jungle, Kizin's weight seemed to drag her pack lower.

She had to trust that Devlin's agent—something Del Rio?—would rescue Doug. And the truth, whatever it was, would come out. *Stay strong, Kate.*

Max looked fresh enough, damn him, as he marched along. No hitch in his step or bowing of the back. Squinting, his head cocked, he stared ahead into the gathering dusk.

"Max, how fa—"

He stopped her with an arm across her chest. "Listen." His voice was low and tight.

At the fierce look in his eyes, her throat tightened. She held herself still as a tree and listened.

No birdsong. No chatter. Only the scratch and rustle of small creatures in the underbrush and the incessant whine of mosquitoes. In the distance the high-pitched hoot of a screech owl. Then she heard something else.

A laugh. Male voices talking.

Icicles pricked her spine. "Bandits?" she whispered.

"Maybe. They're off to the right," he murmured. "We almost walked into them."

"We should hide." She surveyed the shadowed jungle. "Over there, behind the giant agave plant."

"Good call." Grim-faced, he allowed her to tug him into the trees.

They hunkered down among the huge, fleshy spears of the agave, and he tucked their packs beneath the plant. "They're speaking Spanish. Wait here while I check out the situation."

The low rumble of his voice soothed her but only marginally. She gripped his knee. "I'll go with you."

"You'll be fine." He placed his hands on her shoulders. "I can slip through the trees and back before you know it."

Stay here alone? "No, I'll come. It's better if we stay together."

"Too dangerous. I won't risk your life even if you would." His mouth flattened. "Kate, think. I have military training and experience. Can you move silently and unseen across rocky ground and through dense jungle? In the dark?"

Night was nibbling away at the graying daylight. Small bats flitted through the shadows. Darkness deepened the shadows to purple, making the jungle impenetrable to searching eyes. And to city girls who would stumble over rocks and into trees. This wasn't gymnastics or climbing Sedgwick's scaffolding.

If she went, she'd make the situation only more dangerous. For Max.

She slumped, her chest tight. "You're right, of course. I'll wait here."

He rubbed dirt over his forearms and face, then checked his big pistol. He sketched a salute before the jungle swallowed him whole.

****

Keeping low, Max crept from tree to tree. Just enough light remained to show outcroppings of low-growing plants that would muffle his footsteps.

The strangers' laughter died and he heard only conversational tones as he approached. A rising chorus of caws and chirps signaled a return to the normal forest cacophony. He crouched behind a flowering vine to observe.

In the center of a small clearing, soccer-ball-size boulders formed a barrier around a hole about as wide as a child's wading pool.

This *cenote* looked more like a well than a sinkhole.

Somebody had tied a long rope to a plastic bucket for thirsty travelers to dip water from the well's depths. A slender tree anchored the rope's other end. The five men in the clearing took turns dipping water for their canteens.

Uniforms. Gray and green camouflage with Costa Verde emblems. Rifles lay propped against trees and holsters hung from their belts. Not bandits. Were the soldiers on regular patrol or maneuvers? The hairs lifting on his nape said neither.

"Why does he want these Americans?" one grunt asked as he screwed the top on his canteen.

A hook-nosed soldier wearing a sergeant's insignia spat at the ground beside the other's boots. "*¡Bruto!* Fool, that is his business. Yours is to follow orders."

"But it makes no sense, sending us from our regular patrol to search for them here. Why not east, between the city and that temple place?"

"That I will tell you, *bruto*. Reports that their helicopter went down do not say where. Now ask no more."

A third man laughed, poking a fourth in the arm. "Do not give Roano a hard time, *Sargento*. His woman left him, and he heard the *norteamericana* is beautiful. Hair like the sun."

"We must deliver them alive—if they are still alive." Roano grabbed his crotch. "But why not have a little fun with the woman first?"

The sharpness of splintered glass ripped into Max's chest. He clenched his fists against the urge to go pound the man's head on one of those rocks.

Shaking his head, the sergeant made shooing motions. "Time to move out."

The five hoisted their rifles and canteens. Still boasting and jostling each other, they disappeared down the rough trail toward the *sacbé*.

When Max could no longer hear the scrape of their heavy boots on the limestone surface, he pushed through the thick growth back to Kate.

She threw her arms around him. "I was so worried. You were gone forever."

He ached to hold her tight, to absorb her scent and the softness of her body, but she pulled away, brows snapped together like she regretted the impulse.

Fuck his needs. *She* was his priority. Keeping her safe just became harder because of the soldiers, an undisciplined and dangerous bunch. No way in hell could he let her fall into their hands. Monkeys jabbered above him as if in agreement.

He sat back on his heels. "Did you see the soldiers?"

"Soldiers? I heard their boots on the stone, but they didn't come this way." She gripped his arm. "What did they say?"

He gave her the gist of it, omitting the boasts of the *animales*. "They didn't name their commander. President Aguilar or General Lopez, take your pick."

"Does it matter?" Disgust sharpened her voice.

He hesitated to lay out the rest. "More news. The authorities know the chopper went down, but they don't yet know where. There must be more squads of soldiers spread out searching for us."

"Julio was on the radio just before I reached him. He must've reported the trouble."

"But he didn't have time to give the coordinates. Lucky for us."

"And because they didn't come back this way, that

must mean they've gone ahead. They could ambush us."

"Give the lady a hundred dollars."

She swigged water from her canteen, then set it down with the firm hand of a woman who'd made a decision. "You're the expert. What should we do?"

One eyebrow raised, Max pressed a hand to his heart. "You trust me with something? Give me a minute to recover."

She swatted him on the arm. "I trust you to keep us safe. How can we stay out of their way? We can't let them get Kizin."

Or you, Kate. She trusted him with her life but not with her jade statue. He clenched his jaw. He'd take what he could get. For now. "I have a plan, but you won't like it."

"If it'll work, I don't have to like it. Shoot."

"First, we get cleaned up at the *cenote* and have some chow. We can't remain there long. The clearing's too exposed and the soldiers could return. Or others. We'll go ahead a few hundred yards and make camp in the jungle."

She cast a skeptical glance at the dense tangle of trees and vines but nodded. "That makes sense. So what's second?"

"We have to stay out of sight. Leave the track and beat through the bush."

Her worried gaze veered again to the darkening jungle. Roughing it wasn't her thing, and she panicked every time the ground trembled, but she was tougher than he'd thought. Tougher than *she* thought.

"If we do that, how can we get to K'eq Xlapak on time?" she asked, her tone brittle.

"No problem. On the *sacbé* this hike would take

maybe five days. We have three extra." He surged to his feet and held out a hand. "And you can still control our course. We'll need the GPS receiver. What's our position?"

Kate dug the device from her pack. Her face fell. "The screen is smashed. It's dead."

****

The squawking of parrots woke Kate. She stretched and consulted her watch. A little past dawn. Dappled sunlight through the tent's mosquito-netting confirmed her estimate. Rainwater from the night's storm dripped from leaves and bracts. The rising sun coaxed steam from the dampened limestone ground. Her health club sauna had nothing on the Yucatán jungle.

Rolling over, she saw no Max, only his empty inflated mattress. She peered out at the dense wall of vegetation. Probably taking care of personal necessities.

Thank heaven for him. She'd needed his clear head and experience after the close brush with the soldiers. Following a hurried wash and meal by the *cenote*, they'd stumbled through the dark underbrush until they found a space large enough to pitch their tent. They made it inside seconds before the skies opened.

As she settled on her mattress, the incessant jungle noises filtering through the rain battered her senses. And how could she sleep picturing her brother drugged and injured in the hands of sick criminals? Who had yet to call! Something must be wrong, but there was nothing she could do. She had enough to deal with here, her attraction to Max included.

She had finally drifted off, the day's exertion and stress taking their toll. Her last memory had been of owls hooting back and forth.

No makeup and sleeping in her shorts and cami made dressing in pants and a shirt a lot easier than preparing for a workday at the museum. Staying off the trail complicated everything. Somehow they had to find their way. Dammit, the broken GPS was her fault. She should've stowed it in her tote after checking it. Neglecting such an important detail wasn't like her.

Neither was this whole scene. The shooting, the helicopter landing, the jungle noises, the jaguar, and the near-brush with the soldiers had ramped up the stress. Meals consisted of the portable and nonperishable. Her exposed skin bore testament to the jungle's prickliness. Not to mention her hair. She brushed back the corkscrewy mess and confined it with a scrunchie.

As she crawled from the tent, a green parrot swooped above her head, announcing his displeasure at her intrusion. Puddles scattered the ground, but the porous limestone surface would dry soon as the night's downpour drained into the underground rivers and caverns.

Toothbrush, canteen, and other necessities in hand, she headed for privacy behind a stand of bamboo.

When she returned, Max was emerging from the jungle. His cap, carried in both hands, bulged with something. The dark shadow of beard made him look sexier than ever. A thrill of longing swept through her.

"Fresh fruit." He tilted the cap to display four apple-size, golden-skinned globes. "*Zapotes*."

A murky memory rose in her mind. "I know the *zapote*! It's white inside, with a few seeds. Delicious, just what we need with our energy bars."

"A native feast." Max deposited the fruit-laden cap on his pack and dug out a knife.

Moments later, her hunger slaked, Kate broached the subject choking her like the vine strangling the nearby gum tree. "About the GPS, that's my fault. I—"

"Easy, Kate. Everything happened too fast in the chopper. No problem. We'll go low tech." Max flicked away a *zapote* seed and fished in one of the many pockets in his cargo pants. He held up a flat plastic case. "My trusty compass."

Kate gaped. Then it hit her. She jackknifed to her feet. "Why the hell didn't you tell me last night you had a compass?"

A devilish grin lighted his face. He winked. "Reckon I was tired." Opening the case, he stood and held the device level. He oriented it to point north.

She wanted to throw the rest of her cereal bar at him. "You let me stew all night about getting lost."

"You did more snoring than stewing, darlin'."

"I do not sn—"

A rumble like a giant dump truck bore down on them.

The ground shook, making pebbles dance and trees sway. Birds jetted from the trees into the safety of the sky. A ring-tailed coatimundi scurried through the campsite without sparing the humans a glance.

Kate lost her footing but Max caught her. He wrapped her in his strong arms and she clung, burying her face in his shirt. Breathing his familiar scent propped her up. They held onto each other until the tremor's booming stopped after what seemed a century but was mere moments.

Slowly birds settled and jungle chatter increased to its normal chorus.

He lifted her chin. "I reckon Kizin's worried."

Exhaling in relief, she nodded. "Let's hope that's his only warning shot today."

She didn't want to move. For an instant she thought he would kiss her, but instead he stepped away. She wouldn't have allowed it anyway. *Tell yourself that, Katherine.*

She lowered her gaze and gasped at the aftermath of the tremor. The tent lay flat, the stakes askew, and leaves and twigs littered the ground. "We'd better get packed. Then you can consult your magic compass and point us toward K'eq Xlapak."

Max stuffed the remaining fruit in his pack and slapped on his cap. "Think again. *You*'re going to plot our route."

She halted two steps from their collapsed tent. "Me? It's been a while since I used a compass, but I'll see what I remember."

He grinned. The jerk was clearly enjoying himself. "After a lesson from the ol' scout, you'll be Sacajawea."

Sacajawea knew where she was going and had no schedule. If Kate lost her way returning Kizin, the Maya villagers might blame her—and Max—for the coming earthquake. Hell, in the aftermath, they'd probably both perish, along with Doug. Her stomach roiled. She'd push on. What else could she do?

She narrowed her eyes. "And just what will *you* be doing while I'm playing guide?"

He held up the machete.

Chapter Eighteen

SWEAT DRIPPED FROM Max's ears, nose, and chin as he hacked at the vine blocking their way. Bulling through the jungle required protection from thorns and insects. And snakes. Prepared, he wore camouflage cargo pants tucked into snake-proof boots and a lightweight shirt with insect repellant in the weave. Steamed by the sun, now high in the sky, humidity like a damn Houston summer wrapped itself around him, seeking out every millimeter of skin. Clouds were gathering. But still some blue. Maybe the rain would hold off until night.

Behind him, Kate trooped along in a similar outfit. She carried the compass in front of her like it was the Holy Grail. A glance behind him showed frown lines between her eyes revealing how hard she concentrated. She was a quick study. And she'd sucked it up once she realized their situation. They'd plotted the course toward K'eq Xlapak, at 240 degrees southwest. How many days it would take to get there was up for grabs. Not a straight route, not with trees and rocks and who the hell knew what else in their path. So she patiently plotted their route to one visible target after another.

He grinned. *Dios*, the woman made him smile more than he had in a year. And made him hornier than a teenager. Lying beside her in the tent last night was a test of endurance. Trying to concentrate on even breathing and fake snores didn't erase his ache.

He wanted more than her body. He wanted her fire and her stubbornness. And her trust. Those feelings rattled and infuriated him. Shocking as a microburst.

Hacking the last of the vine, he stepped into an open space. Easier going but it meant the sun broiled his head and shoulders. Kate's boots rattled the rocky soil behind him. Good. She was keeping up the pace. He looked back again, saw her swipe at her forehead with a bandana. Game but wilting.

"Let's stop a minute and hydrate." He unhooked his canteen from his pack. Overhead a spider monkey chattered in seeming agreement.

After a few swallows, she said, "I'm trying not to slow us down too much. Jogging in Rock Creek Park doesn't do it as preparation for bushwhacking through backcountry."

Reality must be setting in. A few days ago she wouldn't have admitted this gap in fitness. "I can't make a trail any faster than I am. You're doing okay for a woman who avoids adventure. I reckon you're even enjoying yourself."

She gave a huffy sniff. "Enduring doesn't mean enjoying."

The glow of excitement in her eyes when she'd plotted her first course said otherwise. "What about those expeditions with the professor? No enjoyment even as a kid?"

She lowered her gaze and refastened her canteen. "You ready to go?"

"Kate?"

Aggravation chased across her features. Then she heaved a sigh. "Yes, enjoyment. And discovery and excitement." She gestured at the surrounding vegetation, full of twittering songbirds. "This is bringing it back."

"Like the howler monkeys?"

"And the *zapote*. I remember things—places, food, people, experiences—I'd forgotten. Or made myself forget."

"To please your mother."

She shrugged. "Maybe. I don't know."

"Time to move on." He picked up the machete. "You can tell me about one of those expeditions as we walk. Take my mind off the blisters I'm raising."

"Deal. I'd like to remember more."

He waited as she oriented the compass.

"That way." She pointed. "To the giant agave plant by the boulders."

The target lay about thirty feet ahead. But trailing branches and low vegetation blocked the way. He reached for a tangle of slender vines to move them before swinging the machete.

"Stop, Max! Don't move."

He stilled his hand and the machete in mid-air. "What the hell?"

"Vine snake. Back away."

Half a foot from his outstretched hand, a stiff, straight, gray stem extended from a strangler fig branch to another vine-draped bough. Thinner than a little finger and about six feet long, it could've been a spear stabbing into the foliage. Except for the golden eyes and flicking tongue.

Kate fought to remain calm but trembled when she saw his barely suppressed shudder.

He lowered first one arm, then the other. He retreated one slow step at a time until he reached her side.

Breathing hard, he cupped her head in one hand and kissed her forehead. "Vine snake. Damn. Good call."

She drew in a sharp breath. Unmindful of the backpacks weighing them down, she slid her arms around his waist. His heart beat against her ear. A steady beat, strong and powerful. Unwanted emotions crowded her chest. "Thank God you're all right. You could've died."

He slid a finger beneath her chin and tipped it up. "I'm tougher than that. But once is more than enough. Last time my arm swelled up like a sumo-wrestling costume. I should've spotted this guy."

She gaped at him. "You were bitten before?"

"A few years ago. Like now, I wasn't alert enough. Vine snakes aren't real aggressive. If you grab one, it'll bite."

Memories slithered from the murky past. "We were on expedition somewhere in Mexico. I was about eight. I reached for a flower. Dad yanked me back and showed me the vine snake stretched out beside the stem. I remember the pointy head. And Dad's warning. The venom has no antidote."

"True enough. But a vine snake, whipsnake, whatever you call it, is *semi*-venomous. You probably weighed about sixty pounds, so in that case, your dad could've been right. He was protecting his little girl."

Yes, she'd felt protected. Safe. Until Mom went into hysterics when she heard the story. "I never thought of that. Dad taught Doug and me about the places we camped—the history and people, the animals and plants."

"Sounds like he enjoyed having you with him. He made time for you."

The bitter sharpness in his voice reminded her who was talking. Her face heated, but maybe he'd attribute her red cheeks to the jungle heat. He would so not appreciate lame sympathy at his lack of a father.

But of course he was right. She'd spent too many years treading carefully and letting her mother's fears and put-downs block the good memories. Pain settled in her chest and in her eyes. "When you asked me to tell you my memories, you didn't expect such a graphic demonstration."

He flashed her one of his devilish grins. "I don't mind graphic as long as it includes holding you like this."

With the sudden realization that she was still standing in his embrace, she felt her nerve endings dance with awareness. She could feel his hot gaze, his hands on her waist through the thin cotton of her shirt, his body heat where her palms rested against his rock-hard biceps.

She stepped out of his arms. "Don't we need to keep moving?"

He pointed to the foliage. "The snake seems to have moved on." Picking up the machete, he whacked at the vines in their way.

****

As the afternoon wore on, they faced only a thick green barrier of tangled vines, spindly columnar cacti, and prickly acacia trees. Max reckoned if they met no obstacles, they could keep going until nightfall. He glanced upward at the scudding clouds. Unless the rain hit first.

A while later, he beat past a copa tree and a bush with thick, leathery leaves only to run into a dead end. Spindly trees and low-growing vegetation grew out of sheer stone. Growth was too thick to see right or left to determine how large the barrier was. He bent backward and gazed upward. The green-camouflaged mound arched into the sky three stories high.

His pulse kicked up a notch. This ought to put the sparkle back in Kate's eyes.

"What is it, Max?"

"If I didn't know this plateau has no hills, I'd say we've come to a hill. Look." He hacked away thorny branches and stood aside to give her a view.

Blood spotted her sleeves where thorns had punctured. Fatigue dulled her eyes but her chin had a determined lift. She removed her canvas gloves and swiped sweat from her forehead.

She stepped around him and peered at the obstruction with the same thoroughness he did. "I don't think it's a hill any more than you do." She yanked on her gloves. "Let me have the machete."

Grinning, he handed it to her.

She hacked away until she'd cleared enough to reveal what lay beneath the vines and roots. Blocks of stone held in place with crumbling mortar formed a curved wall.

"Max, look! Maybe a temple of some sort, but not a pyramid. More of a dome shape." When she returned the machete, the excitement of discovery gleamed in her eyes. "We have to keep going but I wish we could stay and explore. Maybe there are more buildings."

A distant rumble drew his gaze again to the sky. Wind drove angry dark clouds far above the trees, devouring the blue.

"Storm's coming. You get your wish. We should get under cover before the rain hits. You think this pile of rocks has an inside chamber?"

Her expression brightened and her shoulders lifted. "Definitely, maybe more than one. Odds are that any doorway is overgrown. Finding it could be a tough order."

He slid the map from his pack. They were traveling to the south of the limestone road. With all the zigzagging, determining just how far they were from the trail was a guess. "I estimate we've gone about eight miles today, to about here. The map shows nothing except green. This temple, or whatever it is, isn't on the map."

She frowned. "So we have six more days to go thirty-two miles."

If his calculations were correct. "Eight miles a day. We can make it. No sweat." He hoped. "Hell, Texas-size sweat. But doable. We need a better source of water than black clouds. We never planned on an overland trek away from the trail or I'd have insisted on hydration packs so we wouldn't have to refill like we do with canteens. We have plenty of hyperiodide tablets for water purification, but funneling rainwater into canteens is problematic."

She agreed. "We need to find a *cenote*. This place is a good bet. The Maya didn't build far from a water source."

"Shelter first. We may have more water than we can handle damned soon."

The boom of thunder backed up his prediction. Trees and undergrowth on the ground blocked most of the wind so he expected the rain to fall straight down.

"From the contours of this structure, I have a feeling it wasn't a temple," she said. "Possibly a way station or storage building. The opening should face the road."

"Maybe this thing's not important enough to restore, but if it was near the beaten path, it'd be on the map. We must be a good distance from the road. Why such a massive building so deep in the jungle?"

"One of the mysteries of the Maya," she said, with a flippant air. "Or it's near the only *cenote* in these parts. Let's try going around the north side." She oriented the compass.

He liked the animation in her eyes, the way her color bloomed with the pleasure of this side adventure. His body tightened. Everything male in him responded to her. If only he hadn't rushed into asking about her brother's deals. Safer if he just thought of her as the client.

Shit.

"Let's find that door before the skies open."

"Yo."

Kate watched Max push past a sapling. Another crack of thunder made her pulse jump. The smell of ozone overlaid scents of flowers and mossy stone. The bees buzzing around the flowering vines vanished.

He whacked at vines and roots, and she pulled the cuttings aside to make a path around the massive structure. A green parrot flew in agitated circles and squawked at the destruction.

Just above their heads, a different layer of flat stones formed a shelf leading to another rise of curved wall. Her pulse quickened. She'd seen a similar Maya structure in Mexico.

A few minutes later, raindrops the size of ping-pong balls began to splatter on their heads and darken the stones. Soon the drops grew to a downpour and lightning flashed all around them in a bigger light show than Independence Day on the Washington Mall.

Water streamed down the stones and sluiced around their feet. The bill of her cap kept the rain out of her eyes but water dripped from her hair. She was soaked to the skin. In spite of the heat, she shivered.

Max came to a halt. Water cascaded off his backpack and from his cap. "This may be the way in. I got a pillar or column."

She came around for a closer look. Two stone pillars and a lintel formed a square opening like a roofed portico. Fallen stones and wood clogged the space.

"Without this junk in the way," Max shouted above the rush of rain, "this opening would be big. The Maya didn't have the wheel but I'd judge the space is wide enough for a Corvette."

She smiled. She'd come to expect his knowledge of the Maya. "They didn't know about arches either, so their flat ceilings sometimes collapsed. We'll have to be cautious."

"No shit. Something could be living in there." He shed his pack. "Clearing one side should give us enough of an entry under cover." He tipped up his head for a drink of the driving rain, then started moving away stones.

Careful to protect the camera bag with its precious cargo, she deposited her pack beneath a tree and set to work beside him. As she rolled away a stone, a scorpion the size of her palm scooted out. She recoiled and shrieked like a howler.

Shaking its venomous stinger in indignation, the scorpion skittered away.

Kate slipped on the wet stones and tumbled

sideways onto the debris. Her hard landing triggered a landslide of rocks and sticks, taking her with it until she crashed against a tree. Pain rocketed through her bones and the breath exploded from her lungs.

Max was at her side, his arm around her shoulders "Take it easy. Where do you hurt?"

She dragged in air. "Everywhere. But I don't think anything's broken."

He ran his hands over her legs and arms. Her left sleeve was torn and red, but the rain was quickly washing away the blood. Her already bruised left shoulder throbbed. "Did the son of a bitch sting you?"

She shook her head and started to rise. "Both of us ran."

He pressed a hand on her knee. "Sit here a minute. I've almost cleared enough space for us to get under shelter. I'll clear the inside in case the chamber has more critters." His headlamp and the pistol came out, and his gaze scanned the littered ground.

She shivered with the aftermath of fear, and her heart thumped like a bongo drum. This stupid fall had earned her bruises and cuts on top of bumps and scratches, but she was okay, just sore. A little bloody. Wetter than she'd ever been in her life. And pissed. She wanted a bubble bath, a glass of sauvignon blanc— French, 2004—and a massage. In any damn order.

Pity party finished, she watched Max work. With his wet shirt nearly transparent, the angles and bulges of his muscles stood out in relief. The ropy sinews of his biceps and forearms contracted as he heaved aside stones and branches.

Heat spiraled through her and tenderness eased her discomfort. She squeezed rain from her hair. This wasn't even his quest. How could she just sit here and let him do everything? She'd damn well hold up her end.

"I feel better now. I can help." Careful where she put her hands, she pushed to her feet. Every bone and muscle protested with stabs of agony. But no dizziness. No concussion. Good. She clambered up behind him, every step painful. Musty and rank odors emanated from the low, dark chamber.

When she put a hand on his back, he held up an arm. "Keep back. Let me check inside first. I'll take no chances with your safety."

She backed up a step, watching as he aimed the lamp beam into the shadowed recess. "Chamber's only as wide as the opening but deeper, like an entry hall. Another doorway in the back but blocked by a cave-in. No critters."

He stowed the Glock and picked up a stout stick from the pile of rocks. "I need to clear away leaves and whatever else is on the floor first. Snakes and scorpions don't like to cross bare ground. Unless you have a hankering to snuggle up to another scorpion."

She grinned at his choice of words. So Texas. "Not anytime soon. I can wait."

"I piled up the stuff on the floor—dry leaves, twigs, even some animal bones. It's dry enough to make good tinder. A fire will help us dry out and repel mosquitoes." He scraped at the debris. "All clear. Let's bring in our gear."

They lugged their packs inside along with a few small logs. She waited in the stone shelter while Max curled up two big leaves as funnels into their canteens before he joined her. In short order, they settled in with the beginnings of a fire. Smoke ribboned up and out the chamber opening. The thick layers of stone deadened the rain's pounding so they could talk in normal voices.

"You should get into dry clothes." He sat cross-legged before the small blaze. "Then we'll doctor those cuts and scrapes. In this climate open wounds can fester. You don't want parasites—"

"Enough, dammit. Thorns, the monsoon, the scorpion. Earthquakes. No more. I don't want to hear a word about parasites." She shuddered, feeling her mouth contort.

"Had enough adventure?" His voice was a gentle rumble.

She straightened her shoulders. "This trip isn't about adventure, remember? And even if it were, it's too damned late now. I'll manage, thank you very much."

She gathered dry clothing and her towel from her pack. When she rose to her feet, the low ceiling forced her to hunch over. The ancient Maya were shorter than their modern counterparts.

"Wait a sec, Kate. I admit I didn't think you could hack it. I was wrong. You wouldn't give up and go back now even if it was possible. You're no quitter. Scorpions, jaguars, and don't forget the vine snake—nothing stops you."

She stared at him, skin tingling as if his words actually caressed her. She licked her lips. Burning wood crackled and sizzled. Lightning flashed and thunder rumbled. "That's the nicest thing you've ever said to me."

"Change your clothes. I'll turn my back and keep watch over the fire to give you privacy."

She cocked her head and sent him a teasing smile. "How can I be sure you won't peek?"

He peeled off his soaked shirt and gripped the stick with both hands. "Darlin', every molecule in my body wants to see you naked again but this isn't the time. I promise not to look."

With that, he turned and jabbed the stick into the fire.

Chapter Nineteen

NO QUITTER. KATE savored the words, let them wrap around her like a blanket. From Max, high praise. He hadn't said she was adept or capable, but at least he respected her determination.

Her headlamp on, she stepped farther back in the chamber. Although he'd cleaned out the space, the scents of decay and mold underlay that of wood smoke. Nose wrinkled, she peeled off her dripping clothes, every stitch soaked. When she finished drying off with her super-absorbent camp towel, she felt warmer even in the stone-cooled space.

Max's rigid back showed he was a man of his word. Puckered scarring dented his left shoulder. Maybe a bullet wound. And a longer, jagged scar gleamed white on his right side.

At the beginning, she'd seen him as only muscle, a brawny protector, and then as a sharp, self-made man. A man who thought her brother a crook, dammit. Actually it was Devlin Security—and Thomas Devlin himself—who mistrusted Doug. Or was she rationalizing because Max Rivera was sexy as hell and as hot for her as that fire? Puckered nipples and twinges low in her body were her answer.

They could go nowhere in this storm. They were comfortable, dry, and safe. Well, relatively safe. So why not?

Warmed inside and out, she smiled as she slipped into clean and dry clothing. Reaching for her boots she said, "Okay, big guy, I'm decent. You can relax."

He swiveled around and raised one dark eyebrow. "Darlin', with you around, I can never relax." His rich voice reverberated against the stone walls and deep inside her.

Was his comment provocative or protective? If provocative, she was ready. If protective, she would change his mind. Soon.

Finished tying her boots, she angled her head to play the light over the walls. "The stonework back here is remarkably intact, even the mortar."

"What do you think is beyond that blocked door?"

His fascination for the ruin matched hers and warmed her further. "Give me a minute."

Her lamplight caught shadowy lines inscribed on the door frame. "The upright pillars are more than framework. They're *stelae*."

"Columns with glyphs."

She nodded, stepping closer and rubbing the stone with her towel. Dampened, the lines showed their design in clear relief. "I think I know what this building is."

"You're killing me with suspense, woman."

She hadn't heard him move, but his voice, low and smoky, tingled in her ear. His body heat and salty, damp scent made her pulse skip.

She swallowed. "I can't read the hieroglyphics but the pictures make the meaning clear enough." She traced the lines with her index finger. "What do you see?"

He trained their halogen lantern on the inscribed drawings. "A beehive?" His tone bordered on incredulous.

"And bees." Kate pointed to the smaller shapes above and below the hive. She wheeled to find him bent over nearly in half. She couldn't help but chuckle. "Hey, old man."

His brows slammed together. "Is there more or can I go sit down before I'm bent permanently?"

She shooed him toward the fire. Peeling off her headlamp, she sank beside him on the hard-packed ground.

"Hold out your arms and I'll have a look at your scrapes." He pulled the first-aid kit from his pack.

"Most of the scratches are from thorns, but my left arm took a hit when I fell." What blood hadn't washed away had dried but her elbow was stiffening up.

"You didn't get this bruise when you fell just now." He was frowning at the purple blotching her shoulder.

She considered a nonchalant shrug but thought better of it. "I took a tumble in the helicopter. No big deal."

"We'll lighten your pack before we head out again. That way it won't *become* a big deal." He held up the iodine. "Parasite prevention next." She winced when he dabbed the antiseptic on the cuts. "Not too bad. Antibiotic ointment later."

"Thank you, Dr. Rivera," she said sweetly.

Grinning, he tossed another stick into their blaze. "Okay, Indiana Fontaine, what is this place if it's not a temple?" He reclined facing her, propped on one elbow.

The heat in his gaze steamed her more than the fire. Huddling together in this ancient stone entry struck her as more intimate than sleeping side by side in a tent.

She edged closer to him and took out her hairbrush. "It *is* a temple, of a sort. There's a similar building in

Mexico, at Cobá. Honey must've been a major trading commodity here as it was there. This structure's shape is a beehive, a temple to the god of commerce. They probably used it as a marketplace. People would've set up huts around the building."

"A trading center." Max glanced at the back wall. "If we could get in, we might find statues or glyphs of the god."

"But—"

He pressed a finger to her lips. "I know. The deadline. Your archeologist pal at K'eq Xlapak might be interested in this temple."

His touch burned, tempting her to lick the callused skin. But he pulled away.

Their gazes held and sizzled as if connected by invisible, live wires. Or was that the fire's heat? The flames reflected on his burnished skin, limning the lean bands of sinew in gold and shadows. The look in his heavy-lidded eyes promised passion, slow, sensual caresses, and dizzying satisfaction.

Hairbrush forgotten, she leaned toward him, blood throbbing in every pulse point in her body. Her tight nipples brushed against the cami's soft cotton.

His fingers slid into the hair at her temples, then trailed down her cheek, to the low neck of her cami, where he stroked just beneath the rolled hem. He could probably feel her fluttering heart.

She could barely breathe, hypnotized by the rasp of his finger against her skin. "Max—"

He feathered a kiss across her lips. "Hold that thought. Gotta put wood on our fire. This stuff burns faster than we will—if we're headed where I think we are."

"We don't need the fire."

"Huh?"

"The rain has stopped."

He went utterly still before he looked out beyond the smoldering fire.

The storm had moved on. Thunder rumbled in the distance. The jungle wept, its tears dripping and trickling from every leaf and tree. Sunlight reflected diamonds on the droplets of water. Rising steam made the setting surreal, dreamlike. Exactly how Kate felt—in a dream.

Don't wake me. Not now.

Max cleared his throat. "I hate to say it but water and safety have to come before pleasure. It'll be dark before long."

She slumped backward, deflated like a pricked balloon. She'd taken a chance at seducing him. She was dirty and smelly and her hair had gone native. Was she making a fool of herself?

"Hey." He cupped her chin. "We'll have all night. If you have in mind what I have in mind, we'll need all night."

The velvet promise of his words tingled her flesh. Gathering her scattered wits, she said, "I'll organize our camp in here."

He laughed. "I expected nothing less. The rainwater probably didn't fill our bottles. You said earlier there must be a *cenote* nearby." After shrugging into a dry shirt, he went outside and stretched. "Ah, feels good to stand up."

This time she wasn't terrified to stay alone. Well, a little. "Be careful."

"Always." With a wink, he plunged into the trees.

****

When Max returned, he found Kate had draped their wet clothing over branches and rocks to dry. He grinned at the tent set up inside the temple entrance. Exactly what he'd have done.

Perched on the rock pile, she was still brushing at her tangled hair. With her dark Cuervo-Gold hair wild around her face and her arms a patchwork of scratches, she was a far cry from the ice princess he first met. They weren't touching. He wasn't within ten feet of her but his body tightened and he burned. Hell, it was just sex. Simple sex.

Except that where Kate was concerned, nothing was simple.

She looked up, first with fear, then with bright expectation. Her welcome wrapped around his chest. Not simple. *De ningún modo.* No way. *Don't go there.*

"How'd you like a bath?" he called.

Her cheeks bloomed with her wide smile. "You found a *cenote*?"

"Not just a *cenote*. The Roman bath of *cenotes*. Wait 'til you see."

"I won't even ask for it to be warm as long as I can shampoo this Medusa do."

As she collected a towel, soap, and her canteen into a mesh bag, he gathered necessities and dry clothes. Leaving their camp unattended was a necessary risk. A no-brainer compared to sending Kate off to bathe alone. Much bigger and more accessible than the small well they'd used the night before, this was a regular watering hole for predators and prey alike, judging from the prints and droppings. He didn't intend for either of them to become prey.

The weights of the Glock against his hip and the

smaller 9mm at his ankle reassured him. For extra insurance, he carried the machete. When Kate gathered what she needed, they set off toward the *cenote*, about twenty yards farther southwest.

After a few minutes pushing through the thick growth, he stopped beside a sprawling acacia tree. He stretched out an arm to halt Kate. "Another step and you'll do a cannonball into the water. No guarantee on the depth."

She gasped as she looked into the hole at her feet. "It's a cavern, not just a well."

The opening in the rocky surface formed an irregular circle big enough to swallow a small house. Vegetation around the edge formed dense camouflage. Sunlight glistened on the ferns lining the walls and on the plant roots like a hundred fine fishing lines dipping into the pool. The air was laden with the fecund odors of a hothouse—lush green growth and fresh water.

"Is there a way down?"

"No worries. The Maya thought of everything."

He led her to the entrance, a stairway carved out of the rocky wall and shored up with the same stone blocks used in the temple's construction.

"Incredible," Kate said in a breathy voice. "You'll find wooden stairs and walkways in caverns in Mexico but only because some modern entrepreneur has made it tourist accessible. I've never seen anything like this."

Max folded his arms and heaved an exaggerated sigh. "You're forced to come to the untamed jungle and you find a shopping mall and a spa. A female's idea of heaven."

She grinned. "Not this female. I hate shopping but lead me to the spa. I was just wishing for a bubble bath and a massage."

He was just the man to provide the massage. Later. "Watch your step. The stones are slippery from the rain."

The stairs angled along the curve of the wall under an overhanging ledge. The scrape of their boots reverberated off the stone. The rock walls arched upward to the wide opening where sunlight poured in. Hundreds of ancient Maya must've bathed down here.

The last step formed a wide platform at the lip of a natural rock bowl. She sat on the edge and removed her boots and socks. Rolling up her pant legs, she fluttered her feet in the clear water. "It's cool but not icy."

"Your bath, milady." He knelt beside her to fill their canteens. "This part of the pool looks shallow enough for wading but it probably drops off farther out."

"Like a swimming pool. A shallow end and a deep end. Perfect. Crystalline water. The Maya believed these *cenotes* were the gateway to the underworld and the lair of Chac the rain god. They sometimes threw in sacrifices as tribute."

"*Ay, chica,* you really know how to set the mood. This commerce god with his beehive temple seems a little friendlier than that. I was all set for a skinny dip but not with skeletons." Sitting back on his heels, he added hyperiodide pills to both canteens and screwed on the caps. Maybe he'd just wash up and get the hell out.

She turned, eyeing him as he retreated to the steps. "Hold on. Let me finish. From what I understand, the *cenotes* they used for sacrifices were ones victims couldn't escape."

"Not ones with stairs. Point taken. No skeletons."

Her gaze browsed him up and down. An odd light gleamed in her blue eyes. "A skinny dip, huh? Are you planning to wash my back?"

"I'm up for that. Any body part you like." Hell, he was up for more than that. "But I should stand guard. I'll be at the top where I can see anything or anybody approaching."

Her face fell for just a second before the necessity of caution sank in. A teasing little smile hovered on her lips. "Then I don't want you to forget what you're guarding."

She reached for the hem of her camisole. Slipped it up and off over her head.

Her bold move knocked the wind from his lungs. The upturned rose-pink nipples of her rounded breasts made his mouth water. Heat shot through him, lighting a fuse into flames. Before his brain cells could coordinate his feet to move, she'd shimmied out of the rest of her clothes and splashed into the pool with the soap.

****

Sitting on the lip of the pool, Kate finished soaping up and glided into the water. She turned her face up to the sunlight. It illuminated rough walls bedecked with ferns and other small plants growing in the layered limestone. The deeper water was dark and impenetrable, but here in the shallows she could see down to the rough rock. The water, up to her breasts, felt merely tepid from the warm rain. She shivered anyway, but from desire put on hold.

She told herself not to be disappointed Max stood watch at the top.

Ironic that the adventurer was being the responsible, safe one and she the reckless one. Knowing the hazards and minimizing the risks had kept Max alive in dangerous places all over the world. She minimized risks by avoiding *life*. Safe job. Safe men. Safe bubble of blah.

Look at me, staying in the shallows. After a shampoo, the deep end. She was already in the deep end in more ways than one. The risk was worth it to feel this alive. She'd felt more alive these past two weeks than she'd ever felt. No small thanks to Max.

A splash of water cooled her hot face. She loved her job but shouldn't there be more to life? When she returned to D.C., she would make changes. What, she didn't know, but she felt like a prisoner given a reprieve.

She poured more soap into her palms and scrubbed away the sweat, grime, and insect repellant. After a second shampoo, she lay back for the last rinse. Then she floated, eyes closed, enjoying the peace.

Something clamped onto her ankle.

Chapter Twenty

KATE WENT UNDER, flailing her arms. The image of a scaly cave monster trying to pull her down to its watery lair flashed in her head. Before she could get her bearings, she was yanked sputtering and coughing to the surface.

"Relax, Kate."

Strong arms supported her. He stood in the shallow pool with her. No cave monster, only Max.

Fury heated her cheeks. She smacked his shoulder. "You scared the bejesus out of me. What the hell were you doing?"

"You were floating away. Falling asleep that way could be dangerous."

He was protecting her. Her pulse slowed and her ire evaporated faster than a puddle under the tropical sun. She finger-combed her wet hair from her face. "You're probably right. Sorry I yelled at you."

"No problem."

Her tight nipples rasped against his chest hairs. His *soapy* chest hairs. She felt the heat and power of his rampant sex against her stomach. Her pulse kicked up its heels again. "Why aren't you standing guard?"

"All quiet up there. I made a booby trap of sticks and rocks. An animal heading down the stairs will make a hell of a racket. Plenty of time to get to my guns. Thought I'd join you… for a bath. Seems you've already washed your back."

The desire in his dark-chocolate eyes stopped her breath. His masculine scent mingled with soap encompassed her. "But you haven't."

His black hair was streaked with suds, and she imagined an older Max, gray at his temples, distinguished. Stowing away a fantasy she'd never see in the flesh, she ran her fingers through his unruly cowlick. She smoothed it back, stroked the chin cleft hazed from two days of beard growth, and trailed her fingers down his strong neck and chest to his flat belly.

Eyes glazed from her sensual ministrations, he blinked. "Haven't what?"

"Washed your back. Turn around."

He obeyed without a word, turning that broad expanse toward her.

Kate poured more soap onto her hands and lathered his shoulders. His jaw clenched at her touch but otherwise he stood still. "Worried?"

"Just be careful with the goods, darlin'."

When her hands slid between the powerful back muscles down the deep cleft of his spine, he sucked in a breath. Her fingers traced the puckered scars but he didn't flinch. The water covered the rest but she couldn't help sampling the resilience of his firm buttocks.

"That's it. I'm done." His voice sounded hoarse and strained. He swam away in two powerful strokes and rinsed off.

Good. She affected his sanity as much as he did hers.

Shaking the water from his shaggy head like a spaniel, he returned to the shallow water. "I came down to the pool for more than washing, Kate. Unless you have second thoughts."

The predatory hunger in his gaze locked her in place. "Not a one."

Stepping into his arms, she rose up on tiptoe and licked the water droplets from his neck. As his heat seeped into her, she pressed her lips to his. He uttered a deep sound halfway between a groan and a growl and kissed her, thrusting his tongue into her mouth and dissolving her bones. He tasted hot and salty and male.

He moved away and tipped up her chin, breathing as if he'd run ten miles. "Kate, a reminder—this is just sex."

He was so wrong for her, but he was gentle and generous and brave. He triggered a throbbing excitement deep inside her and a burn that answered his powerful heat.

"Of course, but I'm not settling for 'just sex.' "

"Throwing down the gauntlet?"

"You up to the challenge?"

His lips curved wickedly. "I'm up all right. Let me show you." He slid his big hands down her back to lift her up and wedge her against his erection, huge and engorged with the same need that engulfed her. This seething volcano of a man had more restraint than she. And he was already prepared to protect her.

She looped her arms around his neck and wrapped her legs around his waist as she met his mouth. His hands journeyed over her body, stroking and caressing, dribbling water over her breasts and capturing her pebbled nipples between his thumb and forefinger. Delicious torture she wanted to go on forever.

Her senses were inundated with him—the clean scent of his skin, the rasp of his beard, the murmurs of pleasure rumbling deep in his throat. His fingers brushed the sensitive spot between her thighs and she went liquid with want.

Sunlight dappled them from above and ripples circled out from their bodies. Something fell into the pool with a soft ping.

Startled by the small sound, Max looked around, straining for his usual iron control. Nothing. Only a stone or a twig from an overhanging tree.

He sucked in a heated breath, seeking her with his fingers. She was ready for him. He forced himself to return his attention to her breasts. Their soft weight in his palms electrified him. No respite, only more intense heat, like fire had ignited his senses, nearly overwhelming him with the urgency to sink into her silky body. He was harder than the rock around them. Every pulse point in his body rioted. But damn, he'd bring her to the same maddening desperation first. He wanted this time to be better than before. He wanted her to cry out his name.

She was responsive to his every touch, clinging to him like fire. Her breathy moans, the fragrance of her bright hair, the way she writhed against him made the blood thunder in his head.

"Max, stop, stop."

Her words penetrated his passion-fogged brain. Stop? Now? He dragged in air, fought for control. "I'll stop, but dammit, Kate, why choose the worst possible moment for your second thoughts? I could be permanently dam—"

Her hand covered his mouth. "Listen."

Only then did he catch the fear edging her voice. Lowering her until she could stand, he heard what she did.

Noises above. Male voices. Laughter and hoots.

Adrenaline spiked inside him, extinguishing desire.

Fuck and damn, he should be shot, for letting his libido overpower his good sense. He should've been protecting her, not making love to her. "Damn!"

"Is it the soldiers?" Eyes wide with fear, she stood with arms crossed and hands covering her breasts.

He'd rather not hazard a guess. "Get dressed. Gather everything. Stay back against the wall, out of sight under the ledge."

Willing away the remnants of arousal and tunneling his focus on the problem at hand, he bounded from the pool. Pulled on his pants without drying off. His options were few. They were outnumbered, probably outgunned. After stepping into his boots, he collected his guns and crept up the stone stairway.

****

Quaking head to toe, Kate dressed and bundled the rest of Max's clothing and canteen with the statue, soap, and towels in her mesh bag. Flattened against the stone wall, she strained to hear. Only the same conversational tones as before. Good. They hadn't discovered Max.

What were they doing? Were they searching for them? Or Kizin? Questions whined in her ears like a mosquito. Maybe they'd just leave with some food. But she doubted it.

Her breath came in short gasps. Hugging herself, she fought tears and dug inside for strength. Max was up there, facing danger, for her. She couldn't just sit by. She had to see. She had to do something.

Clutching her bags, she tiptoed up the stone steps. At the top, she realized that the voices were fainter. Were the men leaving?

Max appeared at the cavern's edge, the Glock in his hand. He returned it to the holster. "They're gone." His mouth was set in a tight line. He gave her a hand up.

"The soldiers, what did they—" Her gaze veered toward the temple as if her vision could bore through the dense foliage.

"Not soldiers this time. Four bandits. With rifles."

Bandits. Cold sweat washed over Kate. She followed Max back to the temple. When the trees parted, what she saw drove her to her knees. No tent, no backpacks. Not even the clothes she'd hung out to dry.

The temple foyer stood empty.

Max spewed a bilingual flood of oaths. Dragging her to her feet, he held her in place. A groan tore from his throat and his arms went around her.

Her head throbbed. Tears swam in her eyes, blurring her vision. "How will we get to K'eq Xlapak? I left my phone in my backpack. What if the kidnapper calls again? How careless can I be?"

"Shh, *querida*. Making sure we were secure was my responsibility. I'm the careless one. Worse than careless. Dumb as dirt." His voice was tight and harsh as he soothed one palm up and down her back and brushed gentle kisses on her forehead. "The best I can say is you still have the statue."

She tore away from him. Her tears had ceased, replaced with a hot coal in her chest. She punched a fist at the trees. "I thought we were safe off the trail. You said—"

"I know. I'm sorry. I blew it." He lifted his hands and then let them fall to his sides. "If I'd thought with my brain instead of my anatomy, I'd have protected you and our belongings. We'll get it all back. Everything."

****

Night was falling as Max gathered palm fronds.

Orange streaked the sky and purple shadows brought down the curtain. Bird calls and monkey hoots provided an off-key chorus. He wanted the shelter finished and a fire going before full dark.

They'd trudged on through the jungle until dusk. A small tremor shook the ground, but they faced no further dangers reaching this site. They took extra care not to leave a trail in case the bandits or God knew who else searched for them. He left it at that, holding his breath. But she didn't press him.

He'd rather not admit his fear that once those *animales* finished celebrating their easy pickings, they might come back for the female who wore those silky panties. Fortunately she was so furious—at him, at them—that she followed his lead without a word.

He cut off another palm frond and headed back to their campsite. An armload had to be enough. He had to stay in sight of Kate through the foliage.

She'd barely spoken since they left the hive-shaped temple, but a glance at the twin lines between her eyes told him she was bouncing back. And she was working. She scraped the ground for their shelter clear with a stick.

He dropped his bundle and hacked at a sapling for the lean-to.

"Did you learn these survival skills in the Army?"

"Most of it. Special Forces training covers survival in all kinds of environments."

She still had a bit of that deer-in-the-headlights look, so he figured she needed distracting. He tied cut saplings with vines and directed her to cover them with the palm fronds, layered from bottom to top so they shed the rain.

As they worked, he talked about Special Forces and working for DSF. About survival training in Georgia swamps and in the Southwest desert. About sad-eyed children in the Afghan countryside and bargaining with vendors in the Cairo souk. She made only murmurs of interest at first, but gradually relaxed and asked questions. Didn't change what he'd done—or not done—but at least she was talking to him.

When the shelter was finished, they gathered deadwood for a fire and chunks of a termite nest for tinder. No matches, so he made a small bow with a stick and a slender vine and used it to twirl another stick in the nest fibers. The effort took a while but finally sparks bloomed into embers. Then a small fire. "I wish we didn't need a fire, but without it we'd have no food. I'll keep the blaze small so we don't send smoke signals."

He tugged over the small armadillo he'd killed earlier and withdrew the big desert knife from his belt sheath to butcher it. When Kate eyed the carcass like it was a rattler about to strike, he drawled, "You worried about supper? In Texas, possum on the half shell's a delicacy."

Eyes narrowed, Kate planted both fists on her hips. "Right. Next I suppose you'll tell me that thing tastes like chicken."

He grinned. "Nu-uh, more like pork. But it'll be a little dry without a marinade. The tail and legs are the edible parts."

Cooking armadillo was tricky. Overcooking turned the meat hard. Undercooking was dangerous because armadillos can carry leprosy. He kept mum on that last and the fact he'd never actually cooked one of these critters.

Kate averted her eyes as he flipped the armadillo onto its back and probed with his knife. "I'll gather more wood for the fire."

"Chicken," he called to her back.

"No, pork. Remember?"

Good. Her sense of humor had returned.

As she ambled away, the sway of her hips drew his gaze. He pictured her naked, standing in the water, all sweet-smelling and flushed with desire—

As he drove the knife into the armadillo's leathery underside, he muttered a Mexican obscenity.

****

Kate gathered another stick into her armload. At least the jungle contained plenty of deadfall. She swatted a mosquito from her nose. Stinging and biting insects were devouring her.

A vague memory stirred of a dark-skinned nursemaid somewhere in South America smearing a plant paste on her skin to repel insects. If only she'd paid attention to the plant's name.

Dad had introduced them to folk remedies and foods, undeterred by Mom's disdain. How many times did she discourage him from teaching Kate practical survival or local lore? What other manipulations had she done? A muscle in Kate's jaw ached.

When she returned, Max had disposed of the carcass. Slices of the meat—actually resembling pork cutlets—were skewered on a green stick propped over the flames. Hunkered over the fire, he turned the spit from time to time.

She knew him well enough to see past that dispassionate surface, as hard as the graven images of his possible ancestors. She read the pulse jerking in his neck and the set of his jaw. Tight as hers had been a few minutes ago.

He'd already reported to DSF so he couldn't be worried she'd complain to Thomas. And he'd stood there and let her yell at him. When was the last time she'd heard a man say he was sorry? Never. Feeling guilty? A good bet. Max took pride in his job, and this mission. He was probably being harder on himself than she could ever be. How could she stay angry?

Night inked out the jungle, blending shadows into a solid, impenetrable wall. Not safe for her to linger away from the fire. Smoke was their only weapon against insects. She brushed off another blood-sucker.

She dumped her firewood onto the pile and went to sit cross-legged beside Max. "How did the bandits find us?"

He turned the meat. His lips twisted around his reply. "They must've followed the four-lane highway I hacked out. Better than a damn neon sign."

"It wasn't that obvious. You had to cut our way through. But what if we'd been in our little temple shelter when the bandits showed up? Then what?"

The sudden clench of his jaw told her he realized what she'd suspected. "My two pistols to their rifles? They'd have killed us."

"And everything would be gone, Kizin included. So being in the pool saved our lives."

He shook his head. "I should've done more to protect the perimeter. Like—" He faltered, frowning and looking upward as if seeking the answer in the stars.

"Like send out two-man patrols with whatever automatic weapons you Delta dudes use?"

"The U.S. Army uses something like an M16." His scowl morphed into a sheepish grin that made her feel all soft inside. "But we have no troops and no assault rifles."

"All you could've done was guard the top of the *cenote*. Or watched in the trees. Your pistol to their rifles, they'd still have stolen everything. Then they'd have killed us."

"You're right. Being in the *cenote* saved us."

"I'm surprised they didn't search for the owners of the tent and packs," she said.

"One man wanted to, but the others insisted they beat feet with what they had." He scraped fingers through his hair. "That much was lucky. But I still screwed up big time."

"That you did, but I'll take some of the responsibility. My little striptease probably fogged your brain."

"Can't argue. Thanks for putting a better spin on the situation."

Laughing, he speared a piece of the armadillo meat with his wicked-looking seven-inch blade. "Looks like supper's done. Hope I haven't overcooked the sucker." He lifted the makeshift spit from over the fire and laid the steaming cutlets on a broad leaf. He picked up a cutlet on his knife blade and took a bite. "It's ready. Not too bad. A little chewy."

She'd rather wait a few minutes. Hunger screamed in her stomach, but armadillo? "Are the bandits working for one of the rivals for Kizin?"

"Don't think so." He slapped at a mosquito on his neck. "From what I heard them say, they were just following us, hoping for somebody to rob. They were as excited as kids at Christmas to find our packs with food and medical supplies. They looked ragged and hungry."

Living in the jungle like animals... She shuddered. She and Max were now doing exactly that. A few more days and she'd be ragged and hungry. Hungrier than now. Another reality slap.

She needed nutrition. Meat was protein. The armadillo was looking better. She took a tentative bite. It did taste like pork. She exhaled. "Why would anyone live from hand to mouth in the jungle like that?"

He slanted a skeptical look her way, clearly chiding her for viewing life from her privileged background.

"Sorry. I wasn't thinking. No one would *choose* that life. Could they be fugitives or illegals heading north?"

"Fugitives is my guess. Back in the capital, I heard the bartender talking about escapees from a national police van. Colombian drug smugglers. The van was taking them from a town on the Mexican border to the prison near Cabo Blanco. They killed the three guards and threatened the driver. When he fought them, the van crashed into the trees. They left him for dead but he survived to tell the police."

"And you think these are our bandits. Hiding out in the jungle."

"Rifles looked like police issue. Probably stolen from the guards."

Drug smugglers. Dangerous and violent men with powerful weapons. A chill rippled through her. She couldn't let herself dwell on those men. She had to lock away any thoughts of what they might do. Her stomach rebelled but she forced herself to swallow the last bite of even more tasteless meat.

Eyeing her with concern, Max held up her canteen. "We have to conserve, but you should drink."

She nodded and sipped just enough to wash down the last taste of the meat.

He turned toward the fire. "Get some sleep. The

bandits won't be wandering around at night. I'll keep the fire going to repel four-legged and six-legged nocturnal predators."

"Wake me later. I'll take a turn at watch." She wrapped her arms around his waist and inhaled his comforting scent, tinged by wood smoke and sweat. He curved an arm around her shoulder and kissed her, first hard and hungry, then softer and sweet. "Rain check on a follow-up to that kiss?"

"You got it, darlin'." He turned away from her and stoked the fire.

He clearly still felt guilty but she didn't know what else to say to him, so she scooted farther into their lean-to and lay on her towel where she could see out. See Max.

At night the jungle ruled, impenetrable and never silent. The ree-o-ree song of the nightjar accompanied the flutter of bats and a choir of insects. The occasional hoot of an owl and the hunting cough of a jaguar. Her own jungle predator prowled inside her. She needed rest but how could she possibly sleep?

Chapter Twenty-One

SUN RAYS SPEARING into the easterly facing lean-to stung Max's gritty eyes. The air hung still and hazy, heavy with humidity. His shirt stuck to his skin like paint.

He'd promised Kate to get their stuff back, but he had no idea how. Yet. They needed her phone above all else. At least she'd transferred the compass to her dry pants when she changed. No map, but he remembered the next village's location. If they made it there tomorrow, he could leave her in relative safety and reconnoiter.

The Colombians might be trained fighters. Some of those drug gangs were damned sophisticated. Still, he had stealth on his side. He could take down the four scum by himself, but Kate had to stay out of danger.

Another suffocating day lay ahead, with the sun broiling them, and they'd lost their hats to the thieves. Their water supply was low. They had to reach the village with no time lost.

Kate stirred behind him. "You didn't wake me," she said, her tone accusing.

He scooted to the side to let her sit up.

Her hair tumbled around her face in the wild curls she couldn't tame without all her female paraphernalia. Her face was flushed with sleep. Mesmerized by her sexy disarray, he almost reached for her.

He settled for looking his fill. "You needed sleep."

"So did you."

"I'm used to living rough. You're not."

She smiled, a soft curve of lips that lit her blue eyes and zapped him with lust. And unexpected tenderness. "Thank you. I guess I needed the rest. I feel much better."

They headed off in separate directions to take care of personal matters. Then before she could launch into questions about finding the bad guys, he steered her into breaking camp.

They had no food but should find fruit as they trekked, he told her. As they were dismantling the shelter, a squall soaked them but passed before he could collect water in either canteen. The rain doused the last embers of their fire, so he mixed the ashes with sticks and leaves to erase their campsite.

"Do you have ideas for getting our belongings back?" She'd finished untying the palm fronds. The anguish in her eyes made his sting.

Feeling a muscle jump in his jaw, he averted his gaze. "Working on it. You ready to go?"

She indicated the compass hanging around her neck. "Good to go, sir. Yes, sir." She flipped him a passable salute.

Her jaunty demeanor was all bravado, judging from her crimped forehead and over-bright eyes. She'd need that and a whole lot more if fate threw more snafus in their path. "I was a sergeant. You don't salute sergeants. Headin' out."

"Heading where, Sergeant? Straight for K'eq Xlapak?"

"Roger. But we'll make a stop at a village I remember from the map. Let's hope they're friendly. We

239

should make it there later today."

He'd have to tell her the rest of his sort-of plan, but not until he knew she was safe. She wouldn't like being left behind one little bit. He dreaded the moment. Damn, he was keeping too much from her. No choice for the time being. Like she'd want to hear it was for her own good that he wasn't telling her the rest of what Mara'd uncovered about her kidnapped brother. Shit.

She smiled at the mention of the village. "They'll have water and food. I can use a hat too. So can you." She squinted in the sunlight.

Scrapes, stings, and sunburn marred her skin. She'd eaten less than he did last night so she must be ravenous. The loss of the phone was eating at her. Yet she wasn't pushing her agenda. Not a word of complaint, only hope.

The pulse jerked in his throat as emotion swept through him. He clenched his jaw. "We should keep a low profile."

"Minimal trail cutting? In case the Colombians are looking for us?"

"Right. And minimal conversation." That would keep her from quizzing him. He'd concentrate on business, put her out of his head... and other body parts.

Following her compass direction, they hit the jungle.

****

Fatigue clawed at Kate. She tramped forward, willing one foot in front of the other. Muscles she didn't know she possessed ached from sleeping on the lumpy ground. Every inch of exposed skin crawled. She shuddered, trying to ignore the itch. Blood might draw more insects, and scratching could cause infection.

Around them, life squawked, hooted, and chirped, but she couldn't dredge up interest. They found another zapote tree but bare of fruit. Probably stripped by monkeys, Max said. He would figure out a way to get their belongings back. They still had four days.

God knew what Doug's kidnappers were doing with him, to him. If Thomas's man Del Rio couldn't rescue him, what in God's name would she do? The dilemma tightened her throat as a tremor shifted the ground beneath her feet. Max helped her stay erect. A little reminder from Kizin not to yield?

The sun was high before they came upon edible fruit—bananas and acerola, sweet red fruit in cherry-like clusters. Not much to sustain them, more an illusion of eating.

A few minutes later Max halted her. "I smell smoke. The village must be just ahead."

She rolled her shoulders. "Maya villages are so poor. I don't want to burden them."

"Poor by our standards, yes. But they have food and water. Sharing with travelers is the custom." His deepening scowl hinted at another concern.

"You think they might not welcome us?"

He hiked a shoulder. "Maybe. But I doubt it. I'd just like to scope things out before we stroll in unannounced."

"Lead on, Sergeant," she said. "I trust your instincts."

They crept through the foliage to the perimeter of the village clearing. Agitated voices came from the right.

"Keep low," he murmured.

Kate followed in a semi-crouch as Max led them around, staying hidden in the dense foliage. Smoke from charcoal cooking fires and the fragrance of flowers drifted on a light breeze.

The village was more substantial than she expected—a settlement with a dozen or more huts. Cut saplings tied together formed the building walls, and new palm fronds expertly overlapped made rain-tight roofs. Chickens and turkeys pecked the soil, and tethered goats grazed in the yards.

A group of people were gathered in front of one hut. Kate and Max knelt on feathery ground cover to observe from beneath a low-growing palm tree. He looked implacable, but her heart drummed so hard she could barely hear the voices.

The hut boasted an overhang to protect the entry from rain. Clay pots and colorful plastic buckets bursting with flowers lined a walkway leading to the door. A ring-tailed coatimundi confined by a thin chain paced and chattered on a wooden perch in the middle of the yard. People clustered there and near the door.

Kate saw mostly women—about seven—and several small children. All had the cinnamon-colored skin, broad faces, and the sturdy build of the Maya. They wore the typical smock dress, embroidered at the neck and hem with bright flowers, and simple sandals.

Two women wept and clutched their little ones close. The barefoot children stared wide-eyed at someone Kate couldn't see. Three other women stood with their backs to the watchers. They hugged each other and rocked, in grief or for comfort. An older, gray-haired man occupied an upturned log, his head in his hands. A naked toddler sat crying on the dusty ground.

The arguing Kate had first heard stopped, replaced by a tense silence.

"What's going on?" she whispered. "Where are the men?"

"Probably out hunting or in the fields." He motioned for her to stay quiet.

When one woman moved toward the crying baby, other figures came into view in the shadows.

Two men with rifles.

Their dusky skin suggested indigenous heritage, but their finer features and ragged clothing didn't blend with the appearance of the villagers. They wore filthy collared shirts and dark cotton trousers with tears and shredded hems. One wore flip-flops, the other no shoes at all.

One man kept a firm hand clamped on a little girl's shoulder. The child's face was a frozen mask of fear. Tears tracked down her brown cheeks. The other man, alert and watchful, his rifle slightly raised, seemed to be standing guard. He stepped into the sunlight.

Kate gasped. "That man's wearing my cap."

Max's adrenaline surged. He clamped a hand over Kate's mouth. "You don't want them to hear us."

"But—" Her eyes flashed blue lasers. Indignation rolled off her in waves.

"Yes, it's two of our bandits," he bit out. Dammit. Why did the Colombians have to find this village? He couldn't catch a fucking break.

She clamped a hand on his wrist. "But, Max, can't you do something?"

"Not unless you want some of those people killed. They have at least one more rifle and some handguns. And we don't know where the other two men are." He had a damned good idea but he hoped to God he was wrong. At the thought, bile crept up his throat.

The intruder wearing Kate's cap shouted to somebody inside the hut to move his ass. Max saw the other man grab his crotch and grin at his comrade. These two were waiting their turn. And not patiently.

His guess wasn't wrong. He cursed silently.

When he saw the second man ruffle the girl's hair and squeeze her shoulders, a chill slid down Max's spine. She would be next. Unless he could stop it. If only he could think of a way to stop this atrocity without endangering Kate.

She narrowed her eyes. "You know what's going on over there."

He heaved a sigh of resignation. She'd know soon anyway. He thrust fingers through his hair. "I think the others are inside with two of the women." The words were dust in his mouth.

She shuddered, her eyes closed against the horror. "They're taking turns... raping the women."

"While this pair stands guard. They sneaked into the village when the only men around are too old to fight them. By the time the other village men return home, these *cabrones* will be long gone." His advantage was that they should be damned easy to track from here.

"Is there nothing we can do to stop them?" Her eyes were pleading. "Your guns..."

He shook his head. "I couldn't take a chance. I might hit one of the women. Or a kid." Then a light flashed on. "There is a possibility. A way my team flushed out some Taliban fighters."

"I knew it! You thought of something. I can help."

Kate help? The ice slid from his spine and congealed in his gut. "I'm going to make them think the menfolk are coming home. What you can do to help is stay hidden. Whatever happens, don't show yourself until I call you."

Her brows lowered, forming the familiar thought

lines between her eyes. This time the lines signaled rebellion. "Okay. But—"

He clamped his hands on her trembling shoulders. "No *but*. I can't do this if I have to worry about you. Promise me."

On a deep sigh, she whispered, "I promise."

He slid the pistol from the ankle holster and checked it. "Do you know how to shoot?"

Eyes wide, she took the gun. "Dad used to take Doug and me target shooting all the time. I haven't held a gun in years, but I remember how to use one."

Seeing her handle the pistol correctly eased his mind. A millimeter. "That'll have to do. If one of those bastards heads for you, blast him in the chest. Don't hesitate."

"I won't."

He half believed her steady voice. But leaving her crouched there under the palm lodged cactus spines in his chest. Damn. If there was any other way…

"Max?"

He looked up from checking his pistol. "Yeah?"

She cradled his head between her hands and pressed her mouth to his for a lightning raid of a kiss. "Be careful."

Blood thundered in his head and longing welled up in his soul. All he could manage to rasp out was his standard reply. "Always."

Kate watched the leaves flutter as Max crept away. She sat and hugged her knees to keep from following. After he disappeared, she listened for his passage. Nothing. How could such a big man move so silently? When dizziness threatened, she exhaled slowly and peered through the foliage.

The same two men hung around the doorway. They seemed to be joking with each other. Only *they* were laughing. The little girl in the one man's grip wept openly. The poor child couldn't be more than eleven or twelve. Kate shuddered.

Hurry, Max.

From somewhere in the jungle behind the hut male laughter resounded. Then another voice spoke, calling out a greeting in Yucatec Mayan, *"Ba'ax ka wa'alik,"* and then random words, numbers and *maskab*, which she recognized meant machete.

Was it Max? Or were the men really returning? Her heart pounded and her jaw was clenched so tightly it hurt.

The crack of gunfire galvanized the group around the doorway. The women's eyes widened in surprise. Children cried out.

The man wearing her yellow cap called to the others, beckoning in frantic motions. *"Ándale. ¡Apúrate!"* That much Spanish she knew—Move it. Hurry!

Another gunshot exploded, closer this time.

Two men dashed from the hut to join the others. Fumbling with the zipper on his cotton trousers, one dropped a handgun in his haste to retreat. As he bent to retrieve it, the second collided with him, cursing. More together, he swung his rifle toward the crowd of women as a warning. A cleared path led away from the village but the four men slammed into thick jungle growth instead.

The child who was spared was enveloped in loving arms and led to the old man. Some of the women entered the hut. To tend to their violated friends, Kate surmised. The others milled around as if uncertain.

Exactly how Kate felt. Until she spied Max, making his way around the village in plain sight.

He spoke to the gaping women in Spanish. *"Norteamericano,"* he said, pointing to himself and showing his pistol, now stowed in its holster. He continued, but she couldn't follow his Spanish.

After a flurry of translation by one of the younger women, they rushed to him, all smiles.

He'd done it.

The laughter, the voices, the gunshots, he'd used them to frighten away those disgusting men. A nova of warmth burst inside Kate, and her throat tightened. The man she loved had stopped that savagery.

The words blared in her ears. *The man she loved.*

Time slowed, pacing itself to the deliberate beat of her heart. She was in love with Max. She'd thought distancing herself and avoiding sex with him would stop the inevitable. But her foolish heart succumbed.

To a brave, compassionate man. But a man who thrived on adventure. A man who'd be gone all the time. A man who lived on the edge.

A loner who wanted no woman's love.

Chapter Twenty-Two

THE VILLAGERS THANKED and welcomed Max and Kate in Yucatec Mayan and halting Spanish. The girl Max had saved from rape came forward with her mother and the old man. She handed him a pink flower and smiled shyly.

Max hunkered down to her level and accepted the flower. He pressed it to his heart. Touched deeply, he cleared his throat to find his voice again. He called her a brave girl and promised those bad men would be punished.

The woman translated for the child, who beamed.

Then the old man said, *"Mi nieta Mora,"* my granddaughter Mora. It was her Spanish name, the one used with outsiders, not her Maya name. He held out his hand. *"Gracias."*

The old man and his daughter, named Jimena, escorted Max and Kate to another hut. For honored guests, Jimena told him. Recovered from her frightening experience in the way only children can, Mora skipped and pranced ahead of them.

Thank God. If his ruse hadn't worked, she'd have had a much worse trauma to deal with.

"What about the other women?" Kate's brow furrowed. "The two who were raped."

He translated for Jimena. She told him in awkward phrases that the women were being tended by their healer. They would be all right, but their husbands would want vengeance.

Kate's indrawn breath said she understood. If the information gave her the same idea it did him, he might have an easier time than he'd expected obtaining her cooperation. Or at least, overcoming her objections.

As soon as they settled in their hut, smaller than a one-car garage, other women brought them food—a simple meal of roasted chicken and onions wrapped in banana leaves, black beans, and small plum-like fruits. Everyone sat on low stools placed on the packed-dirt floor.

Although windows gaped open and air flowed through the hut's pole sides, the heat was stifling. Years of charcoal fires coated the ceiling with creosote. After the meal, they shared strong, bitter coffee and honey-drizzled corn tortillas.

Kate put her hands together in the classic gesture of appreciation. She thanked them in their language. *"Yum botic."* To Max she said, "Such generosity from people so poor. I wish I could help them somehow."

"There may be a way." He stuffed his mouth with a honeyed tortilla. Explanations could wait.

By the time they finished eating, the village men were straggling home from their labors. Two hunters carried a deer carcass. Those from the fields arrived with baskets of corn and yams.

In small groups, every adult in the village came to welcome them and express thanks. They brought more food, more flowers, and carved wooden animals in tribute. Max's cheeks ached from so much smiling.

As night fell, women propped lit torches in holders by the guest hut and around the space in front of its door.

The smoke carried a sharp, sweet resin smell, apparently a natural insect repellent. The clouds of mosquitoes that gathered at dusk evaporated into the darkness.

Jimena and two other young women escorted Kate to their *cenote*, where she could wash.

At last Max had what he needed—time away from Kate to talk with the men. Nobody knew the jungle better than these people who lived here. Nobody could pass through the jungle unseen and unheard better than they could. Compared to the Maya hunter, Max was a howler trumpeting his presence.

One of the hunters who brought in the deer spoke passable Spanish. Franco explained that for a time he had worked in Cabo Blanco but missed his village and the jungle. While he was tracking the deer, he saw where the *malvados*, the bad men, were camped. Max had no difficulty convincing him and the best hunters to join him in a raid.

Convincing Kate to stay behind was another matter.

****

Kate's chest throbbed as Max geared up for battle. He smeared his face and neck with charcoal from the fires so he'd blend into the midnight jungle like the darker-skinned Maya. His eyes had the look of stone, but the camouflage made the rest of his expression difficult to discern.

How could she stand by while he put himself in danger? *Mortal* danger—confronting those vile men and retrieving their equipment. Her body knotting with tension, she'd offered to do her part. But he'd convinced her she'd only be a liability.

Tears clawed at her throat and eyes. The urge to weep and rage threatened, but she swallowed it. "Go then," she choked out. "I'll wait here."

He lifted a hand toward her but she backed away. If he touched her, she might shatter.

"Max, I—" *I love you.* She swallowed the words. "Be careful."

His incandescent grin nearly brought her to her knees. "Always."

She watched until the group melted into the cave-black jungle. The Maya knew what they were doing. They had machetes and rifles. Max had two pistols. He was a trained, experienced soldier, an expert fighter. They would be all right. Max would be all right.

Everything would be all right.

Holding that thought as a talisman, she tucked a curl behind her ear, her fingers brushing against the elaborate braid woven by one of the women after she bathed. These women were skilled and generous, creating healing and beauty from natural materials from the jungle where they lived.

At the *cenote*, she had washed with a soothing green soap that Jimena told her was made from a root. Another woman, their healer, smeared salve on her scrapes and insect bites. Immediately the itch and sting stopped. Clean and with her injuries treated, she felt a thousand times better.

Until Max informed her she must stay behind.

Fighting tears, she walked through the quiet village to the guest hut. The coatimundi chattered atop his perch. Burning torches hissed and crackled, their herb-scented smoke perfuming the night air.

Jimena and a few women and older children sat on stools and talked outside the guest hut. In a mix of halting Spanish and Mayan, Jimena assured her the men would capture the four *malvados* and return safely.

A wide-eyed boy of about ten pulled at the woman's sleeve. He blurted something in Mayan. Jimena stared at him, disconcerted, then reprimanded him in a harsh tone. Whatever it was about, the boy stuck out his chin and stood his ground. He repeated what he'd said, this time in a jumble of Spanish and Mayan.

Although Kate feared she wouldn't understand the answer in either language, she asked, *"¿Que pasa?"*

Dark eyes troubled, Jimena struggled to explain. Her son Tomás happened on the ragged men's campsite yesterday. Today when he saw them approach, he hid in the underbrush. One of them remained hidden like him, watching the path that led from the *sacbé*. The others had gone into the village.

The implication hit Kate in the gut before Tomás said the words. *"Cinco hombres, no quatro."*

That Spanish she understood. Five men, not four.

Max had seen only four when they stole everything at the temple. They must've had a guard in the jungle then too. The villagers didn't see the fifth man either.

Acid bubbled up, sour and stinging in her throat. She swallowed hard and fisted her hands at her sides.

Her pulse racing at warp speed, she rasped in air. No time to waste. She forced her fingers to open, her shoulders to lower, and her breathing to slow. She must focus like Max did, on the situation.

If Tomás could lead her to the bandits' encampment, she might be able to warn Max about the guard. Risky, yes. Foolish, probably. But if she did nothing, the guard could alert his companions to the raiding party's approach. In a firefight, some of the Maya men could die.

Max could die.

She pointed in the direction the five criminals and their trackers had taken. *Where* was one of the few Mayan words she knew. *"Tu'ux?"* she asked the boy. For insurance, she repeated it in Spanish. *"¿Donde?"*

****

Max and his native team slipped through the trees and undergrowth, not even disturbing a pair of owls hooting to each other. Around them insects chirped and clicked. An hour of pushing through the dark jungle took the raiding party close enough to see the red glow from the Colombians' small campfire.

With Franco's help translating, Max directed the men to encircle the camp. They were to wait for his signal, a rock tossed away from the camp to distract their quarry. Or, in an emergency, he'd fire a shot.

To a man, they nodded. In silence, they vanished into the dark.

He crept to the edge of the campsite. Man, if only Thomas Devlin could see these Maya operate. He'd have given his last promotion to have them in his A-Team. Silent, stealthy, and secure in their objective. On the other hand, they were hunters, not warriors. He doubted they'd ever attacked other humans. But the invasion of their village and the rape of their women forged them into warriors reminiscent of their fierce ancestors.

He and Franco edged in behind the stolen tent. Low voices, laughter, and smells of wood smoke and unwashed bodies feathered the air. In pursuit of a moth, a bat flitted between Max and the tent. He scooped away a spider web for a better view.

Two of the Colombians sat cross-legged on the bare ground. The others sprawled in comfort on the stolen sleeping pads. Guns were within easy reach—three rifles, police issue like he figured, plus a couple of 9mm pistols. The two backpacks lay propped against each other, their contents strewn in small piles as if the men had divvied them up. No sign of Kate's phone.

The two lounging on the pads were taunting the others about not having gotten laid. They laughed and poked each other in the shoulders.

Max suppressed a snort. With each lie, their noses should be growing as long as their vaunted virility.

One of the listeners, the man wearing Kate's cap, shifted on his scrawny ass. His mouth twisted and his face grew red. The other, his brow lowered enough to blind him, stabbed a pointed stick again and again into the hard dirt.

Dissension among thieves could work to Max's advantage.

Rustling and a high-pitched cry of pain outside the camp circle halted the bragging session. All eyes turned toward the sounds. Yellow Cap reached for his pistol.

A man stepped into the campsite.

He was greeted with accusation. "What are you doing? It's not time yet."

A fifth man. *Fucking five?*

Max slipped the safety off his Glock.

The fifth man's right hand gripped a pistol. His left hand held something behind him, still out of sight in the inky shadows. Cursing, he dragged a prisoner into view.

Firelight gleamed on golden hair.

"Let me go! You're hurting me!" she spat in English. Crimson blotches stood out against her pale cheeks. She thrashed and kicked at her captor's shins.

Max jerked, almost dropping his gun. The sight of that fucker's hand manacling Kate's slender wrist branded his brain. All the air in his lungs froze. Adrenaline rolled through him like summer thunder.

The other men's jaws dropped and their eyes widened. Otherwise they didn't move, mesmerized.

Franco's hand on Max's arm sobered him. He clenched his fingers around the rock he held. *Think, dammit, think!*

That was it. They were as stunned as he was. Give them no time to think. No time to regroup.

Kate kicked her captor in the knee. He yelped in pain and backhanded her with his pistol. She cried out and crumpled to the ground.

Seeing his opening, Max dropped the rock. Took aim with his automatic. Fired. The pistol exploded from the offender's hand.

The man howled like a wounded coyote and clutched his wrist.

From all sides, Maya warriors roared into the campsite.

A swipe of Franco's rifle knocked one man's pistol from his hand. Before the others could reach their weapons or push to their feet, they were spread-eagled on the ground with machetes and deer rifles jabbed in their necks. Franco cut pieces from a length of rope, and his men tied their wrists behind them.

Max reached Kate as she clambered to her feet. Blood dripped from her right cheek, where the bastard hit her. Already swollen and purpling. His hands shook.

"Max," she said, her voice rough as if her throat needed oiling, "I had to warn—"

"Shh. We'll talk later." He pulled her into his arms, needing tangible proof that she was whole. He splayed his hands across her back and held her flush against his body. *Dios mío*, he'd almost lost her. "Just let me hold you."

The familiar rumble warned him before the ground shook. He spread his feet for better purchase and held onto Kate while the tremor raged through.

Almost lost her? Another tremor rocked him to the core, one that had nothing to do with Kizin. A seismic shift within him that realigned everything. His mouth tightened, the only outward sign he permitted.

She lifted her head. "And the earth moved. Isn't that a line from an old song? Glad that's over."

Numbly, Max nodded. *And the earth moved.*

What the hell was he going to do now?

Chapter Twenty-Three

TWO HOURS LATER, Kate sat on a stool in the guest hut with all their belongings spread around her. Rain pattered on the palm-thatched roof. While Max helped secure the prisoners, she sorted through the retrieved items by the light of the village's only kerosene lantern.

The villagers had greeted the successful raiding party with joyful cheers. The captured thugs were tied to poles beneath a thatched roof, but open on all sides. The Maya men roughed up the offenders but Max persuaded them to let the authorities handle the rest of the punishment.

In the morning, a runner would be dispatched to a village where the people possessed a generator-powered radio. He would contact the national police.

Kate had sent young Tomás back to the village as soon as he pointed out their campsite. Before going to the guest hut, she checked on the boy. Jimena told her he was fast asleep.

The healer applied a salve to her wounded cheek that eased the ache. The woman left a jar of medicine, an analgesic made from yet another native root, thick, with a tangy scent. Her eyes sparkled as she related that when she bandaged the injured man's hand and wrist, she didn't have salve for him.

Kate couldn't bring herself to pity him. He'd

slugged her, and all of the bandits would've raped her. They'd have killed her when they were finished. He deserved pain for his other crimes.

She stood and stretched her back. She recoiled at wearing clothing those men had handled, especially the yellow cap. At least, the soap and other toiletries looked untouched by the filthy beasts.

The borrowed smock dress, embroidered with flowers and birds on the bodice and pockets, was clean but reached only to mid-thigh. Perhaps in the morning, there'd be time to wash some clothing. Except for their meager store of food, everything seemed to be here.

Including her satellite phone. Unharmed. And no record of calls, from the kidnapper or anyone else. A relief. Sort of.

The sound of Max's rumbling voice coming closer revved her heartbeat. When he'd charged into the campsite, eyes blazing and his skin smeared with black, she'd never been so happy to see anyone in her life.

The way he stared at her, as if she'd risen from the dead, and the intensity of his embrace dispelled her panic at being captured. And remembering now turned her insides and her muscles to melted butter. She shouldn't draw any conclusions from his relief she was safe.

He'd clenched his jaw, demanding to know why the hell she followed the raiding party when she promised to remain in the village. Her explanation received only monosyllabic acknowledgment. She said, "It worked, didn't it?"

Then he crushed her to his chest again. She hardly cared he smelled of sweat and charcoal. In Max's arms she felt safe, secure, and cherished. Maybe this closeness, this intense connection was what she needed, not the refuge of a nine to five. Or was it an illusion, a fiction woven by the danger surrounding them? What did she really want? Need?

Outside Max continued talking—in English—but she heard no one else. Probably checking in with Devlin headquarters.

When Max entered the hut, she bit her lower lip against the urge to throw her arms around him. His jaw was clean shaven and his hair sleeked back, dripping and glistening in the lantern light. He'd washed away the charcoal and the two days of grime and wore clean clothes. He looked solid and tough and gorgeous.

"Any word on Doug?" she asked.

He laid the phone on his pack and crossed the hut to kneel beside her. "Nothing yet. But it's hard to hide a *norteamericano* in a wheelchair. Mara said DSF sent a second agent to nose around Cabo Blanco."

Kate closed her eyes in silent prayer Doug was still alive. When she opened them, she looked into Max's unsettling gaze, direct and decisive.

"You gave me a heart attack when I saw that low-life creep drag you into the light. I hate to admit it, but your dramatic entrance was the element of surprise we needed." He tucked a finger beneath her chin and turned her head, checking the damage to her cheek. His touch licked fire across her flesh and deep in her body. "Looks better. Does it hurt?"

"Not much. The salve helped." It ached but not enough to stop what she longed to happen between them.

"Nice outfit. Jimena's?"

Kate nodded.

Their gazes locked. All her muscles drew taut. In his dark eyes she saw the same heat that fired her veins.

"Kate, we can't head through the jungle in the dark. We have tonight."

His words, rasped out, told her what she needed to know. Her heart thundered and desire pulsed lower in her body. "Yes, Max."

Even more heat flickered in his dark eyes. He reached for the smock hem and lifted the dress over her head. "If I'd known you were naked under that skimpy dress, I'd have jumped you as soon as I walked in."

His burning gaze fastened on her bared breasts before returning to her eyes. His hands skimmed over her nipples and down the slope of her hips. Then he tore off his shirt and kicked away his pants and boots.

Still on his knees, he pulled her against his bare chest. His mouth came down on hers like lava on snow, the inside hot and wet and earthy, in a hungry and demanding kiss. The friction of his chest hairs against her breasts drew her nipples into tingling points. Her pulse rate skyrocketed as their tongues met. She kissed him back with feverish need, knowing she might never get another chance, knowing this couldn't last.

She slipped off her stool and eased her legs apart to straddle him. Clinging to him, she clutched his shoulders, the warm and strong shelves of heavy muscle. Aligning herself with his erection, she rocked against him and her breath hitched in pleasure. She quaked and burned with longing. He hissed in a sharp breath and sucked on her left breast. At the pull of his lips on her nipple, lightning flashed through her and both nipples. She swayed closer, aching to tell him how she felt, but she could manage only the one word: *"Max."*

He lavished attention on each breast before returning to her mouth. His tongue explored hers, claiming her with each thrust. He felt so good, so hard and hot, and she wanted the rest of his body to brand her as his. The first time she'd felt only desire but now she craved *him*.

When she reached for him, he stilled her hand.

"Let's take it slow so I can savor every moment." His voice was low and hoarse as he yanked the tent pack closer and laid out one of the sleeping pads. "The Maya get it on in hammocks but that horizontal boogying takes practice."

She cast a skeptical glance toward the other side of the hut where two colorful net hammocks hung between poles. Her breath coming in short gasps, she said, "Maybe later."

"Hold that thought." He slid out of his underwear and stretched out on the pad.

They'd been naked back in Cabo Blanco and again in the *cenote*, but seeing him lounging there, all power and potency, swabbed dry all the moisture in her mouth. Ropy forearms, pectorals and abs thick with sinew, shoulders with heft—male power exuding sensuality. She caressed the hard muscles of his arms, stroked the hard wall of his chest, and when she trailed a finger down his tight abdomen, he sucked in a breath and rolled her on top of him.

She kissed him, reveling in the softness of his lips, the light rasp of whiskers against her lips, the slip and slide of their tongues. Shivers cascaded along her spine as his big rough hands caressed her back and trailed downward. She writhed full length against him, and her heart swelled with love. She couldn't get enough of touching him.

She ran fingers over the puckered flesh on his

shoulder. "This scar. A gunshot wound?"

He moaned. "Not now, darlin'."

"Yes, now. Before you can weasel out of it."

He grinned. "You know me too damn well. Dumb-ass slip-up. A Taliban fighter sneaked up on our patrol. I got him but after he got me."

"Where were you?" She continued her exploration down his flanks.

"I can't tell you exactly."

"Or you'd have to kill me?"

"But you'd love every minute. I'd make sure of that." His tongue on one nipple proved his boast.

She sucked in a breath at the erotic tug but wouldn't be deterred. "Where in Afghanistan? I know Tora Bora and Kandahar are in the eastern mountains near Pakistan."

"Somewhere between them will do." He gave equal attention to the other nipple.

She traced the long, jagged scar on his side. She couldn't imagine the pain these must have caused him. Her chest squeezed. "This longer one isn't from a bullet."

"Knife blade. Same skirmish. Different fighter. Came at me with a wicked-looking dagger. I got him too. Now where were we before you distracted me? Ah, I know."

When his fingers found her, shock waves vibrated outward from where he caressed and circled. She shuddered as he ignited sparks with every stroke. Her mind turned to mush and her body to flame.

He turned her onto her back. Tasting his way down her body, he stroked and sampled until his tongue found her most sensitive spot. A raw jolt of electricity shot to the place he pleasured, eliciting incoherent murmurs. Tension coiled inside until her body clenched and pulsed. "Oh, Max."

He surged upward and grasped her hands, lacing their fingers together beside her head. She wrapped her legs around his waist and urged him to fill her. When he slid home, she shuddered with pleasure and felt him do the same. He held utterly still for a long moment.

Her inner muscles flexed around him in reaction until she could bear the torture no longer. She wanted the feel of him moving within her, the friction of flesh against flesh, the fierce abandon she needed, the conflagration she wanted for him. "Don't stop now."

"Not a chance."

She freed her hands and dug her nails into his back muscles, arching her hips as he rocked against her. They strained together as he surged and thrust and she panted and shuddered. Tension built, climbing and climbing until she fell over the edge in a huge shock wave of liquid flames that curled her toes. Her inner muscles convulsed around him and she cried out.

"*Mi querida!*" He thrust one last time, shaking as his climax took him.

After a long while, Max lay back, holding Kate as she cuddled against him. Amazing, after the Neanderthal way he'd jumped her bones. Seeing her in the grip of that fucking bastard drug smuggler had struck terror in his soul. He needed the reassurance she was whole and safe.

Need. No finesse. Only desperate, ball-burning need.

A need he thought would be slaked after this time. Not even close. Far from it. She'd sneaked over his walls. Hell, she blew them up with a mortar round. He was the poster child for no-strings flings. A soldier of fortune who lived on the road most of the time. She was a wealthy, well-bred socialite, a museum director, for God's sake.

He couldn't keep her. Couldn't let her go.

He felt her roll away and started to tug her back, but she made a throat-clearing noise to get his attention. When he looked up, she sat cross-legged and dressed.

"You covered up the good stuff." He leaned up on his elbows.

"We need to talk."

Her serious expression wilted his most eager part. He met her gaze squarely. "Look, Kate, you wanted—"

Her soft hand on his lips silenced him. "Not about that. Yes, I wanted to make love as much as you did. It was wonderful. You were wonderful."

The warmth in her voice and in her eyes curled inside his chest. "Then what?"

Tears glittered in her beautiful eyes. "What if we don't make it to K'eq Xlapak in time? And Doug—"

When he pulled her into his arms, she didn't resist. She felt delicate and feminine but he knew the steel in her spine. "Hey, we have Kizin. We're safe. We'll make it. And Del Rio will find Doug."

"We have just three days to make it to the temple. If there's a major earthquake, we could be in even more danger."

He looked up to the thatched roof, trying not to picture the devastation and death in the worst-case scenario, but the rain's patter seemed to tick off their limited time together. "What if we make it in time and there's an earthquake anyway?"

She stared at him as if a vine snake was taking a

shortcut through his ears. "I don't know. I can't think that way. I have to save my brother. I have to return Kizin. I have to keep my promises." She made a choking sound as if she hadn't meant to say all that.

He kissed her forehead. "You can't control everything, Kate."

She looked at him with such trust that he felt guilty for keeping secrets from her.

"You've made me think about a lot of things I never have before."

"I did? Dr. Rivera at your service."

"I'm starting to wonder if control is so important after all." She sat up again, but he kept hold of her hand.

He propped himself up with one elbow and rubbed his thumb over the soft skin of her inner wrist. "But commitments—promises—are."

"Dad impressed the importance of keeping a promise when I was a kid."

"Ah, and that's what this is about? Do you want to tell me?"

She smiled. "Are you indulging me because you're sated?"

"Mellowed maybe. Not sated." The dress had inched up, revealing the blond curls at the top of her thighs. He dragged his gaze upward. "But you didn't answer my question."

Her breath hitched. "I was probably fourteen and Doug eleven. He was on restriction because he and two buddies wrote their names in a neighbor's freshly poured cement driveway."

"Yeah, real anonymous. Sounds like a stupid prank I pulled when I was his age." Some were worse. "Go on."

Her grin was nostalgic. "I promised Mom and Dad

I'd walk him home after school, but I hung around school too long yakking with my girlfriends."

"Let me guess. Doug was gone."

"*No one* was outside, and the building was locked. I hoped he'd just gone home but no joy. My parents had received a call he'd been injured. A broken arm." She drew a deep breath. "He'd gone off with some guys to the skateboard park and took a bad spill. Dad had 'The Talk' with me about keeping promises. Disappointing him was the worst part of it."

Clearly something she'd never gotten over. Even if she'd been on time, dollars to pesos Doug had already left. The skateboard spill wasn't her fault. But no point in upsetting her by spouting more doubts about her brother. "I reckon that wasn't the end of it."

She shook her head. "A few months later, Dad promised to come to my first gymnastics meet. Then a colleague asked him to sub for a symposium speaker in New York that same day."

"That had to bite. When somebody doesn't show when it counts, it hurts." Hurt like being kicked in the gut by a mule. But he wasn't going there.

"I was crushed. Mom kept saying Dad would show up. But when it was my turn on the balance beam, no Dad in the bleachers."

"How'd you do?"

Her grin was rueful. "It was my first time in front of an audience. The best I can say about my performance is I didn't fall. On the dismount, I spotted Dad in the gym doorway. He saw the whole thing. He'd persuaded the symposium organizers to let him speak early."

"So keeping your commitments is because of your dad. That includes here in Costa Verde?"

"As he lay dying in the hospice, he asked me to protect my brother and return Kizin to K'eq Xlapak if I could find the statue. So far I've failed at both promises. Doug has gotten in deep trouble, and Kizin may not get home." Her chin wobbled, then firmed.

"Doug is a grown-up," he began. Shit, in years, if not in maturity. "I'm betting your dad meant you should advise your brother, not be his keeper. Doug's the one who drank too much that night in London. He's the one who didn't put the statue in the hotel safe."

"Yes, of course, but—"

"Your dad trusted you, but unless he was clairvoyant, he had no idea what you'd have to face to keep the commitments he asked of you. Right now he'd be damned proud of you. My commitment is to help you keep both. Hold onto that."

He could think of nothing else he should, or could say, so he pulled her back into his arms. The rain on the thatch pattered in the same slow rhythm as his heart. Soothing, comforting. Surprisingly, as ready as he was for her again, just holding her made him feel good, worthy, as if he could actually get her to K'eq Xlapak before the deadline.

They'd used two days tracking the bandits. Slogging through the jungle for forty more miles would take longer than two days.

Kate peered at him with a level gaze. "I've whined about my parents too much. You never knew your dad but you've never said much about your mom. *Mami*, in Spanish, isn't it? Where is she?"

Mami. He hadn't let himself think that word for twenty-five years. Kate meant to be kind. Hell, she was innately kind, beautiful inside and out. And something about her reached places inside him he'd never let anyone touch.

He stared at the flickering lantern. "She left."

"Left you? A mother doesn't just leave her child. What do you mean?"

She had no fucking idea. "We lived in inner-city Houston, the barrio, in a two-room dump. She kept it clean, kept me clean, and kept me hitting the books." Memory took him back. He shifted his voice into neutral, like for a mission report to a superior officer. "She rarely worked the same job from one week to the next. Bussing tables, sorting laundry, cleaning buildings. Whatever she could get."

"Low-skill jobs. That must've been tough."

He nodded, aware of the distance between them, as wide as the Gulf of Mexico. "Brought home men she picked up in bars. She was a dreamer, always hoping to find the one man who'd rescue her and give us a real home. Usually an Anglo like the son-of-a-bitch who impregnated her with me. Sometimes they beat her, took her money. Our money."

"Looking for a prince. An old story. Usually a fairy tale."

"My school ran an after-school program. I took it for granted then, but it must've been subsidized for kids whose working parents couldn't afford day-care. One day she didn't show to pick me up. I never saw her again. I was ten."

"Ten years old? What happened?" Tears laced the shock in her voice.

He managed a shrug. "Social services scooped me up. They looked for her. No trace. After a series of foster homes and a group home, I lit out. You know the rest."

"You must've looked for your mom since?"

"Before I went in the Army, yeah, but I got nowhere."

"But now you'd have Devlin's resources. You could—"

"The bitch dumped me." He shook his head, working his jaw to loosen the muscles. "Why would I want to find her? I never want to see her again."

"But—"

"No. Let it go. I have." He gestured a full stop.

She kissed his palm and lowered his hand. "You haven't let it go. It festers inside you. No wonder you have trouble trusting people. No wonder it bugged you when you thought I didn't trust you to stick to this commitment."

"Works for me."

"But it's lonely." Before he could rebut that, she continued, "If she left you, then she's the unworthy one, not you. Still, the truth might be better than all the dire scenarios you've conjured since you were ten."

She rose to her knees and kissed him, gently and tenderly at first, then with thoroughness and focused attention. She was magical and seductive, and a deep ache welled up within him, the urge to absorb every molecule of her. She kissed him with her tongue, her soft lips, her tender soul, until he was aflame and thrumming with need.

Chapter Twenty-Four

"NOT UNWORTHY, YOU say. Reckon I wasn't unworthy a little while ago, huh, darlin'?"

"Anyone can be potent once." Her bluebonnet eyes danced with enticement and humor as she slipped the dress from her luscious body.

"That sounds like a challenge." He dumped a handful of condoms from his toiletry kit.

Frowning, Kate picked up a foil packet and waved it in front of his face.

"My logical side is relieved you use protection. I obviously wasn't thinking about it earlier. You packed these for the trip. You counted on sex?"

He turned to face her. She did indignation like a pro, with that snotty-princess tilt to her chin. Even naked she didn't flinch.

He took his time browsing her so-fine curves. When he saw the flush climb her cheeks, he said, "Ease up, Kate. Condoms offer more than one kind of protection."

"Such as?"

"From parasites. In some waters down here, there are nasty little critters that like to swim up inside a guy and lay their eggs."

Her lips pursed in disgust. "Eeuw. Wait a minute. What about women? Me?"

He grinned. "Not necessary. These parasites are females."

"Comedian." He could see her sharp mind working on the truth of his words. And when she remembered their bath. "That's why you already wore the condom in the *cenote*."

"Dual purpose in that case. Only I didn't get to make the more pleasurable use of it." He reached for her and pulled her to him. "What say we go again? I promised slow before, but everything got away from us. Now we have the edge off, we can take our time."

Her sultry smile was the sun pushing away a black cloud. "In a hammock?"

****

Sitting on a low stool in the village leader's hut the next morning, Max drank from a mug of strong coffee. In what little Mayan he knew, he thanked the stoop-shouldered leader for his hospitality and for the meat, rice, and tortillas the villagers supplied. For the heroes of his village, the man had said.

Little Tomás knelt beside him, dark features solemn and eyes darting back and forth between the two men. His scrawny chest puffed out with the importance of his translating job. He rattled off Max's words.

The leader rose to his feet, bringing their meeting to an end.

Max's shoulders felt as stooped as the older man's, with the weight of what he'd learned. He thanked his host, but the other man couldn't know that it didn't matter. They couldn't reach the temple site in time. If they arrived at all. Hell, he was starting to believe in the earthquake curse. How would he tell Kate?

One of the men in the raiding party rushed in. He bowed and said something in a low, urgent voice to the leader.

Male voices rose and fell outside, farther down the central village path, but approaching.

The leader nodded to the messenger and turned to Tomás. He barked out what sounded like orders. Max caught only one word, *cenote*.

Tomás clutched Max's hand and tugged. *Soldados. ¡Vamonos!"* Soldiers. Let's go!

As Max followed the boy through a window, he looked back to see the village leader shuffle out to greet the soldiers.

****

Kate hung her freshly washed cap on the clothesline by the village *cenote*, then began washing her borrowed smock.

After the night's rain, the air smelled of new green growth. Steam rose in wispy ghosts as the sun baked the limestone soil. She rolled her shoulders and flexed her fingers, tired and not a little sore from scrubbing on a metal washboard. No way was she wearing what that disgusting bandit had put on his head without cleansing it first.

Village women were chatting nearby as they washed their family laundry. Jimena had offered to help scrub her clothes and Max's, but they couldn't take the time. Kate had forced herself to pretend the bandits hadn't touched the pants and shirt she put on.

As she pictured Max without his underwear or anything else, she hugged herself. They'd tried out her hammock, but ended up on the floor, tangled and laughing like little kids at a sleepover. Then they enjoyed each other more slowly. He took his time discovering what turned her on.

Their lovemaking was tender and as hot and slow as

one of his Texas summers. In the process, they bared their bodies, their souls, and their secrets. He filled the emptiness in her heart. He was romantic and tender, strong and physical, and sexy as hell.

So much for the allure of a stable man.

More than just sex with Max was impossible. They would never work out as a couple. She'd grown up safe with an intact family—even with all the wrangling. After Max's mother left, he'd more or less raised himself. Maybe before.

Fear of uncertainty would no longer keep her confined. Now that she'd tasted adventure, hiding in the security of the museum held less appeal. She'd faced the truth about her past and was coming to terms with her failings.

And Dad, what would he think? Would he be disappointed, or proud like Max said? *If I fail, then what?* Her mind froze, the question too gut-wrenching to contemplate further.

Regardless of her epiphany, she wanted commitment, a home with a husband and children. What did Max want? Excitement, no strings, no permanence. His mother abandoning him like a puppy at the pound had stomped on his heart, made him fear it could happen again. Over the years, that wounded organ had grown scar tissue, an invisible shield to protect him from further hurt. It kept him from trusting easily. From getting close to anyone.

From loving her.

She rinsed the smock and checked her cap. Still damp. What would her mom's reaction be if she saw her scrubbing clothes in a wooden washtub? Or if she saw her callused and scraped hands and ragged nails?

Perhaps she and Mom would have a talk when she got home after all.

If she got home.

No, she wouldn't think that way. Max had brought her this far, pulled them back from disaster time and time again. He'd get her—and Kizin—to K'eq Xlapak. And Devlin's other operative would rescue Doug. What would happen when they found Doug? Could he have committed crimes?

Willing tears away, she cranked the smock through the wringer. Then she hung it on the line. Carrying water from the *cenote* in a pail and washing clothes by hand added to her respect for the Maya women. In primitive conditions, they kept their cotton smocks pristine and pressed smooth. She wondered if her ancestors who settled Virginia had been as happily industrious as these women around her who sang as they did the family laundry.

At the sound of women's giggles, she turned to see Max loping into the clearing. He moved so quietly his boots barely made a sound on the rocky ground. The sight of him quickened her pulse and, despite their lack of a future beyond this wild land, joy burst inside her.

His gaze latched onto her like a heat-seeking missile. He wore his warrior face, only the tight corners of his mouth betraying emotion. She tensed, her breath backing up in her lungs.

"Kate, we have to leave now." He snatched up her pack from beside the washtub and tossed it to her. "Soldiers are in the village. They're asking about two gringos."

Her brain and her knees wobbled at the same time. "Soldiers? Here?"

Max plucked her yellow cap from the line and shoved it at her.

She hugged Jimena. "*Yum botic.* Thank you, my friend."

The Maya woman called softly something that might mean Godspeed as Max hurried her away.

Little Tomás beckoned at the edge of the trees.

They plunged into the dripping jungle. In moments the greenery swallowed them up. She could no longer see the village. They trekked in silence as the boy led them between trees and around agaves and rocks.

She gradually realized they were walking a trail that someone kept cleared of undergrowth and deadfall. She checked the compass. Max had told the villagers they were headed to K'eq Xlapak to help with the restoration. The temple site lay in a southerly direction.

So why was Tomás taking them west?

How could the boy scamper barefoot over the rocky ground? She struggled to clomp along fully shod. After an hour, he stopped the little procession at a clump of palm trees. He stooped and cleared debris away with his hand. Then he used a stick to scrape symbols in the dirt. He spoke to Max in a mix of Mayan and Spanish.

She followed Max's example and knelt.

Her nerves screeched like a parrot. She hated not knowing what was happening. If only she understood one of the languages better. Either one. "What's he saying? Where's he taking us?"

"It's a map to the temple site. Here's the village we left. See?" He pointed to three hut-shaped symbols. He repeated what she thought was the same statement in Spanish.

Tomás's dark head bobbed in agreement. *"Sí, mi*

capamento." Yes, the sketch was his village. To the left of the village, he then drew vertical lines with stylized tops.

"Palm trees," Max said. *"¿Aquí?"* Here? He gestured at the trees above them.

The boy beamed and continued his map, adding where they were to go. Thank God. But by what route? And how long would it take?

Around them, birds sang and twittered. Insects droned. Monkeys chattered. The scents of flowers and loam wafted in the breeze. The jungle accepted their presence without protest.

Max knew the reappearance of soldiers had shaken Kate. Not moving his eyes from the boy's scratchings, he wrapped his hand around her trembling one. He should've expected they'd widen their search. Who sent them, he couldn't guess. Not the kidnappers. General Lopez and President Aguilar each wanted Kizin as their winning card. Neither rival would fold his hand. And Sedgwick? He was the wild card. Shit.

The fear filling her eyes as they fled the village weighed heavier on him than his backpack. No matter what, they would continue toward their destination. They had to keep moving. Maybe the earthquake would fizzle and they'd make it.

As if in answer, a tremor shook the ground, tossing the small pebbles in the boy's scratched map like pieces on a chess board. Exactly how he felt—a rook, not even a knight.

Kate sucked in a breath and clutched the camera bag to her chest.

Staring stoically at the ground, Tomàs sat on his heels and wrapped his arms around his knees. When the tremor eased, he returned to action. Tongue captured in concentration between strong white teeth, he repaired his drawing quickly and added more detail.

Kate's golden head bowed beside Max's as he tried to decipher the rest of the crude design. Circular squiggles and lines between the village and the temple. To the west, parallel lines serpentined southward from a cocked half-circle to a spot near a triangle shape diagonally southwest from the village.

"The Kizin temple," she exclaimed. "My compass work was accurate. We're not lost."

"Of course not, darlin'." If that was the best encouragement he could dredge up, he should just keep his yap shut.

The boy pointed his stick at the circular squiggles in the middle of the map as he explained.

Exactly what the village leader had said. Max's gut knotted.

"Max?"

Hell. "Tomàs says this is the direct way but over rugged terrain. Boulder fields, crevices, blow-downs. The result of a previous earthquake, I reckon."

"We have less than three days. Can we make it?"

Tomás answered Max's repeated question, gazing at them with bright black eyes. He hit his drawing stick against a rock, tapping a rhythmic *snick, snick, snick.* A howler roared and was answered in the distance.

Max swallowed. "He says that way will take us six days or more."

Her eyes widened as if a jaguar was poised to pounce on her. Her lower lip trembled. Wordlessly, she slipped from his grasp and retreated to where she'd dropped her things. Shoulders and mouth pinched, she sank onto the pack.

Max ached for her, ached to go to her, but first he needed more from Tomás.

Tomás continued to chatter as he pointed to the half circle. "*Cenote. Rio.*"

Max's head shot up at the word *rio*. River. He asked the boy to explain. A few moments later, he thanked their young guide, who knocked fists with him. How a kid in the middle of the jungle learned the street-wise salute was a mystery.

Max was tempted to have the boy continue with them. He knew the way and the territory. But leading them farther into the bush meant farther for him to return home alone. He was, after all, only a child, an easy meal for a jaguar. Max praised the boy for a job well done and sent him home.

Wishing them well, Tomás disappeared back along the trail.

With a lighter step, Max crossed to Kate. He squatted on his haunches before her. Removing her yellow cap, still damp from its scrubbing, he tucked a stray lock of hair behind her left ear.

"We're done. I've failed Doug. I've failed my dad."

He kissed her forehead and brushed his mouth across her lips, salty with tears. "Shh, darlin', there's another way. You didn't hear all of Tomás's directions."

****

K'eq Xlapak

In the laboratory shelter, Esteban Morales bent over the table, recording the measurements of the new tiles he and his assistants uncovered that day. His shoulders ached and his eyes burned from working in dim light. Couldn't be helped. Conserving power might extend the life of their aging generator until more funding could replace the damn thing. Funding that would flow once Kizin returned to K'eq Xlapak.

Rubbing his nape with one hand, he closed his eyes. Why hadn't he heard from Kate Fontaine? She should've called to report her progress along the sacbé. If he thought it would hurry her progress, he'd go to the temple and pray to Kizin and all the jaguar gods.

He rose to go fetch one of the tepid beers in the dining tent.

Fabiola Alvarado looked up from working on the radio, another aging piece of equipment. Ascetic features tight with anger, she sputtered curses and flung down her glasses. "I can do nothing with this piece of trash!"

"Give it a rest," he told their illustrator and tech expert. "Sisyphus has nothing on you."

She huffed her frustration. "Rolling a stone uphill for eternity might be easier than trying to repair that devil machine. At least my laptop has given me no problems."

That was because she babied it like a child.

"*Profesor*, you must see." Horacio Flores entered the lab tent with a basket of artifacts.

Morales crossed to the graduate student's table. "Today's finds?"

Horacio nodded. "From the fourth level in the debris pile near the plaza. Finally I'm finding artifacts more than a few millimeters in diameter." From an array of dozens of pieces, he held up the lower body of a jade figurine and a cracked clay whistle.

"Congratulations!" Morales said. "Your patience has paid off. These will be fine specimens to display here alongside the statue of Kizin."

So long as Kate could bring Kizin in time. By Curse

Day.

As if in response, rumbling began and the ground shook like jelly beneath his feet. The light fixtures hanging from the wooden frame swung and clanked. A light bulb shattered.

This shelter and the other large communal structures were wooden-framed with thatched roofs and surrounded by mosquito netting. They had withstood earlier tremors. He prayed they would hold again as he helped Horacio protect the artifacts. Fabiola wrapped her arms around her precious laptop. Her curses nearly reached the decibels of the tumult.

When the tremor ceased, others arrived to help clean up the mess in the lab facility and to check on the damage. Lately that was a twice-daily drill.

As they were finishing, a worker ran into the tent, his eyes wild and his face flushed beneath his dark complexion. "*Profesor, Profesor*, Héctor sent me. You must come."

Could they have arrived? Morales grasped the man's hand. "Is it *Señorita* Fontaine?"

"No, no. It is Arturo!"

Chapter Twenty-Five

In the jungle

THE NEXT MORNING, while Max explored the *cenote*, Kate took down their small tent. She knelt to fold it, but the damn thing wouldn't work right. Or maybe it was her. In her haste to get going, she'd made more lumps than flat folds. What was keeping Max? He'd been down there for too long. Sitting back on her heels, she drew in deep breaths and began again. Finally she smoothed all but a couple of lumps and shoved the tent into its bag.

She crossed the small clearing to the half-moon-shaped cavern entrance, curtained by vines and roots. Biting her lower lip, she stared downward, listening for Max. She detected a faint crunching sound. His boots on the stone maybe? She glimpsed his headlamp winking in the darkness and breathed a thank-you.

Two days to go. Two days until the sixtieth anniversary of the earthquake. *"El Día Maldito,"* she whispered.

Max had added the food the villagers gave them to the tent and pack he carried on his powerful shoulders. Hours of hiking had brought them to this *cenote* on the west side of the boy's map, where they set up camp at dusk. The underground river below would take them south to within what Tomás described as a "short walk" to K'eq Xlapak. The river trip would take less than "two days' light," he'd said. A day and a half.

The villagers fished the underground river during the dry season when the water was low enough for a boat to pass. Because the rainy season hung on, water might fill the cavern to the ceiling. Neither she nor Max possessed gills or scuba gear, so high water would mean— Her stomach tightened, and she pressed her hands against it. No, no, it couldn't be, not the end.

A scrabbling noise below alerted her Max was climbing the rope ladder back to the surface. When he hoisted himself up from the edge, she held her breath.

His expression held guarded caution. "Don't get your hopes up too much but it looks doable." He peeled off his headlamp and ran his hands through his hair, shaggy now and curling around his ears.

She wrapped her arms around his waist, burying her face in his shirt. Breathing in his familiar sun-warmed scent reassured her more than his words.

She lifted her head and saw his expression softening. "Explain *doable*."

He brushed a kiss across her lips. "Boat's there. A fiberglass canoe. Looks water tight. God knows where they got that. About eight feet long. Big enough for us and one pack. We can leave the rest here and collect it later."

Or the jungle would claim it. As the jungle might claim them. *Stop it, Katherine.* Making it alive down the river would demand all her energy and focus. "How high is the water?"

"Hard to tell. That's the question. Starting from the cavern it looks low enough. I might have to hunch over but there's headroom. Flow's steady, not too swift."

The brooding look in his eyes told her there was

more. "So what's your concern?"

"We could be going down a funnel. It could get narrower, and the roof could get lower. High enough here but who knows what happens farther downstream as the water flows through the series of caverns."

Her stomach still ached, and her breath caught. *Please God, this has to work.* "I still haven't heard from the kidnapper, and underground we'll have no reception. Even if a full-on earthquake doesn't happen, they'll—" her voice broke and she inhaled deeply "—k-kill him. We have to try. What are our chances?"

His dark eyes bored into hers. "Hard to say. We'll take it slow, use the lamps to scout ahead. If the tunnel looks too tight and the ceiling too low, we turn back."

He looked too stone-faced for that to be all. "What else?"

"If—and this is a fucking big *if*—tremors hold off until we make it to the other end."

****

Conversation stayed at a minimum as they organized their equipment beside the canoe. They'd brought only essentials and left one backpack behind hidden beneath palm fronds. Moisture dripped down the cavern walls, plinking into the stream and slicking the limestone floor. The damp air smelled of minerals.

Max set the tent bag amidships. Kate hadn't said shit since his doomsday announcement. He slammed a palm on the cool limestone floor. She'd probably figured out the worst-case scenario without his needing to say anything. He blew out a breath. Nada he could do now.

As she buttoned up a long-sleeved shirt, deep thought creased the skin between her brows tight enough for an air seal. She was shivering in the cool underground temps, but they'd both warm up when they started paddling. If only he could come up with some other way.

Dammit, he cared for Kate. Too much. She was a long-term girl; he was a short-term guy. No ties, no lies.

He'd seen a few successes. Some of the guys in his recon unit managed to keep relationships intact from half a world away. But the odds for him were a gazillion to one. Getting involved? Not for him. No way would he put his heart out there to be run over by a Hummer. Hell, whatever they had now would end as soon as she learned the rest about her precious brother.

Stow that. He rubbed his sternum. He needed to think of her only as his principal. Compartmentalize. Be in the zone. Concentrate on protecting her and not possessing her.

Her phone rang. She lifted it from atop her pack, her eyes wide in stark fear.

"If it's the kidnapper, keep him on the line. Give Mara time. She's close." He turned on his phone, extended and rotated the antenna. His pulse hopped like a jackrabbit as he waited for the satellite link.

She set her antenna. "Same as before, a blocked number."

Come on, come on, damn you. When the link icon popped up on the screen, he hit speed-dial.

Mara picked up before the second ring. "I'm on it."

"Fingers crossed," he said to the DSF researcher, then set his phone aside. Leaning close to Kate, he looped an arm around her quaking shoulders. "I'm here."

With a shaking finger, she pressed the button. "Is my brother there?"

A bark of a laugh. "I have him. Time is short. When you arrive K'eq Xlapak?"

Max scowled. Same voice. Less muffled. Definitely male. Fuck, still not sure of the accent.

"Soon. I'm not sure." Her voice shook, and she pressed a hand to her stomach, but she lifted her chin in defiance. "I have to be sure my brother's… all right. You *must* let me talk to him. He—"

The kidnapper grunted. "*I* must do nothing. *You* must meet me and hand over Kizin."

Her phone beeped. Kate frowned and pointed to the warning notice on the screen.

Shit, low battery. They couldn't catch a break, couldn't switch to their last spare in mid call. Nothing Max could do but hope the fuckin' thing lasted a few more minutes. He covered the microphone. "I know. Hang in there. Don't mention the chopper. Tell him we're lost."

"I need time." Her voice rasped like she'd swallowed sand. "Tremors have felled trees and blocked the trails. We have to find our way through the jungle by compass. It's slow. I don't know exactly where we are. How can I meet you?"

"I will find you."

"If you have harmed Doug, you will not get the statue. Let me speak to him. Please."

Muffled voices came across, as if the kidnapper had covered the speaker with his hand.

Kate bent forward, head lowered, her breathing labored.

Damn the bastards to hell. Max couldn't help a silent plea this delay would give Mara enough time. "You're doing good, darlin'. A little longer."

A shuffling sound as the phone was transferred. "Katie?"

She straightened, her headlamp's light flickering on the dripping wall. "Doug." Her breathing hitched and she straightened. "Dear God, Doug, are you okay?"

"Yeah, yeah, but these bas—" A grunt as the receiver was probably snatched away.

These bastards. So the guy in charge who talked to Kate, and God knew how many others.

A sob escaped Kate, and Max squeezed her shoulders. Sucking in a breath, she nodded.

"Kizin will be mine." The kidnapper's tone was flat. "Or your brother is a dead man."

"Don't do it, Katie!" Doug yelled in the background.

The connection went silent.

She sagged against Max. "The battery died."

He picked up his phone. "Mara?"

He could hear her tapping keys. "Call came from near the temple site. We'll find Fontaine. Mr. Devlin says Del Rio's close."

After he explained about the underground river, he disconnected.

Mara had to be right about Del Rio. The next question was what the hell to do if Max and Kate met up with the kidnappers first.

If they lived to find out.

****

Kate dipped her paddle into the inky water.

The river flowed in from the right—the north—and disappeared down a tunnel to the left—toward the south. Stalactites hung here and there in glistening columns. They could be hazardous as the canoe floated southward. Safety would mean staying sharp.

From the canoe's stern, Max said, "It'll be all right. You'll see. We'll make it."

"If anyone can get us through this, it's you. I know you'll do whatever it takes."

"This river's dangerous, but so's the jungle. And none of our pursuers can follow us down here. We have the only boat."

The canoe rocked as he adjusted the tent and pack between them. He turned off the halogen lamp, saving its last battery for emergencies. Only their headlamps would light the way as they paddled into the yawning black maw ahead. If she reached up, she could touch the ceiling. She had headroom, but Max? She twisted slightly.

He slouched in his seat, looking not unlike a surly teenager.

"Comfy?"

He winked. "I'll need a back massage when this is over. Or more."

"Deal." Cheered, she dug in her paddle and pulled back hard.

"Take it easy, darlin'."

Shook her head and stroked hard again.

"Time's short, but so's the reach of our beams. Paddle steady. The current will take us." Max's beam swept a jutting rock to their right.

Her pulse jumped. She'd nearly propelled them into that. If they damaged the canoe or overturned... She yanked her paddle from the water. "Oh God, Max, I didn't think."

"Chill. Oh, right, you're already chilled." His deep chuckle and the bad joke were probably meant to ease her fright. Not working.

Resigned, she smoothed her paddle strokes. Silence settled over them as they glided along. The only sounds were the lap and drip of water, the plash of paddles, and their labored breathing.

Her headlamp caught a sleek, silvery shape undulating past the canoe. "What kind of fish could be down here?"

"Beats me. Mexico has a connected, underground river system where I did some cave diving."

"Even on vacation you do extreme sports?"

"Darlin', on vacation I hardly move except to eat. The only exercise I want is in bed."

The thought of vacation with Max eddied heat through her. Would they even see each other once they returned to the States? That thought wiped out the warmth. "If not vacation, then what?"

"DSF contracted to protect artifacts and fossils for a university team who were researching a connected river system. They found mammoth fossils and smashed pottery where the Maya made offerings. Another team identified dozens of fish and crustaceans. No monsters down here. Don't worry. Tomás said nothing to fear."

Except high water or a tremor. The words whispered through her, and the next dip of her paddle rapped her knuckles on the side of the canoe.

****

Several times the tunnel narrowed then widened again. Max hoped like hell his encouraging words to Kate held true. She'd been nothing but perky when they stopped to eat but he could tell her smiles were only a façade. She was scared. *Dios*, so was he.

But she didn't complain or break down. Kept doing what was necessary. They had to make it. He had to keep his commitment and make sure she did too. If they didn't make it— No, not an option.

But when they stopped for the night, should he tell her how he felt about her? How could he find the words? If he did, she wouldn't laugh. Not Kate. She'd let him down gently. No future for them anyway, but— *Shit. Coward.* A thick constriction bound his chest. Fucking emotions. Action suited him better.

He switched his paddle to his right hand. His neck and his butt hurt. For once he wouldn't mind being shorter by a few inches.

The villagers fished the river but they obviously hadn't ranged down this far. No torch-blackened smears on the walls.

An hour later, they entered a large chamber similar to the entrance but with no surface access. His light-up watch dial indicated night was closing in, and the halogen lamp showed him the tunnel ahead widened yet again. But damn, more twists and turns in this sucker than the Brazos.

He rolled his shoulders as he straightened, grateful for the brief respite.

And then he heard it.

A distant rumble, like thunder. Then louder.

When ripples danced on the water's surface, he knew. One of Kizin's tremors headed this way. A clump of dirt and roots fell from above and splashed beside the canoe. The constriction spread and congealed in his gut.

"A tremor?" Kate had stopped paddling. Her voice was high pitched. "What do we do?"

He scanned the cavern walls with his headlamp. A ledge jutted out about fifteen feet up. Solid looking beneath. High enough, wide enough? Their only chance. As long as it held. "Now's the time to paddle like hell. I'm taking us over to the left. Water's coming. Maybe the tremor or maybe it rained upstream. Gotta get up high."

She dug in with her paddle.

Waves kicked up, splashing into the canoe. A mineral-coated stalactite snapped off with a crack like a pistol shot and dropped to their right.

In a few strokes, they made it to the ledge. A lip below was wide enough to stand on. They climbed out and he dragged the canoe behind him. Waves lapped the rock. The cavern shook, raining pebbles and dirt from the ceiling and walls. The ominous rumbling sound grew to a gurgling roar.

"Will this be high enough?" she yelled over the rumble and the roar of her pulse in her ears. She gripped the bumpy rock.

"No choice. We have to hunker up there. Stuff your camera bag into the pack." When she started to object, he said, "Pack's waterproof. It'll float."

Mouth tight, she complied, making certain the flap was secure before turning to the wall.

He boosted her up so she could climb. Reminded himself she knew what she was doing, even on the slippery rock. She found footholds, cracks to grasp with her fingers. Pushed herself upward with her legs. Slipped backward but caught hold.

Waves crashed against the ledge. Water covered his booted feet. The cavern was cool, the water frigid in comparison. Shivers raced up his spine.

When Kate made it onto the ledge, he handed up the tent and the backpack.

The roar became a muffled booming as rushing water filled the tunnel. They had only seconds before the surge hit the chamber. He followed her up the rock with the canoe's mooring line in his teeth. The ledge could barely hold the two of them and the pack.

His mouth was dry as West Texas and his hands were clammy. Time for balls-to-the-wall effort. He took a deep, steadying breath. Distanced himself from everything but what he had to do. Hauled the canoe up with them. They'd be done for if they lost their transportation.

A liquid monster burst from the tunnel. It churned and thrashed as it clawed up the walls. In no time the roiling flood clawed toward their perch. The entire cavern shook and rumbled like the earth was coming apart.

Chapter Twenty-Six

MAX PLANTED HIMSELF in front of Kate. Pushed the heavy backpack beside her as a buttress. "Stay back against the wall as far as you can."

"Get back here with me." She clamped a hand on his shoulder.

"Better if I stay here. The canoe will be my protection." He gripped the craft by the middle thwart, held it like a shield. His back against Kate, he braced himself. Their rock ledge was lumpy and slimy, smelling of minerals. Soon it would be even wetter.

Waves attacked the canoe's keel. Sucked at the craft. Even without wind, the rushing water roared louder than an entire troop of howler monkeys. His headlamp showed only clawing waves and glistening rock.

Icy water splashed around the canoe. Over it. Over him. The intense cold soaked him. He gasped.

Kate shrieked. The icy water had reached her too, drenching her.

He dug his heels into the limestone. His shoulder muscles burned. He hung on. The rock shivered and quaked, cracking like gunshots when chunks fell away. He prayed to every god he could name, including Chac and Kizin, that enough of this cold, wet slab would hold, that it wouldn't become their grave. The idea of dying down here scared him shitless.

They couldn't even alert Thomas. No satellite

coverage beneath tons of rock.

"Max, the tent!" He felt her reach for the bag as another chunk of ledge broke off.

"Let it go. Stay back!" He propped himself harder against her to hold her in place.

She cried out but did as he said. The tent bag fell away. He couldn't hear the splash over the general cacophony. When her hands gripped his shoulders and hung on, he concentrated on blocking the waves that might sweep them to their deaths.

****

Kate gritted her teeth against the pain radiating from her shoulder—the same shoulder she'd hurt the day before—or two days before. She no longer knew. She'd slammed into a jutting rock when she tried to save the tent. Now she lay sprawled against the ledge with Max's warm bulk pressed against her. She held onto him and the unforgiving rock with every muscle in her body.

The waves subsided as the tremor calmed. Barricading themselves against the water had seemed like an eon, but she guessed lasted only ten or twenty minutes.

"Water's not rising anymore," he said.

"I'm so wet I can't tell the difference."

She let go of his shoulders and sagged, limp and shivering. How some people got a high from an adrenaline rush, she had no idea. Adventure was one thing, but this near-death thing she could do without. The pack lay beside her, drenched on the outside but safe, with Kizin sealed within.

She ought to be numb but her shoulder disagreed. Pain radiated through the bone and muscle.

"We survived," he said. "The water didn't reach us.

Stalactites didn't fall on us."

She pushed against his back. "You're crushing me."

"Darlin', you never complained before."

"First time for everything." He exuded heat but his hard body pressed her injury against the harder rock. She prodded his spine with a finger. "I want to see below."

Sitting up, he slid the canoe aside, keeping it securely on their ledge. He rubbed one arm, then the other. They must ache after holding the canoe to fend off the waves. To protect her. She wouldn't complain about her shoulder.

Their headlamps showed the river swirling about five feet below. Black, the water gleamed like oil, reflecting their twin beams.

He curved an arm around her and she couldn't help wincing. "You're hurt. What happened?"

"It's nothing. I'm okay."

He withdrew his arm and peered at her shoulder. "Not okay. You're bleeding."

She explained as he lit the lantern. The light showed the sharp rock that had dug her like a knife. She let him pull off her shirt and bandage the wound.

"Small but deep. You should have stitches," he said. "But the good news is all that water washed the cut clean."

"Yes, *all* that water. Like you predicted, we're trapped. We'll drown or s-s-starve." Fear and pain added an edge to her voice she couldn't hide.

"No, we'll make it out."

"Have you received a message from Kizin or what?"

He chuckled, a wonderful, resonant sound that warmed her inside. "Water always seeks its level. Look. It's down more. It'll recede. Drain out the downstream tunnel."

"How long?" She heard the desperate hope in her voice.

"Several hours, probably. The chamber will return to the level it was and we can go on. We should get some sleep while we can."

She cast a look around at the wet rock ledge that saved them. Nothing but more rock and loose shale. "I wish we had some wood to build a fire."

Who'd have thought hypothermia would be a problem in Costa Verde? They couldn't afford to lose alertness or their strength. The river's exit lay miles away.

"We need to eat something, put on dry clothes. These will dry when we make camp. You can have a fire then."

She managed a wobbly smile. "Good plan. You can keep me warm while we wait."

"Darlin', we think alike."

Keeping each other warm consisted of holding on tight. For anything more, the ledge was too slippery and narrow, and she hurt too much. Being held in his strong arms revived her more than the change of clothes and cold tortillas. Clicking off the lantern and headlamps threw them into darkness black as... hell, black as a cave. Not even a glimmer of light found its way from the surface. They had only sound and touch to orient them.

She snuggled against his biceps. "This made me remember something that happened on a dig a few years ago in Arizona. One of the grad students drowned in a flash flood."

"In one of those dry washes?"

"You guessed it. We were warned to watch the

weather and keep a lookout up high. Our dig was a mile away, but she thought she saw pottery in the wash. On her time off, she slipped away to search."

"Alone?" He brushed a strand of hair from her cheek.

Kate nodded against his arm. "There'd been a storm up in the hills. The water must've been on her before she knew it. They found her body a few miles downstream."

"That shouldn't happen to anybody. But she was careless. We haven't been careless."

She caressed his chin cleft with an index finger. "Thanks to you."

"Hey, you've done your part. More than I expected. Your dad would be damned proud. And we'll make it. Hold that thought."

They had to make it. If they didn't Mom would lose both her children. She had done her part, hadn't she? More than she'd ever thought she could do. But was Max right, that her father would be proud? Maybe, if he knew everything. *Or maybe you do know, Dad.*

Unable to reply with her heart in her throat, she kissed Max.

"Good night, Lara Croft."

****

In the morning, Max reckoned the flood level had fallen enough that they could paddle onward. Dry, warmer, and rested, they headed into the downstream tunnel. The water hadn't receded to its original level, forcing Max to lie back even lower. Kate barely had head room.

Dammit, her wounded shoulder could be an issue. Too much use and she'd lose blood. Infection could set in. But aspirin eased the pain enough so she could paddle.

This part of the tunnel was wider but they had to maneuver around stalactites that seemed to appear from nowhere. Whiffs of algae and mold clogged his nostrils. Frequent stops to rest Kate's shoulder and for him to stretch slowed their journey. He kept an ear tuned to rumblings and water noises. For whatever good it would do. Here, they had nowhere to go.

Darkness had fallen by the time they reached the *cenote* near K'eq Xlapak. Moonlight and fresh air welcomed them as the canoe floated into the opening, a near vertical, irregular opening. Kate's stifled sob of relief tightened his throat.

The gods or luck and nature stayed with them and they'd met no further disasters. Now he needed some good news from Devlin HQ.

"Are you sure this is the right one?" Her paddle clattered as she rested it against the gunwale.

The anxiety in her voice kicked him in the gut. "Even if it isn't, we've gone as far as we can tonight. We need a fire and rest." He arced the halogen lamp around the jagged, steep walls. At first he saw only a narrow landing with barely enough room to stand.

Then the beam snagged on what he looked for. "This is it. Tomás mentioned a rope ladder, like at the start."

He hustled her up and out. They emerged into a clearing with grasses flattened by much use—probably locals fetching water or swimming.

As soon as they hit dry land, the ground shivered and shook. His pulse took off in a sprint. *Fuck you, Kizin!*

Kate grabbed his arm, and he pulled her close, planting his feet and holding on. A slender palm tree crashed at the edge of the clearing. Cracks formed in the *cenote* rim, and hunks split off.

In a moment, the tremor fizzled on a couple of shudders, as if the ground was relieved to be solid again. He blew out a breath and kissed her forehead before he let her go.

Her hair was disheveled, with wavy strands escaping from beneath her sodden cap. The bruise on her cheek from the Colombian thug's backhand had faded from purple to a green-and-yellow rainbow. She was exhausted. And more beautiful than when he first saw her, the princess in her hands-off suit and perfect hair.

She had her faults. Who didn't? He sure as hell had plenty. But she was warm and loyal, brave and honest. She trusted him and relied on him. She made him want more than his solitary life. He felt more connection with her than anyone ever before. He could get drunk on her smiles. Sex with her blew all his circuits. Just thinking about her heated his blood.

The bonds they'd forged ought to scare the hell out of him. Instead, he dreaded the end of their odyssey. Maybe it was time to take the risk. If she would. The kind of risks he usually took were physical. They didn't make him feel like he had a hot coal in his chest.

But for a little longer, he had to keep her safe. Then they'd talk. Maybe. Hell, how did people do this?

"We've made it, Max." She sank onto a boulder. "Thank you."

He smiled. "Without your fierce determination, darlin', I'd have given up long ago. I'd have told this kidnapper to come get the fuckin' statue if he wanted it so bad." Then he and Lucas Del Rio would've pounded the slime into the next country.

"I know. It's okay. Maybe he'll call again. Or just

show up. Then we can walk to the restoration site." She returned his smile with a weak one as she stood and draped her wet shirt over a branch.

Fuck, yeah, the kidnapper would just dance the two-step over here and exchange the statue for Doug Fontaine. The likelihood of that outcome was as slim as the chance the two of them had a future together.

"You rest while I forage lean-to materials. While I'm at it, I'll check in with my boss."

Away from the clearing, he collected branches, vines, and palm fronds into piles, then turned on his phone. Battery was getting low but good for a while. This late Mara'd be off duty, so he hit Thomas Devlin's private cell number. The drone of nocturnal insects competed with the ring tone.

"About time," Thomas barked into the receiver. "Been trying to raise you for hours. Worried the river might've gotten you."

Max shuddered, picturing the watery grave. He'd rather die in battle. "Nearly did." He brought his boss up to date. "You were right. She's stronger than she looks."

Thomas chuckled. "So you've changed your mind about her."

"We've been through a lot together." Enough said. "Any news?"

"Zip from Del Rio. He's supposed to check in later. Since he's close, you have the go-ahead to connect with him. The other operative reports your downed chopper's been seen from the air. Troops went in."

"Must be the soldiers who came to the village."

"A good bet. Hired killer's name was Rufo Gonzalez. Word on him is good riddance. Spent time in prison for knifing a guy when he was in the army. But no one's saying who might've hired him. All our guy gets about him is shrugs. Except the man was seen with two other former grunts. One of them had a big scar on his cheek."

"Sounds like the same mopes who followed us. They probably offed our guide."

"The *policía* think so too. They're searching for the men, but these things take time."

"Which we don't have."

****

Near K'eq Xlapak

At first light, Max sensed Kate rousing behind him. Her restless movements during the night told him she'd gotten barely any sleep. Worked up about her brother and the kidnapper, and hell, Kizin's tremors and impending earthquake. So was he.

Today was *El Dia Maldito*.

He moved aside for her to scoot out. "Don't go far," he said, when she headed for the privacy of the jungle.

She shook her head. "Can you check in with Del Rio?" Worry roughened her voice.

"Can do. But if the call goes to voice mail, don't worry. He could be saving battery power."

She made no reply, only moved off, holding her shoulder stiff.

Damn, when she returned, he'd check her injury. They must have a medic at the restoration, antibiotics and shit. They ought to head there pronto. But she'd insist on waiting for word from Del Rio about her brother or contact with the kidnapper. He tried his colleague's number. Voice mail, dammit.

Too many fucking players. Soldiers, politicians, kidnappers, murderers. You never knew who'd pop out from behind the next agave.

Max wanted this over. But then he might never see her again. Never touch her again. Never— She was the best thing that ever happened to him. He could talk to her, couldn't he? What the hell was he afraid of? *Fuck.*

Surging to his feet, he stretched and turned his face up to the sun's broiling rays. After the bone-chilling cold below ground, he didn't mind a little sweat. And he needed to shake off the emotions crowding him. Jagged boulders ripping around in his chest. He needed to do something. Anything. He scattered the remaining coals in the small fire with a few hard kicks.

The canteens needed refilling, so he descended the rope ladder. Enough sunlight shone downward so he could see without a lamp, even the nooks and crannies in the limestone walls. But the river tunnel yawned dark and forbidding, the entrance to the Maya Underworld. He and Kate had nearly ended up in that watery Hell.

He knelt on the narrow lip where they'd stashed the canoe. When he finished with the canteens, a few splashes of water on his face revived him, settled him. Now he could talk to her. Face her. Function with calm.

Close enough to the top of the ladder, he swung the canteens onto the ground.

"Ah, there you are, Rivera. Do come up and join us, won't you?"

Alistair Sedgwick stood three feet away. A wormlike smirk curled the collector's lips. He aimed an automatic pistol at Max's head. ESquipped with a silencer.

A surge of adrenaline sent his pulse into warp speed. *Where are you, Kate?* Maybe she was hiding in the jungle.

He'd be no use to her unless he kept his head. He forced the tension from his body and put himself in combat mode. Nowhere to go but up. A given that Sedgwick would take his weapons. Patience and the element of surprise would have to suffice. He pushed up the last two rungs, levered to his feet.

Two men held Kate between them. One had long, greasy hair and a jagged scar on his left cheek.

The breath Max sucked in turned to ashes in his chest. He'd bet his entire paycheck for this gig these were the ex-army mutts the *policía* were hunting.

Scarface pointed a small pistol at Max. The other, the same man with a Fu-Manchu mustache who'd followed Kate and him more than once, covered her mouth with a grubby hand and held a pistol at her temple.

"Kate! You okay?"

Mustache yelped and jerked his hand away from her. "*¡Ay, la puta!* She bit me."

Struggling against the grips on her arms, Kate spat on the ground. "Your filthy hand probably poisoned me."

When Mustache raised his arm to strike her, Max took a step forward. Sedgwick pressed the silenced pistol against his neck.

"Leave the *mademoiselle* alone. I need her conscious and alert."

At the commanding voice from the shadows, Mustache instantly stepped aside. Scarface kept his pistol trained on her.

A man in jungle camo entered the clearing from behind the trees by the lean-to. Face of a bully, body of a linebacker.

Max recognized him from the picture Mara'd sent. "Le Noir, you *cabrone*, at last we meet."

Centaur's chief enforcer dipped his head briefly. "*Monsieur* Rivera, your reputation precedes you."

Chapter Twenty-Seven

In the jungle

DOUG'S LEG ITCHED like a mother where some crawling thing in the fetid mattress had chomped down. He couldn't scratch the damn place, not with his hands bound. The guards had repaired his cot twice after strong tremors. Another big shaker the same day Luis phoned Kate had done in the flimsy wood. After that the mattress—and Doug—stayed on the dirt floor. A guard had to lift him into the wheelchair. His only satisfaction.

Although the sun was up, he pretended to remain asleep. The demons pounding on his brain were on vacation. Gave him a chance to figure things out. Sure.

Where was Kate? She shouldn't try to save him. She couldn't turn Kizin over. Anyone knew how these things worked. He was his kidnapper's leverage with Kate, but in the end, he would die. She would die. Doug's heart pounded like a jackhammer, and frustration burned in his throat.

Luis would get big bucks for the statue—the big bucks Doug had dreamed of.

Now all he dreamed of was getting free. Kate had help. She must, a guide and somebody else looking for him. Maybe they traced that satellite call. An earthquake might bury Doug but being gutted like a Maya sacrifice wasn't in his plans. For now defiance was all he had, and the concealed fork.

The guard entered followed by the Maya woman. As soon as she deposited his breakfast tray on the table, she scooted out without looking back.

Doug yawned and stretched as if he'd just awakened. "Ah, Jeeves, is it time to break my fast already? What is it today, fruit cup, mimosa, French toast with maple syrup?"

Ignoring him, Al wheeled over the chair, which squeaked and groaned after days on rough ground. He set the brake, then bent and hauled his prisoner upward.

Doug sagged. The guard grunted, planted his legs, and gave one more heave. Another. When he plopped Doug onto the seat, the man stumbled back a step, panting as if he'd just run a couple miles. Or dragged a two-hundred-pound man upward. Which he had. A two-hundred-pound man imitating a sack of sand.

Hope you get a hernia, Al ol' buddy.

As soon as Al untied his hands, Doug propped his broken leg on the foot rest. He started to roll forward but the wheelchair remained in place. No rocks in the way. No flat tire. The brake was stuck. Damn chair was falling apart like the cot.

He pointed at the brake lever. "Outta gas, fuckwad."

When Al knelt, Doug caught a movement outside the hut's tiny window.

A bearded man looked back at him through the opening. He put a finger to his mouth before ducking out of sight.

Doug's lungs seized up.

****

Near K'eq Xlapak

"I t-tried to warn you." Kate clenched her jaw against the trembling in her voice, in her entire body.

Rubbing her injured shoulder, aching from the rough treatment, she started toward Max.

"Stop right there, Ms. Fontaine." Sedgwick jabbed the pistol harder into Max's neck.

She froze in place, locking her gaze with Max's. The hard look in his eyes meant he was focused, in that zone he talked about. His head dipped in a small nod, and she lowered her lashes in reply. Bolstered, she drew in deep breaths. He would figure out something, and she had to be ready.

Sedgwick backed away from Max. His gloved hand brushed a dead leaf from his shoulder. He wore designer safari gear—a khaki shirt with epaulets, no less—and polished boots. All he needed was an ascot, the son of a bitch.

Le Noir walked farther into the clearing and stopped ahead of Sedgwick.

The collector scowled and clenched his free hand at his side but made no objection.

Kate shivered. She'd bet people rarely crossed this Frenchman with his deadly calm voice and eyes as flat and opaque as black ice. The pumped-up biceps stretching his sleeves must make bringing a fork to his mouth difficult.

Le Noir said to Max, "Take your pistol from the holster, *s'il vous plaît*."

Max's gaze held Le Noir's for a beat before he withdrew the big Glock with a two-finger grip.

"Now toss it into the *cenote*."

"That's a bottomless well."

Le Noir smiled but his eyes held no humor. His shoulders lifted in a very Gallic shrug. "The pistol."

Max slid the gun to the *cenote*'s rim, then over.

Kate crossed mental fingers it would land on the narrow ledge or in the canoe. A muffled splash was the answer. She sagged.

Edging in front of Le Noir, Sedgwick waved the gun barrel at the knife sheath on Max's belt. "Now the blade."

The knife went into the water with a small plop.

The Frenchman directed Max to sit off to the side, hands in front of him. Farther away, but maybe that was an advantage. They didn't seem inclined to search him. He lowered himself onto a boulder, hiked up his knees, and linked his hands around them, just above the holster on his ankle. Rufo'd noticed the bulge but these men hadn't. Max's back-up weapon was their only hope.

His position was farther to the left, about ten feet from Sedgwick and Le Noir. She'd stopped about that distance from the hired thugs, who remained near the lean-to. The mustachioed thug kept his gun on her, and the other one trained his on Max. Two guns aimed at him, but from there he probably could see all the players. All their moves.

Maybe he could spot an opening but she saw only one possibility—the obvious tug-of-war between Le Noir and Sedgwick. Centaur's thumb sat on the collector's neck, and the scary bulked-up thug exerted the pressure. Sedgwick must resent him but how much did he fear him?

Max's gaze flicked between the two. A twitch in the corner of his mouth suggested he'd noticed the tension. But how to use this falling out of thieves? What if there wasn't time to hit on a plan? What if the kidnapper chose now to enter the clearing? Or one of the Maya villagers?

Her pulse raced. Or— No, she had to stop the worst-case-scenario thinking.

Stepping around the Frenchman, Sedgwick turned to Kate. He kept his gun on Max. "You've caused me a great deal of trouble, Ms. Fontaine. The statue's not in your rucksack or anywhere in your pitiful campsite. Where is it?"

"How did you find us, Sedgwick?" Max asked in a conversational tone. "Dumb luck?"

Le Noir snorted a laugh.

"Certainly not," Sedgwick said. "I—that is, we—arrived two days ago via the limestone trail. Deplorable conditions but one manages. My lads have been monitoring all the approaches to the restoration. I judged it prudent to wait for daylight."

His gaze once again slid to Kate. "The statue."

Her insides churned like a blender, and she clenched her fists. She'd known this demand would come, and she'd made a decision. She wouldn't let them have Kizin. She couldn't. If Del Rio couldn't rescue Doug, she'd need the statue as ransom.

Somehow the thought of not delivering Kizin to his temple, of not keeping that promise didn't bother her as much as before. She was stronger now, capable. Max was right. Dad would be proud of what she'd achieved.

"You're too late." She crossed her arms and hiked out one hip. "The statue's gone."

"I don't believe you, my dear. You arrived only last night. You couldn't possibly have delivered your package to the priest or to whoever has your brother."

"Not what she meant. Statue's lost, down there." Max nodded toward the hole to his left. "Overboard into the drink with the other backpack and the tent. Bottomless, remember?"

308

Thank God, Max had read her intent. She held her breath.

"This is no time to converse politely over teacups, *Monsieur* Sedgwick. I shall 'andle this." Le Noir moved to the other man's left. His fingers, slender for a man with such thick forearms, flexed at his sides.

Max's right hand hovered near his ankle holster and his booted feet were planted.

Her knees felt so liquid she could barely stay on her feet. How could Max make a move? The two pistols on him held steady. Despite the heat and humidity, ice slid down her spine.

Sedgwick held out a hand toward Le Noir in a placating gesture. "Your employer will receive the statue of—the jade statue, but this is my expedition, my negotiation."

"Pah. You bungle this time as you did before. You buy the statue, then you sell it, then you lose it."

Sweat dripped from Sedgwick's chin. His gaze shifted between his adversary and Max. "I was merely maneuvering for the best deal."

"And your visit to Chastain?"

Sedgwick's eyes widened. His already ruddy complexion went crimson. "You know nothing."

"*Non?* I wonder why else you would contact a forger who specializes in figurines." Le Noir's teeth gleamed white against his swarthy complexion. "More maneuvering? Or deception? Or is betrayal more precise a word?"

Riveted by the confrontation, Kate offered a silent plea this confrontation would give Max an opening.

The glare from beneath Sedgwick's amber brows seared the air. The pistol's barrel swung toward the powerfully built thug. "Certainly not. I'll—"

Le Noir snatched away the pistol as he smashed his right boot heel into Sedgwick's knee. The Brit staggered backward. The big Frenchman lunged toward him. Sunlight flashed off the metal object in his hand. A knife. One stroke at Sedgwick's exposed throat cut off his howl of pain. Only a choking gasp came from his mouth as his body toppled backward to the rocky earth.

Frozen in place, a scream trapped inside, Kate clutched her throat.

Behind her, the paid crooks jabbered unintelligibly.

Adrenaline jolted Max to his feet. Everyone else seemed set in stone—Le Noir included—unable to look away from the bleeding man.

A crimson stream gushed from the wound. It soaked the khaki shirt and flowed onto the hard soil, staining the air with a metallic stench. Abruptly the flow weakened, and life drained away from pale, unseeing eyes.

Max surged forward.

Le Noir fired the pistol. *Pfft.*

The silenced bullet struck Max. A thousand fire ants stung his left arm. He groaned and rolled to his side.

Kate staggered to her feet. "No!" Tears clogged her voice. She started toward him.

"Do not move!" Le Noir fired two shots into the ground in front of her. Rock bits spewed upward like shrapnel.

She shrieked and stumbled to a stop, holding up her hands in defense the same way Sedgwick had in his vault. Tears streamed down her beautiful face. "Max?"

Setting his jaw against the pain in his upper arm, he scooted back against the boulder. He plucked his sleeve away from the wound. He'd been shot before. This one wasn't that bad. A deep gouge. Only skin. Not muscle or bone. The bastard only grazed him. On purpose?

The Sig held fifteen to twenty rounds, depending on the magazine, so the gun had plenty more for target practice.

"I'm okay, *querida.*" *Damn, shouldn't call her that. Don't give the Frog more ammo.* "Like in the old Westerns, it's just a flesh wound." Hurt like hell but he would ignore it. Cold focus would get him—them— through. He kept his eyes on Le Noir while, one-handed, he tied his bandana around the bleeding gash.

He ached to go to Kate, to scoop her up and run into the bush, away from this madness. Every muscle in his body tightened against the urge. Black bile churned in his gut. He dug his fingers into the dirt. Hell and high water, for the moment he could do nothing.

The local mutts were dangerous but not bright. Cut off a snake's head and the body flopped around, useless. He had to get his 9mm.

Le Noir sidled past Sedgwick's body. He wiped blood from the knife blade on a clump of weeds, but kept it out, ready. He moved to where he could see everybody, including Sedgwick's hired hands. Not that they'd be loyal now this man had cut off their paycheck. Literally.

"You monster!" Kate mopped her eyes. "You didn't have to kill him."

"But I did," he said. "My employer detests treachery even more than incompetence. *Enfin,* I no long have need of him now he has brought me to you."

Cool and calm, this creep. Martial arts and smooth manners. Probably an expert marksman too. The knife was a switchblade, easily concealed in a pocket, the reason Max hadn't spotted it, but fuck, he should've suspected, knowing Le Noir's reputation for liking blades. This one was an H & K, a deadly dagger in close combat but not a good throwing weapon.

Looked like the murder hadn't been impulsive but a premeditated act. Only the timing was hasty, precipitated by Sedgwick's challenge. Once Le Noir possessed Kizin, he would eliminate Kate and Max.

The silencer. Nobody at the temple site would hear. The bodies would disappear in the depths of the *cenote*. No witnesses.

Not if Max could prevent it.

Le Noir scowled, his black eyes watchful. "The statue, if you please. I should like to be on my way to Cabo Blanco."

"It's over, Kate. Give it to him." Maybe when Le Noir saw the statue, he'd let down his guard.

Her over-bright gaze stared at the fucking Centaur thug. She must know he'd shoot them. For a jade-and-gold statue that meant redemption to her and hope to the Maya. Only another possession to the killer's boss. She hadn't let panic disable her. He could see the steel within her firming as her mind wrapped itself around the choices. Saw decision in the tightening of her mouth.

"I'll get the statue." Swiping away the rest of her tears with one hand, she plodded to the *cenote*'s edge. "It's hidden down there."

Le Noir stalked forward two paces but stopped well away from the sheer rim. "If you try anything, he dies."

Without a word, she climbed down. The only sound was the echo of her hiking boots on the ledge below. Max pictured her reaching into the eroded recess where they'd stashed the camera bag.

Le Noir's watchful eyes remained on him.

Max stared back.

A scant two minutes later, she reappeared at the top, the bag slung over her shoulder. She knelt and opened it. First the Nikon came out, then the bubble-sealed package. When she unwrapped it, sunlight glinted off the emerald eyes and the gold skeleton shape in the jade.

She held up the statue. "Everyone in Costa Verde is looking for this figure of Kizin. You'll never get out of the country with their legendary earthquake god."

One of the local mutts pointed at Kizin and whispered to the other. The second man crossed himself. Accepted religion didn't preclude belief in the old Maya gods. Or in curses. They were fucking afraid. Le Noir didn't need Sedgwick but he did need these two, to lead him out of this wilderness.

If they believed... Apparently Kate had suspected the possibility. Her gaze veered from the frightened men to Max. He nodded.

"Yes, yes." Le Noir hissed. Eager to get out of here. Afraid of the earthquake or something else? "If you smuggled it into the country, I can smuggle it out. Bring Kizin to me."

Max gave a barely perceptible shake of his head.

She lowered the statue. "If you want Kizin, come take him."

"Enough of these games. Gomez, take the statue from her," Le Noir ordered one of the men. "Bring it to me."

"No, señor," Gomez, the man Max had called Scarface, crossed himself again for good measure. His eyes were wild. "Is no good, *señor*. Kizin *muy* bad."

"Do not be idiots. It is only a statue." The killer sneered as he waved Gomez forward.

"Le Noir can't take it from you, Kate," Max said, leveling a confident gaze at the other man. "The big, bad Centaur enforcer with the gun is afraid of heights. He won't go near the *cenote*'s edge. Do you get vertigo, Le Noir? Maybe freeze?"

The other man's lips thinned. Color rose in his cheeks. His gun hand wavered. A second later, calm dropped over him like a blanket. "Bring it to me or I promise more bullets, aimed more precisely. First in Rivera's extremities. Then I shall work my way inward. Methodical but effective. And painful."

Her throat worked as she swallowed. "If you shoot him, I drop it."

Chapter Twenty-Eight

MAX STIFFENED. HAD he heard her right?

The gunman's wide gaze bounced between the two of them. He was rattled. Good.

Lips pressed tightly together, Kate scooted closer to the rim. She held the statue out over the water. Kizin's emerald eyes stared up at the sky.

Le Noir took a step toward her but faltered. "What are you doing? Bring it here now or Rivera loses a kneecap."

"Shoot Max and I let go."

Max's insides cartwheeled. She would do that for him? Give up the quest that obsessed her? He swallowed his question. "You don't have to do that, Kate."

"*Merde, c'est de la foutaise.* You cannot do that." Sweat dripped from Le Noir's chin, spread from his armpits to stain the camo. "You *will not*."

"Put down your gun. Kick it over to Max. Or the statue's gone."

He sneered, his mouth twisting. "You were so dedicated to returning it to the temple, to saving your *bête* of a brother. What about the earthquake?"

"Whether you take Kizin or I drop it in the *cenote*, I can't fulfill my promises. Either way Doug dies. Max and I die. You can't escape. You can't outrun the earthquake. Or the curse. Kizin will have his revenge."

Gomez and Mustache clutched each other, fear stark

on their faces.

"All nonsense. You will not dare to drop it."

"Try me." Her glare should've turned him to stone. Her chin was firm.

Max had never seen anybody more brave or beautiful in his life. "If you don't return to Cabo Blanco with Kizin," he said, "I'm betting Centaur won't let you off easy. What was that about incompetence?"

Le Noir's jaw went slack. The gun lowered a fraction then rose again. His black eyes glittered. "Kizin belongs to Centaur. Bring it to me."

Not deterred, Kate held the statue farther over the void. "This is the official *cenote* for K'eq Xlapak. The ancient priests sacrificed goats and tossed them in this very well. When offerings on the altars, like this statue of Kizin, had served their purpose, the priests smashed them and dropped them in.

"The pool below and the river make up a labyrinth of passages too deep and treacherous for divers. No artifacts have ever been brought to the surface. If I drop Kizin, he's gone forever. And with him, all hope of ending the earthquake curse. You'll never make it out of the jungle."

Spoken like the expert she was. She was magnificent. Max bit his lower lip.

Terror filled the eyes of Gomez and his pal. Their mouths gaped. As one they turned and fled into the vegetation. Palm fronds clattered as they disappeared.

"*Non! Non!* Fools. Come back!" The Frenchman's bellows went unanswered.

Max sprang.

Before Le Noir could turn, Max kicked the Sig from his hand. The pistol skittered across the hard ground, landing out of reach.

Le Noir tossed the switchblade from his left hand to his right and eyed Max like he was choosing his targets. Sweat and the rank odor of living rough poured off the man.

"I hear you like to play with your victims, Frenchie, 'til they bleed to death. Bet you never faced somebody who really knows how to fight." Max beckoned, stretched his lips into a smile. Probably looked like more of a grimace. His wound hurt like a son of a bitch.

Holding the knife in a hammer grip, Le Noir lunged. Max parried the strike with his injured arm. Pain lanced through him. He snapped a side kick into the other man's chin that felled him like a lightning-struck oak. But not enough to loose Le Noir's grip on the knife. He swung the blade at Max's gut, at the same time kicking his ankle. Max fell on his wound and grunted in agony.

The thug struck again with the blade, but Max grabbed his wrist with his good hand and held on in spite of the fire in his other arm. Blood dripped from beneath the soaked bandana. If only he could reach his damn ankle holster.

Sweat and dust covered both men as they traded blows and strained for the knife. Hard to tell who was stronger but Le Noir had the blade and two good arms. Max's punches barely dented the man's skin. How long could he hold out with no weapon?

In his peripheral vision, he saw Kate still kneeling by the *cenote*'s edge. "Get out of here, Kate. Run!" he grunted. "You can make it to the temple."

"No! I won't leave you." She scrambled around, maybe looking for a weapon.

Their arm-wrestling duel was going more and more

Le Noir's way as Max's strength drained away with every drop of blood. Fuck, the French fireplug was using his legs to push their battle inch by inch closer to the pistol. He was bull strong but too bulked-up to be agile in a fight. He seemed to be focused on holding on until he could reach the Sig.

Max scraped up earth with his left hand and flung dirt and gravel at Le Noir's eyes. He drew up a knee and whacked the man in the groin. Finally a blow that fucking distracted him. Torque in the knife arm eased a fraction. Max sucked in air and slammed Le Noir's hand to the ground. The knife clattered free, and Max pushed up and kicked it far away.

A massive punch rocked his bloody arm. Pain like flaming daggers tore through him and he couldn't breathe. He dropped to his side.

A freight-train rumble surrounded them. The ground shook, making footing insecure and trees sway. Dust clouds swirled into Max's eyes and nose. High above, monkeys shrieked in terror.

Shit. Another tremor or was the damn curse real?

Le Noir scrambled to his feet and scooped up the pistol. He stumbled over the trembling earth toward Kate. Leaves and twigs shaken from the trees littered his path. "Bring me the statue."

"No!" She backed closer to the *cenote*. "I'll never let you have it."

Heart pounding like it could break through his ribs, Max staggered erect. His arm hurt like ten rattlers had latched on. Blood ran down his arm. He had to stop Le Noir. Couldn't let him hurt Kate.

Gritting his teeth, he pulled out the 9mm and flicked off the safety. Would it fire after getting wet?

The ground wobbled and bounced beneath him, but he planted his feet and raised the weapon. He stood off to the side, not the best position, but the Frenchman's thick body made a wide target. If he waited, ordered the man to drop his weapon, he might not get another chance.

Le Noir raised the pistol toward Kate. *Fwip.*

Kate cried out and crumpled to the ground. The statue fell from her limp fingers into the *cenote.*

"Kate!"

"*Non! Non!* It cannot be gone." Le Noir turned the silenced pistol on Max.

The crack of Max's shot reverberated around the clearing. The round struck Le Noir in his side. Blood bloomed on his shirt.

He dropped to his knees. Aimed the pistol at Kate.

Max discharged the pistol again and again until the big man fell face down and didn't move. Beneath the sun, now high overhead, the acrid smell of gun smoke mingled with the meaty scent of blood.

Kate didn't answer. She didn't move.

Rage vibrated through every cell in his body. His heart thumped wildly.

She moaned.

Gracias a Dios, she was alive. He trudged toward her.

Writhing in pain, she clutched at her left thigh where blood was spreading.

"Max." His name was barely a whisper but rang in his ears like "The Hallelujah Chorus." She gripped his arm weakly. "Le Noir, is he—"

"He won't be doing any more enforcing." He ripped the cloth to look at her wound.

"How bad is it?"

"We're in that same old Western, darlin'. Just a flesh wound." Hers went deeper, into muscle, but telling her would scare her more than she already was. The bullet had gone all the way through. Tore up that tender flesh on exit.

He yanked off his shirt and tied it around her leg. "Keep pressure where you can. I'll get the medical kit."

The spasms in Kate's thigh came in waves, chewing a path to her brain, and she breathed deeply to swallow down nausea. She kept her hand where she could reach, but blood was already soaking the makeshift tourniquet.

Oh, God, worse than the pain was her utter failure—in everything she'd set out to do. Her eyes stung, and she could barely swallow past the tightness in her throat. Kizin was lost forever. And Doug, she could lose him. Still no call from the DSF agent. If he failed, she had no way to ransom her brother. Once she'd obtained the statue, she should've allowed Devlin Security to handle the rest. Without the drag of her incompetence.

But then she wouldn't have known Max.

He'd brought her almost to K'eq Xlapak. He'd kept his commitment and gotten shot in the process. He was braver and more honorable than she deserved. A wave of pain swept her, inside and out.

****

In the jungle

Had to be really bad when Doug didn't wince at Al's fetid breath as the guard rolled him back into the hut. On the trip to and from the latrine, no sign of the bearded guy. Dammit, that would've been the perfect time.

This better be a rescue. If he didn't have a bum leg and wasn't weak as a baby, he could take Al, but not that

GI Joe. Not knowing if the guy was on his side was eating him as bad as the bedbugs. He sagged against the seat back. So why in hell was GI guy here? And where'd he go?

The guard squatted down and folded the footrests.

Shit, why couldn't he just sit in the fucking chair? Horizontal was good for sleep and sex, but for now he'd rather be vertical. "Hey, Al, give your back a break. Let me sit here?' He shifted in the sagging seat.

Something clanked against the wheel.

Al lifted the fallen object from the dirt floor.

Doug's heart thumped. *Shit. The fork. The damn fork.*

He knew no Mayan but recognized angry cursing when he heard it, probably something like *"What the fuck is this?"* The fork went winging across the room. A back-handed blow knocked his head to the side. Rang up that headache that had finally subsided. He lowered his head and concentrated on breathing.

Before he could do anything but recover, footfalls crunched at the doorway.

The bearded guy swung in, bent in a crouch Doug had seen a thousand times in war movies. He carried a honkin' big semi-automatic. *Holy shit.*

The guard pulled a pistol from somewhere. Aimed it at GI Joe, who ducked back behind the door frame.

With all his strength, Doug rolled the wheelchair forward, rammed it into Al.

The guard jerked, yelled, but his forefinger tightened on the trigger.

Dammit, if only Doug had the fork. With both hands, he hoisted up his leg, weighted with the cast. He swung for the bleachers with all his strengths.

The leg cast whacked the back of Al's knees. He yelled. His gun went off. Doug, the wheelchair, and Al crashed to the ground. The bullet blasted through the thatched roof. Brown shreds of palm fronds rained down.

The GI guy jumped the guard and decked him with one meaty fist to the chin.

A gleaming white smile greeted Doug from the depths of the dark beard. "Nice save. You must be Doug Fontaine."

"Maybe. Who the hell are you?"

****

Near K'eq Xlapak

Max gathered the med equipment where the thugs had dumped them. He cleaned the bullet holes and applied wound sealant. After binding her thigh with gauze and tape, he carried her to the lean-to. Ibuprofen would take the edge off her pain until he could get her to K'eq Xlapak. "I'll phone your archeologist buddy. Get him to send a litter. A medic if they have one."

"No, first call Del Rio. Doug," she gritted out, her breath shallow. She pushed up onto her elbows as he punched the number.

The anguish in her eyes stabbed more pain into him than his arm scrape. May be some way to salvage this cluster fuck as long as Del Rio could rescue Doug. *Dios*, he hoped he could give her good news.

A familiar voice answered the call. "Hey, Texas, you calling me for help already?"

Tension drained from his shoulders and jaw as if siphoned away. "Del Rio, you bum. We had some issues here but nothing I couldn't handle solo. Situation report."

"Fontaine seems okay except his cast just got busted. I got some mopping up to do here first, and then

I'll take him to that temple restoration place."

When Max gave Kate a thumbs-up, she sank down, eyes closed. Tears streamed from beneath her lashes and her lips formed the words *thank you*.

He swiped at his eyes. Must be grit left over from the tremor. He listened as his buddy rattled off the rest of his situation report.

"Two guards, according to Fontaine. One outside jumped me, got his neck snapped for his trouble. The other was inside this hut with his prisoner. Had a pistol, but Fontaine helped deck him. How he broke the cast." Max could hear the smile in his buddy's voice. "Guard number two is trussed up and gagged. Have to hang out here awhile. Waiting for—"

In the receiver, Max heard yelling and a clunk as the phone dropped.

"What's happening?" Kate asked.

"Dunno. Hold on." He listened. A scraping sound. A grunt. Then a new voice.

"This Max Rivera?"

"Roger. What's going on? Who's this?" Except he knew damned well who it was. He sounded winded but strong, as if he just kicked butt. Which he did, according to Del Rio.

"Doug Fontaine here. My fucking kidnapper arrived for his daily visit when your guy was talking to you. He tied up Luis with some of those zip ties."

"You *know* who he is?"

"Hell of a thing. Don Luis, chief priest at K'eq Xlapak. My sister, she all right?"

Max smiled. "She's had a rough time but she wants to talk to you."

Kate's hands shook but she barely felt the pain in

her leg as she reached for the phone. "Doug?"

"Hey, Katie, don't cry. I'm okay. Hell, not totally, but I will be."

"I'm so sorry you had to go through this." Her voice caught on a sob. "If only—"

"*You're* sorry? I'm the one who fucked up, but good."

That much was true, but she couldn't help laughing. "Let it go for now. I'll get you home and we can argue later about whose fault this mess was."

She smiled at Max, but he wasn't looking at her. He sat nearby wrapping his arm with gauze. Cuts from flying rock splinters dotted the left side of his handsome face. The bullet gouge in his arm was raw and red. He'd only winced at the antiseptic, but she'd squealed like a monkey. No amount of thanks would be enough. Her chest ached as if the bullet had struck her there.

She looked away when she heard Doug's voice.

"About going home. It's like this. Your buddy's ordering up a chopper to take me out of K'eq Xlapak. Then the FBI wants to talk to me. Questions about black market deals with Centaur. A guy doesn't say no to the Feds, right?"

The bottom dropped out of her stomach. "The FBI?" She shot a glance at Max. Mouth tight, warrior face on, he stared straight ahead, not at her. Pain raked her, grinding like serrated knives into her wounded thigh and radiating through her body. Did she hear her brother correctly, or was the pain dulling her mind?

"Katie, you okay?"

She gritted her teeth against a groan. "But your buys were legitimate, with documented provenance. Tell this Del Rio you don't know anything about the black market or this Centaur."

Throat-clearing noises came through the receiver. "I wish I could do that, Katie, but I can't. I have to answer their questions."

"But, Doug, this makes no sense."

"I've done some things I'm not proud of. No time to explain now. Del Rio needs to call the professor at the restoration to send us some help. Hey, cool we're both not far from there. Bye." His strained tone belied his flippant words.

After the phone went dead, she stared at nothing. Dizziness rocked her. A lungful of air wasn't enough to clear her head of the ugly truth. In spite of the heat, she felt encased in ice, numb. Even though Doug was safe now, it was her fault he'd been injured to begin with. She'd blinded herself to his dealings, let him become involved with criminals. She hadn't kept her promises to her dad, either of them. She'd even screwed up by falling for Max, an adventurer she shouldn't have trusted from the outset.

Mom was right. She wasn't tough or brave or capable. She would return to the museum and stay there. Put Max out of her head and her heart, or the memories would crush her like an earthquake.

She levered herself to a sitting position. The throbbing in her leg was a mosquito bite compared to what she had to do now.

Chapter Twenty-Nine

MAX HAD KNOWN this moment would come, but maybe now that Kate knew what her brother had done, she'd understand.

The anguish in her eyes said he was wrong. His heart sputtered and knocked like a dying engine.

"You lied to me, Max. You never mentioned the FBI, only suspicion by DSF."

"The FBI was part of the plan all along." No reason not to 'fess up. Might as well dive off the cliff and end it all. "Interpol too. The reason I had to ask you about what Doug bought and sold."

"The bronze helmet and the Nike amphora. Were they… illegal?"

"Stolen from a small museum in Athens, along with a gold bracelet I saw in Sedgwick's safe. Scotland Yard found the other two in a raid on a Centaur guy."

"You knew they were illegal but you said nothing. If you'd told me, I'd have understood."

He hadn't reckoned she would, one reason he didn't explain after Mara found out the rest. And he didn't want to hurt her. Shit, she was hurting now, probably worse. A lie of omission was still a lie. He'd made a fucking mess of it. No excuses. He shook his head, kept his sorry yap shut.

Pain crimped her forehead and tightened her mouth. "I paid Devlin Security Force for protection, but they used me, *you* used me to find dirt on my brother. Thomas will hear about this." She picked up her phone. "I'll call for that litter. When the helicopter arrives, I'll leave with Doug. You and I have no more to say to each other."

Her tears had dried, but the raw pain and accusation in her eyes struck hard and deep, spearing between his ribs. He could barely breathe.

He'd fucked up bad. He'd betrayed her trust. Look what happened when you got involved. Kate was leaving him, like *she* did. He must've deserved it then and he sure as hell deserved it now.

****

In the jungle

Fucked up was right. How could he ever explain all he'd done to his sister? Hell, how could he even face her? Telling the K'eq Xlapak Maya their chief Jaguar priest had kidnapped him would be no picnic either. *Suck it up, Fontaine.*

After his excruciating conversation with Kate, Del Rio had called the restoration. The professor knew nothing about Doug's kidnapping, so Del Rio told him the basics. Then he'd wheeled Doug from the hut and marched out the two kidnappers, pushing them down to sit against the hut wall.

"You okay? Is it your leg?" Del Rio said.

Doug's pain wasn't in his leg. Or in his head this time. Rubbing his chest, he lifted his face to the sun and inhaled the clean air. Ah, green plant smells, not dirt laced with smoke from cooking fires.

"A little achy. No big deal. Those fuckers probably hurt worse." Dried blood stained the priest's split lip and Al's eye had swelled shut. Damned right.

Voices approached from a shaded trail. Several men,

some with hunting rifles, one carrying a stretcher, entered the clearing.

"Me llamo Héctor," a wiry man in khaki pants said. His eyes widened as he caught sight of the prisoners.

Del Rio and he shook hands and rattled on in Spanish too fast for Doug to follow. When they finished, Héctor walked over to Luis and shouted at him, then at the guard. Neither man had said fuck all since Del Rio kicked their asses. They said nada now. Only stared straight ahead.

Doug hitched around in the wheelchair and beckoned to Del Rio. "Care to translate?"

The other man cocked his head. His big fingers probed his thicket of a beard and scratched. "Most of it was my explanation and his shock. Main thing—your kidnapper's not the chief Jaguar Priest. Real name's Jago, assistant to Don Luis."

****

K'eq Xlapak

Max trudged behind the stretcher as the little procession entered the archeological encampment. Kate needed more medical care than his field kit could supply. Once he saw to that, he had to know why the priest wanted the Kizin statue as ransom when Kate was bringing it to him anyway.

Men had arrived at the *cenote* clearing with a stretcher. An older woman carrying a medical kit introduced herself as Dr. Pilar Morales. She pronounced Max's first aid as satisfactory and organized the men to lift Kate onto the stretcher. A ten-minute walk had taken them along a trail to K'eq Xlapak, and the midday sun's heat. Professor Morales met them at the temple and accompanied them here.

People clustered around them, talking in Spanish and Mayan, making sympathetic noises. More than one spoke the name Fontaine. Shit, they probably thought she'd brought Kizin.

For days Max had anticipated viewing the ruins, but now all he saw was Kate, gravely injured, barely conscious. If it was possible, he'd absorb all her pain.

"Rivera, hold up."

Shaking himself to awareness, he turned toward the voice. A larger group than theirs emerged from the jungle, led by Lucas Del Rio carrying a wheelchair. A few Maya men holding rifles held onto two men whose wrists were tied. And a few others carried a stretcher bearing a tall blond man—Doug Fontaine.

Max sketched his friend a salute.

"Kate, I see Del Rio and your brother." When she raised her head and started to speak, he put a hand on her shoulder. Had to touch her one last time. "I'll bring Doug soon. Hold on and let the doc take care of you." Dragging away his hand, he closed his fingers on his palm.

He turned to Dr. Morales. "I need to go talk to my colleague."

"But your arm!" She held up a hand to stop the parade and made clucking noises. "You need proper bandaging."

As a man rushed forward, Max tensed, hand on his side holster. Smiling, the man bowed and pressed his hands together in the Maya gesture of thanks. *Arturo*, Constantino's brother. Thank God he made it to safety. Max shook his hand and sent him to Kate's side.

"Doc, I'll catch up with you later." He peeled off and jogged toward the other group.

"Lucas, those bums look like you dragged 'em

through the jungle." He shook his friend's hand.

"Not me, but their buddies here didn't take it well when they heard what they'd done."

Max turned to Doug Fontaine, who was settling into the wheelchair.

"Might've done them some good." Doug grinned and pumped his hand. "Thanks for protecting my sister."

"No thanks necessary. My fault she got hurt. Some of the time she protected me." The less Kate's brother knew the better.

"Can't wait to hear about that." Doug jerked a nod toward the two prisoners. "Can't wait for their story either. So far they're not talking."

****

Kate adjusted the aluminum crutches beneath her arms. She'd slept away the afternoon on a cot and was still wonky. The pain in her thigh hammered at her, but she'd refused anything but ibuprofen until she could explain the loss of Kizin. And apologize. Not much but all she could offer.

And she had to see Doug. They'd had a few moments of hugs and tears—her tears—and he told her the kidnapper wasn't the actual chief priest but a usurper, who'd planned to enter K'eq Xlapak with Kizin and declare a miracle. "The creep figured they'd anoint him the new Jaguar Priest," Doug sneered. A medical assistant had interrupted and whisked him away to change his cast.

Kate needed to know more, especially how he'd gotten involved with Centaur. Was there more bad news? Why hadn't she pressed Max for the facts after he quizzed her? Her eyes stung and she ached for her brother. No, no more tears. *But why, Doug...*

330

Shaking herself to alertness, she took a few steps along the wall of the medical building, a basic structure with screened walls and a thatched roof. "Thank you for everything, including braiding my hair and the shorts and T-shirt." Blood and grime and tears had ruined what she'd been wearing, and rather than search for the backpack, the doctor had shared. At least she had her yellow cap.

"Good thing we're about the same size." Dr. Pilar chuckled, and laugh lines crinkled her dark eyes. "I've had lots of practice braiding hair." She flipped her own French braid, a glossy red softened by gray strands.

"My brother, where is he?"

"Oh, *sí*. I should have told you. He and my husband are at the temple plaza. Some villagers are outside to help you there. I'll come along shortly."

Good. She wanted to see the temple, maybe more of the restoration, and then leave this place behind. Along with her memories. As if that were possible. "I'll be okay." Her progress would be slow but she could make it as long as another tremor like the one this morning didn't hit.

Outside, she squinted in the sun and inhaled the baked-dust scent of the open air.

Nearby ranged other semi-permanent buildings for the project's work and rows of tents for the project personnel. No one seemed to be around except for those waiting for her.

Max stood to one side, a clean bandage on his wounded biceps. Pilar had stitched his wound, then administered a tetanus shot and antibiotics to both. To the doctor he'd said, "Only a flesh wound. No big deal."

He hadn't spoken to Kate since those few words

when they arrived at the compound. She could hardly blame him. He wore his warrior face now. Back in professional mode, her protector but only as employee. She bit back the pain that threatened to blow her composure and turned to the two Maya men who waited, ball caps in hand.

One of them was Arturo. He nodded and smiled.

When he'd greeted her, pain roughened her voice but she managed a few words of sympathy for Constantino's death. "Someday… please forgive me."

Esteban translated between Arturo and her.

"No, no, *señorita*," Arturo said, walking alongside the stretcher. "The blame goes to the bad men. My brother should not have gone to the cantina with them."

Esteban explained that late that night Arturo had gone looking for Constantino and found him dead. He was terrified and thought only of running away. He was packing up when the same men tried to jump him, but he fled into the jungle and raced home.

"Hand me your crutches," Max said. "Your brother has the only wheel chair but Arturo and Marco will take you to the temple plaza."

The two stocky men stepped forward with a folding camp chair. Arturo bowed as she eased onto the canvas seat.

Chapter Thirty

THE TWO MEN carried her, Max trailing in their wake, past scattered stone blocks and excavations in the rocky ground. If Kate could muster even a dollop of good humor, she'd joke about traveling in a sedan chair like Cleopatra. Under other circumstances, she'd expect Max to laugh.

She couldn't catch sight of much but clumps of trees, but finally the view opened up at the plaza. Her great-grandfather had found it only as a mound of earth with trees growing from the top. The project still had to tackle untouched buildings that could yield information about the ancient Maya. But now the steps forming the temple shape stood out in stark relief in the growing afternoon shadows. *Stelae* with reliefs and inscriptions lined the entrance. She'd seen Esteban's photographs but nothing could compare to the actual temple pyramid.

Her breath caught. Incredible.

Work had moved quickly so that on Curse Day, the Jaguar Priest could place the figure of Kizin inside. And stop the curse. Now there'd be no ceremony. And the curse? Who knew?

Then why were so many people at the temple? A throng of villagers and project staff. Foolish of her to think she could arrive unnoticed with or without the statue.

Where was her brother? She searched the crowd.

Maya women wearing flower-embroidered dresses and blossoms in their hair. Men in collared shirts and dark trousers. The restoration team in clean shorts, not work clothes smeared with limestone dust and dirt.

Expectation brightened some faces, but not all. A woman made the sign of the cross. A man planted his feet apart, bracing himself. A young mother clutched her bare-bottomed infant so tightly it began to wail. Other furrowed brows and surreptitious glances toward Kate betrayed the crowd's fear the earthquake would ravage them and their country at any moment.

Professor Esteban Morales and another man stood before the temple entrance. A slanting sunbeam caught on Doug's blond hair. He grinned and pointed to the new gray plastic cast covering his leg. He looked pale and drawn but otherwise fine. He'd need strength to face interrogation, and more. As she reached him, she struggled to breathe past the giant boulder in her chest. They managed to embrace with their chairs side by side, and she finally could inhale deeply.

Behind him stood a bearded man, every bit as military and muscular as Max, in jungle camouflage. Lucas Del Rio, the man who'd rescued her brother. She thanked him for saving her brother's life.

"Ma'am, it was a pleasure. Your brother and I made a good team." The DSF operative looked as ferocious as a bear but a beautiful smile gleamed in the midst of his dark beard.

She couldn't speak, for the emotion constricting her throat and binding her chest. All she could do was hold Doug's hand.

"Del Rio here said that bastard Sedgwick was responsible for my tumble off the balcony. I can't imagine you doing all the stuff Rivera tells me went on in the jungle. You... hell, you *crushed* it, Katie." Doug sagged in the chair but then squared his shoulders. "Getting kidnapped was the pits, but it got me to K'eq Xlapak. And it made me think. Made me examine my sorry life. I'm ready to face what I did."

"Something good had to come of all this." Sniffing back her tears, she hugged him again. "We'll talk more later."

She pushed to her feet and found Max on the spot with her crutches. He stepped aside, standing at military attention, his expression set in granite. They'd hurt each other, and the pain of it was too raw, too deep. How could she bear it? She tore her gaze away from him and faced the dark doorway to the temple.

For weeks, she'd anticipated seeing this, but today everything was blurred in a haze of tears and pain. She swayed on her crutches. When Max and then the doctor started forward, she shook her head.

Max stepped aside but remained close, his stern gaze on her as if he was ready to rush forward and support her.

"At last you are here at the temple." Esteban's lined features bore an expression of kind concern. "I trust my wife took good care of you."

"Yes, yes, of course. But what is going on here? Why all the people?" She'd failed in her mission. Were they here to witness her humiliation? She raised her chin.

He indicated the gray-haired Maya beside him, wearing ceremonial garb, a striped bandana and matching sash. "Don Luis, the chief Jaguar Priest, has called us together for a small ceremony. Not the one planned, of course. *El Presidente* and General Lopez will not attend."

335

A ceremony? Really? Or maybe she was still groggy.

The Jaguar Priest nodded solemnly, then spoke in Spanish.

Esteban translated. "I apologize for my assistant's cruelty and ambition. Jago forced your brother to suffer. He has disgraced the Maya people. We would mete out a harsh punishment, but we understand Jago has committed international crimes and must face justice elsewhere."

Kate tightened her fingers around the crutch grips. She steadied her good leg, fighting to remain standing. She faced the priest, guessing the sadness in his eyes mirrored hers. True, murderers and thieves prevented her from returning Kizin. But saying so would seem self-serving.

"Don Luis, it is I who must apologize to you and to your people. I promised to return the statue of Kizin to this temple. I failed. Kizin is lost, and Curse Day—"

Don Luis interrupted with a flurry of words.

Esteban held up his hand. "Wait, *señorita*. Don Luis reminds me you do not know the tremors have lessened. Some of the people are still fearful, but Don Luis believes that this *Día Maldito* will bring no earthquake. We are hopeful the curse is finished."

The words whirled in her brain. Could it be true? Or only a temporary reprieve? She glanced at Max, who shrugged and shook his head. Even if real, it didn't negate her failure to keep her promise.

"That's amazing, wonderful," she said, "but Kizin is still lost, gone forever."

The priest held out his arms as if to encompass the entire plaza full of people. He declaimed loudly, a proclamation that had the Maya villagers cheering.

Esteban translated. "Kizin is not lost, but deposited in the *cenote* as the gods and our ancestors intended. In ancient times, Maya queens contributed their blood in honor of the gods. Because *Señorita* Fontaine has given of her blood, the villagers have prepared a feast to honor her as a brave Maya queen."

Two small girls in embroidered smocks trotted to Kate and handed her bouquets.

Blood roared in her ears, and her heart clattered against her ribs. Had she succeeded after all? The Maya believed Kizin was where it should be. And maybe Doug would straighten out his life. Now she could go back to her normal life.

Without Max.

A shuddering breath rocked her. She could only nod and press her palms together in return thanks.

****

"This *poc chuc* is damned good. The Maya know how to put on a feast," Lucas Del Rio said. "But if you don't want yours, dump it. The mess you made of your food makes me want to puke." Frowning, he shoveled in another forkful of the char-grilled pork, black beans, and tomatoes.

Max snorted, ready to overturn his plate on his friend's head. "Fuck off, Del Rio, or go hurl your cookies in the latrine. Your ragging's a pain in the ass."

On the other side of the project dining tent, the location of the feast, Kate was listening to her brother. And picking at her food like him. A tossup whether ol' Dougie was feeding her a line of bull or whether his stay in the thatched hotel had changed his outlook. Not Max's business. Kate would be outta here soon and there wasn't a damn thing he could do about it. Her transport, an official Costa Verde military helo had landed as they began to eat. Or not eat.

"Ragging ain't working. Better I haul you into the bush and hammer some sense into you. All *you*'ve done since we sat down is growl and stare at Kate. What's up between you two?"

"Nothing's up," Max growled. "Enough or I'll pound you into the jungle floor." He took a long drink of herbal tea in hopes he wouldn't have to talk to the Hulk here anymore.

"What's up now is your temper. Looks to me like something else *was* up. If I had a thing going with a woman like that, I'd be a coward if I let her fly off without fixing it." He pulled a chunk of tomato out of his beard before plucking a papaya from the table's big bowl of fruit.

Max shot to his feet. "And when was the last time you had a "thing" going? Oh, yeah, your ugly mug scares away females and small children. I'm going outside to check in with the boss." He glimpsed hurt in his friend's eyes before he turned and stalked out. Shit, that was cruel, but hell, why couldn't Lucas leave him alone?

He dumped his dishes and crossed the dusty ground to a vegetation-covered mound. His phone in hand, he stared at the stones that formed the base of what Professor Morales had said was the palace. The anticipation of seeing all this had excited him but now he couldn't rouse much interest.

Damn, he'd never let a woman get to him like this. But Kate wasn't like any female he'd ever known. Honorable and brave, loyal to a fault. How could he forget all the ways she'd shown her trust in him? Trust he'd betrayed. Slashed all the insight and caring they'd woven around them like liana vines and left them in shreds.

She made him want more. Del Rio was right. If he didn't try to talk to her, he was a coward, too afraid to hear she didn't love him back. Like he was abandoning himself. What did Nestor say? *"Truth is better than believing the worst."* Kate had told him almost the same thing.

"Dammit to hell!" Because of his stubbornness—or cowardice—he could lose the best thing in his life. She'd dared and changed. Could she forgive?

He'd catch her before the helo took off. But he'd put off reporting in too long. He was about to punch in the DSF number when his phone rang.

"You were supposed to check in this morning. What's up?" Thomas Devlin barked.

"I've been sorta busy," Max drawled. He recited a quick sit rep.

Devlin gave a low whistle. "Good riddance to that pond scum Le Noir. I still don't have much on Centaur but looks like their honchos know things are FUBAR. So Sedgwick paid for his greed, the bastard. Don't know what Scotland Yard will do about his black-market loot. They're searching his place. Got something else. Give me a sec." The swish of papers being shuffled. "Interesting development that could change things down there. Seismologists in Guatemala and the States are puzzled as to why, but they find no signs of stress or movement along the fault. No earthquake likely this Curse Day."

Max shook his head. So it wasn't just the locals being hopeful. "Hard not to believe just a little bit in the power of Kizin."

"Anything else?"

"Doug Fontaine told us three men abducted him, but one of them stayed behind in D.C. Maybe from Costa Verde but not Maya. Finding him might be tough, but that's on the FBI."

"Copy that. How's Kate doing?"

Max's gut tightened. "Down about losing the statue but she'll be okay. Tough like you said." Tougher than him. *"The truth is better…"* He was twice a coward if he didn't follow through on what he'd been thinking.

"You there?"

"Sorry. Got a personal request. You think Research could find out what happened to my mother? It's been years, so maybe it's too late, but—"

"Right. I thought you might never ask," Devlin said gently. "I did that search myself when you came on board DSF. Security issue. Had to be certain she couldn't cause problems if she came looking for you. You want this now?"

Max hesitated, then nodded, but of course Devlin couldn't see him. "Affirmative."

Keys clicked on Devlin's laptop. "I'm sorry, Max. She's dead. She died the day she didn't come back for you."

The news rocked him like Kizin's mega earthquake. His vision blurred. After a moment, he managed to make himself speak. "Go on."

Following the explanation took all his strength. His mother had ridden a city bus and obtained a transfer. She used to do that all the time to find work and to get to work. The police report said her purse contained a flyer about technical training in a suburb of Houston. But the bus stop where she waited for the transfer put her in the middle of a gang war. She was cut down in a drive-by shooting.

"Why didn't they find her back then?" His legs wouldn't support him, and he sank onto a stack of numbered building stones.

"Her ID was fake. No address or phone. Could she have been in the States illegally?"

"Possible. I don't know."

"Houston Social Services might've found her if they'd looked hard enough but most of those organizations are overloaded with work and understaffed. The police kept her effects and a blood sample. They hoped for a blood match if a relative came looking. DNA's how I found her, with the sample of yours the company has on file."

"What happened to her… body?"

"She's buried in a municipal cemetery for John and Jane Does. I can give you the case number and what else you need when you return."

Max rocked on his hard perch. His throat felt like he'd swallowed the dust at his feet. "Thanks," he choked out. "Reckon I'll take care of her."

"Thought you would."

He barely listened to the rest of Devlin's news. All he could think about was telling Kate.

****

"I'll be right back, Katie," Doug said, backing up his wheelchair. "Gotta get a couple more of those honey cakes. The bastards fed me okay but no desserts."

Kate stretched her lips into a smile. Sweets had always been one of Doug's "treasures." Treasure was how Centaur had reeled him in. He'd sold them one artifact of shaky provenance, then procured another for them, and another, until he was doing more shady deals for Centaur than legitimate ones for himself. When he finished his story, he heaved a sigh of relief to be free of those leg irons.

He'd committed crimes—international crimes—and might go to prison. Her throat closed up. *No, stop it.* He'd have the best attorney and her support, but not her guilt. No more. She raised her eyes toward the setting sun. *Dad, he's finally growing up. He'll make it.*

The initial shocks of losing Kizin and hearing Doug's admission of guilt had blinded her to the truths she'd learned these past weeks of hazards and hardships. The upheaval of her childhood had led to her need for security, leading a life as static as a museum exhibit. And she'd allowed her mom's fears to become her own. Until now. Wasn't she capable outside her safe museum, capable in the face of danger and in the jungle? She learned to navigate and survive, didn't she? And the whole adventure was exciting. So she'd make it too. Except for the emptiness inside.

Movement on the other side of the tent caught her eye. Max. A wave of longing swept through her. She'd forced herself not to look his way, but her excellent peripheral vision tortured her by keeping track of his movements. He was on his feet, phone in hand, glowering at Del Rio. Then he stalked outside. Likely to call Devlin.

Del Rio stood and headed toward the desserts. He'd be leaving with Doug and her on the helicopter, but Max was staying until the runners carrying back the canoe could return with the rest of their equipment.

Intrepid, wonderful, proud Max. Her chest squeezed

as if it might crack.

She'd been so wrong, rejecting him, as he believed his mother did. How painful that must be. Betray her trust? How blind and selfish could she be? She'd expected him to choose between loyalty to her and loyalty to Devlin Security Force, to the men he'd served with under fire.

She hadn't known it, but Max was what she'd been missing in her life. His arms around her that gave her a sense of safety, of belonging. His confidence in her that made her feel good about herself. Their deep connection that felt like physical vibrations in the air between them.

The helicopter would take her away in a few minutes. Her heart pounded so hard it hurt.

Chapter Thirty-One

MAX HAD JUST ended the phone call when the whirring of helicopter rotors jarred him to alertness.

Kate's transport. *Shit!*

He took off at a dead run.

He raced through the project's compound of tents and burst through the trees into the clearing. No old Huey rust bucket, this was a new military bird. Its rotors deafened him with their powerful *whomp, whomp, whomp.* Dust devils swirled, blinding him, as the chopper lifted off. The big craft banked and turned before disappearing over the treetops.

Too fucking late.

She was gone.

Winded—had to be blood loss, not the adrenaline pumping his heart out of his chest—he propped his hands on his knees. Figuring things out took too fucking long. Pain ripped through him wearing acid-tipped spurs.

Through the haze, figures emerged. The two Maya carrying Kate's camp chair and her crutches. And Kate.

She eyed him silently, her face solemn and drawn and so beautiful the sight split him in two.

Blood roared in his ears, and his pulse stumbled. "You…. you didn't leave." He barely managed to get the words past the pile of sand in his mouth.

Her taxi service set down her deck chair a few feet away. "What with the soldiers, the bad guys, the bodies,

Doug's wheelchair, and his giant chaperon, there wasn't room for me." She gave him a shaky smile, and emotion glittered in her eyes. She shook her head. "I couldn't go. Not until I cleared up some things."

His brain was sluggish, like it couldn't dare hope what her words might mean. He vibrated like a tuning fork. Where was the damn zone when he needed it? He fisted his hands at his sides.

She took the crutches from Arturo. Thanked each man in turn, *"Yum botic."*

Smiling and bowing, they jogged away.

Kate pushed to her feet and adjusted the crutches under her arms. They stared at each other across the dusty ground. A monkey meandered across the clearing. In the branches above, songbirds trilled. He'd take anything as a good omen.

"Max, I was wrong and I'm sorry." When he opened his mouth, she held up a hand, nearly unbalancing herself. He started forward, but she shook her head and held on, upright, her chin lifted. The Maya queen. "I didn't listen to my own advice about knowing the truth. In my case, I hung onto self-delusion. I see now that didn't press you about Doug's criminal involvement because I was afraid of what I'd learn. I'm still going to talk to Thomas about this, but I shouldn't have put myself between him and you."

"You deserved to know. You were already hurting bad with worry for Doug and I didn't want to cause more pain. Reckon it hurt worse finding out the way you did."

She dismissed that with the lift of one shoulder. "I wouldn't have believed you. I should've caught on to his shady dealings myself. He verified what you said happened in Istanbul. You were right that he's an adult and should be responsible for his actions." She drew a shaky breath. "Even if that means prison time."

"Maybe not much time. Del Rio says your brother has information to trade about Centaur—names and places."

"That's a comfort." Her brow crinkled. "Except Centaur might come after him."

"No more blinders, huh?" He jabbed fingers through his hair. "Yeah, if the Centaur boss found out, it could be dicey for Doug. I can think of some possibilities, like keeping him an anonymous source. Thomas has connections at the Justice Department."

"And I know an excellent attorney." She tilted her head. "I've been thinking."

"Dangerous, like you told me."

"True. But not this time. You helped me see the truth. And more."

"Damn straight. Brave and determined, that's my Kate."

She stood only inches away, so close he could smell the fragrance of her hair, see her pulse fluttering in her throat, see her eyes widen at his last words. Longing welled up inside him, bounded only by the racing of his heart. The urge to touch her, to absorb her softness, her sighs—*her*. Could he take the chance? He started forward.

"No, I'm all right. But if another tremor hit or, heaven forbid, an earthquake, I'd drop like a coconut."

He forced from his mind that she'd just refused his help, his touch—him. At least he was close enough to catch her if she started to fall. "About the tremors, seems like they're done with for now. DSF got reports. The tremors haven't just subsided. They've stopped altogether. No stresses on the fault line, at least for now. No earthquake, like the priest said."

Her eyes widened in amazement. "The end of the curse? Hard not to believe in Kizin."

"Who knows? But no guarantees. Those fault lines didn't magically disappear."

When she swayed on the crutches, alarm flashed in his mind. Dammit, he was a selfish son of a bitch. "Your wound. I'll get the chair. Don't you want to sit down?"

"No. Let me finish." Determined Kate's brow had those lines. "We're alike, you and I. We allowed our pasts to control us. You're afraid to trust, to open yourself, and I've been afraid of... living. When I was growing up, I felt pulled along in my parents' slipstream, not in control of my life. The gymnastics wasn't even my idea. Mom thought it would improve my coordination. No one considered my wants or feelings. No one needed my ideas or my opinion, or—"

"You."

"Yes, but *you* did. From the start." Her smile was brighter than the rays of the sun dipping below the treetops. "I like my museum work, but I've boxed myself in, where I know I'm capable. And, yes, needed. But now I want more. I've dealt with my past. What about you?"

He swallowed. When Devlin told him, he couldn't wait to tell Kate, but now, how to start? "You were right. About everything." He stabbed fingers through his hair. "Damned tough for a soldier to admit this, but I was afraid, like you said."

She stared at him intently. "You asked Mara to search. When?"

His throat felt too tight for speech. He swallowed hard. "I talked to Thomas after the feast. He did the research when he hired me, sat on it."

"Until you were ready." Her hands white-knuckled on the crutches.

"She's dead. Killed on the street. Shot. Got caught in a gang shootout. Same day she disappeared."

Her face crumpled. "I'm so sorry. How—"

"False papers. Not her real name. I'll tell you later." If there *was* a later.

"Would you tell me her name?" The sympathy and sadness in her eyes nearly undid him.

"She was Maria Lourdes Rivera." For the first time in twenty-five years, he said it with pride. "She'd gone to sign up for job training, for a better life for the two of us. She didn't reject me. Didn't abandon me."

"She loved you." She hiked up the crutches and hopped a step closer. Her blue eyes darkened and she licked her lips. "Max, you just called me your Kate. What did you mean?"

Her words punched him in the gut. She'd opened the door. He took a giant step and pulled her against his chest. Her crutches clattered to the hard ground and she wrapped her arms around him. His whole body sighed at the feel of her in his arms again. He held her hard against him. Everything inside him said hold on and never let go. The soft shift of her body surged hunger through him. She moaned his name into his mouth and kissed him back with a passion that matched his. He slid his mouth along her jaw, kissed her ear, her neck. *Dios.* He had to stop before he combusted.

"Thank God you didn't leave, Kate. Never thought I'd say this to anybody but here goes. I love you. I realized it a while ago but couldn't handle it. And now I can't handle losing you." His voice came out too rough but he had no water to wash the last of the sand from his throat.

Her eyes brimmed with tears. "Can I hear you say those words again? Those three little important words?"

He sighed, pressed his forehead to hers. Reveled in the touch of her soft skin. "I love you. Those three words?"

She kissed the cleft in his chin. "Perfect. And now I'd like to sit down, but only if it doesn't mean letting go." The smile on her lips was teasing.

He picked her up, taking care with her bandaged thigh. "Am I hurting you?"

"Not a bit." She wrapped her arms around his neck and laid her head on his shoulder.

Not confident the chair wouldn't collapse under his weight, he inched down onto the canvas seat. The contraption creaked but held. He settled Kate on his lap. The movement of her delectable butt hardened him like a damn tree trunk. The gleam in her eyes said she felt it. "Careful, sweetheart. You're starting something we can't finish."

Another wriggle was her revenge. "Along with protecting me—and the statue—from more dangers than I care to list, you helped me deal with my past and my insecurities. Because of your confidence in me, I could face bandits and floodwater and Le Noir. The man who did all that is the wonderful, gentle, sensitive, strong man I fell in love with. I love you, Max."

Her words and the softness in her bluebonnet gaze ignited a wildfire in his chest. Kate cupped his jaw and kissed him, the sweetest kiss he'd ever received.

"Hell, we have about as much in common as a Thoroughbred and a burro. I've avoided relationships like scorpions but I want to give us a try. If you do."

"We'll make it work. You can help me with that lingering issue of control." She snuggled closer and their gazes locked. Her eyes sizzled with the same heat firing his veins.

"No sweat. You aren't the only one with issues." He sent her a wicked grin. "If you'd like to build my self-esteem, I have some ideas. Once you're healed, that is."

"My house in D.C. has four bedrooms." She nibbled his neck, pressed tiny kisses there, punctuated by her warm, wet tongue.

Her touch was flame licking his skin. He could barely think. "Ah, sweetheart, we can try every one."

"Kiss me, Max."

"That's the controlling Kate I love. The Kate I need." He lowered his mouth to hers. Everything would be all right.

He connected with her as with nobody else. She fit in his arms as no other woman ever had, ever could. She was his friend and his lover and his other half. That she loved him too was nothing short of a miracle, and he'd do whatever it took to keep things that way. He trembled as if Kizin shook the earth.

A word about the author…

Occasional bouts of insomnia led to Susan Vaughan's writing career. When she couldn't sleep, she made up stories to fill the long, dark nights. Her stories throw the hero and heroine together under extraordinary circumstances and pit them against a clever villain. Besides curling up with a good mystery or romance, Susan enjoys walking her dog, boating, traveling, and volunteering. A former teacher, she is a West Virginia native, but she and her husband have lived in Maine for many years. Find her at www.susanvaughan.com, where you can sign up for her newsletter or contact her, or at https://www.facebook.com/susanvaughanbooks.

Thank you for purchasing
this publication of The Wild Rose Press, Inc.

For questions or more information
contact us at
info@thewildrosepress.com.

The Wild Rose Press, Inc.
www.thewildrosepress.com